SCOTTISH FAIRY

Scottish Fairy Belief:

A History

Lizanne Henderson and Edward J. Cowan

TUCKWELL PRESS

First published in Great Britain in 2001 by
Tuckwell Press
The Mill House
Phantassie
East Linton
East Lothian EH40 3DG
Scotland

Copyright © Lizanne Henderson and Edward J. Cowan, 2001

ISBN 1 86232 190 6

British Library Cataloguing in Publication Data

A catalogue record for this book is available
on request from the British Library

Typeset by Hewer Text Ltd, Edinburgh
Printed and bound by The Cromwell Press, Trowbridge, Wiltshire

Contents

Plates vii
Figures and Tables viii
Acknowledgements ix
Abbreviations x

Introduction: Beware the Lychnobious People 1

1. The Nature of Fairy Belief 8
   What's in a Name? 14
   Betwixt and Between: What are Fairies? 17
   Fairy Origins: Folk and Learned Ideas 19
   Extinction of a Species: The Retreat of the Fairies? ... 24

2. The Wonderful World of Fairy 35
   The Road to Elfland 36
   Liminal Worlds: The Location of Elfland 39
   Ferlies to Find: Descriptions of Fairyland 45
   The Wee Folk? 47
   Fairy Life-Styles 57
   Activities and Pastimes of the Fairy Folk 61
   The Politics of Fairyland: Social and Political Structures 65

3. Enchantments of the Fairies 74
   Fairy Glamourie: The Modes of Enchantment 74
   Breaking the Spell: The Modes of Disenchantment 87
   Changelings: 'of nature denyit' 94

4. The Rise of the Demonic 106
   The Reformation Centuries 107
   Redefining the Supernatural 116
   The Scottish Witch Hunt 118
   Satan's Greatest Enemy: King James VI 121
   The Assault on Fairy Belief 125
   Motifs in Common 137

5. Writing the Fairies 142
True Thomas 142
Eldritch Explorations 152
Fairies in Flyting................................. 158

6. The Reinstatement of Fairy Belief: Robert Kirk and
The Secret Common-Wealth......................... 171
'The Fairy Minister': Robert Kirk.................. 172
The War Against Atheism and the Sadducees 176
Seers, Second Sight, and the Subterranean People .. 181
Robert Kirk and Fairy Belief 184

7. Farewell Lychnobious People...................... 193
Fantastical Fictions 193
Folklore and Fairyology 206
Figuring the Fairies............................... 209

Bibliography...................................... 224
Index... 235

Plates

1. Hawthorn at Merlin's Grave, Drumelzier
2. The Fairy Hills, Balnaknock, Skye
3. Eildon Hills from Scott's View, Bemersyde
4. The Rhymer's Stone, Melrose
5. Tamlane's Well, Carterhaugh, Selkirk
6. Lynn Glen, haunt of Bessie Dunlop
7. Robert Kirk's Bell, Balquhidder
8. Doon Hill, Hill of the Fairies, Aberfoyle
9. The Clootie Tree, Doon Hill, Aberfoyle
10. Grave of Robert Kirk, Kirkton, Aberfoyle
11. Grave of Will o' Phaup, grandfather of James Hogg, Ettrick

Tables

1. Liminal Space 40
2. Robert Kirk's Universe 188
3. Witch Trials 217
4. Folk Motifs 218

Figures

1. The King of France's Cellar 38
2. King James interrogates Agnes Sampson 122
3. 'The Fairy Rade', by K. Halsewelle. 158

Acknowledgements

Although they conjure images of ethereal, and, in the minds of some, small creatures, the fairies of Scotland represent rather a colossal subject which tends to grow on acquaintance. We are conscious that we could have spent much more time in search of them and that, as in the best fairy tales, all has not been quite resolved at the end.

Part of the research for this book was carried out at the Folklore Department of Memorial University, St. John's, Newfoundland. L.H. owes many thanks to her supervisors, the late David Buchan, and Martin Lovelace, for their encouragement and many helpful comments. She is also indebted to Louise Yeoman, Miceal Ross, and Joyce Miller. E.J.C. has been exploring fairy belief as a reflection of folk mentalité for longer than he cares to admit. He is grateful to students at the universities of Guelph and Glasgow for their invaluable participation in the quest. Theo van Heijnsbergen, Cathair Ó Dochartaigh and Douglas Gifford all most generously gave advice on literary matters. Needless to say, the authors alone are responsible for the errors that undoubtedly remain.

The friendly assistance of the staff at the National Archives of Scotland, the University of Guelph Library's Scottish Collection, Stirling Archive and of Special Collections at Glasgow University Library has been greatly appreciated. We also thank John and Val Tuckwell for their faith and interest in this project.

Lizanne Henderson
Ted Cowan
Glasgow, 2001

Abbreviations

APS	*The Acts of the Parliaments of Scotland*, ed. T. Thomson and C. Innes (Edinburgh 1814–75)
Child	F. J. Child, *The English and Scottish Popular Ballads*, 5 vols (Boston and New York 1882–1898)
Court Books	*The Court Books of Orkney and Shetland, 1614–1615*, ed. and transcribed Robert S. Barclay (Edinburgh 1967)
Court Book of Shetland	*Court Book of Shetland, 1615–1629*, ed. Gordon Donaldson (Lerwick 1991)
Daemonologie	King James VI, *Daemonologie in forme of a Dialogue 1597* (London 1924)
Extracts . . . Aberdeen	*Extracts From the Council Register of the Burgh of Aberdeen, 1570–1625*, Spalding Club (Aberdeen 1848)
Extracts . . . Strathbogie	*Extracts from the Presbytery Book of Strathbogie* (Aberdeen 1843)
Good People	*The Good People: New Fairylore Essays*, ed. Peter Narváez (New York and London 1991)
JC	Justiciary Court Records (NAS)
Kirk	Robert Kirk, *The Secret Common-Wealth*, 1691, ed. Stewart Sanderson (Cambridge 1976)
Letters	Walter Scott, *Letters on Demonology and Witchcraft* (1830; London 1884)
Maitland	*Maitland Club Miscellany* (Edinburgh 1833)
Miscellany	*Miscellany of the Spalding Club* (Aberdeen 1841), vol. 1.
Minstrelsy	Walter Scott, *Minstrelsy of the Scottish Border*, 4 vols, ed. T. F. Henderson (Edinburgh 1932)
NAS	National Archives of Scotland

NLS	National Library of Scotland
NSA	*New Statistical Account of Scotland*, compiled by John Sinclair 15 vols (Edinburgh and London 1845)
OED	*Oxford English Dictionary*
OSA	*The Statistical Account of Scotland*, compiled by John Sinclair 21 vols (Edinburgh 1771–1799)
Pitcairn	Robert Pitcairn, *Ancient Criminal Trials in Scotland* 4 vols, (Edinburgh 1833)
POAS	*Proceedings of the Orkney Antiquarian Society* (Kirkwall 1923–5)
PSAS	*Proceedings of the Society of Antiquaries of Scotland*
SCA	Stirling Council Archives
SND	*Scottish National Dictionary*
TGSI	*Transactions of the Gaelic Society of Inverness*
Trial . . . Irvine	*Trial, Confession, and Execution of Isobel Inch, John Stewart, Margaret Barclay & Isobel Crawford, for Witchcraft, at Irvine, anno 1618* (Ardrossan and Saltcoats 1855)

INTRODUCTION:

Beware the Lychnobious People

... who in the sixteenth century lacked familiarity with angels and demons? Who did not carry inside himself a strange, phantasmagorical universe haunted by strange species?

Lucien Febvre[1]

The world is full of spirits. 'As thick as atomes in the air', wrote Robert Kirk in 1691, they populate every nook and cranny. They are 'no nonentities or phantasms, creatures, proceeding from ane affrighted apprehensione confused or crazed sense, but realities'. Not all tales of pygmies, fairies, nymphs, sirens, or apparitions can be true, but so many are the stories, and so universally told, that surely they 'could not spring of nothing?'[2] The Reverend Kirk believed the fairies to be one of several orders of spirits inhabiting the world. To him, and the many others who shared his views, the fairies were just another species awaiting scientific analysis like the many animals, birds and insects that were being discovered as the world's horizons widened.

This book seeks to investigate the nature of Scottish fairy belief from the fifteenth to the nineteenth centuries and aims to reach some conclusions about the role of fairies as a cultural phenomenon. Despite J. R. R. Tolkien's cautionary observation that 'faërie cannot be caught in a net of words; for it is one of its qualities to be indescribable though not imperceptible', we attempt to describe as well as perceive. Most of the tropes and metaphors associated with the fairy experience are by no means unique to Scotland, but are found throughout the length and breadth of Europe with analogues much further afield. The pantomime question annually roared at laughing children, 'Do you believe in fairies?' would have baffled people in pre-industrial societies; everybody did, for the contrary was unthinkable. The only dispute concerned what fairies represented, questions of whether the guid neighbours were manifestations of divine providence or the legions of hell. As late as the 1840s sober ministers compiling their parish reports for the *New Statistical Account* were quite capable of suggesting that just as the capercaillie or the pine marten had not been seen in their districts for seventy years, neither had the fairies. Consideration of the latter affords an opportunity, too seldom available or seized in historical investigation, to explore the *mentalité* or mindset of the Scottish folk to learn something of their hopes and fears, their assumptions and their concerns, as they struggled to comprehend the world around them and the unfamiliar, yet momentous, forces to which it was subject.

Interest in the folklore of past generations has always been with us, although the investigative motives have sometimes been questionable. For instance, the antiquarian approach toward folk beliefs and traditions often took a patronising view of the subject as a means of validating the beliefs of the present, lauding the rational and the learned, at the expense of the 'ignorant' and the 'superstitious'. Yet even in the writings of the most complacent and censorious of commentators it is possible to detect an element of nostalgia for an 'idealised rural past', an imagined idyll in total harmony with nature.[3] Those engaged on such a quest have often been doomed to disappointment for there is seldom much trace of the idyllic in a past which witnessed an unprecedented assault on fairy belief, and on folk culture generally. The religious impetus, both protestant and catholic, to remodel the world, subjected the fairies to a process of demonisation, with frightening consequences for the people who resisted these reinterpretations and steadfastly held on to their beliefs. Such was the climate of suppression and persecution that it is often difficult to understand how fairy belief survived, relatively unscathed, if somewhat refurbished and sanitised, into the modern era.

This book is concerned with the 'real *dramatis personae* of fairy narrative, the people in them'.[4] We are not concerned with proving the reality, or otherwise, of fairies; such an endeavour would be as futile as it is irrelevant. What we can prove is that many Scots people, who lived mainly in the period from c.1450 to c.1750, had no doubt that fairies actually existed. The dictum that the 'folk' in folklore 'can refer to *any group of people whatsoever* who share at least one common factor',[5] is suitably broad to be applicable to this study, the common factor being, in this case, an opinion about fairies, whether that be a strongly held conviction that they existed, or, less commonly, rank disbelief. Having said this, our focus is directed toward the 'esoteric' rather than the 'exoteric' factor,[6] toward the 'culture *produced by* the popular classes' rather than the culture '*imposed* upon them,[7] ever-mindful that most of our sources were produced by the literate and learned, forcing us to view the esoteric perspective through an exoteric lens.

Belief is not the easiest of subjects to study. In approaching the *mentalité*, or mental world, of a past age it is important to shed anachronistic attitudes, to be aware that our predecessors' response to events and perceptions was not the same as our own. Since there was no assumption of the natural as opposed to the supernatural, folk across the wide spectrum of society had no sense of the impossible and thus

> in the whole fabric of life nature and supernature were perpetually intertwined ... They were at home in a peculiar world where phenomena were not located precisely, where time did not impose a strict sequential order on events and existences, where what came to an end could nevertheless continue ...[8]

Carlo Ginzburg's argument for the existence of ecstatic cults in continental Europe includes references to fairies within Scottish witch trials, as a uniquely Scottish manifestation of this ecstatic experience. As he points out, the 'thoughts, the beliefs, and the aspirations of the peasants and artisans of the past reach us (if and when they do) almost always through distorting viewpoints and intermediaries',[9] thus posing problems for the folkloristic approach. For example, to say the least, the use of witch trial evidence 'to classify beliefs or practices in folkloric culture, known via indirect, casual, often stereotyped testimonies interspersed by hiatuses and silences, is difficult'.[10] The nature of the documentation available to the folklorist should not, however, deter one from attempting to study the folklore of the past: 'the fact that a source is not 'objective' ... does not mean that it is useless'.[11]

Witch trial testimonials are of crucial importance to this study. Investigators such as Walter Scott and John Dalyell used the fairy material in witch trials for purely anecdotal purposes, thus trivialising the experiences of the victims. The first systematic approach was taken by J. A. MacCulloch in his study of the mingling of fairy and witch beliefs (1921).[12] No one else has extensively used the witch trial evidence to establish the nature of Scottish fairy belief. Aside from the fact that the Scottish witch-hunt is an understudied phenomenon in its own right, the reluctance to use the depositions of those accused of witchcraft has sprung from the prevailing attitude that the confessions are no more than the effect of torture and leading questions by the inquisitors. The confessions are thus somehow divorced from those who utter them as testimonies and accused alike are manipulated by cynical puppeteers.

Another problem is that the tendency has been to study persecution, 'giving little or no attention to the attitudes and behaviour of the persecuted', but there is no difficulty in agreeing with the assertion that although the testimonies are fragmentary and indirect, 'individuals articulate in a distinct manner, each with his (or her) own accent, a core of common beliefs'.[13] Accessing these beliefs through the use of documentation originating from, or filtered by, demonologists, inquisitors and judges, a process whereby 'the voices of the accused reach us strangled, altered, distorted', involves looking at the trial evidence in a different way. It is the importance of 'the anomalies, the cracks that occasionally (albeit very rarely) appear in the documentation, undermining its coherence',[14] that we must seek. The anomalous material in the Scottish witch trials that this book will attempt to investigate are the alleged encounters with the fairy folk, in several examples the sole reason accusations of witchcraft were made against the victim. In many cases we prefer to quote what purport to be, and sometimes clearly are, the actual words of the informants. Their voices have been silent for too long.

A frustrating aspect of the trial records is the frequently abrupt termination of the transcript, presumably at the behest of the judges who were, in the main, only interested in recording certain types of evidence, namely those which they wished to hear. This is very noticeable in Isobel Gowdie's trial (1662), where so often the copyist stopped writing down the details about the fairies, which she so amply provided.

The bias shown, even by relatively recent scholarship, toward the witch trial evidence is also problematic. Commenting on the case of Bessie Dunlop, Robert Chambers opined, 'the modern student of insanity can have no difficulty with this case: it is simply one of hallucination, the consequence of diseased conditions'. The confession of Isobel Gowdie is frequently dismissed as the product of insanity. Sir Walter Scott commented, 'it only remains to suppose that this wretched creature [Isobel] was under the dominion of some peculiar species of lunacy'. J. A. MacCulloch accused Isobel of 'delusions and erotic ravings'. Even Katharine Briggs' response to this case was highly prejudicial: 'these strange, mad outpourings at least throw some light on the fairy beliefs held by the peasantry of Scotland in the seventeenth century'.[15]

Another source which may be controversial, but which may also be held to represent the authentic voice of the folk, is that of Scotland's rich ballad heritage. The historical value of ballads has, like witch trial evidence, been devalued and ignored. Contrary to the view that the ballads 'present no coherent record of either historical event or of popular belief and custom at any one particular period',[16] we would claim that the ballads do preserve valuable material and that they do indeed provide an important articulation of folk belief. When we study the ballads, we are studying not only the 'poetry of the folk' but stylistic representations of belief as well. In the late nineteenth century the American scholar, F. J. Child master-minded the five volume edition of popular ballads which turned out to be preponderantly Scottish in origin. Though fairies do not feature prominently in the classical ballads (only 11 of the 305 Child ballads contain fairy material), we would argue that they are most worthy of investigation. Of the Child corpus (numbers in brackets are those ascribed by the editor), we have identified the following which mention the fairies: [2] 'The Elfin Knight', [4] 'Lady Isabel and the Elf-Knight', [19] 'King Orfeo', [35] 'Allison Gross', [37] 'Thomas Rymer', [38] 'The Wee Wee Man', [39] 'Tam Lin', [40] 'The Queen of Elfan's Nourice', [41] 'Hind Etin', [53] 'Young Beichan' and [61] 'Sir Cawline'.[17]

Child, who was sceptical toward the historical value of the ballads, stated in his introduction to 'The Battle of Harlaw', 'A ballad taken down some four hundred years after the event will be apt to retain very little of sober history'. The late David Buchan refuted this claim, and the general attitude that ballads cannot be taken seriously as history. He found that 'Harlaw' was 'historical in a rather extraordinary way', reflecting the kind of 'historical truth' that rarely finds its way into the documents, 'the ways in which the folk imagination reacted to, moulded, and used for its own emotional purposes, the raw material of historical event'. The ballads, we suggest, similarly provide a heavily figurative and motifemic expression of the fairy beliefs of the folk, for 'ballads can contain factual truths not found in the often scanty records, and can contain certain emotional truths, the attitudes and reactions of the ballad-singing folk to the world around them'.[18]

Researching Scottish fairy belief is rather like confronting a huge obscure painting which has been badly damaged and worn through time, great chunks totally obliterated and now completely irrecoverable, portions repainted by poorly skilled craftsmen, and other parts touched up by those who should have known better. Nevertheless, enough remains – much more by far than we have been able to retain in this book – to present a reasonably vivid picture of what fairy belief once was and meant to the believers. In assembling this material, we have not worked toward some deconstructionist end, but rather have tried to synthesise the individual components, to reconstruct the whole essence of fairy belief as a distinct phenomenon. It has been sensibly observed that 'the attempt to attain knowledge of the past is also a journey into the world of the dead'.[19] As we embark upon a similar journey, we feel some envy for Thomas Rhymer who enjoyed the assistance of the Fairy Queen to show him the road. In our case, however, we must find another way to Elfland.

Notes

1 Lucien Febvre, *The Problem of Unbelief in the Sixteenth Century: The Religion of Rabelais*, trans. Beatrice Gottlieb (1942; Cambridge 1982), 446.
2 Kirk, 62, 64.
3 Jacqueline Simpson, intro., *Examples of Printed Folk-Lore concerning the Orkney and Shetland Islands*, collected by G. F. Black, ed. Northcote W. Thomas (1903; London 1994).
4 Barbara Rieti, *Strange Terrain: The Fairy World in Newfoundland* (St. John's 1991), 215.
5 Alan Dundes, 'What is Folklore?', in *The Study of Folklore*, ed. Alan Dundes (N. J. 1965), 2. Personally we prefer the definition of 'folklore' as given by Robert A. Georges and Michael Owen Jones, 'The word *folklore* denotes expressive forms, processes, and behaviours (1) that we customarily learn, teach, and utilize or display during face-to-face interactions, and (2) that we judge to be traditional (a) because they are based on known precedents or models, and (b) because they serve as evidence of continuities and consistencies through time and space in human knowledge, thought, belief and feeling'. *Folkloristics: An Introduction* (Bloomington and Indianapolis 1995), 1.
6 Wm. Hugh Jansen, 'The Esoteric-Exoteric Factor in Folklore', in *The Study of Folklore*, ed. Alan Dundes (N. J. 1965), 43–51.
7 Carlo Ginzburg, *The Cheese and the Worms: The Cosmos of a Sixteenth-Century Miller*, trans. John and Anne Tedeschi (1976; Harmondsworth 1982), xv.
8 Febvre, *Problem of Unbelief*, 440–444. What is now called an act of nature was once considered an act of God.
9 Ginzburg, *The Cheese and the Worms*, xv.
10 Carlo Ginzburg, *Ecstasies: Deciphering the Witches' Sabbath*, trans. R. Rosenthal (New York 1991), 213.
11 Ginzburg, *The Cheese and the Worms*, xvii.
12 J. A. MacCulloch, 'The Mingling of Fairy and Witch Beliefs in Sixteenth and Seventeenth Century Scotland', *Folk-Lore* 32 (1921): 227–44.
13 Ginzburg, *Ecstasies*, 2, 23.
14 Ginzburg, *Ecstasies*, 10.
15 Robert Chambers, *Domestic Annals of Scotland: From the Reformation to the Revolution*, 3 vols. (Edinburgh 1874), vol. 1, 110; *Letters*, 235; MacCulloch,

'The Mingling of Fairy and Witch Beliefs', 238; Katharine Briggs, *The Vanishing People: A Study of Traditional Fairy Belief* (London 1978), 25.
16 Gordon Hall Gerould, *The Ballad of Tradition* (Oxford 1932), 161.
17 *The English and Scottish Popular Ballads*, ed. F. J. Child. 5 vols. (Boston and London 1882–1898). Single volume edition *The English and Scottish Popular Ballads*, ed. Francis J. Child. Eds. and intro. by Helen Child Sargent and George Lyman Kittredge (London n.d.). On Child and his collection see *The Ballad in Scottish History*, ed. Edward J. Cowan (East Linton 2000).
18 David Buchan, 'History and Harlaw', in *Ballad Studies*, ed. E. B. Lyle (London 1976), 29–40.
19 Ginzburg, *Ecstasies*, 24.

CHAPTER ONE

The Nature of Fairy Belief

> Gin ye ca' me imp or elf,
> I rede ye look weel to yourself;
> Gin ye ca' me fairy,
> I'll work ye muckle tarrie [trouble];
> Gin guid neibour ye ca' me,
> Then guid neibour I will be;
> But gin ye ca' me seelie wicht,
> I'll be your freend baith day and nicht.[1]

There is, arguably, as much evidence of one kind or another for the activities of the fairies from the fifteenth to the early nineteenth centuries as there is for the existence of either the Picts, the Britons, the Angles or the Scots during the first millennium of Scottish history. In strictly historical terms, they appear on the scene with tales about Thomas Rhymer at the end of the thirteenth century. They figure in medieval and renaissance poetry and they have a prominent presence in the ballads. Witch trial testimonials record their activities. Such judicial indictments, processes and decisions would normally be regarded as representing some of the soundest types of historical evidence, affording a dilemma for the investigator who must be inclined to intellectually reject the bizarre reportage which they contain. None other than King James VI considered it worth his while to write an influential treatise, *Daemonologie*, which included some material on fairies. A hundred years later the respected and scholarly minister of Aberfoyle, Robert Kirk, produced a learned tract about them in which he drew upon oral informants and local traditions in the manner of a modern folklorist. He was the first person writing in English or Scots to use the expression 'fairy tale' though he conceived his dissertation as a serious contribution to contemporary science and theology, written, in part, for friends and acquaintances who were members of the Royal Society in London. He was by no means alone since a number of his contemporaries were turning their attention to matters of the occult and the supernatural. By the eighteenth century traditions about the 'fairfolk' were eagerly sought out and published by a host of so-called authorities who believed that the objects of their interest were no more, though the fairies continued to hold their place in the folk tradition. Writers such as Walter Scott and James Hogg fostered a massive interest through poetry, story and ballad collection. Throughout the nineteenth century the elves littered the pages of Scottish literature, from which inspirational source they impacted upon painters and book illustrators. Folktale collections significantly added to the corpus of lore, as did the energies, or imaginations, of legions of antiquarians. Andrew Lang, inspired no doubt by Kirk, whose tract he edited, is generally credited with being the first to truly popularise some of the traditional material which he described as fairy tales, while J. M. Barrie, from Kirriemuir in Angus, invented one of the most famous of modern sprites when he introduced the malevolent Tinker Bell in his much-loved play, *Peter Pan*.

Like the early peoples of Scotland, the fairies left their legacy in place names which are abundant throughout the length and breadth of the country. A pair of chambered cairns on Cnoc Freiceadain in Caithness are known from their shape as Na Tri Shean, the three fairy mounds. Now over 5,000 years old, these impressive monuments overlook the nuclear power station at Dounreay which harbours sinister materials that will be lethally active for ten times the age of the cairns. Every county in Scotland has fairy hills or fairy glens. The magnificent Schiehallion on the edge of Rannoch Moor is the fairy mountain of the Caledonians. *Sith* (fairy) names are numerous throughout Gaelic-speaking Scotland. Tomnahurich Hill at Inverness is an abode of the elves, as is Dumbuck Hill in Dunbartonshire. Perhaps most famous of all are the Eildon Hills in the Borders, where true Thomas met the queen of the fairies. Names containing the local element 'troll' or 'trowie', are plentiful in the islands of Orkney and Shetland. Just when such countrywide names were first conferred is problematical, for while some may be old, we may suspect that many others post-date the fairy craze which took hold in the late eighteenth century, in much the same way as a majority of the topographical features of Glen Etive in Argyll were renamed following the publication of James Macpherson's purported translations of Ossianic poetry in the 1760s, or MacBeth names were applied to landscape features around Dunsinane, in the beautiful howe of Strathmore, as the play became familiar to an increasingly literate public.

The fairies even bequeathed their own archaeology in the prehistoric graves, brochs, souterrains, and 'Picts' houses' which they were thought to have inhabited. The landscape contained many 'downie' or fairy hills which provided access to Fairyland. Wells, confluences of rivers and burns, and ancient trees were places frequented by the elves. Fairy rings preserved the imprints of spritely feet dancing the light fantastic, standing stones representing the dancers themselves fossilised in the cold, cruel light of dawn, as at Haltadans on the island of Fetlar. There were caves where human musicians, most often pipers and fiddlers, trapped forever by the enchanters, could be heard to play on certain eldritch nights.

Although many writers have pretended that the so-called fairy faith constituted folk belief in all its pristine purity, they were sadly deluded for, from earliest times, ecclesiastical authorities well versed in the classics persistently traced popular lore back to classical or biblical sources. The practice can be charted in the works of Augustine and Gregory the Great, to name but two luminaries in the christian panoply. *Superstitio* to the Romans meant any non-Roman belief, just as it later came to bear such semantic burdens as non-christian, non-protestant or non-rational. But 'somebody else's belief' could be rendered more intelligible by assimilation, which was what, as often as not, the Church recommended, or by the manufacture of a pedigree which foregrounded such beliefs in the mythology of the bible or of Greece and Rome. To this heady brew antiquaries later added ingredients from Scandinavia, Germania, the Celtic areas, the Near and Far East and ultimately, the World at large.

Dichotomies such as 'elite and folk', 'literate and illiterate', 'official and unofficial', and other such 'them and us' couplings are easy to understand in theory, but in practice the issues are much more complex. Further unwitting obfuscation was created by the model of the 'little tradition' and the 'great tradition', the one of the people at large, the other of the learned, which recognised that popular or folk culture is not a closed system. The assertion that the 'great tradition and little tradition have long affected each other and continue to do so' acknowledged the mutual flow between the two, although as Peter Burke noted, 'the elite participated in the little tradition, but the common people did not participate in the great tradition'. The distinction is offensively patronising, as are labels such as 'the little people' to describe those who were, or are, the non-elite. In Scotland the people at large were called, quite simply, as they still are, 'folk'. Most observers would now agree with Carlo Ginzburg, following Mikhail Bakhtin, that the key lies in 'circularity': 'between the culture of the dominant classes and that of the subordinate classes there existed, in preindustrial Europe, a circular relationship composed of reciprocal influences, which travelled from low to high as well as from high to low'.[2] Thus, a synthetic and holistic model is to be preferred, composed of many interlocking and overlapping spheres of belief and activity, one influencing the other.

Anthropological concepts of 'official culture', maintained through formal documents and laws, and 'real culture', or culture as it is actually practised, fail to encapsulate that exchange and rapport between the two; 'official culture stands in relation to real culture as the elite value system stands in relation to that of the folk'.[3] This is not to lament the passing of a merry, rosy-cheeked peasantry dancing on the village common; rather it is to celebrate, and in some measure to recover, the non-exclusive culture that virtually everyone took for granted. For long in western culture the progress of 'civilisation' has been marked by the distance which the elite have been able to place between themselves and the folk, by stressing the superiority of learning over supposed ignorance, of literacy over orality and by emphasising the importance of the rise of manners, widely interpreted. A possible means of studying such phenomena is provided by the unifying discipline of folklore.

One of the functions of folklore is to maintain the stability of culture:

> the basic paradox of folklore is that while it plays a vital role in transmitting and maintaining the institutions of a culture and in forcing the individual to conform to them, at the same time it provides socially approved outlets for the repressions which these same institutions impose upon him.

People who have had a supernatural experience do not always interpret it as such themselves: 'the social group that surrounds him [or her] may also participate in the interpretation'. Furthermore, while some people may be prone to phenomenal experiences, others may be better able to provide an explanation. Ultimately, 'the group controls the experiences of its members'. To formulate the matter in another way, in terms postulated by the Italian Marxist Antonio Gramsci, there is a cultural hegemony in effect which operates from the bottom up so that, culturally speaking, certain phenomena cannot be disbelieved.[4] It was as impossible, at certain times in history, to question the existence of witches as it is today to query Einstein's Theory of Relativity, either on the grounds of supposed invincible authority or the certainty of invincible ignorance. So it was with fairy belief, but the group itself was subject to the historical influences being exerted upon it, sometimes perceived, but often impersonal, unknown and incomprehensible – and thus, in turn, the beliefs themselves were affected by remote forces originating far from the community.

That many people in pre-industrial Europe believed in fairies cannot be disputed on the basis of available evidence. They were a part of everyday life, as real to people as the sunrise, and as incontrovertible as the existence of God. While fairy belief was only a fragment of a much larger complex, investigation of the fairy tradition is potentially rewarding. Through the study of folk beliefs, it may be possible to understand the worldview of people who lived in a past which was very different from our present. Too often the study of history is concerned with recognition and relevance, or worse is approached with a sense of presentism which is as much the conceit as it is the curse of scholarly enquiry at the commencement of the twenty-first century. People in our past did not think or act as we do, yet they experienced anxieties and bewilderments as profound, or more so, as those which affect us all, and like many of us they sought explanations outside themselves.

It has been observed that the supernatural is the least studied of all topics in the folklore discipline, a circumstance that can be attributed to an academic bias against supernatural beliefs on ideological grounds: namely, that such beliefs 'arise from and are supported by various kinds of obvious error'. A great deal of scholarly work has taken this perspective, a 'tradition of disbelief', as its starting point, the adoption of an attitude in which both belief and disbelief are suspended and an external point of view taken. The approach adopted in this book is that which has been termed 'experience-centred' and focuses not on whether a belief is true or untrue, but on the reasons such beliefs are held to be credible. It should be possible to believe one's informants without believing their explanations. When dealing with the beliefs of people in the past there is the additional problem of trying to understand the world in which they lived, a world constantly subject to modification by the identical beliefs that we are attempting to recover. The study of alien belief-systems requires a 'temporary suspension of the cognitive assumptions of our own society'. The role of the folklorist with regard to folk belief scholarship has been, and will doubtless continue to be, a hotly debated issue. The stance taken in this study is that it is irrelevant whether or not fairies existed; what matters is that people believed in the reality of the phenomenon. The folklorist is thus interested, as should be the historian, in the 'reality of the supranormal experience and not in the reality of paranormal phenomena'.[5]

This book is largely, but not exclusively, concerned with fairy belief in pre-industrial Scotland. The assumption is that before revolutionary economic changes engulfed both rural and urban Scotland, generally in the eighteenth and nineteenth centuries but at different times in different places, life had remained much the same for several hundred years. People in 1450 lived in pretty much the same type of house, ate the same sort of food, worked on the land in much the same sort of occupation and died the same sort of death as folk in 1750. People alive in the latter years would have more in common with their predecessors than they would with their successors in 1850. Before the mass exodus to the cities, or overseas, most people still lived on estates subject to the whim of the local laird in his castle or 'big house'; they inhabited a world that, economically, socially and culturally, was still essentially medieval.[6] Such a model confers a validity upon the work of the collectors in the late eighteenth and early nineteenth centuries frequently denied by the more severe of their critics. These men – for they were almost exclusively male – were still in touch with traditions which were vital and persistent. While some embroidery and invention did take place, much of their evidence must be evaluated, scrutinised and corroborated like any other historical source material. When subjected to rigorous analysis, it very often passes the test.

The fairies of Scottish folk, and for that matter the learned, tradition bear little or no resemblance to the vast majority of modern stereotypes of fairies. Rather, the images inherited by the twenty-first century find their inspiration in the butterfly-winged, diaphanously clad, frolicking nymphs of writers such as Shakespeare, and artists such as Blake and Fuseli, with a hefty infusion of later accretion. The romantic Cottingley Fairies, the materialistic Tooth Fairy,[7] and Walt Disney's mischievous Tinker Bell are the pervasive iconographic forms in current popular culture. The approach of the third millennium generated a spate of fairy books, often profusely and imaginatively illustrated, and frequently inspired by the New Age movement. Many of these, unfortunately, depend much more on faith, fantasy and intuition than upon any shadow of respect for the disciplines of History and Folklore. Although the literary, artistic and mass media creations were undoubtedly inspired by folk tradition, they are by no means representative of their often wilfully ignored, and frequently disparaged, folk roots.

If it were possible to ask the people of pre-industrial Scotland what they thought about the 'guid neighbours', they would probably admit to a fascination (from Latin *fascinum*, a spell, witchcraft) but they would deny that there was anything very merry, or coy, or playfully mischievous about the fairy folk in their experience. The fairies were dangerous, capable of inflicting terrible harm, even death upon people and their livestock, and every precaution had to be taken to keep them at bay, or at least placated. Though they were occasionally benign, their proclivity towards cruelty and general malevolence meant that they were best avoided at all costs. The northern 'light-hearted, night-tripping elves',[8] so dear to the hearts of a number of investigators during the past two hundred years, can no longer be said to reflect the fairy traditions that once impacted upon the Scottish consciousness.

What's in a Name?

James Hogg, the Ettrick Shepherd, wittily distinguished the problem besetting the study of fairy belief:

> That fairies *were*, was not disputed,
> But *what* they were was greatly doubted.
> Each argument was guarded well,
> With 'if' and 'should', and 'who can tell'.

Because of their unfavourable reputation, fairies were frequently given amiable and agreeable names. Such placatory appellatives were thought to please and mollify the fairies, thus reducing the risk of inducing their wrath. Robert Kirk's *The Secret Common-Wealth* affirmed that *sluagh-maith*, or 'good people', was a name often used by Highlanders, 'it would seem, to prevent the dint of their ill attempts'. It was a rule best obeyed *ad infinitum* as they were supposed always to be invisibly present, so at all times must be spoken of with respect. Kirk used a variety of designations: subterranean people, invisible people, and lychnobious people (those living by lamplight). Of this last appellation he explained, they 'instead of day, useth the night, and liveth as it were by candle night'. He also distinguished between lowland names such as elves, fauns, and fairies, and Gaelic terms '*hubhsisgedh, caiben, lusbartan & siotbsudh*'.[9]

Throughout the whole of Scotland there were several different euphemisms for fairies: the good neighbours, the good people, the honest folk, the fairfolk, the green goons, the gentry, the little people, the forgetful people, the still people, the restless people, the seelie and unseelie court (from *sellig* meaning blessed), and the people of peace. Other terminology for these eldritch (weird, unearthly) beings included elves, the hill folk, fanes, and the klippe. Gaelic words for fairy were *sith*, *sluagh* (the fairy host), and *Daoine Síth* or *maithe* (people of peace). The Dame of the Fine Green Kirtle, a fairy woman who is usually friendly, features in many Highland folktales. Within the rich, and heavily Norse influenced, traditions of Orkney and Shetland they were known as the peedie and peerie (small) folk, ferries, the grey folk, the huldre-folk or hidden people, and the hillyans, but the most common term was troll, trow or trowies. A related species, known as the kunal-trow, was male only and therefore obliged to marry a human bride, but on the birth of their child the mother died. The hogboy or hogboon (from Old Norse *haug-búinn*, meaning mound-dweller) inhabited Orkney burial chambers and guarded them from intruders. Over time, the hogboy traditions became intermingled with the brownies from mainland Scotland.[10]

Brownies or broonies, who were the answer to the peasant's prayer since they could accomplish a superhuman amount of work without demanding payment, attached themselves to particular households or families. In appearance, they have been variously described, from squat, shaggy, naked creatures to tall, handsome and well proportioned. They usually kept to themselves, being mostly solitaries, unlike the fairies who were notably gregarious. Generally brownies were thought to be male, with only occasional references to the female of the species, though the gruagach has been described as 'a female spectre of the class of Brownies, to whom the dairy-maids made frequent libations of milk'.[11]

One generic term frequently used is 'wicht' in the primary sense of 'a supernatural being or one with supposed supernatural powers', as in the label 'the guid wichts' for the fairies. In the centuries of persecution and demonisation the word fell together with 'witch', and although the term survived in the sense of 'wight' (warrior or man), much damage was done in the intervening period.

In some cases the personal names of individual fairy folk are given, though such occurrences are fairly unusual. The most interesting name of all, used to specifically denote the queen of the fairies, is NicNiven or Neven, which appears to derive from Neamhain, one of the Gaelic and Irish war furies better known as Badb. The matter is complex since Neamhain and Badb may represent different aspects of the same persona, but *badhb* in some Irish dialects is the word for the supernatural death messenger more familiarly known in Ireland and Scotland as the banshee, *bean-shithe* literally 'fairy woman' in Gaelic. *Badhb* also means a hoodie-crow and carries the sense of 'deadly' or 'ill-fated'; it can also translate as 'witch', which is apposite since in Scotland NicNiven was also queen of the witches. This intriguing name therefore, it would appear, originated in the Gàidhealtachd whence it was imported into the Lowlands and even found its way to Shetland. W. B. Yeats was therefore incorrect when he stated that 'the gentle fairy presences' which haunted the imagination of his countrymen became 'formidable and evil as soon as they were transferred to Scottish soil', since this truly terrifying death messenger seems to be shared by both Ireland and Scotland while her associations give some indication of how the Scots regarded the fairy queen.

Self-confessed witch, Isobel Gowdie, supplied several names during her trial in 1662, such as Robert the Jakis, Sanderis the Read Reaver, Thomas the Fearie [Fairy?] and Robert the Rule. An old lady from Quarff, Shetland was reported early in the twentieth century as having known some trows by name, such as 'Sara Neven' (NicNiven again) and 'Robbie a da Rees' (obscure but possibly Norn *russa* a mare or horse). In the ballads, the only cognomen given to a fairy is Hind Etin, the lusty lover from the ballad of the same name. In the genre of folktale personal names are occasionally ascribed. The nasty Lowland fairy, Whoopity Stoorie, whose name must be guessed to break the spell, and the benevolent Habetrot, a fairy patron of spinning, are examples from the genre. The brownies are also generally innominate, though there are a few exceptions. The best known is perhaps Galloway's Aiken Drum, the Brownie of Bladnoch, but there are others, such as Wag-at-the-wa' from the Borders, Puddlefoot from Perthshire and Meg Mullach (or Hairy Meg), a female brownie from Strathspey.[12]

The etymology of the word 'fairy' is about as vague and amorphous as the creature which it signifies, though there has been no lack of theories about its derivation. Many have favoured etymologies derived from words that denoted female supernatural beings, such as the Arabic *Peri*, or the Latin *nympha*. Others sought out derivatives from words with supernatural associations, such as the Old English *fagan*, or the Latin *fatua*.[13] One popular idea is that in the Roman period the Latin *fata*, meaning 'fate', came to be associated with native goddesses. Hypothetically as the Latin language was subsumed by Old French the /t/ was omitted, producing *fae*, but unfortunately, there is no concrete evidence for such a change. Noel Williams, who has conducted a thorough study of the word and its mystical connotations and denotations, points out that the main problem with this etymology is its reliance upon the 'vague processes of 'identification' and 'misunderstanding''. The majority of Old French *fee* and Middle English *fay* citations rarely indicate a female enchanter, but rather denote a 'quality of phenomena or events which may or may not be associated with creatures'. Although *fay* could be used to mean 'enchantress', this was not the primary sense of the much more common *fairy*, which seems to convey the concept of 'fatedness', a quality 'which can control and direct the actions of humanity'. The etymology may not derive from *fata* and *fae*, but from a term denoting fatedness. There were also words in Old English, such as *faege*, 'fated, doomed to die', *aelf* meaning 'supernatural', and the problematical *scinu* which could mean 'skin', or 'shining', 'apparition' or 'appearance', all in a supernatural context. It is possible that when the term *fairy* was imported into Britain it incorporated some of the connotations of these Old English words. But whatever the precise etymology, the notion of 'fatedness' has been central to the development of the word *fairy* since its earliest occurrences.[14] It is in this sense that it was utilised in Scotland by medieval makars, or poets, such as Blind Harry and Gavin Douglas. To say that a person was 'surely fey' meant that he was near his end; to be 'fey taikin' was to have a presage of impending death. 'Fey' in Douglas's poetry conveyed the sense of 'unfortunate' or 'producing fatal effects', ideas implicit in the Scottish notion of fairies.

It is an important consideration that the word *fairy*, as it emerged in twelfth-century England, was initially a literary term. The people at large would have retained Old English words.[15] It is not clear when *fairy* was incorporated into everyday language, though there is some evidence to suggest that the term was becoming reasonably well established in Scotland by the fifteenth century.

Betwixt and Between: What are Fairies?

The importance of Robert Kirk's work to the understanding of the nature of fairy belief, and other supernatural phenomena, cannot be stressed enough since he greatly enhanced his account by drawing upon a range of informants and tradition-bearers. His invaluable contribution provides an unrivalled corpus of information and a rare insight into various aspects of belief in the latter half of the seventeenth century. Kirk opined that fairies were a distinct order of created beings, possessing intelligence, and having 'light changable bodies' that could be 'best seen in twilight', though usually only by 'seers or men of the second sight'. In many ways their lives paralleled those of humans, whom they resembled in size and appearance, but they lived in a state 'betwixt man and angell', which rendered them difficult to define, often leading commentators to describe what they were not rather than what they were. To Sir Walter Scott 'the fairies were a race which might be described by negatives, being neither angels, devils, nor the souls of deceased men',[16] but, needless to say, such doubts did not prevent him from formulating his own opinions on the nature of these puzzling beings. In his incomparably influential *Minstrelsy of the Scottish Border* (1802–3) he characterised fairies as a capricious, diminutive race who dressed in green, rode horses in invisible processions, and inhabited conical-shaped hills. They frequently danced on the hills by moonlight, leaving behind circles or fairy rings in the grass; they attacked humans and cattle with elf-shot, and they enjoyed hunting. The 'Wizard of the North' considered that Scottish fairies never received the 'attractive and poetical embellishments' enjoyed by their English counterparts. He speculated that this was perhaps due to the stricter persecutions these creatures suffered under the presbyterian clergy, which had the effect of 'hardening their dispositions, or at least in rendering them more dreaded by those among whom they dwelt'. He also suggested that the landscape of Scotland might have been conducive to a more malevolent and terrifying breed, since

> we should naturally attribute a less malicious disposition, a less frightful appearance, to the fays who glide by moon-light through the oaks of Windsor, than to those who haunt the solitary heaths and lofty mountains of the North.

The idea that certain landscapes facilitated fairy-spotting was widely held. One visitor maintained in 1794 that the Isle of Man was the only place where there was any probability of seeing a fairy. Man was, at one time, briefly part of the kingdom of Scotland and links remained close, particularly with Galloway, for hundreds of years. His informant – 'an aged peasant of a pensive and melancholy aspect' – had told the visiting investigator that the elves were most likely to be seen sitting beside brooks and waterfalls, half-concealed among bushes, or dancing on mountain tops. These creatures were 'generally enveloped in clouds or in the mountain fogs, and haunted the hideous precipices and caverns on the sea-shore'. The visitor considered that Manx people were more susceptible to fairy sightings because of scenery and 'a sombrous imagination heightened by traditionary terrors'.[17]

Fairy Origins: Folk and Learned Ideas

Speculations as to the origins of fairies are almost as numerous as the different types of their kind who once haunted Scotland. Some authorities considered them to be ghosts, or the souls of the pagan dead, existing in a limbo between heaven and earth, while others thought that they were originally nature spirits. To some commentators they were representative of a folk memory of an actual race of people driven by their conquerors into remote and inaccessible areas, or a similarly remembered race who were believed to be diminutive in size, or a shady recollection of the druids. Alternatively, they might be fallen angels cast out of heaven by God. In the Irish tradition the fairies were derived from mythological deities. The legend of the Tuatha Dé Danann owes much to erudite Irish monks well-versed in a highly developed antiquarian tradition. It relates that the Tuatha were a divine race, descended from the Greek mother goddess Danu, who were conquered by the Milesians (humankind). The mortal victors struck a bargain to the effect that while they would inhabit the surface of the earth, the defeated pantheon would either retreat west to the island of Tir Nan Og (Land of Youth) or make new homes inside the earth; thereafter they were known as the *sidhe*. Stories of the Tribe of Danu circulated in Scotland from at least the sixteenth century, and doubtlessly long before. Bishop Carswell identified the fairies as the Tuatha Dé Danann in the introduction to his Gaelic Prayer Book of 1567. Whatever the theories as to origin, there was, as might be expected, considerable overlap, as the folk absorbed elements of the learned tradition.[18]

That fairies represented the souls of the dead, or ghosts, was for long a fashionable opinion and, at times, a confusingly entwined yet distinct tradition of the folk. To discover something of the persistence of the connection one need look no further than the depositions given by accused witches Bessie Dunlop (1576) and Alison Peirson (1588), who both clearly maintained a linkage to the fairy realm through men who were once ordinary living, breathing mortals. Folk customs, such as the offering of meal and milk to appease the fairies, were carried out to placate the dead. In 1656 there were reports at Kinlochewe of the 'pouring of milk upon hills as oblationes'.[19] Often, as for example in Orkney, the offerings were decanted into, or left on top of, neolithic burial chambers. Kirk's parishioners held divided opinions about the nature and origin of the inhabitants of Fairyland, though most believed that the dead were in some way connected with, or shared a relationship with, the fairies.

Some thought the fairies to be caught in a state of limbo, a condition which seems to have distressed them: 'their continuall sadness is because of their pendulous state . . . as uncertain what at the last revolution [Judgement Day] will becom of them, when they are lockt up into an unchangable condition'. Others averred that the 'subterranean people' were 'departed souls attending a whil in this inferior state, and cloth'd with bodies' procured through their good deeds in life. Second-sighted people told Kirk they often saw fairies attending funerals, where they would partake of funereal food, or might carry the coffin 'among the midle-earth men to the grave'. A fairy might appear as a 'double-man' or doppelgänger, also known as a 'reflex-man' or a 'co-walker', a kind of mirror-image or wraith. Places distinguished as fairy hills were also popularly believed to house the souls of the ancestors, and 'a mote or mount was dedicate beside everie church-yard, to receave the souls, till their adjacent bodies arise, and so become as a fayrie-hill', a notion which spawned the idea that fairies were the guardians of the dead.[20]

Tales and legends accumulated through the fieldwork of the American Evans-Wentz, in the first decade of last century, indicated that some people believed fairies were spirits of the dead, while others thought they were both spirits of the dead and other spirits not the dead, while others again explained they were like the dead, but were not to be identified with them. He contrasted Breton death legends and customs with fairy traditions found in Scotland, Ireland and Wales and uncovered several overlapping areas. His conclusions, which were conditioned by a pan-Celtic approach no longer convincing, may have been influenced by his Oxford teacher Andrew Lang who, commenting on the creatures of Robert Kirk's treatise, found them like 'a lingering memory of the Chthonian beings, "the ancestors"', and who pronounced that 'there are excellent proofs that fairyland was a kind of Hades, or home of the dead'. Another American, Lowry C. Wimberly, found striking resemblances between the ballad ghost and the ballad fairy, thus reinforcing the idea, well established in the folk tradition, but ultimately to be traced to literary notions of Pluto and Hades, of a close relationship between fairies and the souls of the dead.[21]

Postulations based on the premise that fairies constitute a folk memory of former races, conquered peoples who were pushed out beyond the periphery of settled areas, have fuelled the imagination of many scholars on this subject.[22] Of particular significance was a theory advanced by David MacRitchie that fairies were an actual race of small or 'little' people, the original Pictish peoples of Scotland. Although MacRitchie is often credited with first suggesting this idea, it had been long anticipated. Thirty years earlier it had been argued that the first fairies were Picts. He was also pre-empted by the esteemed collector of Highland folktale, John Francis Campbell of Islay, who in 1860 wrote:

> Men do believe in fairies, though they will not readily confess the fact. And though I do not myself believe that fairies *are*, in spite of the strong evidence offered, I believe there once was a small race of people in these islands, who are remembered as fairies . . . the fairy was probably a Pict.

Campbell argued that there were more reasons to assume fairies were once real people rather than 'creatures of the imagination', or 'spirits in prison', or fallen angels, because the evidence of their 'actual existence is very much more direct and substantial', not to mention that all European nations have had similar beliefs 'and they cannot all have invented the same fancy'.[23]

Walter Traill Dennison, a collector of Orkney folklore, associated the fairies with the Picts, but he also pointed out that prehistoric burial mounds were believed to be trowie homes. Folk traditions were not entirely devoid of the Pictish association, as is indicated by stories about the 'pechts' and the numerous 'Picts' houses' marked on nineteenth-century Ordnance Survey maps to denote archaeological remains of indeterminate origin, yet it is difficult to establish how far back in time the identification of Picts with supernatural entities can really be traced and whether or not this was a 'learned' imposition upon folk ideas or vice versa. Late nineteenth- and twentieth-century commentators generally state that folklore concerning the Picts confused them with gnomes, brownies and fairies because of the nature of Pictish archaeological remains. Brochs, tower-like structures found mainly, but not exclusively, in the Western and Northern Isles and dated to the period 500 B.C. to 200 A.D., have small entrances and tiny steps. Souterrains, possibly cellars or storage chambers which are low-roofed and underground, dated from around Roman times to c. 700 A.D. but built by local people, contributed to the supposition that the Picts were of small stature. In fact, the fallacious idea that the Picts were short and lived underground can be traced back to the eleventh-century *History of the Archbishops of Hamburg-Bremen* by Adam of Bremen, and the anonymous *Historia Norwegiae*, written c.1200. The latter noticed that 'the

Picts little exceeded pigmies in stature'. Morning and evening they worked hard at building their brochs, 'but at mid-day they entirely lost all their strength, and lurked, through fear, in little underground houses'.[24] Both histories are reflective of the type of propaganda that must have followed the subjugation of Pictish life and culture by the Vikings and the Scots. There is no archaeological evidence to suggest the Picts, or for that matter any of the other peoples of early Scotland, were of particularly small stature. Nonetheless, the folk were capable of making their own rationalisations. If they found inland deposits of shells or sand they assumed that such sites had once been covered by the sea, just as fishermen figured out that some parts of the ocean had inundated dry land or people finding tree roots in peat bogs assumed the sometime existence of a forest that had otherwise totally disappeared. They were perfectly capable of working out for themselves that structural remains, whatever their size, on moors or hillsides had been placed there by their predecessors.

The theory that fairies represented a folk memory of druids, on the other hand, clearly owed much to book knowledge, as did the far-fetched assertion that fairy changelings were actually children stolen by druids in order to procure 'the necessary supply of members for their order'. Over-enthusiastic antiquaries were capable of the wildest fantasies beside which the supposed ignorant superstitions of the folk pale into insignificance. One such antiquarian bizarrely maintained that the belief in fairies

> doubtless arose from the circumstance that the priestesses or female Druids, who performed some of the rites of their religion while living in retired places, were called by the poets the 'nymphs of the groves', which gave rise to the fancy of ignorant people that charming fairy women, clad in green apparel, inhabited remote places, such as woods, valleys, hills, and rude dens.[25]

Such views were an echo of the Ossianic craze sparked off when James Macpherson published his *Fragments of Ancient Poetry* (1760) to the accompaniment of Hugh Blair's *Critical Dissertation* on same, both men conspiring in a sort of well-intentioned literary fraud which seized the imagination of their readers. So widely read were the putative poems of Ossian, the ancient Gaelic bard, druids and all, that they entered the popular tradition.

Yet another theory of origin appears in the intriguing tale of a reputed giant living in the North of Scotland, called 'Balkin, the Lord of the Northern Mountains', which identified him as the father of the fairies:

> . . . he was shaped like a satyr and fed upon the air, having wife and children to the number of 12 thousand which were the brood of the northern fairies, inhabiting Southerland [Sutherland] and Cateness [Caithness] with the adjacent islands.

His multitudinous progeny spoke ancient Irish, lived in caverns and mountains, and engaged in regular combat with the fiery spirits of Mount Hekla in Iceland. The supposition that fairies were more likely to be found in the remotest of regions was of longstanding. Ever since medieval times mention of either of the two northernmost mainland counties automatically equated with supernatural habitats. A fourteenth-century English map noted of the empty spaces of Sutherland, *hic habundabant lupu* (here wolves abound).[26] Wolves, witches and fairy wichts co-existed in the wilderness.

The idea that the fairies were sired by a superior being was not uncommon, though by far the most pre-eminent 'father' was none other than God himself. The notion of fairies as the fallen angels expelled, with Lucifer, from heaven is particularly prevalent in both written record and oral tradition, a theory which gained particular prominence because there is good biblical authority for their existence, in the many passages which mention spirits and demons. Such interconnections between fairy and christian belief are surprisingly frequent. On his visit to Orkney and Shetland in 1700, John Brand surmised that fairies were evil spirits and fallen angels. Alexander Carmichael recorded these evocative lines from an old man of Barra, quoting the fairies:

> Not of the seed of Adam are we
> Nor is Abraham our father,
> But of the seed of the Proud Angel
> Driven forth from Heaven.

Another Barra man reasoned that though the fairies must be spirits, it was his firm belief 'that they are not the spirits of dead men, but are fallen angels', a belief paralleled in Shetland:

> When the angels fell, some fell on the land, some on the sea. The former are fairies [the latter were often said to be the seals]. A fairy once met a man and asked him if he might be saved. The man said, Yes if you can say 'Our Father which art in heaven.' The fairy tried

but could only [say], 'Our Father which wert in heaven,' and went away lamenting.[27]

Extinction of a Species: The Retreat of the Fairies?

It is a curious phenomenon that each generation perceives that the former generation was, not only more superstitious, but generally had more folklore. Hugh Miller's metaphorical explanation encapsulates this sentiment:

> I see the stream of tradition rapidly lessening as it flows onward, and displaying, like those rivers of Africa which lose themselves in the burning sands of the desert, a broader and more powerful volume as I trace it towards its source.

His sadness at the decline in supernatural belief in general was widely shared:

> These credulous times are long, long gone by, and we can see no more the flitting sea-trow or the peculiar Finnman. Civilisation has crept in upon all fairy strongholds and disenchanted the many fair scenes in which they were wont to hold their courts . . . the light of science has shone upon every green mound and dispossessed it of its fairy inhabitants.[28]

The notion that the fairies were always slightly out of reach, slipping beyond human ken as they vanished into the mists of time, is exceedingly tenacious and of long duration. Almost every generation has apparently been convinced that fairy belief was stronger among its predecessors. This was equally true during periods when fairies were taken very seriously indeed. However, even at the height of their baleful influence it is possible to find this theme of what one scholar has neatly distinguished as 'the perpetual recession of the fairies'.[29]

The theme was picked up by such an impeccable authority as Chaucer whose works were very well known and appreciated in Scotland. A passage in the *Canterbury Tales* blames the decline of fairies on the priests and holy men:

> In th'olde dayes of the Kyng Arthour, . . .
> Al was this lond fulfild of fayerye.
> The elf-queene, with hir joly compaignye,
> Daunced ful ofte in many a grene mede, . . .

> I speke of manye hundrid yeres ago;
> But now kan no man se none elves mo,
> For now the grete charitee and prayeres
> Of lymytours and othere hooly freres, . . .
> This maketh that ther ben no fayeryes . . .[30]

William Cleland, poet, commander of the Cameronian Regiment and victor at the siege of Dunkeld (1689) in which he was killed, attributed their disappearance to the Reformation; it is interesting to note the connection he made between the catholic faith and the existence of fairies. Addressing Parnassus he declared:

> There's als much virtue, sense, and pith,
> In Annan, or the water of Nith,
> Which quietly slips by Dumfries,
> Als any water in all Greece.
> For there, and several other places,
> About mill-dams, and green brae faces,
> Both Elrich elfs and brownies stayed,
> And green-gown'd fairies daunc'd and played:
> When old John Knox, and other some,
> Began to plott the Haggs of Rome;
> Then suddenly took to their heels,
> And did no more frequent these fields;
> But if Rome's pipes perhaps they hear,
> Sure, for their interest they'll compear
> Again, and play their old hell's tricks.

Scotland's writers and antiquarians have proved no strangers to the recessive qualities of the fairies. An Orkney minister lamented:

> No more shall they be found,
> Travel all the country round,
> Over hill, through dale, up river:
> They are all underground,
> And hidden from the sound
> Of our voices, should we call on them forever.[31]

Hugh Miller saw the dimming of the fairies as a product of growing up. He sadly related:

But the marvels of his childhood had been melting away, one after one – the ghost, and the wraith, and the fairy had all disappeared; and the wide world seemed to spread out before him a tame and barren region, where truth dwelt in the forms of commonplace, and in these only.

J. F. Campbell noted a decline in fairy belief in the Western Isles and its passing out of oral culture and into the pages of books:

> Fairy belief is becoming a fairy tale. In another generation it will grow into a romance, as it has in the hands of poets elsewhere, and then the whole will be either forgotten or carried from people who must work to 'gentles' who can afford to be idle and read books.

John Firth, writing of Orkney in the 1920s, thought it remarkable that enlightened people, 'even within the last generation, believed in, and feared, the malicious tricks of the fairies on the occasions of births and deaths, though long since they had ceased to believe in their interference in the ordinary affairs of life'.[32]

Sometimes it was not the fairies that seemed to be disappearing but their cousins, the brownies. Reginald Scot wrote, as early as 1584, that Robin Goodfellow, the English equivalent of the brownie, was not as feared as he had been a hundred years previously, and had been replaced by a fear of witches. The process was apparently slower in Scotland. When George Low visited the Northern Isles in 1774 he found that 'witches and fairies and their histories, are still very frequent in Schetland, but Brownies seem, within this century, to lose ground'.[33] However, brownies continued to fascinate and they were fictively popularised in the early nineteenth century by such publications as James Hogg's *The Brownie of Boddsbeck* and William Nicholson's poem 'The Brownie of Blednoch', so admired that it entered, in tale form, the oral tradition of Galloway. As to why there has been a general contagion throughout history of ascribing certain traditions or beliefs to a previous age there is no easy answer, save that each generation seems to preen itself on being superior to its predecessor, though there have been many who have recognised the symptom:

> Educated Europeans generally conceive that this sort of belief is extinct in their own land, or, at least their own immediate section of that land. They accredit such degree of belief as may remain, in this enlightened age, to some remote part . . . But especially they accredit it to a previous age.

Recent fieldwork in Newfoundland, to take but one example, has demonstrated that fairy belief is by no means extinct, even if somewhat reduced in status. Interviews with informants disclosed that conversation about fairy belief was a means of discussing the past and of reflecting on how times had changed. The fairies' 'perceived recession makes them an evocative symbol of the past, and conveys an image of a time in which the way of life and worldview were more amenable to fairy tradition than today'.[34]

The reasons as to why the fairies were fading were many and varied. If Cleland attributed decline to the Reformation, others credited the growth of science and technology, the rise of rationality and reason, and changing economic circumstances.

The synonymity between the past as an age of irrationality and darkness, and the present as an age of reason and light, was a sentiment that was strong among the educated classes of the late eighteenth and early nineteenth centuries, and left a legacy of prejudice well into the twentieth. Adam Ferguson, at the height of the Scottish Enlightenment, wrote that superstition had been defeated due to the 'light of true religion, or to the study of nature, by which we are led to substitute a wise providence operating by physical causes in the place of phantoms that terrify or amuse the ignorant'. An English tourist, Sir John Stoddart, who visited Scotland in 1799–1800, furthered the equation between the irrational and rational in geographical terms; for him Scotland equated with the former and England with the latter. He was not surprised that a country like Scotland should be 'marked by superstitions'. Expressing a view which (as was noted above) would later be embraced by Scott, it was the very landscape that made the Scots a more 'superstitious' race: 'the scenery here is very favourable to the excursive flights of the imagination'. However, Stoddart was gracious enough to point out that there was still hope for Scotland since he found that, in general, superstitions were fast wearing away: 'Every peasant spoke of the belief in them, as originating in times of darkness, and contrasted it with the clear and accurate knowledge of the present day'. For visitors like him, however, the noting of supernatural belief traditions was an essential part of the Scottish experience, a confirmation of the backwardness of the place. Though Scotland as a whole was targeted for such stereotyping, the Highlands and Islands bore the brunt of it, sometimes with native complicity. It was noted that the 'barbarous' Highlanders 'are much addicted to a kind of sorcery and charming; and it is commonly said that (in the remottest places especially) there are still several among them who deall with familiar spirits'. Folklore has the potential to patronise and the practice has not yet ceased. It was thus a delightful irony when Robert Burns contributed his 'Tam o' Shanter' to the second volume of *Antiquities of Scotland* by the boozy and comical Francis Grose, practitioner of the antiquarian trade who eagerly looked forward to consorting with the devil's crew in 'auld, houlet-haunted' biggins and ruined kirks.[35]

Another idea was that agrarian transformation defeated the fairies:

> The land once ripped by the plowshare, or the sward once passed over by the scythe proclaimed the banishment of the Fairies from holding residence there forever after. The quick progress of Lowland agriculture will completely overthrow their empire; none now are seen, save solitary and dejected fugitives, ruminating among the ruins of their fallen kingdom!

James Hogg believed that the fairies had totally disappeared, 'and it is a pity that they should for they seem to have been quite the most delightful little spirits that ever haunted the Scottish dells'.[36] Even Scott, who was regarded as the great doyen of Scottish fairy belief, was convinced by 1826 that the fairies had been consigned to the cottage and the nursery.

It was believed, in some quarters, that nineteenth-century religious revivalism weakened the power of the fairies. In 1838 a Shetland laird was quoted as having told a tenant: 'the Methodist preachers are driving away all the trows and bogues and fairies'. It was also said in Shetland that the prayers of a Free Church minister, James Ingram, forced the trows to leave Unst and emigrate to the Faroe islands. The reporter for the parish of Kilmuir in Skye in the *New Statistical Account* (1840) pronounced the age of superstition to be gone. One prevalent view credited industrialisation with driving the fairies from their homes. A curious example was cited by Evans-Wentz who asserted that Glen Shee was once teeming with the spirits after whom it is named until the steam-whistle scared them underground- a somewhat inappropriate metaphor since there has never been a railway in the vicinity of Glen Shee!

A minister in South Ronaldsay (Orkney) attributed the retreat of the fairies to the march of progress, as he saw it. He reported in 1912:

> Times have changed, surroundings are different, and the atmosphere seems to be healthier, and life itself more wholesome. People are more practical and less sentimental, they have less time to muse on the past, or to be amused with fairy tales. The Hill Trows, the Water Trows,

and even the Kirk Trows, have nearly all disappeared before the advance of light and truth. Perhaps we are all indebted to the Penny Post, the daily papers, and the weekly steamers, [rather] than anything else for the disappearance of the old fairies. The best way to dispel darkness is to pour in light.

A Highlander named John Dunbar, drawing partly on his own experience and on what his parents had taught him, believed that people had seen fairies in the past, but no longer, 'because every place in this parish where they used to appear has been put into sheep, and deer, and grouse, and shooting'. He placed a new spin on the history of the Highland Clearances by recounting a story that the fairies had a premonition of the coming of the sheep and told of the ensuing fight between them as the fairies tried to protect their ancient domains. R. Menzies Fergusson, who so deplored the decline of supernatural belief traditions in general, attributed their waning to the new wave of mercantile greed and capitalism:

> At one time Orkney must have been teeming with trows or fairies, witches, elves, mermaids; but these imaginative superstitions are fast giving way before the stern fight for gain, that so often dulls the lively imagination and robs life of all its poetry.

A highly sceptical, if humorous, explanation is given in an 1850s guidebook to the Highlands. The fairies were awa' wi' the exciseman!

> There are still some who have seen and can tell wondrous stories of the fairies before the gaugers put them to flight by their odious tax upon the generous liquor which was required to warm and expand the heart ere those airy inhabitants condescended to reveal themselves to the eyes of man.

It is truly remarkable that until comparatively recently the fairies could be used to reflect upon wider concerns, viewed as symptoms of the great historical forces sweeping over the Highlands and Islands just as such bewildering movements as the Reformation or agricultural improvement had once impacted upon the rest of the country. One suggestion concerning the Gaelic-speaking areas of Scotland was that when 'English grammar invaded the highlands . . . the fairies retreated before it'. The opening by archaeologists of an Orkney chambered cairn, believed to be the home of the fairies, had the psychological effect of stripping away any mystery the place had once held.[37] The absence of mystique and magic is one of the great conundra confronting moderns, but they are not alone, for all generations seem to have been possessed of the belief that as the present slipped into the past they lost a little of themselves.

Notes

1. Robert Chambers, *Popular Rhymes of Scotland* (Edinburgh 1870), 324.
2. Robert Redfield, *Peasant Society and Culture* (Chicago 1956), 41–2; Peter Burke, *Popular Culture in Early Modern Europe* (New York 1978), 23–8, 58; Ginzburg, *The Cheese and the Worms*, xii.
3. Carl Lindahl, *Earnest Games: Folkloric Patterns in the Canterbury Tales* (Bloomington and Indianapolis 1989), 74.
4. William R. Bascom, 'Four Functions of Folklore', *The Study of Folklore*, in ed. Alan Dundes (N. J. 1965), 298; Lauri Honko, 'Memorates and the Study of Folk Beliefs', *Journal of the Folklore Institute* 1 (1964) 18; Antonio Gramsci, *Selections From the Prison Notebooks* (New York 1971), 12.
5. David J. Hufford, 'The Supernatural and the Sociology of Knowledge: Explaining Academic Belief', *New York Folklore* 9.1–2 (1983): 21; David J. Hufford, 'Traditions of Disbelief', *New York Folklore* 8.3–4 (1982): 47; David J. Hufford, 'Rational Scepticism and the Possibility of Unbiased Folk Belief Scholarship', *Talking Folklore* 9 (1990): 19; David J. Hufford, *The Terror That Comes in the Night: An Experience-Centered Study of Supernatural Assault Traditions* (Philadelphia 1989); Gillian Bennett, *Traditions of Belief: Women, Folklore and the Supernatural Today* (London 1987), 16; J. D. Y. Peel, 'Understanding Alien Belief-Systems', *British Journal of Sociology* 20.1 (1969): 82; Donald Ward, 'The Little Man Who Wasn't There: Encounters With the Supranormal', *Fabula* 18.3–4 (1977): 216.
6. Edward J. Cowan, 'The Hunting of the Ballad' in *The Ballad in Scottish History* (East Linton 2000), 12–13.
7. For an excellent appraisal of this topic see Paul Smith, 'The Cottingley Fairies: The End of a Legend', in *Good People*, 371–405. On the Tooth Fairy see Tad Tuleja, 'The Tooth Fairy: Perspectives on Money and Magic', and Rosemary Wells, 'The Making of an Icon: The Tooth Fairy in North American Folklore and Popular Culture', in *Good People*.
8. Thomas Keightley, *The Fairy Mythology* (1828; London 1981), 13. Keightley was one of the first scholars to undertake a comparative study of fairy traditions.
9. *The Works of the Ettrick Shepherd Centenary Edition*, ed. Thomas Thomson 2 vols. (Glasgow n.d.) vol. 2, 22; Patrick Graham, *Sketches Descriptive of Picturesque Scenery on the Southern Confines of Perthshire* (Edinburgh 1806), 120. Graham adds 'on Friday, particularly, they are supposed to

possess very extensive influence . . . if they are spoken of on that day, it is with apparent reluctance; and they are uniformly styled the *Daoine matha*, or good men'; Kirk, 49, 102, 117.

10 The 'green-goons' or gowns, was a Clackmannanshire term. John Ewart Simpkins, *Examples of Printed Folk-Lore Concerning Fife with some notes on Clackmannan and Kinross-shires County Folk-Lore. Vol vii,* Publications of the Folklore Society, lxxi, London 1914, 312; On the seelie (kindly) and unseelie (malignant) court see Katharine Briggs, *A Dictionary of Fairies* (London 1977), 353, 419. Jamieson's *Scottish Dictionary* says 'fane' is an Ayrshire name for fairy. The *SND* traces the coinage of this word to poet Joseph Train, *Poetical Reveries* (Glasgow 1806), possibly influenced by English 'fay'. Briggs, *Dictionary* says 'in default of further evidence, the name should possibly be listed as literary'. For 'Klippe', a Forfarshire name, see Eve Blantyre Simpson, *Folklore in Lowland Scotland* (1908; Wakefield 1976), 93; Hillyans is a Papa Westray term, Alan Bruford, 'Trolls, Hillfolk, Finns, and Picts', in *Good People*, 116–41. Giants and trows of the Northern Isles were introduced by Viking settlers in the 9th century. Words 'troll' or 'trow' appear in several place names and local words, e.g. Trowie Glen, Hoy, and Trolhouland, Shetland. On the trow and hog-boy see Ernest W. Marwick, *The Folklore of Orkney and Shetland* (London 1975), 30–3, 39–42, and 'Creatures of Orkney Legend and their Norse Ancestry', *Norveg Folkelivsgranskning* 15 (1972): 177–204. Jessie M. E. Saxby, *Shetland Traditional Lore* (Edinburgh 1932), 127–65, discusses the kunal-trow.

11 As reported by the minister in the Parish of Kilmuir, Skye, in 1840, *NSA*, vol. 14, 275.

12 On Neamhain and Badb see Patricia Lysaght, *The Banshee: The Irish Supernatural Death Messenger* (Dublin 1986), 34–9, 191–218, James MacKillop, *Dictionary of Celtic Mythology* (Oxford 1998), 27, 303, and Evelyn Kendrick Wells, *The Ballad Tree. A Study of British and American Ballads, Their Folklore, Verse and Music* (London 1950), 76. We are indebted to our friend Professor Cathair O'Dochartaigh for his helpful elucidation of this derivation; Trial of Isobel Gowdie, Pitcairn vol. 3, 606–615; E. S. Reid Tait, ed., *Shetland Folk Book* 9 vols. (Lerwick 1947–95) vol. 2 (1951) 24–5; On the Dame of the Fine Green Kirtle see John Francis Campbell, *Popular Tales of the West Highlands* 1860. 2 vols. (Edinburgh 1994) vol. 2, 156–76, Whoopity, or Whuppity, Stoorie, see Hannah Aitken, *A Forgotten Heritage, Original Folk Tales of Lowland Scotland* (Edinburgh 1973), 61–5, and Marwick, *Folklore of Orkney and Shetland* 144–6 provides an Orcadian version of this tale type called Peerifool. For Habetrot and Wag-at-the-wa' see William Henderson, *Notes on the Folk Lore of the Northern Counties of England and the Borders* (London 1866), 220–6. The name Aiken Drum was given by William Nicholson, see Malcolm M'L. Harper, *The Bards of Galloway: A Collection of Poems, Songs, Ballads, &c., by the Natives of Galloway* (Dalbeattie 1889), 72–

6; For Meg Mullach, first cited in John Aubrey's *Miscellanies*, and Puddlefoot see Briggs, *Dictionary*, 284–5, 337.

13 Keightley, *Fairy Mythology*, 4–13. Keightley devotes a sub-chapter to this topic. For an up-to-date reassessment consult Noel Williams, 'The Semantics of the Word *Fairy*: Making Meaning Out of Thin Air', *Good People*, 457–78.

14 Williams, in *Good People*, 462–7. There is no definitive proof of the influence of Old English *faege* on Old French *faer*, but Williams thinks that the possibility is strong; The earliest occurrences of *fairy* are found in French Medieval Romances of the 12th century. Such Romances would have been known to the educated classes within Scotland. The earliest recorded usage of 'Elf' is found in *Bald's Leechbook*, a mid-10th c. Anglo-Saxon manuscript including cures for 'elf-shot', Karen L. Jolly *Popular Religion in Late Saxon England: Elf Charms in Context* (Chapel Hill & London 1996), 145–67.

15 Williams, in *Good People*, 468–70. Many of these words, though they almost vanished from official usage, survived in the oral tradition.

16 For examples of Kirk as folklorist see 52, 54, 59, 61; Kirk, 49–51; *Letters*, 121.

17 *Minstrelsy*, vol. 2, 352–3; David Robertson, *A Tour Through the Isle of Man. To which is subjoined a review of the Manks History* (London 1794), 75–82.

18 Carolyn Whyte, *A History of Irish Fairies* (Dublin 1976), 10–12, Briggs, *Dictionary*, 400, 418. On Bishop Carswell see below p. 112–3.

19 Donald A. Mackenzie, *Scottish Folk-Lore and Folk-Life* (Glasgow 1935), 219; Pennant noted that dairymaids in the Hebrides still retained the custom of pouring milk on to stones associated with the Gruagach, a type of Brownie, *A Tour in Scotland and Voyage to the Hebrides*, 1772 ed. Andrew Simmons (1774, 1776; Edinburgh 1998), 313, 759.

20 Kirk, 52–61.

21 Walter Yeeling Evans-Wentz, *The Fairy Faith in Celtic Countries* 1911 (New York 1990), 84–116, 218–21. See also 'A Dead Wife Among the Fairies', in *Scottish Traditional Tales*, eds. Alan James Bruford and Donald Archie MacDonald (Edinburgh 1994), 357; Andrew Lang, intro. *The Secret Commonwealth*, by Robert Kirk. 1691 (London 1893), xxiii; Wimberly, *Folklore in the English and Scottish Ballads*, 165.

22 For example, Elwood Trigg, *Gypsy Demons & Divinities: The Magic and Religion of the Gypsies* (New Jersey 1973), 161–3, speculates the popular image of fairies may have derived from the appearance and activities of gypsies, and 'brownies' originated from a connection between the complexion of gypsies and descriptions of fairies as being 'dark'. The suggestions do not convince.

23 David MacRitchie, *The Testimony of Tradition* (London 1890) and *Fians, Faeries and Picts* (London 1893); Herbert Hore's article, 'Origin of the Irish Superstitions Regarding Banshees and Fairies', was written not later than 1844. MacRitchie maintained he and Hore arrived at their conclusions independently and were not known to one another, in *Scots Lore* 1.7 (Glasgow 1895) 404; Campbell, *Popular Tales of the West Highlands* vol. 1, 66–7, 72.

24 Dennison also speculated that the fin folk and sea-trows may have been confused with Lapps, Finns or the 'Esquimaux'. See Walter Traill Dennison, *Orkney Folklore and Traditions* (Kirkwall 1961), 16; A. O. Anderson, *Early Sources of Scottish History A.D. 500 to 1286* 2 vols. (Edinburgh 1922), vol. 1, 331, Anna Ritchie, *Perceptions of the Picts: From Eumenius to John Buchan* (Rosemarkie 1994), 20.

25 Graham, *Sketches Descriptive*, 113; Robert Dinnie, *History of Kincardine O'Neil* (Aberdeen 1885), 103. That the belief in fairies could be accounted for as Druids, who had fled from their enemies and hidden inside 'Picts' Houses' (chambered cairns), is a view also shared by James Cririe, *Scottish Scenery: or, Sketches in verse, descriptive of scenes chiefly in the Highlands of Scotland* (London 1803), 347–8.

26 Anon., 'A Discourse concerning Devils and Spirits', appended to Reginald Scot, *Discoverie of Witchcraft* (London 1665), 511; Edward J. Cowan, 'The Middle Centuries', in *The Sutherland Book* ed. Donald Omand (Golspie 1982), 186.

27 John A. Brand, *A Brief Description of Orkney, Zetland, Pightland Firth and Caithness*, 1701 (Edinburgh 1883), 170; Alexander Carmichael, *Carmina Gadelica* 6 vols. (Edinburgh 1928–54), vol. 2, 352–3; Evans-Wentz, *The Fairy Faith*, 113; Marwick, *The Folklore of Orkney and Shetland*, 46.

28 Hugh Miller, *Scenes and Legends of the North of Scotland* (1835; Edinburgh 1994), 2; R. Menzies Fergusson, *Rambling Sketches in the Far North* (Kirkwall 1883), 121–2.

29 Katharine Briggs, *The Fairies in Tradition and Literature* (London 1967), 3; The 'perpetual recession of the fairies' is a theme elaborated by Rieti, *Strange Terrain*, 51. Wirt Sikes, *British Goblins: The Realm of Faerie* (1880; rep. 1991), 4, thought that the practice of 'relegating fairy belief to a date just previous to its own' was not applicable to 'superstitious beliefs in general'. The validity of this statement remains inconclusive, though it would seem that similar comments have been made about other supernatural entities, such as witches, banshees, and selkies.

30 Geoffrey Chaucer, 'Wyf of Bathes Tale', *The Canterbury Tales*, 1387–1400. *The Complete Works of Geoffrey Chaucer*, ed. F. N. Robinson (London 1957), 84. According to Noel Williams, Chaucer used *fayerye* primarily to denote a kind of place or experience, and used *elf* for a type of creature. On four occasions he used *fayerye* collectively of creatures, but never to describe an individual. See William, 469.

31 William Cleland, *Effigies Clericorum*, qtd. in Charles Kirkpatrick Sharpe, *A Historical Account of the Belief in Witchcraft in Scotland* (Glasgow 1884), 22–3. Cleland was a covenanter who also fought at Drumclog and Bothwell Brig. He played a prominent part in defeating the first Jacobite Rising; D. W. Yair, 'Lament for the Departure of the Fairies', qtd. in R. Menzies Fergusson, *Rambling Sketches in the Far North* (Kirkwall 1883), 110–2. Fergusson also

quotes the English poet Lord Lytton, who composed the 'Complaint of the Last Faun', 'The youth of the earth is o'er/And its breast is rife/With the teeming of life/Of the golden tribes no more'.

32 Hugh Miller, *Scenes and Legends of the North of Scotland*, 1835 (Edinburgh 1994), 323–4; Campbell, *Popular Tales of the West Highlands*, vol. 1, 17; John Firth, *Reminiscences of an Orkney Parish together with Old Orkney Words, Riddles and Proverbs* (Stromness 1920), 74–7.

33 Reginald Scot, *The Discoverie of Witchcraft* (1584), 131; George Low, *A Tour Through the Islands of Orkney and Schetland, containing hints relative to the ancient, modern and natural history collected in 1774* (Kirkwall 1879), 82.

34 Sikes, *British Goblins*, 3; Rieti, *Strange Terrain*, 181.

35 'Account of the Highlanders and Highlands by Lord Grange for Viscount Townshend, Secretary of State' 29 Dec. 1724 and 2 Jan. 1725. NAS, GD/124/15/1263; Edward J. Cowan, 'Burns and Superstition', in *Love & Liberty: Robert Burns, A Bicentenary Celebration* ed. Kenneth Simpson (East Linton 1997), 235.

36 Adam Ferguson, *An Essay on the History of Civil Society*, 1767, ed. D. Forbes (Edinburgh 1966), 90–1; John Stoddart, *Remarks on Local Scenery & Manners in Scotland during the years 1799 and 1800*, 2 vols. (London 1801), 58, 66; R. H. Cromek, *Remains of Nithsdale and Galloway Song: with Historical and Traditional Notices Relative to the Manners and Customs of the Peasantry* (London 1810), 309–10; Hogg, *Works*, vol. 2, 24 note.

37 James Catton, *The History and Description of the Shetland Islands* (London 1838), 117; James R. Nicolson, *Shetland Folklore* (London 1981), 83. Ingram died in 1879. See also, 'The Last Trow in Yell', Bruford and MacDonald, *Scottish Traditional Tales*, 372–3; Evans-Wentz, *The Fairy Faith*, 86; A. Goodfellow, *Sanday Church History* (Kirkwall 1912), 374–5, qtd. in George Marshall, *In a Distant Isle: The Orkney Background of Edwin Muir* (Edinburgh 1987), 73; Evans-Wentz, *The Fairy Faith*, 94; Fergusson, *Rambling Sketches in the Far North*, 109; George Anderson and Peter Anderson, *Guide to the Highlands and Islands of Scotland including Orkney and Shetland* (Edinburgh 1850), 682; Isabel MacDonald, *The Fairy Tradition in the Highlands and Some Psychological Problems* (Keighley 1938), 35; Marwick, *The Sufficient Place*, unpublished autobiography, referred to in Marshall, *In a Distant Isle*, 73.

CHAPTER TWO

The Wonderful World of Fairy

Diamond . . . had not been out so late before in all his life, and things looked so strange about him! – just as if he had got into Fairyland, of which he knew quite as much as anybody; for his mother had no money to buy books to set him wrong on the subject.

George MacDonald[1]

The supernatural ballad, like folktale or folk song, while functioning primarily as entertainment, also had a didactic purpose – 'the portrayal of both the personnel and the environment of the Otherworld conveys important cultural information about not only the world around, but the world around that'. Such knowledge can only be communicated if the audience of ballad performances is aware of the figurative language employed. For example, the usage of green, or particular plants and trees, the combing of hair or plucking of fruits, is only significant if the connotative meaning is understood as well as the denotative meaning. The majority of the audience must recognise the figurative language or the meanings are lost.[2] The same argument holds true in considering folk belief.

From childhood onwards folk acquired a knowledge of symbols and codes through the medium of ceilidhs and other types of social gathering where tales were told and songs sung. Throughout northern Europe – and Scotland was no exception – neighbours would take it in turn to hold open house for these events, thus reducing heating costs for the community as a whole, especially during the dreary nights of winter when, in 1792, brownies and 'gyar carlins' were still to be heard curling on frozen lochs and lochans.[3] It was on such occasions that people learned about fairies, among other things, about their appearance, their clothing, customs and conventions. They would hear of individuals who had visited with the guid neighbours, of the awesome place that was Fairyland, the splendour of its landscape and buildings, the beauty of its near perpetual music, the lusciousness of its fruits and food, but above all, they would shudder to learn of the sinister enchantments which lurked in this flawed paradise to jeopardise mortal souls.

The Road to Elfland

Elfland was a place that many contemplated but few had the opportunity to visit. Indeed most who found it did so unwillingly or by accident. The most remarkable depiction of the journey to Fairyland, in the ballads or any other source, is of that made by Thomas Rhymer. It is the most elaborately described of its kind, alluring in its attention to detail and the phantasmal atmosphere which suffuses the story. Seduced by the Queen of Elfland at the Eildon tree, Thomas is taken, part way on horseback, on a fantastic expedition to her mysterious abode. He travels through subterranean caverns and bountiful orchards, in a land of perpetual twilight, from where he can hear the roaring of the sea. The crossing of some sort of water barrier is a common requirement for many travellers to the Otherworld, found time and time again in myths, legends, sagas, poetry and medieval romances. Robert Henryson's poem described how Orpheus had to cross water on his descent to Hell while trying to find his wife Eurydice: 'He passit furth ontill a ryvir deip, our it a brig'. Although Thomas cannot escape this obstacle and in at least one variant of the ballad must wade across water, in most versions he is faced with a much more horrific prospect in order to attain his ultimate destination: 'For forty days and forty nights/He wade thro red blude to the knee'.

Thomas Rhymer's sanguinary trek vividly depicts this crucial stage of the journey. Another notable conjuncture is the point at which the queen indicates the option of 'ferlies three' (marvels or wonders), three possible roads, that could be taken. The cosmography given preserves a startling juxtaposition of christian and non-christian ideas. Thomas cannot see these roads until he places his head on the queen's knee, which seems to be a variant of the idea that non-seers could have access to visions through touching the seer's foot or shoulder, or both, though the bold Rhymer appears to have secured a more acceptable berth, so reinforcing the erotic spiciness of fairy contact. The queen explains that the first route is the path of righteousness, whereas in other versions it leads, more convincingly, straight to the gates of Hell. The second track, in most versions, leads to Heaven. The third trail is the one they seek:

> And see not ye that bonny road,
> Which winds about the fernie brae?
> That is the road to fair Elfland,
> Where you and I this night maun gae.

There is a suggestion here that Elfland is to be identified with Purgatory or Limbo, the halfway house between Heaven and Hell, which was outlawed by the reformers as surely as it had been invented in the late twelfth-century. It is of note that Robert Kirk believed that the fairies were perpetually sad in Limbo, uncertain as they were about the fate that awaited them on Judgement Day.[4]

Since no details are given of the eponym's journey in the ballad of 'Tam Lin', the assumption must be that he too is led there by the Queen of Elfland. Janet's visit to the magical site of Carterhaugh can perhaps be interpreted as an excursion to the verge of the Otherworld, waters meeting at the confluence of the Ettrick and the Yarrow. For good measure, in some versions, they also meet at a well, one splendidly refurbished in recent years since posterity appears, as it long has been, to be intent upon the inventive creation of fairy landscapes. In 'The Wee Wee Man' the sparse account implies only that the mortal is accompanied by a fairy guide and both travel on horseback.

Interestingly enough, not much is made of the actual journey to Elfland in the confessions of accused witches either. There is nothing to compare with Thomas Rhymer's exotic excursion. Generally speaking, the witch trial testimonials indicate that the accused were escorted to the abode of the fairies, or else they accidentally stumbled across their homes or favourite haunts, while out walking. In other cases the fairies transported the human visitor by way of a whirlwind or some other form of levitation. There are several accounts of people claiming to have been taken quite significant distances, to find themselves in places totally unknown. At her trial in 1588 Alison Peirson of Byrehill related that her uncle was 'careit away with thame out of middil-eird': 'and when we hear a whirlwind blowing in the sea the witches will be around somewhere or will appear soon thereafter'. Bessie Flinkar of Liberton, tried in 1661, said she was taken 'upon the hills by a whirle of wind & masked herselfe, & ther danced with the rest'.[5]

When Isobel Gowdie of Auldearn was tried in 1662, she referred to a saying that would enable flight: 'I haid a little horse, and wold say, "Horse And Hattock, in the Divellis name!" And than we wold flie away', and also, 'we wold ryd', placing grass stalks, or beanstalks, between their feet and thrice repeating '[Horse] and hattok, horse and goe, horse and pellattis [pellets], ho! ho!'[6] The *Miscellanies* of John Aubrey (1626–97) noted two cases involving the phrase 'Horse and Hattock' and fairy levitation. They were communicated to him in a letter dated 1695 by a Scot named Stewart, tutor to the Duffus family. The first incident was the subject of a seventeenth-century legend concerning a Duffus ancestor who, when walking in fields, heard a whirlwind and voices saying 'Horse and Hattock'. The man repeated the phrase, was promptly swept up in the mêlée, and woke up the following day in the King of France's cellar with a silver cup in hand. The legend, unsurprisingly, came to be known as 'The Fairy Cup'. The second incident was witnessed by Stewart himself who, when a schoolboy, was in a churchyard with friends when they heard a whirlwind. One of the boys shouted 'Horse and Hattock, with my top', which resulted in his spinning-top being lifted in the air and carried over the roof of the church,[7] a neat example of how an occult explanation might be sought for an utterly mundane incident. The phenomenon of the fairy whirlwind is a frequent theme of nineteenth- and twentieth-century folktales. J. G. Campbell wrote of 'eddies of wind . . . whirling about straws and dust, and as not another breath of air is moving at the time, their cause is sufficiently puzzling'. In Gaelic the eddy is known as *oiteag sluaigh* or 'the people's puff of wind'.[8]

Fig. 1. The King of France's Cellar, from *Newes from Scotland*, 1591.

There were thus many ways to enter Fairyland. For most folk the problem was not arriving but returning home.

Liminal Worlds: The Location of Elfland

As fairy activity was generally associated with specific temporal and spatial locations, so humans were most likely to meet with the lychnobious people at certain times or dates, in particular places. Such locations of time and space can be described as 'liminal', a term derived from Latin *limen* (threshold). The concept of liminality, applied here to the supernatural landscape, is usually associated with the work of Arnold van Gennep on rites of passage. He identified 'liminal rites' as 'rites of transition', that ambivalent in-between state during a rite of passage when a person moves from one biological (as in puberty) or social situation to another. Following the lead of folklorist Peter Narváez on the subject of fairy belief in Newfoundland, van Gennep's temporal usage of liminality can be supplanted with a spatial interpretation and applied to the fairy landscape of Scotland. Fairy belief, as with many folkloric traditions, established 'proxemic boundaries on the cognitive maps of community residents, boundaries which demarcated geographical areas of purity, liminality, and danger'.[9] It was in the area between known space (purity) and unknown space (danger) that encounters with the fairies frequently took place. Those who found themselves in this transitional state have been described as 'physically and magico-religiously in a special situation for a certain length of time during which he [or she] wavers between two worlds'. The diagram created by Narváez, used here in slightly modified form, exemplifies how these worlds intersect [Table 1].[10]

There is a good deal of information with regard to the location of Elfland, although the details are fragmentary and often confusing. One pioneering student of folklore in the classical ballads discovered that the dwelling places of the fairies were remarkably diverse. He asked:

> Is the abode of the departed, or the land of the elves and demons, associated with the forest; is it on a hill or mountain; is it subterranean, submarine, over the sea, or on an island; is it far away; is it terrestrial or celestial?[11]

The answer is a resounding affirmative to all of the above. Not the clearest directions, perhaps, for those in search of Fairyland, which may explain why so many mortals had to be escorted by a fairy guide, or else stumbled upon it inadvertently. Sir David Lyndsay in the 'Complaint of the Papingo', imagined the entrance to Fairyland to be in a wilderness, inhabited only by wild animals:

> Bot sen my spreit mon from my bodye go,
> I recommend it to the quene of Fary,
> Eternally into her court to tarry
> In wilderness amang the holtis hair [lonely dens].

The Fairyland of the ballad tradition similarly existed in a kind of wilderness, albeit one suffused in preternatural light. As already indicated, Thomas Rhymer's Elfland was situated in some sort of subterranean locale wherein 'he saw neither sun nor moon/ But heard the roaring of the sea'. Likewise, the enchanted wood in 'Tam Lin' lacked solar and lunar illumination: 'Seven days she tarried there/Saw neither sun nor meen'.[12] 'Leesome Brand' visited 'an unco land, where the wind never blew, nor cocks ever crew', a significant detail because cock-crow heralds the end of supernatural time in many ballads and legends, a signal that revenants and other night visitors must return whence they came.

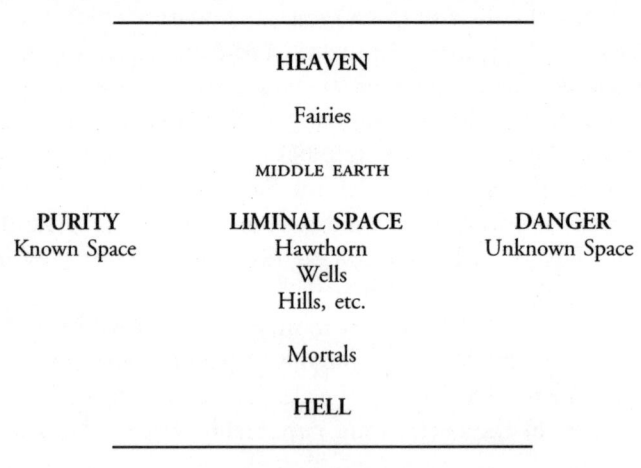

HEAVEN

Fairies

MIDDLE EARTH

PURITY	LIMINAL SPACE	DANGER
Known Space	Hawthorn	Unknown Space
	Wells	
	Hills, etc.	

Mortals

HELL

Table 1. Liminal Space

There were several different gateways to the Land of Fairy. Tam was taken 'In yon green hill to dwell'; 'The Elfin Knight' 'sits on yon hill'; and 'Sir Cawline' fought the elf king at 'Eldrige [Eldritch] Hill' upon which grew a thorn. In 'The Wee Wee Man' a mortal was taken to 'yon bonny green', as the woman in 'The Queen of Elfan's Nourice' was led to a glen. 'Lady Isabel and the Elf-Knight' preferred a forest in one version, a well in another. 'Tam Lin' merged both of these locations, appearing to Janet by a well in a forest. The fairy lover in 'Hind Etin' took his mortal wife to 'Elmond's [Elfman's?] wood' where he built her a bower made from the highest tree in the forest. In a variant, while still within the woods, the mortal bride was kept more or less a prisoner inside a very deep cave.

Frequent mention is made of the location of the home of the elves in the witch trials, virtually every example placing the fairies beside or inside hills. The trial of Lady Fowlis or Katherine Ross in 1590 reported that she 'wald gang in Hillis to speik the elf folk'. In 1615, Jonet Drever was convicted for the 'fostering of ane bairne in the hill of Westray to the fary folk, callit of hir our guid nichbouris'. In Shetland Katherine Jonesdochter, tried in 1616, saw trows on a hill called Greinfaill. John Stewart, tried in Irvine in 1618, regularly met with the fairies on top of Lanark Hill and Kilmaurs Hill. When asked if she had any 'conversatioun with the farye-folk', Isobel Haldane, tried in Perth in 1623, said that she had been taken out of her bed one night 'quhidder be God or the Devill scho knawis nocht' and was carried 'to ane hill-syde: the hill oppynit, and scho enterit in'. At Livingston in 1647, Barbara Parish confessed to a regular rendezvous with the good neighbours on the Ministers Brae where she received her baptismal nip or bite from the devil and entered into his fold.[13] Robert Kirk was aware that 'there be manie places called fayrie hills, which the mountain-people think impious and dangerous to peel [interfere with] or discover'. Another much more famous Robert referred affectionately to 'certain little, romantic, rocky, green hills'. The Downans of Burns' poem 'Halloween' recalls the Downie Hills near Auldearn mentioned in Isobel Gowdie's trial, and the various Dunans that dot the landscape elsewhere. Such nomenclature seems to have signified fairy hills in Scotland.[14]

Nowhere in the witch trials did anyone specifically refer to the forest as a location for Elfland, though a hawthorn tree was mentioned by Bessie Dunlop, from Lyne, Ayrshire as a place to meet with fairies. Bessie, whose trial occurred in 1576, once encountered Thomas Reid at the 'Thorne of Damwstarnok', while on another occasion she saw the laird of Auchenskeigh, at a thorn, beyond Monkcastle. This reference is of particular interest because Auchenskeigh, or Auchenskeith as it now is, means the field or farm of the hawthorn (Gaelic *sgitheach*). Bessie also witnessed a fairy host on horseback gallop straight into Restalrig Loch

(Leith). She related how they made such a din 'as heavin and erd had gane togidder; and incontinent, thai raid in to the loich, with mony hiddous rumbill'. Elspeth Reoch, tried in Orkney in 1616, also first met the fairies at a lochside in the district of Lochaber. Bessie's fairy contact, Thomas Reid, explained that they were the 'gude wichtis that wer rydand in Middil-zerd'. Alison Peirson also spoke of her uncle being taken from 'middil-eird'.[15] 'Sir Cawline' is the man from Middle Earth who defeats the eldritch king, and cock-crow heralds another day in Middle Earth in 'Sweet William's Ghost'. In medieval parlance Middle Earth signified the actual world of mortals, between Heaven and Hell; it is only with the advent of Tolkien that Middle Earth is transformed into a truly magical place.

Thomas Rhymer, in the ballad, may have been liberated from Elfland after his seven-year sojourn, but in Scottish legend he still lies sleeping, within the Eildon Hills like King Arthur and his knights, waiting for his time to return. Indeed, the Avalon of Arthurian lore is apple-land which recalls the forbidden fruit of Elfland. However, there is more than one candidate for the precise location of his slumber; Dumbuck Hill, near Dumbarton, is one such, while MacCodrum, a Uist bard, referred to Tomnahurich (Hill of the Yew Trees) in Inverness as the Rhymer's resting place: '*Dar thigedh sluagh Tom na h-iubhraich, Co dh'eireadh air tùs ach Tòmas?*' (When the hosts of Tomnahurich come, who should rise first but Thomas?)[16]

What begins to emerge in discussing locality is that there are specific places connected with fairies – a supernatural landscape coinciding with the natural landscape, an observation which has also been made regarding places associated with witches and their sabbats. The locations, when given in trial confessions, are almost always very specific. Placenames reflect mentalities as well as toponymic information. 'Man takes and makes the outside world to be like himself, a sort of second self', often, in Gaeldom, naming features of the landscape after parts of his own body.[17] The suggestion that human beings define the world around them in relation to themselves could be greatly expanded. In a similar fashion placenames and landscapes can also be seen to incorporate and reflect the beliefs and ideas of people. It is, however, impossible to resolve the conundrum of whether supernatural encounters were more likely to happen at a place which bore a portentous name or whether such names followed the alleged happenings.

A native of the Appin region, Donald McIlmichall, tried in Inveraray in 1677, stated that 'on a night in the moneth of November 1676 he travelling betwixt Ardturr and Glackiriska at ane hill he saw a light not knowing quhair he was'. Inside the hill he encountered several fairies. On other occasions he met the fairies in Lismore and at the Shian of Barcaldine. Between Ardtur and Glaceriska, there is a place called Dalnasheen (lit. the field of the fairy hill).[18] In Gaelic *sìthean* means 'a green, little pointed hill, a fairy hill'. The words 'sheen' and 'shian' are clearly an anglicisation of the Gaelic. The Shian of Barcaldine is South Shian on the south side of Loch Creran, and there is indeed a small hill there. It is adjacent to a skerry named Sgeir Caillich, probably referring to the *cailleach bheur*, the old woman of winter, a figure of great prominence in Gaelic traditional lore. On the other side of the loch and east of Eriska is North Shian.

Recent work on myth and mythtellers argues that myths are, in a sense, tangible, in their strong interconnections with nature and with place. A map of mythtime 'wouldn't be a unified map, of course, because there is no singleminded order to mythtime. Instead, there would be places of local meaning where mystery is felt'. Fairy belief is also demarcated by a temporally and spatially specific geography. What we have in the description given by Donald McIlmichall is an example of such a region: an 'oral narrative map of a landscape touched everywhere by footprints of the supernatural'. The recording and plotting of all known fairy related locations in Scotland would create a significant and informative map in its own right.[19]

Not exclusive to, but nonetheless of great significance to the supernatural landscape, is the concept of boundaries which are applicable to many areas of folklife and lore, such as folk customs, material culture and folk beliefs. Any discussion of supranormal creatures, metaphysical experiences or supernatural landscapes is almost impossible without some grasp of the fundamental role boundaries play; they exist at the junctures between the world of the natural and the supernatural. Like a membranous film they separate and delineate one place or one state from another:

> this separation of the mysterious and the familiar has a practical advantage. It segregates the world of mystery from the world human beings have some control over. Without that boundary, the world of mystery does not stand apart from the world of human making; each world contaminates the other.

Boundaries between regions and territories, 'like boundaries between years and between seasons, are lines along which the supernatural intrudes through the surface of existence'.[20] Crossing them can prove a physical, a spiritual, or a mental event. They can be intersected intentionally or unintentionally, by humans or non-humans, symbolically or substantively. Every human being, indeed every living thing, has crossed some sort of boundary, for instance, in the eternal cycle of birth, copulation and death.

When Janet went to Carterhaugh to boldly meet Tam Lin, she was on a threshold, tenuously separating her from the Otherworld. Though she was able to communicate, and indeed to have sexual relations with Tam Lin, she herself did not cross the boundary that so fatefully ensnared her lover. Although Janet clearly recognised the markers delineating this liminal space, Tam Lin, being less shrewd than she, evidently did not or could not. Fairies, or those in a fairy state, were not as confined as were humans by the bounds of liminality and could move much more freely between the two worlds.

The fairies themselves were liminal creatures. For example, Kirk mentioned that fairies were best seen in twilight, and lived in a state 'betwixt man and angell'. Elfland existed in other-space, a place that was so near and yet so far. It was, in many ways, an inversion of the human world, with its own laws, but unlike Heaven and Hell, Fairyland existed on earth.[21]

The demarcation of particular areas as fairy places may have served a larger social purpose: to protect community members from known, or presumed, dangers. To be alone on the hills, by water, in the forest, basically away from the home, the village or town, and away from the social group was to be imperilled.[22] Death from exposure, drowning and, in earlier centuries from wild animals, was by no means unknown. Hence the endless fascination in medieval literature with such perennial topics as the quest, or outlawry, which explore the predicament of the outsider but which generally result in the getting of wisdom. The desire to belong comes across time after time in narratives of fairy belief. One is lost without family and friends or the relative security of community, a matter of considerable concern in kin-based Scotland whether one was a member of a Lowland family or a Highland clan; regnal authority did not distinguish between the nature of 'clannit' societies in the Borders or the Gàidhealtachd. However, in some instances that very separation, to be alone or individuated in some way, could lead to increased power or status in the community through alleged communication with the Otherworld, resulting in the acquisition of second sight, prophecy or healing. To be alone, among fairy-infested places, was potentially empowering.

While examining the key elements of the stereotype of the witch, Ginzburg suggested that night flights taken to diabolical sabbats constituted, however distorted they were, a very ancient theme, 'the ecstatic journey of the living into the realm of the dead', concluding that the folkloric nucleus of the witches' sabbat could be found therein.[23] It may be suggested that beliefs surrounding the sojourn in Fairyland shared a similar origin or root, a venture into the beyond, and hopefully, a return.

Ferlies to Find: Descriptions of Fairyland

Once prospective travellers made it to Elfland, they invariably found it to be a land of peerless beauty and compelling mystique, a sort of subterranean paradise. Literary sources, such as the anonymous poem 'The Maner of the Crying of ane Playe', at one time, but no longer, attributed to William Dunbar, frequently tell that the sojourner in Fairyland went there in search of wonders:

> I am the nakit Blynd Hary,
> That lang has bene in the fary
> farleis (wonders) to fynd.

In this case he probably sought solace, for the speaker was a giant who had problems finding a wife. He could not expect much comfort from his monstrous mother who 'spittit Loch Lomond with her lippis' and of whom it was said 'In Irland when quhen scho blewe behynd/at Noroway costis scho raisit the wynd'.[24]

Similarly, balladry emphasised the marvels of this subterranean kingdom. 'King Orfeo' described a hall where fine music was much appreciated. 'Thomas Rhymer' evoked images of a place luxuriant and luscious, abundant in fruit trees, flowers and fine clothes. The Queen of Elfland resided in a splendid court. 'Tam Lin' referred to a fairy court that was 'a pretty place, In which I love to dwell'. In 'The Wee Wee Man' the elfin world was described as a 'bonny green', filled with music and dancing, in a bonny hall: 'Whare the roof was o the beaten gold/ And the floor was o the cristal a'.

Descriptions of Fairyland in the witch trials were also remarkably favourable. Alison Peirson, though admitting the fairies were often cruel to her, commented that the 'Court of Elfane' was a place of piping, merriness and good cheer. Isobel Gowdie's confession recorded: 'we went in to the Downie-hillis; the hill opened, and we cam to an fair and lairge braw rowme, in the day tym. Thair ar great bullis rowtting and skoylling ther, at the entrie'. The presence of large bulls bellowing and roaring was an indication of much wealth and status so far as members of an agricultural community were concerned.

Donald McIlmichall, attracted by light emanating from a hill, approached to discover 'a great number of men and women within the hill quhair he entered haveing many candles lighted'. He was doubtless impressed by the extravagant illumination since at this period humble domestic dwellings were ill-lit, if at all, after dark. At first the inhabitants seem to have been in two minds whether they should allow the intruder to stay or not: 'sum of them desired to shutt him out and others to have him drawine in'. However, Donald was eventually admitted. Kirk described fairy homes as 'large and fair, and (unless at som odd occasions) unperceivable by vulgar eyes . . . having for light continuall lamps, and fires, often seen without fuel to sustein them', another indication of conspicuous consumption, contrasting with the small, poorly illuminated cot-houses in which most people lived.[25]

Fairyland, however, had a propensity to vanish into thin air without notice. In the 'The Wee Wee Man' it disappeared 'in the twinkling of an eye', despite the fact that only moments before there stood a great hall filled with activity. Analogous sudden disappearance is noted in the 1597–8 trial of Andro Man:

> Thow grantis the elphis will mak thee appeir to be in a fair chalmer, and yit thow will find thy selff in a moss on the morne; and that thay will appeir to have candlis, and licht, and swordis [presumably the weapon], quhilk wilbe nothing els bot deed gress and strayes.

In 1773 an Orkney farmer told George Low that he observed at the Broch of Burrian 'near his house in Harray, on a Christmas day, a large company dancing and frolicking', but upon his approach they all disappeared. Low's suggestion that the vision was nothing more than the effects of the 'cakes and strong ale' he had eaten on Christmas morning was apparently not welcomed by the canny informant.[26]

Many people claimed to have seen the dead in Fairyland, sometimes known to them but sometimes not. Bessie Dunlop saw the laird of Auchenskeith riding with the fairfolk, though he had died nine years earlier. Alison Peirson claimed she had 'freindis in that court quhilk wes of hir awin blude'. Andro Man knew 'sindrie deid men in thair cumpanie', and he recognised James IV, who was killed at the Battle of Flodden (1513), and Thomas Rhymer. J. F. Campbell was still able to hear, in the mid-nineteenth century, tales of people thought to be dead who were seen alive in Fairyland.

Often the sojourn in Elfland involved a severely distorted sense of time. What had seemed only a few minutes, or an evening, frequently turned out to have been weeks, years, or if particularly unlucky, centuries. Even more problematical, for the captive whose departure had exceeded an ordinary human lifetime, was that upon returning to the natural world they rapidly aged or simply crumbled into dust.[27]

The Wee Folk?

Although descriptions of Fairyland and the activities of its inhabitants are relatively consistent, one area of dispute concerns the stature of the fairy folk. J. M. Barrie's observation reflects most modern assumptions – 'Fairies have to be one thing or the other, because being so small they unfortunately have room for one feeling only at a time'.[28] Yet Kirk indicated that fairies were indistinguishable from humans in size and garb, with the implication that people could never know when they might be in fairy company. The impression conveyed by witch testimonials is that fairies resembled their human associates in stature and appearance. Manx fairies were said to be not so diminutive as the English variety. There is no evidence whatsoever for childlike, semi-clad sprites darting around on hovering wings as if hybrids between insects and humming-birds. On the other hand, there are some references to little people or pygmies, the latter doubtless inspired by the new spirit of exploration and scientific enquiry; as Tolkien once remarked 'pygmies are no nearer to fairies than are Patagonians'. There is enough evidence, however, to warrant speculation as to whether these smaller creatures represent regional variants, the remnants of an older tradition, a particular type of fairy, or, what seems most probable, competing traditions. There was, after all, nothing logical about the fairies. They could appear in different sizes from human stature to a shape-shifter disappearing through a hole in a dyke.

Scotland's southern neighbour certainly seems to have had a smaller type of fairy.[29] Two Anglo-Saxon books of remedies known as the *Leechbook* and *Lacnunga* might permit the speculation that Scottish elves almost certainly originated as English immigrants, albeit with a significant infusion from Scandinavia. Such works contain plentiful advice on how to defend oneself against the malignant attacks of these tiny creatures for whose existence there is no comparably early Scottish evidence.[30]

Gerald of Wales, while on a tour of Wales in 1188, recorded a story, stunning in its wealth of detail, and purportedly true, which involved a young boy's encounters with a group of diminutive folk, who, although not described as such, were notably evocative of the fairies.[31] A priest named Elidyr claimed to have been the person involved; at the age of twelve, he ran away from home, hiding for two days in the hollow bank of a river. In due course he was approached by two tiny men, 'no bigger than pigmies', who announced, 'If you will come away with us . . . we will take you to a land where all is playtime and pleasure'. Elidyr followed the small men to their subterranean domicile, of which he gave a rich and fulsome account. He seems to have lived there for quite some time, learning the language of the inhabitants – which bore a remarkable resemblance to Greek – and he was allowed frequent trips back to the 'upper world', making himself known only to his mother. His account began with a journey, reminiscent of that made by True Thomas:

> They led him first through a dark underground tunnel and then into a most attractive country, where there were lovely rivers and meadows, and delightful woodlands and plains. It was rather dark, because the sun did not shine there. The days were all overcast, as if by clouds, and the nights were pitch-black, for there was no moon nor stars.

He went on to describe the beings he met, having been introduced to their king, in the presence of the entire court:

> They were amazed to see him, and the king stared at him for a long time, . . . All these men were very tiny, but beautifully made and well-proportioned. In complexion they were fair, and they wore their hair long and flowing down over their shoulders like women. They had horses of a size which suited them, about as big as greyhounds. They never ate meat or fish. They lived on various milk dishes, made up into junkets flavoured with saffron. They never gave their word, for they hated lies more than anything they could think of. Whenever they came back from the upper world, they would speak contemptuously of our own ambitions, infidelities and inconstancies.

Elidyr's visit to this twilight world was eventually brought to a grinding halt when he unpardonably abused the hospitality he had received by attempting to steal a golden ball from the little folk. Thereafter, he was never able to find the tunnel entrance again. Regrettably, no such detailed account, of such an early date, has yet been uncovered for Scotland though there are ample parallels to Elidyr's tale at later periods. Since Welsh speakers survived in some areas of Southern Scotland perhaps as late as the twelfth century, it is just possible that some Scots were aware of this story or others like it.[32] However that may be, the parallels between the adventures of Elidyr and Thomas Rhymer are fairly obvious.

Turning to Scotland, there is some indirect evidence for smallness as a trait of fairy folk (or at least of their kinsfolk the brownies) in the somewhat surprising personage of Blind Harry, author of the much-loved poem, *Wallace*. In a highly speculative, though not entirely unconvincing, critical work W. H. Schofield postulated that Blind Harry was not the writer's real name but a pseudonym borrowed from a mythical character known within fifteenth-century popular culture.[33] Though he drew on several disparate sources in seeking to prove his thesis, he relied heavily upon the poem written c.1500, 'The Maner of the Crying of ane Playe', also known in the Bannatyne MS as 'Ane Littill Interlud of the Droichis [Dwarf's] Pairt of the Play'. In this interlude the dwarf, who arrived in Scotland 'with the whirlwind', declared he was 'the nakit Blynd Hary', engendered from a race of giants and mythical heroes, and a recent returnee from Fairyland. Schofield, reasonably enough, questioned any identification with the actual Blind Harry of *Wallace* fame. Indeed, the Bannatyne MS credited the poem to Hary Hubbulschow whose surname means 'hubbub' or 'commotion', so presumably in dramatic terms he was a kind of 'lord of misrule', usually associated with festivals such as Yule or Beltane. The character of the dwarf, however, intriguingly has several experiences characteristic of the sojourner in Fairyland (e.g. whirlwinds, skewed temporal perception, prophecy), at times recalling Thomas Rhymer who also went in pursuit of 'ferlies'. Repercussions meted out to the dwarf for breaking taboo by leaving that land (e.g. blindness, nakedness, ageing) similarly threatened Tam Lin.

Yet this dwarf also resembles a shape-shifting, tutelary figure akin to a brownie or Robin Goodfellow. Schofield also speculated upon possible correlatives, such as 'Blind Odin', 'Blind Ossian' and 'Billie Blin', a creature of equal mystique who has been dubbed 'a serviceable household demon'. The latter is encountered in at least one English and four Scottish ballads. A small book could be written about Billie Blin the brownie. Like most of his kind he could perform superhuman tasks and usually attached himself to a particular family until offended in some way and it was time to move on. Since he enjoyed a three-hundred-year life span, he worked for several masters, or rather mistresses, for brownies had a particular attachment to women. In the ballads Billie pops up to advise ladies in distress and to resolve their predicaments. Having mitigated any courtship problems, he would then attend his mistress on her honeymoon, or in childbirth, as well as taking care of the housework. All that might be demanded in return was a lock of the lady's hair, or a dish of brose, though in some traditions Billie had a particular fondness for honeyed cakes. The brownies were

> to all appearances, beings of a very superior race; invulnerable to the spells and cantraips of deadly witchcraft, and proof against everything but baptismal affusion. They bore neither bows nor shafts like the Fairies, but relied upon their own superior endowments. Their love of women and dainty food, proves them of earthly mixture; but they conducted themselves in a way worthy of their celestial origin.[34]

Hary Hubbulschow was unusual since there are very few, if any, references to brownies paying a visit to Fairyland.

Firmer evidence for a species of small fairies surfaces in the work of Donald Monro, High Dean of the Isles; his *Description of the Western Isles of Scotland* (1549) is the earliest known description of the Hebrides from personal observation, and, as it happens, the first documented visit to the tidal island of Luchruban (off the north-west coast of Lewis), 'ane little Ile callit the Pygmeis Ile, with ane little kirk in it'. His informants, whom he described as 'the ancients of the cuntrie' of Lewis, were able to tell him that within this kirk the 'pygmeis hes bene earthit [buried] thair'. It is unclear how long the story of Pygmy Isle had been around, but however old the tradition, it clearly ignited the curiosity of Monro and subsequent travellers:

> Mony men of divers cuntries hes delvit up deiply the fluir of the said kirk, and I myself amangis the lave [rest], and hes fundin in it deip under the earth certane banes and round heids of verie little quantitie [very small in size], alledgit to be the banes of the saids Pygmeis, quhilk may be licklie according to sindrie storeis that we reid of the Pygmeis.[35]

That well-known sceptic, George Buchanan, surprisingly, seems to have accepted Monro's evidence, noting the discovery of 'small and round skulls, and little bones belonging to different parts of the human body, which coincide with the ancient report'.

An anonymous account entitled *The Description of the Isles of Scotland*, dated to somewhere between 1577 and 1595, refers briefly to the Pygmy Isle. The document, due to its appearance as an official report, was possibly intended for the use of James VI who was, by the 1590s, casting acquisitive eyes at the Hebrides in hopes of increasing royal revenue:

> In this Ile thair is ane little cove biggit in form of ane kirk, and is callit the Pygmies Kirk. It is sa little, that ane man may scairslie stand uprichtlie in it eftir he is gane in on his kneis. Thair is sum of the Pygmies banes thairinto as yit, of the quhilkis the thrie banes being measurit is not fullie twa inches lang.[36]

The persistence of the pygmy tradition was carried on through a few more generations, for in 1695, 146 years after Monro's visit, the legends associated with Luchruban were still very much alive, as Martin Martin was to discover. He referred to the island in *A Description of the Western Isles of Scotland* (1703) as 'The Island of Pigmies, or, as the natives call it, The Island of Little Men'. He mentioned that small bones, resembling human bones, had been found, giving 'ground to a tradition which the natives have of a very low-statur'd people living once here, call'd *Lusbirdan*, i.e. Pigmies'.[37] This story was, in Martin's opinion, 'superstitious', though he was concerned to stress that such traditions were disappearing as protestantism advanced. Like most observers from that day to this he believed that folk beliefs were in recession, many of them having disappeared during the previous generation:

> There are several instances of heathenism and pagan superstition among the inhabitants of the islands, related here: but I would not have the reader to think those practices are chargeable upon the generality of the present inhabitants; since only a few of the oldest and most ignorant of the vulgar are guilty of 'em. These practices are only to be found where the reform'd religion has not prevail'd; for 'tis to the progress of that alone, that the banishment of evil spirits, as well as evil customs, is owing, when all other methods prov'd ineffectual. And for the Islanders in general, I may truly say, that in religion and virtue they excel many thousands of others, who have greater advantages of daily improvement.

It is of considerable interest and significance that Martin gives two alternative names for Luchruban; 'The Island of Pigmies' seems to be the learned version, while the natives called it 'The Island of Little

Men'.[38] What had changed, at least in the written descriptions, was the introduction of the theory that the bones were perhaps the bones of birds, a 'rational' as opposed to a supernatural explanation. From then on, the bones were to be treated as 'evidence', either in support of the existence of pygmies or as proof against them. The empirical approach to supernatural phenomena and superstitious belief had taken a firm hold.

It is probable that Martin's chief informant was *Iain mac Mhurch' 'c Ailein*, John Morison, a tacksman from South Bragar and the first identifiable *Leòdhasach* to write a geographical description of the island. Morison's brief narrative, composed sometime between 1683 and 1685, was inspired by Sir Robert Sibbald's geographical project which involved the distribution of questionnaires requesting information on topographical details or notable features of the local area. Entitled *A Descriptione of the Lews by John Morisone indueller there*, he reports:

> There is a little Island hard by the coast where it is said that Pigmeis lived some tyme by reason they find by searching some small bons in the earth; but I can not give much faith to it, since greater mans bons would consume in a shorter tyme but I hold them to be the bons of small foulls which abound in that place.[39]

Lewis was not the only island to claim a pygmy race. Martin's visit to Colonsay and Benbecula elicited similar evidence. A fort on Colonsay, by the name of Dun-Evan, was believed to have once been the dwelling place of 'a very little generation of people' called '*Lusbirdan*, the same with Pigmies'. On Benbecula the locals had 'lately discover'd a stone vault' containing many small bones. However, in the Benbecula findings, theories as to the origins of the bones were divided:

> Some said they were the bones of birds, others judg'd them rather to be the bones of Pigmies. The Proprietor of the Town enquiring Sir Normand Mackleod's opinion concerning them, he told him that the matter was plain as he suppos'd, and that they must be the bones of infants born by the nuns there.[40]

Martin displayed his protestant bias by suggesting that the catholic inhabitants, though they outwardly laughed at such an insinuation, must have been inwardly displeased with this particular explanation since they took the precaution of covering over the vault, thus concealing potentially embarrassing evidence and preventing further hostile speculation.

Martin's account inspired the English poet William Collins, whose 'Ode on the Popular Superstitions of the Highlands of Scotland' drew heavily upon his two publications. The poem, written in 1749 though not published until 1788, makes reference to Luchruban:

> Thy Muse may like those feath'ry tribes which spring
> From their Rude Rocks extend her skirting wing
> Round the Moist Marge of each cold Hebrid Isle
> To that hoar Pile which still its ruin shows
> In whose small vaults a Pigmie-Folk is found
> Whose Bones the Delver with his Spade up-throws
> And culls them wondring from the hallow'd Ground![41]

Perhaps not unexpectedly, though unfairly, Monro and Martin's reputations as reliable writers came under attack by geologist John MacCulloch who published his own *Description of the Isles* in 1824. He ridiculed the dean's open-mindedness towards the possible existence of pygmies and also cast Martin as a credulous observer, stating that both 'supposed them to be realities'.[42] It can only be assumed that he did not read Martin's *Description* very carefully, for nowhere does he give the impression of believing the pygmy tradition: in fact, quite the opposite. MacCulloch himself travelled through the Hebrides and published his observations as a series of letters to Sir Walter Scott. He may have based his scepticism on the fact that he was unable to locate either the Pygmy Isle or its 'little kirk' and thus concluded that the reports were false. In one fell swoop he attempted to destroy not only the legend, but the credibility of Monro and Martin as well.[43] Why MacCulloch was so dogmatic on this point is something of a mystery, particularly since other visitors had confirmed the dean's information, including an English traveller, Captain John Dymes, in 1630, who said the place was popular with certain Irish antiquaries who came to retrieve some of the miniature bones for themselves.[44] What MacCulloch's experience might suggest is that by the time of his visit, in the early nineteenth century, visible remains of the anchorite's cell had disappeared and with it perhaps, though this is unlikely, the legend. Either that or MacCulloch, for some reason, did not endear himself to the people of Ness – given his attitudes, a distinct possibility – and thus received no assistance or co-operation.[45]

Traditions about tiny creatures have a relatively long history. In the anonymous poem 'King Berdok' written c.1450, and in which, incidentally, the first recorded Scottish usage of the term 'fairy' appears, there is a line which states that Berdok lodged in summer in a cabbage stalk, but in winter in a cockleshell. An anonymous and somewhat eccentric author, writing in 1665, associated pygmies with northerly climes, specifically Greenland whence, he thought, they emigrated to America.[46]

Robert Kirk included in his title page the word *lusbartan*, which is probably the same as Martin's *Lusbirdan*. Although Kirk did not allude to the smallness of the fairies themselves anywhere within the body of his text, in his glossary he defined the elves as 'a tribe of the fayries that use not to exceed an ell [37 inches] in stature'. In Gaelic *luspardan* means a dwarf, pigmy or sprite. A connection may also possibly exist between the Scottish *luspardan* and the Irish leprechaun, or *lupracan*. The most reliable etymology traces leprechaun to *lucharmunn*, a 'pygmy, dwarf, or small gentleman'. The place name Luchruban almost certainly preserves this same element. The *luridan*, a brownie-like creature associated with Mainland Orkney, may also be related. Leprechauns were, until the late nineteenth and twentieth centuries, peripheral to Irish fairy belief, most of the characteristics now associated with this creature resulting from literary emphasis.[47]

The earliest reference to *luprachans* appears in a tenth century poem, while a fuller account of the *lucorpan*, ancestor of the leprechaun, is found in the *Ancient Laws of Ireland*, compiled in the mid-eleventh century. The tale tells of King Fergus who, while he sleeps, is carried away by the lucorpans to the sea. The king awakes when his feet touch the water; he grabs three of the tiny creatures, and agrees to exchange their lives for the grant of a wish. This story is vaguely reminiscent of a confused custom recorded by Martin which involved the consultation of an 'invisible oracle' in order to gain knowledge of future events. A man was chosen, by lot, to be carried by a company of his fellows to a river whereupon his body was bumped against the bank. One man would customarily shout, 'let his invisible friends appear' and 'relieve him by giving an answer to our present demands'. After a few minutes, a number of 'little creatures' would come from the sea, answer their questions, and then suddenly disappear.[48]

A description given by Walter Ronaldson from Kirktown of Dyce, brought before the Aberdeen court in 1601 for 'familiarity with a spirit', furthers the possibility that a race of smaller supernatural beings was popularly believed to exist. Some twenty-seven years before his trial, a spirit first came to Ronaldson's door, and continued to come twice a year for several years thereafter. Initially he never saw the spirit but one

Michaelmas night, while he slept, it came and 'sat down anent the bed upon a kist, and callit upon him, saying "Wattie, Wattie!"' When Ronaldson awoke he 'saw the form of it, whilk was like ane little body, having a shaven beard, clad in white linen like a sark'. The creature spoke to him and told him where to find 'baith silver and gold' hidden in a house. This little man may have been of brownie cast rather than of fairy kin. His benevolent gesture of informing Walter where valuable booty could be found is in keeping with certain traditional associations with brownies as guardians of hidden treasure.

Another description of great interest is found in the 1662 witchcraft trial of Isobel Gowdie, who confessed to meeting with the fairies and visiting with them inside fairy hills on several occasions. She claimed to have witnessed the manufacture of elf arrowheads by 'elf-boys' who were, in appearance, 'little ones, hollow, and boss-baked'; they spoke 'gowstie lyk'. Since 'boss-baked' seems to mean diminutive and humpbacked, while 'gowstie' conveys the sense of roughly or gruffly, it could be that Isobel was talking about a brownie or trow-like creature and hence, the closest thing so far found in the witch trials to the wee wee man of the ballads.

The ballad of 'The Wee Wee Man' is the only example in the Child ballad corpus of small fairies. In every other case the ballad fairy is of human size. The wee wee man is different in other ways also:

> His legs were scarce a shathmont's [6 inches] length,
> And thick and thimber [heavy] was his thigh;
> Between his brows there was a span,
> And between his shoulders there was three.

As described, he recalls a creature similar to the dwarf, gnome or kobold found in Teutonic and Scandinavian traditions. His hideous appearance and superhuman strength – 'He took up a meikle stane, And he flang't as far as I could see' – add credence to this theory. On the other hand, the fairy ladies described in the ballad are also diminutive – 'jimp and sma' – and they danced with 'wee wee knichts'.[49] These latter creatures are closer in form, excepting size, to the beautiful fairy folk of 'Thomas Rhymer' and 'Tam Lin'. Generally speaking, it would seem, groups of small fairies were considered to be attractive in appearance (as were the human-sized variety), but solitary male fairies were usually regarded as plain, ugly, or misshapen in some way.

One last proposal on the vexed question of stature is the popular assumption that a fairy could alter its own height at will, a form of shape-shifting. After all, Andro Man attested that the fairy queen could drastically alter the appearance of her age at whim. J. G. Campbell's work on Highland fairy tradition suggested that fairies had an ability to change their size, but he started out with a prior assumption that the fairies were a small race, 'the men about four feet or so in height, and the women in many cases not taller than a little girl', and that over time the human proclivity to exaggeration took the descriptions of their littleness to even smaller extremes.[50]

In Scott's version of 'Tam Lin' some stanzas referred to the ability of fairies to alter their shape: 'Our shapes and size we can convert/To either large or small'. Child was suspicious of these stanzas, putting them in an appendix, in spite of the fact that a central motif in this ballad is shape-shifting, though it is entirely possible that the lines owe something to Scott's editorial interference. Further evidence occurred at the trial of Bessie Dunlop, who reported that her fairy contact Tom Reid 'went away fra me, in throw the yard at Monkcastell; and I thocht he gait in at ane naroware hoill of the dyke nor ony erdlie man culd haif gane throw'. The account is ambiguous; perhaps Reid had the ability to disappear or maybe the suggestion is that he was able to become smaller and thus pass through an entrance to Fairyland. Kirk does report of the fairies that, 'their bodies of congealed air, are som times carried aloft, other whiles grovell in different shapes, and enter in anie cranie or cleft of the earth (where air enters) to their ordinary dwellings'.[51]

The small creatures that Martin Martin heard about from the islanders of Lewis, Benbecula, and Colonsay cannot be considered peculiar to these islands, since there is evidence for small fairies in other regions, as in the witch-trial testimonials cited from Aberdeenshire and Ayrshire. They may, however, represent the remnants of an even older tradition since both Monro and Martin appear to describe what was already felt to be a past belief by the islanders themselves. There is some evidence that smallness was characteristic of some fairies, for example brownies, or the 'peedie' folk of the Northern Isles, a suggestion which receives some support from Scandinavian and Germanic parallels. But what seems most probable is that we are dealing here with competing traditions. The *luspardan* were clearly believed to occupy that island off the coast of Lewis long before they were usurped by the pygmies of the learned. The pygmy motif brought together ingredients from many sources: Celtic, Germanic, English, Scandinavian, and perhaps, to a lesser extent, classical mythology, tradition overlapping tradition, both learned and folk, in a process, over centuries, of hybridisation. It also seems likely that, as a general rule, fairies became smaller the further they receded into the past, an idea which is hardly surprising given that human beings always seem to believe, often erroneously, that their ancestors were of smaller stature than themselves.

Fairy Life-Styles

Strength is a characteristic of several fairies apart from the wee wee man. For example, the fairy lover in 'Hind Etin' casually ripped a tree out by the roots and then proceeded to carve out a cave 'monie fathoms deep'. The elf king in 'Sir Cawline' was described as the eldritch king that was 'mickle of might, who stiffly to the ground did stand'. The possession or temporary acquisition of superhuman strength permitted the heroine of 'Tam Lin' to overwhelm the power of the fairy queen. The notion of invisibility, which was touched upon earlier in 'The Wee Wee Man', also occurred, though in another form, when it was said of the bower that Hind Etin built, 'appearance it had nane'. Tam Lin also seemed to possess the ability to appear and disappear at will. He chose to reveal his presence to Janet only after she had picked a rose. Kirk related that the bodies of fairies were 'so plyable through the subtilty of the spirits, that agitate them, that they can make them appear or disappear at pleasure'. He also learned that the fairies could make humans vanish when it suited them. In full view of witnesses, a man possessed of the second sight became invisible:

> His neighbours often perceivd this man to disappear at a certane place, and then about one hour after to become visible, and discover himselfe neer a bow-shot from the first place: it was in that place where he becom invisible, said he, that these subterraneans did encounter and combate with him.[52]

The ballad fairies were repeatedly portrayed as lavishly adorned and accoutred beings. They lived in opulent courts, ate sumptuous foods, and dressed in equally sumptuous clothes. They owned or guarded treasures beyond the imagination of most mortals, decorating even their horses in golden bridles and silver bells. The steeds themselves were of the finest stock, usually milk-white, and ran swifter than the wind.

The fairies almost always dressed in green, a sometimes ill-omened colour connected with bad luck and death. When Thomas first met the Queen of Elfland, she wore a 'grass-green silk' skirt and a mantle of green velvet. The four and twenty little fairy women of 'The Wee Wee

Man' were similarly 'clad out in green'. The woman who makes an impromptu appearance in 'Young Beichan' is identifiable as a fairy due to her choice of attire – 'up starts a woman, clad in green'.

A passage in James VI's *Daemonologie* (1597) sets out very plainly some of the main characteristics of the fairy tradition:

> . . . there was a King and Queene of Phairie, of such a jolly court and train as they had, how they had a teynd, and dutie, as it were, of all goods: how they naturallie rode and went, eate and drank, and did all other actiones like naturall men and women.[53]

At this stage of his career James was by no means sympathetic towards this supernatural tradition, though his assertion that the fairy monarchs enjoyed the levy of a teind is unusual since more commonly it was the fairies themselves who had to pay the teind to Hell. He believed that fairies were nothing less than wicked demons sent by the devil to undermine christianity, and those who claimed acquaintance with them were a threat to society at large.

The witch trials provide quite detailed information about the appearance of the fairy folk. Andro Man said the elves were in the shape of, and clothed like, people. The queen of fairies, he confided, could be old or young at will and would lie with any man she happened to like. Andro himself admitted to producing several children with her. Bessie Dunlop described the fairy men as clad in gentleman's clothing and the women in plaid. Elspeth Reoch saw two fairy men: one who was 'cled in blak and the uther with ane grein tartane plaid about him'. Isobel Haldane met a man with a gray beard. Janet Trall of Blackruthven, tried in Perth in 1623, said the fairies appeared, 'some of them red, some of them grey and riding upon horses', while their leader resembled a 'bonny white man, riding upon a grey horse' though on another occasion he was clad in green. A Livingston witch, Margaret Alexander, saw a fairy man who wore green clothes and a grey hat. Isobel Gowdie described not only the attire of the sprites she knew, but she was able to give their names as well:

> Robert, the Jakis; Sanderis, the Read Reaver; Thomas, the Fearie; Swein, the roaring Lion; Thieffe of Hell, Wait wpon hir self; Makhectour; Robert, the Rule; Hendrie Laing; and Rorie. We wold ken thame all, on by on, from utheris. Som of thaim apeirit in sadddun [turf-brown?], som in grasse-grein, som in sea-grein, and som in yallow.

Isobel also divulged that 'The Read Reiver . . . is my owin sprit, that waittis on my selfe, and is still clothed in blak'. Of Robert the Jakis she reported that he was 'clothed in dune [brown], and seimes to be aiged. He is ane glaiked [stupid] gowked [foolish] spirit!'[54]

Robert the Jakis may have been so called because he wore armour of some kind. A comparable, though somewhat unusual, description was offered by John Brand, a contemporary of Martin Martin and Robert Kirk, writing about Orkney where 'evil spirits also called fairies are frequently seen in several of the Isles dancing and making merry, and sometimes seen in armour'. But fairy clothing was frequently less exotic. Like Bessie Dunlop and Elspeth Reoch, Kirk described elfin attire as native Scots garb: 'their apparel and speech is like that of the people and countrey under which they live: so are they seen to wear plaids and variegated garments in the high-lands of Scotland and suanochs [tartan] heretofore in Ireland'. Of their voice and language he remarked: 'they speak but litle, and that by way of whistling, clear, not rough' and 'answer in the language of the place: yet sometimes these subterraneans speak more distinctly then at other times'.[55]

Just over a hundred years later another minister gave a description of local beliefs in his parish of Kirkmichael in Banffshire:

> Notwithstanding the progressive increase of knowledge and proportional decay of superstition in the Highlands, these genii are still supposed by many people to exist in the woods and sequestered valleys of the mountains, where they frequently appear to the lonely traveller, clothed in green, with dishevelled hair floating over their shoulders and with faces more blooming than the vermeil blush of a summer morning.

The eloquence of his description seems to owe more to post-Ossianic romanticism than it does to actual experience. Furthermore, his tone is more suggestive of a day spent bird-watching than an encounter with dangerous supernatural forces. He continues:

> At night in particular, when fancy assimilates to its own preconceived ideas every appearance and every sound, the wandering enthusiast is frequently entertained by their musick, more melodious than he ever before heard.[56]

The spirit that had an acquaintance with Bessie Dunlop for four years is somewhat of an enigma. Though he acted in most ways like a fairy, and certainly lived and associated with their kind, he was not, or at least was not always, a fairy. Of his appearance, Bessie gave a full account:

he was ane honest wele elderlie man, gray bairdit, and had ane gray coitt with Lumbart [Lombardy] slevis of the auld fassoun; ane pair of gray brekis and quhyte schankis [legs], gartanit [gartered] abone the kne; ane blak bonet on his heid, cloise behind and plane befoir, with silkin laissis drawin throw the lippis thairof; and ane quhyte wand in his hand.

What was most startling about him was his claim to have died at the Battle of Pinkie, fought twenty-nine years earlier on 10 September 1547 and ever after recalled painfully as a devastating defeat. In order to prove his assertion, he told Bessie that if she doubted him she should 'gang to Thom Reid, his sone, now officiare in his place, to the Lard of Blair, and to certain utheris his kynnismen and freindis thair, quhom he namit'. Reid was somewhat reminiscent of a ghost, and there was another incident that pointed to his revenant nature. When Bessie was asked whether she had observed him 'gangand up and doun the warld', she said that she had seen him in the kirkyard of Dalry, among the people. Fairy sightings within consecrated ground were not altogether unusual. In Shetland, at the trial of Katherine Jonesdochter, the accused reportedly saw trows or trolls rise out of the Kirkyard of Hillswick and Holycross Kirk of Eshaness.

In ways quite similar to Bessie's case, Alison Peirson claimed a mortal intermediary between herself and Fairyland, though this man was known to her before his capture by fairies as he was her uncle, William Simpson, who seemingly had quite a history of abduction. Alison said he had been kidnapped 'be ane mann of Egypt', that is a gypsy, and returned to Scotland twelve years later only to be carried off by fairies.

It would seem that both Reid and Simpson were ghosts of men once mortal, now under the sovereignty of the fairy queen. Reid told Bessie that the Queen of Elfame was his mistress and had commanded him to wait upon her, and to do her good.[57]

Another hint that the dead could be subsumed into the realm of fairy occurs in the trial of Elspeth Reoch. She related that the black man who came to her, and called himself a fairy man, was 'sumtyme her kinsman callit Johne Stewart quha wes slane be McKy at the doun going of the soone [sunset]'. He told her he was neither dead nor alive but was forever trapped between heaven and earth. What Reid and Stewart shared in common was violent, sudden death. They were taken before their time with no opportunity to prepare for impending death; as Robert Service once wrote, they 'were killed so bleeding sudden that they hadn't time to die'. Kirk himself stated that the seers avouched that 'severals who go to the siths (or people at rest and in respect of us in peace) befor the natural period of their lyf expyr, do frequentlie appear to them', and that the Highlanders averred that the 'souls goe to the sith [fairies] when dislodged'.[58]

Interplay between the words 'fairy' and 'spirit' is encountered in October 1675, when the bishop and synod of Aberdeen were engaged in considering 'divers complaints that some, under pretense of transes and familiaritie with spirits by going with these spirits commonly called the fairies, hath spoken . . . of some persons whereof some ar dead and some living'. That the dead were often seen in the company of fairies is by now well established. Sightings of dead witches were also occasionally seen at fairy/witch gatherings, as attested by Margaret Alexander (1647). She witnessed a number of cats shape-shift into the form of twelve men and women, many of whom she knew personally to be witches, though some were now deceased. She was 'carried away' by them, a distance of sixteen miles, to a place where they ate and drank, and was returned within the space of an hour. Margaret continued to attend meetings with this troop and sometimes they would come to her house and she would offer them ale to drink. On one occasion she confessed to having gone from Calder to Linton brig with two men and two women 'that she called the Faries' adding that one of the men, who was the king of fairy, 'laye with her upone the brige'. The company with whom Margaret associated was a blend of living witches, dead witches, and fairy folk.[59]

Anxiety about death is universal, but perhaps it had a particular sting in Reformation Scotland, where, while the good and the godly were predestined for salvation, there must have been legions of less fortunate and less confident souls who had severe doubts about what awaited them in the afterlife. For some the home of the fairies, imperfect though it was, provided some sort of an alternative, just as the very idea of Fairyland permitted some assuagement of the grief attending the death of a loved one. It is even quite possible that a number of disoriented Scots in this period really did believe, to cite the old adage, that it was better to serve in Hell than reign in Heaven.

Activities and Pastimes of the Fairy Folk

It was well known that the fairies were 'a sociable people, passionately given to festive amusement and jocund hilarity'. The ballads certainly support this image and relate the fairy love of hunting, of music and dancing, and, let us not forget, of abduction. They were gourmets who also enjoyed good wine. They were promiscuous tempters who happily indulged their sexual passions. They appreciated the best of everything, be it silver and gold or magnificent horses, and in their spare time they liked nothing better, by way of recreation, than to foment mischief and mayhem for their human neighbours. Beaten by the knight in 'Sir Cawline' the elf king promises nevermore to 'sport, gamon, or play' on Eldritch Hill.

The Fairy Rade or procession, as mentioned in the romance 'Sir Orfeo' and in the ballads 'Allison Gross', and 'Tam Lin', was probably their favoured and best-known activity.[60] The Scots spelling 'rade' is retained to emphasise that the word had at least two meanings. It was frequently used in the fifteenth and sixteenth centuries in the sense of a predatory expedition, or foray, by mounted men, an outing which might culminate in battle or in the seizure of plunder and prisoners. Such was the Rade of the Reidswire (1575) when a party of Scottish reivers routed the English Warden of the Marches after a fight broke out as a truce was supposedly being negotiated near Carter Bar on the slopes of the Cheviot. In the Rades of Holyrood (1591), Falkland (1593) and Leith (1594) the target was the person of James VI. But although the two words stemmed from different roots there was also an element of 'parade' in 'rade', in the sense of ostentatious display or show of strength; parade is French, rade Old English. In 'Sir Orfeo' the Fairy Rade seized Eurydice but in 'Allison Gross' and 'Tam Lin' the 'seely court' merely went 'ridin by'. The most remarkable literary example of a Fairy Rade was provided by Alexander Montgomerie's 'Flyting of Montgomerie and Polwart.' His evocative and brilliant description undoubtedly owed something to accounts of Diana and her nymphs riding the night sky but in addition to classical sources there are echoes of the Wild Hunt drawing upon Gaelic, Irish and Norse lore. All of these elements were to be captured in Noel Paton's consummate artistic statement of 1867, 'The Fairy Raid', perhaps the greatest and most authoritative fairy painting ever executed, rooted as it firmly was in Scotland's traditional and legendary past.

Andro Man affirmed that the elves 'have playing and dansing quhen thay pleas'. On Donald McIlmichall's first sighting he saw them dancing by candlelight. On subsequent visits he 'playd on trumps to them quhen they danced'. Sometimes the site where fairies danced was detectable by circular impressions left in the grass, of which Samuel

Hibbert cautioned: 'within such unholy precincts it is hazardous for a Christian to enter'. In Shetland, the trows were notoriously eccentric dancers. They were said to 'henk' or 'lunk', which seems to infer a limping motion. At Haltadans above Skutes Water on the mystical island of Fetlar in Shetland are two concentric circles of stones, the physical embodiment of dancing trolls caught by the sunrise. Two taller uprights are said to be the figures of the fiddler and his wife transmogrified for their tunes.[61]

Kirk discovered that several fairy activities were remarkably similar to human pursuits: 'they are sometimes heard to bake bread, strike hammers, and to do such like services within the little hillocks where they most haunt'. Fairy women were said to 'spin, verie fine, to dye, to tissue and embroyder'. However, enquiring and scientific as ever, he was unsure if their goods were produced by 'manual operatione of substantiall refin'd stuffs with apt solid instruments, or only curious cob-webs, impalpable rainbows, and a phantastic imitation of the actiones of more terrestriall mortals'.

With regard to how and what the fairies actually ate, Kirk surmised:

> Some have bodies or vehicles so spungious, thin and defecate, that they are fed by only sucking into some fine spiritous liquor that pierce like pure air and oyl: others feed more gross on the foyson or substance of cornes and liquors, or on corne itselfe.

Humans who ate a lot yet never seemed to gain any weight were believed to have 'a voracious elve' called '*geirt coimitheth*, a joynt-eater, or just-halver, feeding on the pith and quintessence of what the man eats, and that therefore he continues lean like a hauke or heron, notwithstanding his devouring appetite'. He also explained how food was stolen by these greedy elves:

> they convey that substance elsewhere, for these subterraneans eat but litle in their dwellings, their food being exactly clean, and served up by pleasant children like inchanted puppets. What food they extract from us is convey'd to their homes by secret pathes, as some skilfull women doe the pith of milk from their neighbours cows.

MacCoan of Mull, an eighteenth-century seer, confided to John Ramsay of Ochtertyre, that the fairies consumed the goodness of meat, removing the nourishment, but that they never touched whisky.

Indulging in malevolent mischief, including poltergeist activity as in the following extract, was, above all, what the troublesome fairies loved most:

> The invisible wights which haunt houses seem rather to be some of our subterranean inhabitants . . . than evill spirits or devils, because tho they throw great stons, pieces of earth, and wood at the inhabitants, they hurt them not at all, as if they acted not maliciously like devils, but in sport like [well-wishers] buffoons and drols.[62]

Visitors to Fairyland very often became involved in the general activities of their hosts. The well-known account of the 'Boy of Leith', written by George Burton and reproduced in Richard Bovet's *Pandaemonium, or the Devil's Cloyster* (1684), is a fairly good indication of this. Burton, who went to Leith on business, was told of the 'fairy-boy' and desired to meet him. He was brought to where the lad was playing and 'by smooth words and a piece of money' managed to persuade him to be interviewed in the presence of other witnesses. Burton was utterly astounded by the ten-year-old child's revelations that every Thursday night he met with a multitude of fairies underneath a hill between Edinburgh and Leith (most likely Calton Hill) where he played for them on a drum. He also accompanied them on overnight excursions. His descriptions, not only of what he did with his nocturnal companions, but of what their world was like, were fulsome:

> they are entertained with many sorts of musick, besides my drum; they have, besides, plenty of variety of meats and wine, and many times we are carried into France or Holland in a night, and return again, and whilst we are there we enjoy all the pleasures the country doth afford.

When asked how he got inside the hill, he replied that 'there was a great pair of gates that opened to them, though they were invisible to others; and that within there were brave large rooms, as well accommodated as most of Scotland'.

The boy was also gifted with the second sight, presumably an inheritance from time spent with the fairies, and was able to answer Burton's astrological questions with 'great subtilty' and a 'cunning much above his years'. He proceeded to tell fortunes and informed Burton that he would have two wives, both very handsome, but to a woman also present he revealed that 'she had had two bastards before she was married; which put her in such a rage that she desired not to hear the rest'. This was a clear case of a boy who knew too much and whose sojourn with the fairies rendered him unfit for human society.

Another widely reported case concerned the Boy of Borgue, in

Kirkcudbrightshire, Johnny Williamson who would visit the fairies for days at a time. On one occasion he emerged from a hole in a peat-bank, with 'his folks', the fairies, that no-one else could see. His grandfather, on the advice of a neighbour named Brown, sent the boy to consult a priest who provided him with a cross necklace:

> When the minister and kirk session heard of it they excommunicated the old grandfather and old Brown for advising such a thing. They believed in fairies, but not in anything a papist priest could do.

There were old men in Borgue in 1859 who could remember the boy when he himself had attained advanced old age. Both accounts suggest unfortunate individuals who were 'not all there' but who were best treated with respect, a common phenomenon in small close-knit communities which tended to look after their own, whatever their circumstances.[63]

The Politics of Fairyland: Social and Political Structures

It seems clear, given the majority of descriptions, that fairies were aristocratic, engaging in the hunt, playing music, and dancing. In many cases their home was described as a hall or court: 'thai war the gude wychtis that wynnit in the Court of Elfame'.[64] The very title of queen and king of fairy, so prevalent in the descriptions, is a pretty good indicator of their political structure. The power yielded by this unearthly monarchy was awesome and, according to the protagonist in 'The Wee Wee Man', the queen of fairy was a match for even the most powerful of earthly mortals: 'Though the King of Scotland had been there/The warst o them might hae been his queen'.

As he had discovered with the daily activities of fairies, Kirk similarly found the social and political infrastructures of Fairyland were parallel to those of their human counterparts. They were organised into tribes and orders and had children, nurses, marriages, deaths and burials. They lived under 'aristocratical rulers and laws, but no discernible religion, love or devotione towards God', and would disappear on hearing the name of God or Jesus. They were subject to the same conflicts and controversies that people experienced, having 'doubts, disputes, feuds, and syding of parties'. In Kirk's eyes this was due to 'there being som ignorance in all creatures', and the supernatural world was by no means exempt. They were certainly not free from the follies of vice and sin, for as he explains, 'whatever their own laws be . . . they transgress and committ acts of Injustice', by abducting women to nurse fairy offspring, and by stealing human children. The promiscuity, he sternly asseverated, of their '*leannain Sith* [fairy lovers] or succubi who tryst with men, it is abominable . . . But for swearing and intemperance they are not observed so subject to those irregularities, as to envy, spite, hypocrisy, lying and dissimulatione'.[65]

Donald A. MacKenzie asserted that in Gaelic folktales there is no mention of a queen of fairies, and that her arrival in Gaelic poetry was of relatively recent date, adding that the work of Stewart and Campbell on Gaelic folktales makes no mention of either a queen or king of fairy, and concluding that the 'genuine fairies of folk-belief are nameless and devoid of titles'. However, there is evidence from a Highland witch trial that some sort of leader or ruler, though not specifically called a king, did exist at one time in at least a part of the Gàidhealtachd. Donald McIlmichall claimed he saw 'ane old man as seemed to have preference above the rest' and that this man 'seemed to be chief, being ane large tall corporal Gardman' of ruddy complexion.[66]

If there is some doubt about traditions of a fairy queen or king in the Gaelic speaking areas of Scotland, though probably less than MacKenzie has suggested, the same could not be said of Lowland folk tradition or of the traditions heard within the courtly chambers of Scotland's monarchs. The earliest documented evidence for the personage of a fairy queen and king appears in two poems previously mentioned, the anonymous 'King Berdok' and Robert Henryson's 'Orpheus and Eurydice'. James IV was treated to William Dunbar's burlesque about a knight whose father was of the giant kindred while his mother was 'ane farie queyne'. At the court of James VI, Alexander Montgomerie's 'Flyting between Montgomerie and Polwart' mentioned 'the king of pharie, with the court of the elph quene'.[67]

Elite traditions aside, the notion of a fairy queen and king was also well-known in the folk tradition of Lowland Scotland. Bessie Dunlop was in labour when she first made acquaintance with the Queen of Elfland. Unlike the majority of descriptions, this queen was far from regal. Rather, as one commentator noted, she was 'a stout carline who begged for a drink'. Alison Peirson of Byrehill was tried for 'hanting and repairing with the gude nychtbouris and Quene of Elfame'. The king of fairy, with whom Margaret Alexander claimed to have had sex, was a black man dressed in green, though the love-making was not pleasant for she found his 'nature was cold', a diabolical trait for the devil's semen was notoriously chill. Isobel Gowdie, while inside the 'Downie-hillis', was fed meat by the 'Qwein of Fearrie' whom she described as 'brawlie clothed in whyt linens, and in whyt and browne cloathes'. She also met the 'king of fearrie, a braw man, weill favoured, and broad faced'.[68]

Isobel was one of those, together with others discussed in this chapter, who not only conveyed information, in David Buchan's model, about 'the world around' but also about 'the world around that'. Such notions about fairies clearly owed much to the subjectivity and experience of those who talked about, wrote about, or commented on them. For many the fairies were simply a reflection, projection or inversion of contemporary concerns and preoccupations. Nonetheless fairies could only be encountered in very special circumstances, which, in the literal sense of the word, were truly enchanting.

Notes

1 George MacDonald, *At the Back of the North Wind* (1870; Ware 1994), 25.
2 David Buchan, 'Taleroles and the Otherworld Ballads', in *Tod und Jenseits im Europäischen Volkslied*, ed. W. Puchner (Ioannina 1989), 254; Barre Toelken, 'Figurative Language and Cultural Contexts in the Traditional Ballads', *Western Folklore* 45:2 (1986): 128–42.
3 Robert Heron, *Observations on a Journey through the Western Counties of Scotland in the autumn of MDCCXCII* 2 vols. (Perth 1793), vol. 2, 228.
4 Kirk, 57; Jacques Le Goff, *The Birth of Purgatory*, trans. Arthur Goldhammer (Chicago 1984).
5 Trial of Alison Peirson, 28 May 1588. Pitcairn vol. 1, 164; Trial of Bessie Flinkar, 7 Aug. 1661. NAS, JC/26/27/9 and 13. Among other 'notorious witches', who confessed alongside Bessie, to have attended this meeting with the Devil 'amongst the hills' were Bessie Wilson and Isobel Dodis.
6 Trial of Isobel Gowdie, 13 April, 3rd and 15 May 1662. Pitcairn vol. 3, 604, 607. Isobel's trial is unusual in that it was given 'without ony compulsitouris'. In other words, her confession was voluntary and no torture or compulsion was used. Isobel appears to be referring to what we can identify as a well-known migratory legend, ML 3045, Motif F241.1.7. A Shetland version, recorded in 1875, told how the trows could transport themselves on bulrushes to Norway by saying 'Horsick up haddock, weel ridden bulwand'. Letter from Robert Cogle, Kunningsburgh in Gilbert Goudie 'Shetland Folk-Lore – Further Tales', *Old-Lore Miscellany of Orkney, Shetland, Caithness and Sutherland* ed. Alfred Johnston and Amy Johnston (London 1912), vol. 5, 16–20.
7 Another legend involving 'The Fairy Cup', recorded by William of Newburgh, involves a man who happens upon a fairy banquet, is offered a drink but pours out the contents and makes off with the vessel. Though pursued he

escapes. The cup became the property of the English King William the Elder. Later, the cup passed to the Scottish King David and was kept in the treasury of Scotland until the reign of William the Lion, at which point it passed back to Henry II of England. *Guiliemi Newbrigensis Historia, sive Chronica Rerum Anglicarum* Book I. Chapter 28, 95–6. See also Pitcairn vol. 3, 604 footnotes, and *Minstrelsy*, vol. 2, 367–8. Burns has a story of a shepherd boy who found himself in Bordeaux after using stalks of ragwort as the mode of conveyance, Cowan, 'Burns and Superstition', 235.

8   For examples of the fairy whirlwind see 'The Tale of Donald Daoilig' J. F. Campbell, *More West Highland Tales*, 1960 (Edinburgh 1994), vol. 2, 17–20, and 'A Man Lifted by a Sluagh', Bruford and MacDonald, *Scottish Traditional Tales*, 71–2. J. G. Campbell, *Superstitions of the Highlands and Islands of Scotland* (Glasgow 1900), 24. Campbell, *More West Highland Tales* vol. 2, 18.

9   Victor Turner, *The Ritual Process: Structure and Anti-Structure* (Ithica 1979), 94–130; Arnold van Gennep, *The Rites of Passage* (Chicago 1960), 11. Examples of other such folk traditions are mummering or guizing, ghost legends, witch beliefs, anomalous lights, and so on. Peter Narváez, 'Newfoundland Berry Pickers 'In the Fairies': Maintaining Spatial, Temporal, and Moral Boundaries Through Legendry', in *Good People*, 337.

10 van Gennep, *Rites*, 18; *Good People*, 338.

11 Wimberly, *Folklore in the English and Scottish Ballads*, 121.

12 Medieval chroniclers Ralph of Coggeshall and William of Newburgh both record the Suffolk story of the 'Green Children' who came from St. Martin's Land where 'they saw no sun, but enjoyed a degree of light like what is after sunset'. Ralph of Coggeshall's original account is found in *Radulphi de Coggeshall Chronicon Anglicanum*, ed. Joseph Stephenson, *Rolls Series* (1875) No. 66, 120–1. William of Newburgh's confirmation of the story appears in his *Guiliemi Newbrigensis Historia*, Book I. Chap. 27, 90–3. See also Keightley, *Fairy Mythology*, 281–3, and Briggs, *Dictionary*, 200–1.

13 Trial of Katherine Ross Lady Fowlis, 22 July 1590. Pitcairn vol. 1, 196; Trial of Jonet Drever, 1615. *Court Books*, 18–20. Jonet allegedly had 'conversatioun with the fary' for 26 years. Westray is an Orkney island; Trial of Katherine Jonesdochter, 2 Oct. 1616. *Court Book of Shetland*, 38–43; Trial of John Stewart, 1618, Irvine. *Trial . . . Irvine*, 9, and also see *Letters*, 134–5. Scott says a copy of a record of this trial was sent to him by a friend who wished to remain anonymous; Trial of Isobel Haldane, 15 May 1623. Pitcairn vol. 2, 537; Trial of Barbara Parish, 10–15 April 1647. Angus MacDonald, 'A Witchcraft Case of 1647', *The Scots Law Times* 10 April 1937, 78.

14 Kirk, 61; Cowan, 'Burns and Superstition', 235n. Kirk reported that two women saw a vision of hidden treasure in a hill called '*Sith bhruaich* or Fairie-Hill'. Scott also mentioned that mountain lakes, pits on top of high hills, or wells were thought to lead to Fairyland, *Minstrelsy*, vol. 2, 313–4. Magic wells, according to Juliette Wood, function in Scottish tradition 'as the extreme

limit of the known world'. See 'Lakes and Wells: Mediation Between the Real World and the Otherworld in Scottish Folklore', *Scottish Language and Literature, Medieval and Renaissance* eds., Dietrich Strauss and Horst Drescher, *Scottish Studies* 4 (Frankfurt 1986), 526.

15 Trial of Elspeth Reoch, 1616. *Maitland*, 187–91. Elspeth was born in Caithness; Trial of Bessie Dunlop, 8 Nov. 1576. Pitcairn vol. 1, 52–53, 58. A 'thorne' or hawthorn tree. In Thomas Rymer, the Eildon tree, under which he sits, is almost certainly a hawthorn; Trial of Alison Peirson, Pitcairn vol. 1, 164.

16 Legend says the last person to enter Dumbuck Hill saw Thomas resting his head on his elbow. Thomas asked the man 'Is it time?' at which the man fled. MacKenzie, *Scottish Folk-Lore and Folk-Life*, 107.

17 Christina Larner, *Enemies of God* (London 1981), 154; H. Cameron Gillies, *The Place-Names of Argyll* (London 1906), 7. A suggestive study of people and landscape is Kirsten Hastrup, *Culture and History in Medieval Iceland. An anthropological analysis of structure and change* (Oxford 1985).

18 Trial of Donald McIlmichall, 27 October 1677. J. N. R. MacPhail, *Highland Papers* 3, (Edinburgh 1928), 37; The assize of McIlmichall declared him to be 'a common vagabond', accused of stealing horses and cattle, and for 'consulting with evill spirits . . . giveing out himself to have skill of discoverie and finding out all lost goods by which means he wes guiltie of cheating and abuseing ignorant people and getting money from them for such discoveris . . .' *The Justiciary Records of Argyll and the Isles, 1664–1705* ed. John Cameron. *The Stair Society* (Edinburgh 1949), vol. 1, 80–2; Gillies, *The Place-Names of Argyll*, 7, 73.

19 Sean Kane, *Wisdom of the Mythtellers* (Peterborough 1994), 61, 75; For localised studies on aspects of Scotland's supernatural landscapes see E. B. Lyle, 'A Reconsideration of the Place-Names in 'Thomas the Rhymer'', *Scottish Studies* 13 (1969) 65–71; and Louis Stott, *Enchantment of the Trossachs* (Stirling 1992).

20 Kane, *Wisdom of the Mythtellers*, 102–3; Rees, *Celtic Heritage*, 94.

21 Kirk, 49–51. Sometimes Hell is believed to be located in the earth's core. According to Howard Rollin Patch 'the Other World of the Celts was . . . located on this earth, often in the west, and sometimes took the form of the Isles of the Blessed, the Land-beneath-the-Waves, the hollow hill, or the land beyond the mist, or varying combinations of these'. *The Other World: According to Descriptions in Medieval Literature* (Cambridge 1950), 27. Modern scholarship would dispute that such locations are particularly 'Celtic'.

22 Narváez constructs a convincing argument about the various dangers associated with being removed from the community in some way (such as berry picking), and the fairy narratives that developed around this theme, in his article 'Newfoundland Berry Pickers 'In the Fairies'', *Good People*, 336–68.

23 Carlo Ginzburg, *Ecstasies: Deciphering the Witches' Sabbath* trans. R. Rosenthal (New York 1991), 101, 307.

24 'The Maner of the Crying of ane Playe', in John Asloan, *The Asloan Manuscript* 1515. ed. W. A. Craigie, 2 vols. (Edinburgh 1925), vol. 2, 149, 151.
25 Trial of Alison Peirson, Pitcairn vol. 1, 163; Trial of Isobel Gowdie, Pitcairn vol 3, 611; Trial of Donald McIlmichall, *Highland Papers*, 37; Kirk, 54.
26 Trial of Andro Man, 1597–8. *Miscellany* vol. 1, part 3, 121–2; Low, *A Tour Through the Islands of Orkney and Schetland*, xlii.
27 On the dead in Fairyland refer to the trial of Bessie Dunlop, Pitcairn vol. 1, 57, trial of Alison Peirson, Pitcairn vol. 1, 162, trial of Andro Man, *Miscellany* vol. 1, part 3, 121, and Campbell, *Popular Tales of the West Highlands* vol. 1, 432; Walter Map *De Nugis Curialium* (1209) has the story of 'King Herla' who was led to the underworld by a dwarf for what seemed three days but was two hundred years. Also see J. F. Campbell, and Bruford and MacDonald for 19th and 20thc. folktale examples.
28 J. M. Barrie, *Peter Pan* (1911; Bristol 1998), 44.
29 Though fairies of medieval romance are human size, some medieval chroniclers discuss smaller fairies, eg. Map's 'King Herla' and Gervase of Tilbury's *Otia Imperialia* (1211) which discusses 'portunes' or 'small agricultural fairies', see Briggs, *Dictionary of Fairies*, 333.
30 Jolly, *Popular Religion in Late Saxon England*, 132–68.
31 The following account is from Gerald of Wales, *The Journey Through Wales*, 1188, trans. Lewis Thorpe (Harmondsworth 1978), 133–6.
32 William J. Watson, *The History of the Celtic Place-Names of Scotland* (Edinburgh and London 1926), 135. See also Edward J. Cowan, 'Myth and Identity in Early Medieval Scotland', *Scottish Historical Review* vol. LXIII. (1984): 130–3.
33 William Henry Schofield, *Mythical Bards and the Life of William Wallace* (Cambridge 1920). See also W. MacKay MacKenzie who says 'Blynd Hary' is a degenerate god derived from Odin, possessing supernatural powers, and having only one eye, *The Poems of William Dunbar* 1932 (London 1970), Appendix D.
34 Cromek, *Nithsdale and Galloway Song*, 337–8. Schofield, *Mythical Bards*, 73–6, 100–3; Child, 67. 'Billie Blin' is found in Child ballads [5] 'Gil Brenton'; [6] 'Willie's Lady'; [53] 'Young Beichan'; [110] 'The Knight and the Shepherd's Daughter'; and the English ballad [30] 'King Arthur and the King of Cornwall'.
35 R. W. Munro, ed., *Monro's Western Isles of Scotland*, 1549 (Edinburgh 1961), 82–3. The island appears on the ordnance survey map today as Luchruban.
36 James Aikman, *The History of Scotland Translated from the Latin of George Buchanan* 4 vols. (Glasgow 1827), vol. 1, 52; William F. Skene, *Celtic Scotland: A History of Ancient Alban* 3 vols. (Edinburgh 1880), vol. 3, 440; *The Description of the Isles of Scotland*, in Skene 3, 429.
37 Martin Martin, *A Description of the Western Isles of Scotland*, 1703. 1716. (rep. Edinburgh 1976), 19. It was written c. 1695. The author was himself a Gael

and one of the Martins of Bealach, Skye. Samuel Johnson, whose own tour to the highlands was inspired by Martin, deplorably and patronisingly said of him, he 'was a man not illiterate: he was an inhabitant of Sky, and therefore was within reach of intelligence . . . yet with all his opportunities, he has often suffered himself to be deceived . . . he probably had not the knowledge of the world sufficient to qualify him for judging what would deserve or gain the attention of mankind'. In *Johnson's Journey to the Western Islands of Scotland and Boswell's Journal of a Tour to the Hebrides with Samuel Johnson, LL.D.* 1774, 1785 ed., R. W. Chapman (Oxford 1979), 57–8.

38 Martin, *A Description of the Western Isles of Scotland*, xiv, 19.

39 Iain F. MacIver, 'A Seventeenth Century 'Prose Map'', *Togail Tìr, Marking Time: The Map of the Western Isles* ed. Finlay MacLeod (Stornoway 1989), 23, 30. We are grateful to Finlay MacLeod for bringing this material to our attention. Robert Sibbald's statement on the pygmy bones in his *Description* (MS. 44) must have been taken directly from John Morison. Sibbald said the bones, 'when examined are found to be the bones of some small fowls, which abound in that place'.

40 Martin, *A Description of the Western Isles of Scotland*, 82, 249.

41 William Collins, 'Ode to a Friend on his Return &c' and later called 'An Ode on the Popular Superstitions of the Highlands of Scotland, Considered as the Subject of Poetry.' It does not appear that Collins ever visited Scotland himself, but obtained his information from a friend John Home (to whom the poem is addressed), and the work of Martin Martin. For more on Collins see Mrs. Barbauld, ed. *The Poetical Works of Mr. William Collins* (London 1797), iii-xlix, 108–24, and Richard Wendorf and Charles Ryskamp, eds. *The Works of William Collins* (Oxford 1979), 56–63, 161–72.

42 John MacCulloch, *A Description of the Western Isles of Scotland* 3 vols. (London 1819) and *The Highlands and Western Isles of Scotland* 4 vols. (London 1824), vol 4, 329. These accounts were based on journeys made between 1811 and 1821.

43 W. C. MacKenzie, *History of the Outer Hebrides* (Paisley 1903), 498–9, and *The Highlands and Isles of Scotland: A Historical Survey* (1937; Edinburgh and London 1949), 152–3. MacKenzie was able to prove the existence of the Pygmy Isle and its attendant legends and thus restore the Dean's reputation on this issue.

44 Dymes reports '. . . the Pygmeys Island is a round high hill contening about one acre of land. This Ile is ioyned to the Lewis by a narrowe necke of land, which is in lenght about halfe the distance of a paire of Butts, wherein there is the walls of a Chappell to bee seene which is but 8 foote in length and 6 foote in breadth, the ground whereof hath bene often tymes digged up espetially by the Irish which come thither of purpose to gett the bones of those little people which they say were buryed there. At my beinge upon the Ile I made search in the earth and found some of those bones, which are soe little that my beleife is

scarce bigg enough to thinke them to bee the bones of humane flesh'. MacKenzie, *History of the Outer Hebrides*, 591–5.

45 See (James Browne) *A Critical Examination of Dr MacCulloch's Work on the Highlands and Western Isles of Scotland* (Edinburgh 1825) for a devastating critique of the author and his opinions.

46 'A Discourse concerning Devils and Spirits', appended to Reginald Scot, *Discoverie* (1665 edit.), 514.

47 Definition in 'An Exposition of the difficult Words in the forgoing Treatises', Kirk, 115; 'A Discourse concerning Devils and Spirits', 511; John J. Winberry, 'The Elusive Elf: Some Thoughts on the Nature and Origin of the Irish Leprechaun', *Folklore* 87 (1976): 63–75. We thank Miceal Ross for suggesting a possible connection between the two traditions.

48 Michael Slavin, *The Book of Tara* (Dublin 1996), 13; *Introduction to Senchus Mor or Law of Distress, Ancient Laws of Ireland* vol. 1 (Dublin 1865), 71, 73. Qtd. in Winberry, 66; Martin, *A Description of the Western Isles of Scotland*, 110–1.

49 Trial of Walter Ronaldson, 20 Nov. 1601. *Aberdeen Presbytery Records* (Aberdeen 1846). Ronaldson, with friends, searched for the treasure but was unsuccessful. However, he maintained that 'there is gold there, gif it was weel sought'. On brownies and hidden treasure see Lewis Spence, *The Fairy Tradition in Britain* (London 1948), 38; Trial of Isobel Gowdie, Pitcairn vol. 3, 607. For more on trows see Ernest W. Marwick, *The Folklore of Orkney and Shetland* (London 1975), and Alan Bruford, 'Trolls, Hillfolk, Finns, and Picts', in *Good People*, 116–41; Wimberly, *The Folklore of the English and Scottish Ballads*, 171.

50 Campbell, *Superstitions of the Highlands and Islands of Scotland*, 10.

51 Trial of Bessie Dunlop, Pitcairn vol. 1, 52; Kirk, 50–1.

52 Kirk, 50, 59.

53 *Daemonologie*, 74.

54 Andro confessed 'to have carnall deall with that devilische spreit, the Quene of Elphen, on quhom thow begat dyveris bairnis, quhom thow hes sene sensyn'. Trial of Andro Man, *Miscellany* vol. 1, part 3, 119; Trial of Elspeth Reoch, *Maitland*, 112; Trial of Isobel Haldane, Pitcairn vol. 2, 537; Trial of Janet Trall, 22 May 1623. *Extracts . . . Strathbogie*, xi-xiii; Trial of Margaret Alexander, 12 March, 10 April 1647. Angus MacDonald, 'A Witchcraft Case of 1647', *The Scots Law Times* 10 April, 1937, 77–8; Trial of Isobel Gowdie, Pitcairn vol. 3, 606– 615.

55 Brand, 63; Kirk, 55.

56 Minister of Kirkmichael, 1793. *OSA* vol. 12, 462.

57 Trial of Bessie Dunlop, Pitcairn vol. 1, 51, 55–7; Trial of Katherine Jonesdochter, *Court Book of Shetland*, 38. Trial of Alison Peirson, Pitcairn vol. 1, 164.

58 Edward J. Cowan, 'The War Rhymes of Robert Service, Folk Poet', *Studies in*

Scottish Literature 28 (1993) 12–27; MacCulloch, 'The Mingling of Fairy and Witch Beliefs', 227–44, also thinks that the grey bearded man who led Isobel Haldane out of the fairy hill was a 'kind of familiar or ghost, like Thomas Reid and William Simpson', 237; Trial of Elspeth Reoch, *Maitland*, 113; Kirk, 80, 93.

59 NAS, CH2/1/2 *Presbytery Records of Aberdeen* October 1675. The recommended action, to warn people of the dangers of fairy belief, was to call before them 'the seducers' to be publicly rebuked 'and if the seducers be compots mentis to proceed in censure against them as lykewayes against the consulters'; Trial of Margaret Alexander, *The Scots Law Times*, 77. She further confessed that her father was carried back and forth over St. Mungo's Well by her fairy/witch associates.

60 William Grant Stewart, *The Popular Superstitions and Festive Amusements of the Highlanders of Scotland*, 1822 (London 1851), 90; Cromek, *Remains of Galloway and Nithsdale Song* (1810) gives an account of a Rade, 298–9.

61 Trial of Andro Man, *Miscellany* vol. 1, part 3, 121; Trial of Donald McIlmichall, *Highland Papers*, 38; Samuel Hibbert, *A Description of the Shetland Islands* (Edinburgh 1822). He adds, 'Their nightly dancing ring I always dread/ Nor let my sheep within that circle tread/ Where round and round all night, in moonlight fair/ They dance to some strange music in the air', 449; James Nicolson, *Shetland Folklore* (London 1981), 77; Jessie Saxby, *Shetland Traditional Lore* (Edinburgh 1932), 116–7; John Spence, *Shetland Folklore* (Lerwick 1899), 39.

62 Kirk, 50–5, 85. 'Well-wishers' was deleted from text and 'buffoons and drols' substituted later.

63 George Burton, letter to Richard Bovet, *Pandemonium, or the Devil's Cloyster* (London 1684), 173–4. This quotation may reflect an echo of the legend of 'The Fairy Cup', see above p. 38 and note. J. F. Campbell, *Popular Tales of the West Highlands*, vol. 1, 425.

64 Trial of Bessie Dunlop, Pitcairn vol. 1, 53.

65 Kirk, 51, 56, 62.

66 MacKenzie, *Scottish Folk-Lore and Folk-Life*, 195–6; Trial of Donald McIlmichall, *Highland Papers*, 38.

67 William Dunbar, 'Now Lythis off ane Gentill Knycht', Bawcutt vol. 1, 133–4.; Alexander Montgomerie, 'Flyting between Montgomerie and Polwart: The Secund Invective: Montgomeryes Answeir to Polwart', *Alexander Montgomery: A Selection From His Songs and Poems*, ed. H. M. Shire (Edinburgh 1960), 81–90.

68 MacCulloch, 'The Mingling of Fairy and Witch Beliefs', 234; Trial of Alison Peirson, Pitcairn vol. 1, 162; Trial of Margaret Alexander, *The Scots Law Times*, 78; Trial of Isobel Gowdie, Pitcairn vol. 3, 604.

CHAPTER THREE

Enchantments of the Fairies

> They bore her far to a mountain green,
> To see what mortal never had seen;
> And they seated her high on a purple sward,
> And bade her heed what she saw and heard;
> And note the changes the spirits wrought,
> For now she lived in the land of thought.
> She looked, and she saw nor sun nor skies,
> But a crystal dome of a thousand dyes;
> She looked, and she saw nae land aright,
> But an endless whirl of glory and light:
> And radiant beings went and came
> Far swifter than wind, or the linked flame.
> She hid her een frae the dazzling view;
> She looked again, and the scene was new.
> 'Kilmeny', James Hogg

Of great importance to the vast majority of people living in the Reformation centuries was knowledge of the ways in which creatures from beyond Middle Earth were believed to ensnare human beings or lead them astray. Since the fairies had many ways of casting their glamour, or enchantments, it was essential to take certain precautions, or to make placations, to avoid their lures and traps. Inevitably, not all would be successful at eluding beguilement, so it was of even greater importance to know if, once captured, there was any hope of escape. In other words, how could people break the fairy spell and disenchant themselves, their friends and loved ones, and even their animals?

Fairy Glamourie: The Modes of Enchantment

Although the fairies had special days and times which they favoured for glamouring ill-fated humans, they could strike at any time and, if they were so minded, there was very little that one could do to avoid these persistent and capricious creatures. The word 'glamour' conveys the sense of charming the eye, of casting a spell, of making an object appear more beautiful or alluring than it is in reality, hence the modern meaning of the term. The *Oxford English Dictionary* notes the modern English word as deriving from Old French via archaic Scots and subsequently revived by Scott, but Allan Ramsay, in the early eighteenth century, used the expression 'glamourit sicht'. The reasons behind enchantment – not that the fairies always required a motive – might be to obtain a mortal lover, an earthly nurse or midwife, or a human baby. Humans were also required for the more sinister and frightening purpose of serving as a payment or a 'teind' to Hell. Activities such as eating, drinking, speaking, or sleeping in a taboo place were all common mistakes made by luckless mortals. Physical contacts with an Otherworld being who bestowed gifts, music, or charms were equally common forms of entrapment. Mortals were sometimes enchanted through the use of fairy darts, arrows, or blasts. Encounters with fairies were prone to occur beneath apple trees, or close to wells, hills or woods, invariably known, or suspected, to be frequented by the elves. Childbirth was also a highly vulnerable time.

Thomas Rhymer was warned against the consumption of fruit when he arrived in Elfland; he was also forbidden conversation. The dangers of eating fairy-contaminated food were known to Kirk, who reported that men with second sight had seen fairies 'eat at funerals, banqueetts: hence many of the Scotish-Irish will not tast meat at those meetings, least they have communion with, or be poysoned by them'.[1] Bessie Dunlop was forbidden by Thomas Reid to speak during a visit to a fairy tryst, even when asked direct questions. Likewise, he warned her not to speak to him if ever she saw him in public unless he first addressed her.

Janet in 'Tam Lin' outwits the Queen by refusing the offer of fairy gifts:

> 'O stay, Tomlin,' cried Elphin Queen,
> 'Till I pay you your fee;'
> 'His father has lands and rents enough,
> He wants no fee from thee.'

She was well advised to avoid fairies bearing gifts for they generally compromised the recipient or turned to dust, as with fairy gold, upon receipt.

Another type of gift could reside in a name. Tam Lin may have received his appellation to keep him trapped in the Otherworld, a sort of naming magic, a possibility suggested by

> 'First they did call me Jack,' he said,
> 'And then they called me John,
> But since I lived in the fairy court
> Tomlin has always been my name'.[2]

In both 'The Elfin Knight' and 'Lady Isabel and the Elf-Knight' the lady was seduced by the sound of a fairy horn or harp:

> If I had yon horn that I hear blawing,
> And yon elf-knight to sleep in my bosom
>
> This maiden had scarcely these words spoken,
> Till in at her window the elf-knight has luppen.
>
> It's a very strange matter, fair maiden, said he,
> I canna blaw my horn but ye call on me.

Thomas Rhymer was much taken with the queen's bugle horn. Music was a seductive medium which figures again and again in accounts of the fairies.[3]

In some versions Tam Lin was sleeping under an apple tree at the time of his capture (in others he had fallen from his horse), while the Rhymer was taken from under the Eildon tree. In other variants Tam Lin was abducted while he was beside a well, and Lady Isabel escaped death by the Elf-Knight at 'Wearie's Well'. Magical woods are featured in 'Tam Lin' and 'Hind Etin', two ballads in which love and seduction are key motives, as they are in 'The Elf-Knight', 'Lady Isabel and the Elfin-Knight' and 'Thomas Rymer'. Payment of the teind to Hell is exemplified best in 'Thomas Rymer' and 'Tam Lin'.

The fairy need for human midwives and nurses was the theme of the ballad, 'The Queen of Elfan's Nourice', but for some, such as accused witch Barbra Parish in 1647, the tale was recounted as frightening reality. A group of twenty green-clad fairies told Barbra, at one of their regular gatherings on the Ministers Brae, Livingston, that they were in search of a nurse. She suggested a suitable candidate who was, surely by no coincidence, a woman with whom she had fallen out. A green kirtled fairy entered the home of the chosen nurse-to-be but was, for some unstated reason, unable to abduct her. Not content to leave empty-handed the fairy killed the woman's child and announced to Barbra and the rest of the fairy troop, 'If I have not gotten the gouse I have gottene [the] gaizline [gosling]'.

'King Orfeo' lost his wife to the fairies when she was struck by a fairy dart: 'For da king o Ferrie we his daert/Has pierced your lady to da hert'. The infamous elf arrowheads or fairy darts were widely believed to have been a favoured form of weaponry against humans and animals. Fairies, according to Kirk, did not have any weapons made of iron; rather they were 'stone like to yellow soft flint, shaped like a barbed arrow head, but flung as a dart with great force'. The impact of these darts was 'of the natur of thunder-bolt subtilly and mortally wounding the vitall parts without breaking the skin'. Kirk himself claimed to have seen such wounds on animals and had held the offending weapons in his own hand.[4]

Agnes Sampson, Bartie Paterson, and Isobel Gowdie, could identify elf-shot victims. Isobel testified that she saw elf darts being made. First, the Devil would 'shape them with his awin hand', then elf-boys would fashion and trim the arrows. She also went on forays with other 'witches' to shoot them at unsuspecting victims:

> . . . we may shoot them dead at owr pleasour. Any that ar shot be us, their sowell will goe to Hevin, bot ther bodies remains with us, and will flie as horsis to us, als small as strawes.

She explained that no bow was used to shoot the elf arrowheads, they were flicked off the thumbnail. She regretfully admitted to killing people by this method: 'Som tymes we will misse; bot if thay twitch [touch], be it beast, or man, or woman, it will kill, tho they haid an jack [armour] upon them'. She was remorseful over the deaths for which she believed she was responsible: 'Bot that quhich troubles my conscience most, is the killing of severall persones, with the arrowes quhich I gott from the divell'.

There are numerous references within the witch trials to animals, especially cattle and horses, being 'shot to dead', a term which implies a sudden attack of illness or death as a result of a fairy dart. Witches were often implicated for directing these particular assaults, with or without the assistance of the fairies. Isobell Young of Eastbarns (1629), Katharine Oswald in Niddry (1629), Alison Nisbett from Hilton, Berwickshire (1632), John Burgh at Fossoway (1643), and Jane Craig in Tranent (1649) were all alleged to have the ability to cast elfin darts. John Burgh could also cure afflicted cows by sprinkling them with water in which 'two inchantit stanes' had been placed. He said he learned his remedies from a widow woman (Neane VcClerich) who was a relative of a famous witch called Nik Neveing from Crieff, probably Catherine NicNiven (c.

1615) who was said to have been burned alive, and who bore a very suggestive surname.[5]

Protective charms against elf-shot were occasionally recorded, for example in the testimony of Bartie (Barbara) Paterson in 1607, who sought to defend against specialist types of shot aimed at the portals of buildings or at different parts of the body:

> And for useing of thir charmes following, for charmeing of cattell; 'I charme thé for arrow-schot, for dor-schot [door-shot], for wondo-schot [window-shot], for ey-schot, for tung-schote, for lever-schote [liver-shot], for lung-schote, for hert-schot, all the maist, in the name of the Father, the Sone and Haly Gaist. Amen'.

Bartie had no problem in combining magic and religion. She anointed one of her patients with green salves made from herbs, gave him 'drenches' or potions, and ordered him to fall down on his knees three times 'to ask his health at all living witches above or under the eard, in the name of Jesus'. After the ritual, she gave him nine 'pickles', or berries, of rowan-tree to keep upon his person.

Janet Trall's diagnosis for one anxious mother was that her 'bairn had gotten a dint of evil wind', which may refer to the fairy blast. Jonet Morrison of Bute, tried in 1662, supplied detailed and fascinating information about a sabbat, including the rather touching circumstance that a woman who was asked by the Devil why her husband was not present replied that 'there was a young bairne at home and they could not both come. Clearly no diabolical crèche was provided! Jonet claimed that she healed three people who had been blasted by the fairies:

> And being questioned anent her heiling of Mcfersone in Keretoule his dochter who lay sick of a very unnaturall disease without power of hand or foot both speichles and kenured [meaning is obscure]. She answered the disease quhilk ailed her was blasting with the faryes and that she healed her with herbes. Item being questioned about her heileing of Alester Bannatyne who was sick of the lyk disease answred that he was blasted with the fairyes also and that she heiled him thereof with herbs and being questioned anent her heileing of Patrick Glas dochter Barbra Glas answred that she was blasted with the faryes also.

Jonet Morrison made a clear distinction between elf-shot and the blast:

quhen they are shott ther is no recoverie for it and if the shott be in the heart they died presently bot if it be not at the heart they will die in a while with it yet will at last die with it and that blasting is a whirlwinde that the fayries raises about that persone quhich they intend to wrong and that tho ther were tuentie present yet it will harme none bot him quhom they were set for.

A victim of the blast, Jonet confided, could be healed using herbs or by charming: 'all that whirlwind gathers in the body till one place; if it be taken in time it is the easier healed and if they gett not means they will shirpe [shrivel] away'. Robert Kirk was told that to cure elf-shot a man simply had to find the point of entry with his finger 'as if the spirits flowing from a mans warme hand were antidote sufficient against their poyson'd darts'. This method was also employed on the island of Arran, by Farquhar Ferguson who was brought before the kirk session of Kilmory in 1716 for practising charms and pretended skill in elf-shot. He admitted that he was frequently called upon to 'search for holes in people that were suspected to be shot' and provided medicines, which consisted of 'a little black soap' and a drink made from the herb, agrimony. He learned his technique by watching and observing people on the mainland searching for holes in cattle, and, having a child who was ill, decided to try out the technique himself. After successfully healing his child, he continued to practice his new-found talent.[6]

Falling asleep on fairy territory was a dangerous business, as Tam Lin learned to his cost and as Dame Heurodis or Eurydice discovered when she fell into a slumber under an 'ympe' tree, one May morning, and soon found herself in the hands of the king of fairy.[7] The discovery by Arthur Edmonston in Shetland of 'King Orfeo', a ballad version of *Sir Orfeo*, an early fourteenth-century English romance which drew upon Breton lays to retell the story of Orpheus and Eurydice, was truly sensational. In the ballad, Lady Isabel is smitten by the fairy dart but she is rescued by Orfeo whose music enchants the fairies. The story must have struck a certain resonance in Shetland where traditionally music and fairies 'gang thegither' like whisky and freedom elsewhere in Scotland. Edmonston personally knew of a young woman, who had fallen asleep on a hill at midday and later died; her father believed that she had been taken by the fairies and an image, or 'stock', left in her place.[8]

As 'The Queen of Elfan's Nourice' shows, women were particularly susceptible to fairy enchantment when in childbirth. Unfortunately, the ballad survives in a fragmentary state but there is sufficient to indicate that a grieving mother was taken from her four-day-old son to wet-nurse the Queen of Elfan's child. Bessie Dunlop was 'new rissine out of gissane [child-bed]' when first she met Thomas Reid. Janet Trall was likewise 'lieing in child bed lair' from which, as she said, 'I was drawn forth to a dub (stagnant pond) near my house door in Dunning, and was there puddled and troubled' by vexing spirits.[9] Kirk also told of women 'taken away when in child-bed to nurse fayrie children, a lingring voracious image of theirs being left in their place'. The fate of women abducted to serve as midwives or wet nurses to their captor's brood differed quite markedly, however. When the child was weaned, there were three potential outcomes for the nurse — she might die, be returned home unharmed, or be given the option of remaining with the fairies:

> But if anie superterranean be soe subtile as to practise sleights for procuring a privacy [knowledge] to any of their misteries . . . they smit them without pain as with a puff of wind, and bereave them of both the naturall and acquired sights in the twinkling of ane eye . . . or they strick them dumb.

Kirk was told of another incident in which a woman was stolen out of childbed and a stock in her likeness left in her place, which dwindled and eventually died, to be duly buried. Two years later she returned and was reunited with her husband. Of her time away she said she had seen very little that went on in her spacious lodgings until she anointed one eye with an unction that she found. The unguent allowed her to see a 'place full of light without anie fountain or lamp from whence it did spring'. Her newly acquired vision was quickly uncovered by her hosts who promptly 'fann'd her blind of that eye with a puff of their breath'. Kirk reported other ointments which, like 'Gyges's ring', could render individuals invisible or evanescent. Such applications might cast them in a trance, alter their shape or 'make things appear at a vast distance'. Such assertions raise the possibility that some sort of hallucinatory substances were on occasion employed, as was the case with the Benandanti in Italy who experienced group trances, and with poor wretches in Germany who were accused of witchcraft and were said to have applied salves to their bodies.[10]

A greatly dreaded occurrence, and arguably the worst act attributed to the fairies, was the payment of a teind to Hell, perhaps one of the most feared prospects that a captured mortal could face. The teind, or tithe, was the tenth part of a person's income which notionally was gifted to, or uplifted by, the ecclesiastical authorities. Needless to say it was bitterly resented as the Church appeared to grow richer in proportion to the aggravated poverty of the laity, a theme memorably tackled, for example, by Sir David Lyndsay in his hard-hitting play, *Satyre of the Thrie Estaitis*. Farmers complained that standing crops rotted while awaiting ecclesiastical appraisal which might result in the requisition of the best part of the harvest, grown perhaps in a tenth of the field but exceeding that amount in yield. Some fishermen in Fife were said to have thrown a tenth of their catch into the sea, before returning to harbour, donating it directly to God, in order to avoid grasping ecclesiastical intermediaries. The idea that the fairies had to sacrifice one tenth of their kind to the fiends of Hell on an annual basis was therefore one which would strike chords of sympathy and terror alike in the hearts of the human population. In some cases it was believed that the queen of fairies was pledged to the Devil to submit the teind, but in order to save members of her own population from this fate human adults and children were stolen and proffered as the obligatory stipend instead. Alison Peirson's uncle told her to sain (bless) herself so 'that scho be nocht tane away with thame agane; for the teynd of thame gais ewerie yeir to hell'.[11]

In almost every case, the time of day or year is specified in the ballads, with respect to the appearance of the fairies. In 'Lady Isabel and the Elf-Knight' the fairy appears on the 'first morning in May', which is Beltane (1 May), a festival which could enthuse even the often over-solemn George Buchanan, lambaster of Mary Queen of Scots and rigorous tutor of the young James VI:

> Hail! sacred thou to sacred joy
> To mirth and wine, sweet first of May!
> To sports which no grave cares alloy,
> The sprightly dance, the festive play.[12]

The queen of fairies in 'Allison Gross' breaks the witch's spell on Halloween (31 October):

> But as it fell out on last Hallow-even,
> When the seely court was ridin by,
> The queen lighted down on a gowany bank,
> Nae far frae the tree where I wont to lye.

Tam Lin must also be rescued on Halloween: 'Just at the mirk and midnight hour/The fairy folk will ride'. The elf king arrives, heralded by a bugle, at midnight in 'Sir Cawline'.

Accused witches frequently mention specific times and dates also. Bessie Dunlop's fairy contact usually appeared to her at the twelfth hour of the day. Katherine Ross highlighted Halloween and Midsummer, while Euphemia Makcalzane pointed to Lammas as a fairy time. Katherine Jonesdochter met a fairy man every year for forty years on Halloween and Holy Cross Day (14 September) and mentioned that the trows would come to any house where there was 'feasting, or great mirrines and speciallie at Yule'. Katherine Caray, tried in 1616, said that when she went to the hills 'at the doun going of the sun, ane great number of fairie men mett her'.[13]

The relationship of fairy activity with specific temporal and spatial locations has been noticed already. It was no accident that particular times and places were denoted, or that fairies would appear to have a fondness for special occasions. Frequently the time and place specified were significant in a broader supernatural or customary context, and did not necessarily pertain only to fairies. In addition, as the discussion about the landscape of the supernatural suggested, place and periodicity operate conjointly with the concept of boundaries – 'the magic points where worlds impinge'.[14] For example, calendar customs associated with Halloween and Beltane, which were repeatedly mentioned in connection with fairies, were important dates for many other reasons.

Halloween can be traced directly to the ancient Celtic day of Samhain, or Samhuinn, one of two major festivals of the Celts; the other was Beltane. Samhain marked an entry into winter and the beginning of a new year. Beltane celebrated the coming of summer and its attendant renewal of vegetation and fertility. Samhain solemnised the arrival of winter, a time of decay and impotence when bonfires were lit to banish darkness and hasten the return of the sun. Beltane fires were kindled at dawn to welcome the awakening of the sun from its slumber. The duality of life and death were celebrated on these days. On the evening of Samhain the normal order of the world was suppressed, the curtain between the natural and supernatural temporarily lifted, leaving the spirits of the dead free to wander into the realm of the living.[15]

Even the fairies themselves, according to Kirk, recognised special days, dates when they were compelled to shift their abodes, and times when their world collided with that of humans: 'They remove to other lodgings at the beginning of each quarter of the year . . . and at such revolution of time, seers or men of the second sight' have frightening experiences with them. Not surprisingly, Kirk commented that church attendance on Sundays closest to the four Quarter days increased as people came to sain 'or hallow themselves, their corns and cattell, from the shots and stealth of these wandring tribes'.[16]

The numbers three and seven[17] are repeatedly encountered in the ballads. The most frequent lapse of time in Elfland was seven years. Thomas Rhymer was enchanted for seven years and Hind Etin lived with a mortal wife for the same period, during which time she managed to produce one son a year. Tam Lin was the third rider in the Halloween procession. He also warned Janet that if she failed to rescue him he would languish in Elfland for seven more years, assuming he managed to avoid becoming the payment of the teind to Hell. In 'Lady Isabel and the Elf-Knight' the elfin assassin had murdered seven times: 'Seven king's-daughters here hae I slain'. In 'Allison Gross' the queen of fairy cured the metamorphosed man, restoring him from dragon form to human shape by stroking him three times over her knee.

Though repetition of particular numbers in the witch trials is not as standardised as in the ballads, it is not altogether absent. In 1598–9 Thomas Lorn from Overton of Dyce was brought before the provost of Aberdeen on charges that could be interpreted as communication with, and repeated abductions by, fairies. He was accused of 'hearing of spreits, and wavering ofttimes frae his wife, bairns, and family, by the space of seven weeks, they not knowing where he has been during the said space'. Isobel Haldane's first visit inside a fairy hill lasted three days, from Thursday till Sunday at noon.[18] Janet Trall's cures specify three and nine as operative numbers. James Knarston and Katherine Cragie performed magical rituals, which were repeated three times and involved the use of three stones.

Interludes or relationships with fairy folk could be, on occasion, of some benefit to a mortal. Encounters might leave the human with special gifts or qualities. Thomas Rhymer was given a 'tongue that can never lie', hence his reputation for prophecy. Gifts of second sight or an ability to heal were commonly a consequence of involvement with the fairies. Steven Maltman from Gargunnock confessed in 1628 that he had the healing abilities of the fairy folk. Isobel Sinclair, tried in 1633, claimed that over seven years, six times at the 'reathes of the year [Quarter days], she hath bein controlled with the Phairie; and that be thame, she hath the second sight: quhairby she will know giff thair be any fey bodie in the hous'.[19]

Musical talents were often bestowed upon human visitors to Elfland. Orkney and Shetland are saturated in traditions about people whose musical accomplishments were attributed to the teachings of the trows, who, it was believed, liked to lure human fiddle players to their abode, generally for a space of one year and a day. Of course, to the human involved, it seemed like only an evening in their company. Several Shetland fiddle tunes were accredited to the recollections of such visitants. Similarly, on the island of Skye, the gifted MacCrimmon family of pipers were said to have received their musical gifts courtesy of the fairies. The first MacCrimmon to inherit this gift, Iain Og, was playing his pipes when he was approached by a fairy woman who gave him a magical silver chanter:

> *Thug do mhaise 's ceòl do phìoba*
> *Leannan sìthe air do thòir,*
> *Sineam dhuit an sionnsair airgid*
> *A bhios binn gun chearb fo d' mheòir.*
>
> Your beauty and the music of your pipe
> Have attracted a fairy lover to you,
> Let me hand you the silver chanter
> That will be sweet and faultless in your fingers.[20]

Usually, however, there was a price to pay for these gifts, and what initially might have seemed a welcome boon turned out to be a dangerous liaison. Before endowing Andro Man with the ability to 'knaw all thingis, and suld help and cuir all sort of seikness', the Queen of Elfin caused one of his cattle to die upon a hill called 'the Elphillok, bot promeist to do him gude theireftir'. Two fairy men taught Elspeth Reoch a ritual so that she could gain the power of second sight, but one of them arrived at her bedside at night and would not let her rest, relentlessly harassing her until she slept with him. After three nights of this abuse she succumbed, but when she awoke the next morning she had 'no power of hir toung nor could nocht speik'. Isobell Strathaquin from Aberdeen, tried alongside her daughter in 1597, was similarly obliged to sleep with an 'elf man' in order to acquire her occult powers.[21]

Bessie Dunlop, the Ayrshire healer accused of witchcraft, while initially appearing to enjoy the favour of the fairies, underwent a reversal of fortune. For Bessie it all started when she received a visit from the Queen of Elfame while she lay in childbed. The queen asked for a drink and Bessie obliged. The fairy told her the child would die but that her husband, who was ill, would recover. In return for Bessie's kindness the queen decided to send one of her minions, Thomas Reid, to wait upon her. Before long Bessie was acquiring a reputation for medical knowledge, solicited even by the elite, though she claimed that 'sche hirself had na kynd of art nor science' but rather she consulted about each case with her fairy contact, Reid. When asked if she could 'tell of ony thing that was away, or ony thing that was to cum', Bessie said that she herself was not gifted with second sight, but when people asked for her help to find stolen property she consulted Reid who would tell her where it was. Again, Bessie was able to boast some very distinguished customers including the chamberlain of Kilwinning who approached her about stolen barley and Lady Blair who, on numerous occasions, asked about the theft of clothes and other purloined possessions.[22]

Though Bessie was, on the whole, quite well treated by the fairies, she was also threatened by them in various ways for her refusal to join them. After her visit with the 'gude wychtis' from Elfame, she testified that a 'hiddeous uglie sowche of wind followit thame' and left her feeling sick. Reid then tried to persuade her to join them, arguing that she could share in his prosperity: 'seis thow nocht me, baith meit-worth, claith-worth, and gude aneuch lyke in persoun; and I suld make hir far better nor euer sche was?' All he asked of her, in return, was that Bessie deny christianity 'and the faith sche tuke at the funt-stane', the baptismal font. Bessie, however, was not convinced by his promise of a better life and was probably appalled at the suggestion of renouncing her baptism. She flatly told him 'that sche duelt with hir awin husband and bairnis' and could not leave them. At this Reid 'began to be verrie crabit [angry] with hir' and cautioned 'gif swa sche thocht, sche wald get lytill gude of him'. This threat was repeated once again when Bessie had dared to refuse a meeting with Reid who shook his head and said that he 'suld caus hir forthink it'.

Like Bessie, Alison Peirson was given instructions on various types of medicinal cures through an intermediary who was once a mortal man. William Simpson taught her 'of everie seekness, and quhat herbis scho sould tak to haill [heal] thame, and how scho sould use thame'. She claimed that she frequently went to St. Andrews to heal people over a sixteen-year period and sensationally revealed that she was instructed by the fairies on how to cure the Bishop of St. Andrews, Patrick Adamson.[23] Unlike Bessie, Alison visited Fairyland and received more than simple threats to her well-being for refusing to co-operate with or join the fairy company. For failing to remain silent about the things she witnessed in their world, thus breaking the taboo of secrecy, she received a 'sair straik' from one of them that 'tuke all the poistie of hir car syde fra hir, the mark quhairof wes blae and ewill faurrit' [took the power of her left side from her and left a discoloured and ill-looking blue mark]. Conditions were not to greatly improve for Alison who said that the fairies became

> feirfull sumtymes, and fleit [frighten] hir verry sair, and scho cryit quhene thay come . . . and quhene scho tauld last of it, thay come to hir and boistit [threatened] hir, saying, scho sould be war [worse] handlit nor ofbefoir [than formerly]; and that they tuke the haill poistie of hir syde, in sic soirt, that scho lay tuentie oulkis [weeks].

Throughout her ordeal they frequently came and sat by her bedside, promising that she should never want, if only she agreed to be 'faithfull and keep promeis'.[24]

Christiane Lewingston, or Livingston, from Leith, tried in 1597, had some psychic ability and could cure a variety of ailments as a result of fairy intervention. However, she herself claimed not to have met with fairies but to have received her information through an intermediary, her daughter. Christiane affirmed

> her dochter was tane away with the Farie-folk, and declarit to [Guthrie's] wyff, than being with barne, that it was a man chyld scho was with; as it provit in deid: And that all the knawlege scho had was be hir dochter, wha met with the Fairie.

Isobel Haldane's ability to predict future events was similarly explained as information proffered from a contact in the fairy world. The trial reported two instances of Isobel's accurate predictions of death communicated to her by a grey-bearded man who met with her and took her to Fairyland. The first incident involved Isobel warning a man not to bother making a cradle for his child since his heavily pregnant wife would not give birth for another five weeks, but worse, 'the bairne suld never ly in the craidill, bot be borne, bapteist, and never souk, bot die and be tane away'. The second incident sent Isobel to warn a seemingly healthy woman that she must prepare herself for death since before Fastern's Eve, Shrove Tuesday, 'quhilk wes within few dayis', she would be 'taikin away'. Both predictions were said to have been fulfilled.

Janet Trall was tried alongside Isobel Haldane in 1623. In her confession, which is remarkably similar in detail to Isobel's, she testified that she learned her healing skills from the fairies; the 'bonny white man' told her to speak of God, and do good to poor folks: and he shewed me the means how I might do this, which was by washing, bathing, speaking words, putting sick persons through hesps [hanks] of yarn, and the like.

However, Janet found herself the victim of trickery and deception, as the next time she was visited by the fairies their agenda was significantly different. Janet was terror-struck: 'they drave me down, and then I was beside myself, and would have eaten the very earth beside me', because 'the principal of them' had told her 'to do ill, by casting sickness upon people'. For her impudent, and imprudent, refusal of the fairy demands she was pestered by them for many years.[25]

Breaking the Spell: The Modes of Disenchantment

Though it was possible for the fairies to bestow good luck or assistance upon mortals, the risks were often too high or the price too much to pay. For most people avoidance, or at least propitiation, was the best policy; various precautions and placatory measures were taken to avoid fairy enchantment.

One option was to evoke the power of God, whether through prayer, using a cross, a Bible, or holy water. In the ballad 'Sir Cawline' the mortal knight overcomes the elf king because he negates his supernatural powers at the outset of battle by calling on the name of Christ: 'For because thou minged [named] not Christ before/Thee lesse me dreadeth thee'. When Alison Peirson was visited by a large group of fairy folk, she attempted to ward them off by saining and praying for herself, and it has already been indicated that Robert Kirk attracted a particularly healthy flock to church service on quarter days.

Kirk also noted that the 'Tramontaines', or Gaelic speakers, 'to this day, put bread, the Bible, or a piece of iron, in womens bed when travelling [travailling, i.e. in labour]' to protect them from being stolen in childbed. Helen Bull was sharply rebuked by the Haddington presbytery (1647) for placing bread on the breast of children when they were baptised, which she did 'onlie becaus it was an old custom: which she had ever sein used'. A Dalkeith midwife, Beatrix Lesley (1661), confessed that when women were brought to bed she would 'stick a bair knyfe betwixt the bed and the straw', sprinkle salt about the bed, and then recite: 'Lord let never a worse wight waken thee nor hes laid thee downe'. Presumably this ritual would ensure the baby was kept safe from supernatural abduction. The protective power of iron was, of course, not limited to expectant mothers. A seventeenth-century manuscript described how bewitched persons could be cured by placing a knife under them. Isobell Bennet from Stirling (1659) admitted that she used a horseshoe to fend against 'our good neighbours'. Horseshoes were deployed throughout Scotland to guard against fairies but were also put on stable doors to protect the horses from witches riding them at night. Iron was also an effective deterrent against ghosts. The kirk session of Pencaitland reprimanded Agnes Bennet in 1651 for putting a nail 'betwixt the winding sheit and ye corpse which she said was to keep her [the dead woman's] spirit from coming again'. Kirk had spoken to a man with the second sight who had 'cut the bodie of one of these people in two with his iron weapon' to avert fairy enchantment; he was told that iron was so effective because

> all uncouth unknown wights are terrified, by nothing earthly so much as by cold iron, they deliver the reason to be, that Hell lying betwixt the chill tempests, and the fire-brands of scalding metalls, and iron of the North . . . by an antipathy theirto, these odious far-senting creatures shrug and fright at all that comes thence, relating to so abhorred a place, whence their torment is either begun, or feared to come heirafter.

J. F. Campbell was curious to know why iron was invested with magical powers over supernaturals in so many folktales of the Western Isles. He deduced the fairies to be a dim remembrance of 'savage times and savage people':

> Who were these powers of evil who cannot resist iron? These fairies who shoot stone arrows, and are of the foes of the human race? Is all this but a dim, hazy recollection of war between a people who had iron weapons and a race who had not, the race whose remains are found all over Europe?[26]

As suggested above, the 'conquered race' thesis, although widespread, is not entirely convincing, owing more, perhaps, to learned rather than to popular tradition. On the other hand the Irish favoured a long-established tradition of waves of invaders, each of whom triumphed only to be defeated by their successors. These legendary activities were recounted in the *Lebor Gabála Érenn* or *The Book of the Taking of Ireland* which was compiled between the eleventh and the fourteenth centuries. Since the *Book* was put together under the aegis of the

Church in Ireland and since there was close contact between the two areas, this material was probably quite well-known in Gaelic-speaking Scotland where it very probably entered the oral tradition. It is somewhat noteworthy that unlike England and Ireland, – and for that matter Wales – Scotland did not suffer from an invasion complex. On the contrary Scottish propaganda harped on for centuries about how the Scots were an unconquered people with the possible consequence that Campbell's theory had less application in the Lowlands. However, Lowland and Highland Scots alike were always aware, through the 'ruins in the landscape' that other peoples had gone before them and it was always necessary to find stories to account for the disappearance of the folk of olden time.

While some trees, such as apple and hawthorn, were known to be favoured by the fairies, holly and rowan (or mountain ash) were a potent protection against them. Similarly, holly and rowan offered protection from witchcraft and the evil eye and were thus particularly useful trees to plant near to the home. Sprigs with red berries were considered doubly potent because of the protective nature of the colour red. In Argyllshire stories, as elsewhere, the fairies were unable to resist rowan-tree crosses, and, like witches, they were incapable of following potential victims over a running stream.[27]

For many, it would seem, the assuagement came too late or was forgotten altogether, with predictable results. Once people believed themselves or someone else to be under fairy power, it was crucial to know what to do to break the enchantment or to attempt a rescue. A story collected in Barra tells of a man named Lachlann who had fallen in love with a fairy woman. However, Lachlann grew afraid of the fairy and in an attempt to be rid of her emigrated to Cape Breton, Nova Scotia. His first letter home stated that the same fairy woman was haunting him still.[28] Distance was clearly no object to the fairies.

Everyone now knows that every time a child disbelieves in fairies one of them dies. Tinker Bell was saved from death when Peter put out the word to all children -'If you believe in fairies clap your hands!' 'Many clapped. Some didn't. A few little beasts hissed' but the outcome was happy. As it happens fairy death is not mentioned much in the sources. According to Kirk, fairies were invulnerable to human weapons, and if struck by normal weaponry their bodies were 'as air, which when divided, unitts again'. Even if, by some remote chance, any damage was incurred, – and fairies sometimes displayed wounds and gashes – 'they are better phisitians then wee, and quickly cure it'. He seemed rather uncertain about what happened to fairies. They lived longer than humans 'yet die at last, or at least vanish from that state'; elsewhere he asserted that 'they dwindle and decay at a certain period,' all at about the same age. There are some late reports of fairy funerals presaging the human variety, small creatures in bowler hats transporting tiny coffins.[29] What seems clear is that nobody ever saw a dead fairy, changelings excepted.

The modes of disenchantment from fairy power were curiously similar to those of enchantment. In other words, what in one case might act as a spell could, in another, act as a counter-spell. In 'King Orfeo' the music that the fairies loved so much was used as a way to win back Lady Isabel. As is seen in 'Allison Gross' and 'Tam Lin,' physical contact produced both enchantment and disenchantment. The fact that Janet, in 'Tam Lin', wore a green dress, garb traditionally worn by fairies themselves, was probably no accident and had counter-magical significance. The heroine of 'Lady Isabel and the Elf-Knight' lulled the elf-knight to sleep with a 'sma charm' before stabbing and killing him with his own dagger. She thus employed two counter-magical methods, the charm and the dagger, to overcome the supernatural knight. Significant dates, such as 1 May in this ballad, could prove dangerous times when mortals might succumb to the power of the fairies. Conversely, such dates were often when people could be extricated from their Otherworld entrapment, as in 'Allison Gross' and 'Tam Lin', in both of which the bespelled managed to escape on Halloween. In the former, rather baffling ballad, the helpless anonymous man is enchanted by the horrific, repugnant witch, Allison Gross who, by blowing three times on her 'grass-green horn' transforms her unco-operative victim into 'an ugly worm', forcing him to 'toddle around the tree' to which she has tethered him. His dire situation is relieved by weekly visits from his sister and regular hair treatments from his captor. The unhappy object of enchantment has been transformed into a dragon, one furthermore who is in the invidious position of being rescued by a maiden – of a type – for his liberator is the queen of fairy.

> She took me up in her milk-white han,
> An she' stroakd me three times oer her knee;
> She chang'd me again to my ain proper shape,
> An I nae mair maun toddle about the tree.

If 'Thomas Rymer' can be said to be the best description of the journey to Elfland, then 'Tam Lin' is surely the most memorable description of a rescue from the fairy realm, which has no equivalent in the witch trials. Janet, the real protagonist in this story, decides to win the father of her child back from Fairyland. In order to do this, she must observe a series of rites, leading to an incredible sequence of shape-shiftings, and the eventual metamorphosis of Tam Lin into a mortal man once more. Firstly, Janet must know when and where the rescue can take place:

> The night it is good Halloween,
> When fairy folk will ride,
> And they that wad their true-love win,
> At Miles Cross they maun bide.

In some versions Janet is required to make special preparations:

> You may go into the Miles Moss,
> Between twelve hours and one;
> Take holy water in your hand,
> And cast a compass round.

Tam Lin tells Janet that when the procession arrives she will be able to identify him as he will be the third rider to pass mounted on a splendid horse. To avoid any possible confusion he gives her a few more clues:

> For I'll ride on the milk-white steed,
> And ay nearest the town;
> Because I am an earthly knight
> They gie me that renown.

> My right hand will be gloved lady,
> My left hand will be bare,
> Cockt up shall my bonnet be,
> And kaimed down shall my hair,
> And thae's the tokens I gie thee,
> Nae doubt I shall be there.

She must pull him down from his horse and hold on to him, a tall order at the best of times but compounded by a hideous succession of frightening shape changes which he must undergo before the enchantment is broken:

> They shaped him in fair Janet's arms
> An esk (newt) but and an adder;
> She held him fast in every shape,
> To be her bairn's father.

He is then transformed into a grim bear, a bold lion, a red-hot band of iron and finally a fiery flame which must be tossed into well water. Janet, of course, succeeds brilliantly, immersing him in water (or sometimes milk) and then wrapping the naked Tam in her green mantle.[30] The ritual in which both participate, in the name of their child, resembles a rite of purification, in this case the purifier shifting from serpent to animal, iron, fire and water, until Tam is literally born again, helplessly dependent throughout upon his lover who is also the protective mother clothing his nakedness at the end. So concludes one of the greatest love stories to come out of Scotland. After all they have endured, there seems little doubt that they will live happily ever after. The gloriously self-willed Janet, beautiful, bold, brazen and tenacious as she is, represents the ideal of womanhood for both women and men. She, after all, had sought a liaison with Tam after being warned by her father against a visit to Carterhaugh lest Tam have his way with her. She is the one who takes responsibility for her pregnancy, contemptuously dismissing the cravens at her father's court. It is she who contemplates abortion,[31] pulling the roses, because she fears that Tam is an otherworldly being, and she it is who heroically frees her lover from his elfin spell. Tam is apparently no mean catch either and both triumph over the fairy queen who closes the ballad, nursing her wrath to keep it warm, while incidentally revealing the true depths of her cruelty:

> Out then spak the Queen o Fairies,
> And an angry woman was she:
> 'Shame betide her ill-far'd face,
> And an ill death may she die,
> For she's taen awa the bonniest knight
> In a my companie.
>
> 'But had I kend, Tam Lin,' she says,
> 'What now this night I see,
> I wad hae taen out thy twa grey een,
> And put in twa een o tree'.

There is, however, a strong hint that there was more to the story. Tam, like Thomas Rhymer, was regarded as something of a buffoon, or worse a reprobate, in certain quarters. One short ballad relates how Tam refuses to take any more part in the care of his baby son and he goes off to sea; 'And a' women's curse in his company's gane'. In later tradition he was often a figure of fun, a fate which also befell, for example, George

Buchanan in the chapbook literature. The dramatist Joanna Baillie (1762–1851) neatly captured something of his folk reputation in her poem 'Tam o' the Lin':

> Tam o' the Lin he married a wife,
> And she was the torment, the plague o' his life;
> She lays sae about her, and maks sic a din,
> 'She frightens the baby', quo' Tam o' the Lin.[32]

The predicament from which Janet rescued Tam at Carterhaugh could be avoided by taking certain precautions. Elf arrows could be put to counter-magical use as amulets. Sometimes set in silver by the wealthy, they were worn around the neck as protection from elf-shot. On Stroma, in the Pentland Firth, elf arrowheads were kept as a protection against the fairies gaining power over oneself or one's cattle.[33]

Pebbles and stones, specially chosen for their apotropaic qualities, could be utilised as part of a larger ritual to ward off evil influences. The confession of Euphemia Makcalzane, tried in 1591, makes reference to a bored stone, used for relieving the pains of childbirth. Among her alleged crimes, Euphemia was charged with seeking help from 'Anny Sampsoune, ane notorious wich, for relief of your payne in the tyme of the birth of youre twa sonnes; and ressaving fra hir to that effect, ane boird-stane, to be layit under the bowster [bolster], putt under your heid'. Bored stones, naturally created by erosion, have been mainly associated with second sight, as well as with fairies and witchcraft. The legend of Coinneach Odhar, the Brahan Seer, says that he was given the gift of prophecy, by means of a bored stone, while sleeping on a fairy hill.[34] Coinneach Odhar, or Kenneth Mackenzie, executed as a witch in 1577, was to become (as he remains) one of the best-known prophets in Gaelic-speaking Scotland. Since seers very seldom, indeed hardly ever, used artificial implements of this type, it may be assumed that the story of Coinneach's acquisition of the stone was a comparatively late addition implicitly linking him to the fairy tradition. Looking through the hole in these 'fairystones', 'charmstones', and in England 'witchstones', sometimes produced visions or an ability to see fairies, but hung on a wall they served as amulets against fairy attack.[35] It is possible that Anny Sampson was prescribing a form of counter-active magic to protect Euphemia and her newborn baby from the fairies.

In some cases certain rites or special medicines were required to disenchant the unfortunate mortal. A preliminary ritual, to determine precisely the nature of the supernatural entity in question, was described in two Orkney trials, those of James Knarston (1633) and Katherine Cragie (1640). Knarston collected a stone 'from the ebb, another from the hill, and the thrid from the kirk-yaird', heated them in a fire and put them in water, thereafter placing them above the door lintel for a night or more. Finally the stones were immersed in a tub of cold water; he then recited words 'knowen unto himselff', and the identity of the spirit was revealed to him. Katherine Cragie carried out an almost identical rite which involved placing three stones in the fire before dawn, taking them out after sunset, and lodging them under the threshold until just before the next sunrise. The stones were next put in a vessel containing water. At this point Katherine would know if it was a 'hill-spirit, a kirk-spirit, or a water-spirit'. The person afflicted with the spirit was then washed with the water. The entire ritual was repeated three times. Katherine spoke of another ritual cure for those who had been gripped by trows. She wrapped the sufferer three times in a 'Trowis glove [foxglove]', and after three days the person would be healed.

The ritualistic usage and medicinal properties of elf arrowheads are well and widely attested. One example indicates the significance of water as a component of the healing ritual: 'He put one elff-arrow stone in the water, becaus it wes ane remedie against the fairies schott'. The importance of bodily contact with the fairy weapon is seen in another: 'He rubbed his breist and his bak with ane elff arrow stone'.

Other implements, such as threads, cloth, or specific plants and herbs, were also used as part of the process to rid the afflicted of their unholy pests. Janet Trall explained how she cured Robert Soutar by putting him through a 'hesp of yarn, and afterwards cut it in nine parts, and buried it in three lords lands'. She testified that the house shook while the ritual took place. Thomas Geace of Fife passed one of his patients nine times through loops of yarn in order to cure her; another was treated in a similar fashion 'and thairefter burning the said hesp in ane grit fyre, quhilk turned haillilie blew'.[36] Humankind was not entirely defenceless against fairy magic.

Changelings: 'of nature denyit'

Childbirth was an occasion of great anxiety on account of the high rate of infant mortality, roughly one in four between 1600 and 1800, and because of the significant risk to the mother. Such fears were more than justified. Women generally delayed marriage until their mid-twenties, thus increasing the chances of complications since, as a rule, the younger the mother, the better the chances of a healthy birth. Rates for death in childbirth are not available before the eighteenth century when it is estimated that they varied from 3% to 18%, but in the previous century such rates would probably have been higher due to famine and plague, which impacted upon maternal well being. Diseases such as typhus tended to strike more at adults but the toll which smallpox took among children was horrific. In the outbreak of June and July 1636 at Dumfries, 89 out of 92 reported deaths were of children; at Kelso the rate was 36 out of 41 deaths.[37]

General concerns about such matters were manifested, in part, by what amounted to something of an obsession with the phenomenon of changelings, of human babies stolen by the fairies who left fairy children in their place. Such beliefs were among the most commonly held and widespread of traditions, found not only throughout Europe but all over the world. It was also widely believed that the fairies, existing in a state between Heaven and Hell, sought out contact with humans in an attempt to acquire a soul. Furthermore midwives, 'who surpass all others in wickedness', were universally distrusted by the Church and were deemed likely, for twisted reasons known only to churchmen themselves, to either kill the child at birth or else offer it to the Devil. But the authorities were always worried about processes such as childbirth which were the near-exclusive preserve of women. The kirk session of Kinghorn in 1645 attempted to ban 'cummerscales', toasts made to the new-born child, avowedly to protect the mother's health but also because 'persons of the better sort carrie a secrit dislike' to the custom.

Kramer and Sprenger, the deluded German Dominicans who conspired in the production of the repugnant *Malleus Maleficarum* (1486) and celibate as they must be assumed to have been, were nonetheless supposedly as knowledgeable about children and changelings as they were about sexual relations and women. However, using the appropriate authorities, they rather neatly described changelings:

> Substitutions of children are, with God's permission, possible, so that the devil can effect a change of the child or even a transformation. For such children are always miserable and crying; and although four or five mothers could hardly supply enough milk for them, they never grow fat, yet are heavy beyond the ordinary.

That such children existed, they asserted, was due to the sins of the parents.[38]

The English word 'changeling' was first used in the sixteenth century in the sense of a waverer or turncoat, but Shakespeare was aware of its specific association: 'Such, men do chaungelings call, so chaung'd by Faeries theft'. Some versions of 'Tam Lin' relate that he was carried off to Fairyland either when he was a baby or when he became three years old.[39] Presumably a changeling was left in his place though, strangely perhaps, given the general anxieties about such phenomena, there is no mention of changelings in the Child ballad corpus. A Scottish pasquil, or lampoon, of 1639 characterised three hated bishops as changelings. The word soon came to be applied to a mentally disabled person, in which sense it was used, for example, of certain unfortunate individuals in the kirk session records for Ardnamurchan in the late eighteenth century. Alexander Montgomerie touched on widespread fears of changelings or monstrous births when he entertained the court of James VI with a gruesome, if humorous, account of the birth of a changeling of a kind: 'Vyld venymous viper, wanthreivinest [most stunted] of thingis, Half ane elph, half ane aip, of nature denyit'.[40]

There are a number of references to changelings in witch trials, generally regarding cures to be rid of the unfortunate creatures. Janet Trall of Perth was consulted by Isobel Haldane and Duncan Tawis, a man who believed his child had been replaced by a fairy changeling, 'it being stiff as an aik tree, and unable to move'. Janet agreed to see the child:

> And when she came she took the bairn upon her knee before the fire, drew every finger of its hands, and every toe of its feet, mumbling all the while some words that could not be heard, and immediately the bairn was cured.

Isobel was not so fortunate. Her attempt to cure a changeling, or 'sharg', with a potion was described at her trial:

> David Moreise wyff com to hir [Isobel], and thryse for Goddis saik askit help to hir bairne that wes ane scharge: And scho send furth hir sone to gether sochsterrie leaweis, quhairof scho directit the bairnes mother to mak a drink. – Bot the bairneis mother deponit, that the said Issobell Haldane, on-requirit, cam to her house and saw the bairne; said, 'it wes ane scharge taikin away;' tuke on hand to cure it; and to that effect, gaiff the barne a drink; efter the ressait quhairof the bairne died.[41]

It was often assumed that any sick child had been affected by the fairies or the Devil. In 1643 John Sharp deponed that Margaret Dickson had treated his crippled daughter, advising that if her condition was due to 'evill wichts', then John should take a peck of meal which was to be baked with a dozen eggs. He was then to place the bread and the eggs in front of the fire and his daughter behind it. At midnight he should walk nine times around his house, on his return ordering the spirits to depart 'in the divel's name and give me my daughter againe, and if the bairne mend the bread and egges wald be away, and if not the shells and bread wald be still, and bad him keep quyet'. Margaret confessed to the foregoing but claimed she had told John to go round the house three times at ten o'clock, not midnight. Another woman, Isobell Johnson, testified that Margaret had washed her bairn and its sark in south-running water twice, whereupon the child sweated profusely. Three weeks later, when the child was still pining, Margaret told Isobell to 'put on a good fyre, and cast the bairne into it, for the bairne was not hirs, for shee [presumably the bairn] was a hundredd yeare old'. Instead Isobell blessed the child, which began to recover. Later Margaret asked Isobell's forgiveness if she 'had done the bairne ony wrang'.[42] The intriguing details of this case suggest that it concerned a changeling.

Martin Martin, while visiting Benbecula, was told of the 'fire-round' ritual. This involved carrying fire around a woman and her baby shortly after childbirth to protect them from evil before their churching. The result of neglecting such precautions could be devastating since

> evil spirits, who are ready at such times to do mischief . . . sometimes carry away the infant; and when they get them once in their possession, return them poor meagre skeletons: and these infants are said to have voracious appetites, constantly craving for meat.

In the event of a child being taken away the parents had to 'dig a grave in the fields upon Quarter-Day, and there lay the fairy skeleton till next morning'. The parents would return hoping to find their own child in place of the skeleton.

Leaving suspected changelings out overnight as a means to cure them was a widespread belief, though it is impossible to gauge how frequently it was put into practice. At a well in Ross children and adults, of whom the fairies had 'abstracted their substance', were left overnight.[43] Hugh Miller had heard of a stone trough called 'the fairies' cradle' that was used until about 1740 for the treatment of changelings. Parents would lay the suspect child inside the trough and wait for their own baby to be restored to them. It had been situated very near to a chapel in Cromarty dedicated to St. Bennet, or Benedict, but it was apparently destroyed shortly before the '45 rebellion by a zealous minister and two of his elders. Interestingly the chapel-site was significant in other ways since it was not yet 'twenty years since a thorn-bush, over the spring of St. Bennet, used to be covered every season with rags, as offerings to the saint, by sick people who came to drink the water'. There were several of these 'clootie wells' in this area, so-called because the sick would bathe affected parts with pieces of cloth, or rags, dipped in the well water which would then be hung on nearby trees and bushes. Objects such as coins or pins might be thrown into the well as offerings. The efficacy of such curing processes varied but might not be complete until the rags had completely deteriorated. The best-known surviving example is probably the Clootie Well at Munlochy on the Black Isle which is still heavily patronised and which nowadays is no longer calendrically limited. Wells generally were best visited before sunrise at Beltane but Munlochy is available at any time and the clooties are highly conspicuous.[44]

Among the alleged crimes of Barbara Thomasdochter of Delting, Shetland, tried in 1616, was witnessing a visit from a changeling though it is not known whether Barbara lost any of her own children in the process: 'she saw ane litle creatour in hir awin hous amongis hir awin bairnes quhom she callit the bowmanes [fairy man's] bairne'. The implication may be that Barbara, like the fairies, was promiscuous, and that the story of the fairy cygnet joining the mortal ducklings was a way of explaining a love child. When a former lover tried to leave her she rendered him impotent. Another individual who had a relationship with her daughter lost all of his bodily strength for some six months after Barbara 'grippit his member'.

A story collected by Charles Kirkpatrick Sharpe may be rather late but it contains nothing which jars with the earlier tradition. Tibbie Dickson of Duns was the mother of a thriving boy, but when she went to the well one day a great commotion sent her running back into the house to discover in place of her bonnie bairn 'a withered wolron, naething but skin and bane, wi hands like a moudiewart [mole], and a face like a puddock [frog], a mouth frae lug [ear] to lug, and twa great glowrin een'. She suspected the worst, particularly when he refused the breast in favour of huge quantities of porridge. 'It was aye yammerin and greetin (a whingin, screechin, skirlin wallidreg), but never mintet to speak a word; and when ither bairns could rin it couldna stand'. But when Wullie the tailor was called upon to babysit, the creature sat up in its cradle and offered to play a set of pipes hidden in its bedding straw. Wullie, realising this must be 'a deil's get', grabbed him by the scruff of the neck, pipes and all and threw him into the fire and 'awa flees the fairy, skirling "Deil stick the lousie tylor!" a the way up the lum [chimney]'. Among the miners of Fife it would be said of a child that persistently cried, 'If this gangs on we'll hae to pit it on the girdle', a reference to a practice that did once take place when children supposed to be changelings would be placed on the cooking plate in the fireplace, or on a sheet of hot iron. Sometimes, of course, they died, but the expectation was that the shock would drive out the fairy and restore the human infant.[45]

First published in 1788 was another chilling tale, leavened with a hint of humour to quell the nightmares:

> Then wake (forwell thou canst) that wond'rous lay,
> How, while around the thoughtless matrons sleep,
> Soft o'er the floor the treach'rous fairies creep,
> And bear the smiling infant far away:
> How starts the nurse, when, for her lovely child,
> She sees at dawn a gaping idiot stare!
> O snatch the innocent from demons vilde,
> And save the parents fond from fell despair!
> In a deep cave the trusty menial wait,
> When from their hilly dens, at midnight's hour,
> Forth rush the fairy elves in mimic state,
> And o'er the moonlight heath with swiftness scour:
> In glittering arms the little horsemen shine;
> Last, on a milk-white steed, with targe of gold,
> A fay of might appears, whose arms entwine
> The lost, lamented child! the shepherds bold
> The unconscious infant tear from his unhallowed hold.

By this date the elite could mock and sentimentalise the changeling predicament but there were still plenty of worried parents for whom the whole subject was deadly serious. One nineteenth-century informant – and many had similar stories – told of an acquaintance who rid himself of a changeling by burning its toes though his natural child was never returned to him. Less fortunate was a woman carried off by the fairies and who repeatedly appeared to her husband beseeching him to win her back from her captors, but since he had remarried, he refused. It was considered unlucky for newborns to be given new cradles. The clothes of such children were passed through the smoke of a fire to ward off evil. Precautions that could be taken during the birthing process were to place a nail or a piece of iron, a bible, some bread or a pair of the father's breeks in the childbed. In some places the newborn would be immediately wrapped in clothing belonging to the parents, sometimes with amber beads or other charms sewn into the seams. These latter practices were not so very different from the custom of importing saintly relics into childbed at royal births. The sark or chemise of St Margaret, wife of Malcolm Canmore, was used by expectant Scottish queens until the birth of James V. Less elevated women in labour could only invoke the saint's name and hope for the best. Soeur Jeanne des Anges was horribly abused and tortured during the sensational case of the devils of Loudun, France, in the 1620s and '30s. John Maitland, later Duke of Lauderdale, the powerful secretary of Charles II, actually visited the accused in the case but was unimpressed, claiming there were more convincing witches in Scotland. Sister Jeanne survived to undergo an ecstatic experience when St Joseph anointed her, some drops of the heavenly balm attaching to her chemise. The garment was later spread over Anne of Austria (who was already protected by the girdle of the Virgin Mary, but one had to be sure) when she was giving birth to Louis XIV. Superstition then, as now, could be acceptable; whether it was good or bad depended upon the object of veneration.[46]

An elderly woman in Rousay (Orkney) in 1895 told the story of a baby which began to pine and waste. The local wise woman advised that the fairies had lifted the child and had left one of their own in its place. The mother was told to visit the Hammers of the Sinians above Muckle Water in Rousay, taking with her a wedge of steel and a bible. At a certain rock cleft she was to drive in the steel whereupon the rock would open, and inside she would find a fairy with the child on her knee. Without uttering a word she was to strike the fairy three times on the face with the bible and return home. She followed her instructions to the letter, stoutly resisting the fairy's attempts to make her speak, and her baby was duly restored to her as fat and healthy as he had been before. The informant knew of what she spake for she had actually known the subject of the story, the changeling himself, who was an old man at the time.[47] The twist in the tale, the concluding validation, renders the story an example of contemporary legend, and indeed the names of the principals were suppressed because the old man's descendants were still living in Kirkwall in 1924 when people in the beautiful island of Rousay who suffered from some mysterious disease, physical or mental, were still said to be 'in the hill'. The fairies, feared as they were, could be invoked to dull the pain of the incomprehensible.

Notes

1 Kirk, 52.
2 Lewis Spence did not approve of this suggestion and said he could not 'recall any kidnapped hero in fairy legend whose name underwent a change once he became a denizen in the land of the fays'. *The Magic Arts in Celtic Britain* (London 1945), 65. But see above for a list of possible fairy names. To name is to control in folk belief; however, this stanza is a formulaic commonplace of ballad so is not necessarily proof, in this instance, of a direct reflection of belief in naming magic. See Child [110] 'The Knight and the Shepherd's Daughter'.
3 On this subject see now Karen Ralls-MacLeod, *Music and the Celtic Otherworld, from Ireland to Iona* (Edinburgh 2000).
4 Trial of Barbra Parish, *The Scots Law Times*, 78; Kirk, 58–9.
5 Trial of Isobel Gowdie, Pitcairn vol. 3, 604–609; For 'shot to dead' cases see *Selected Justiciary Cases, 1624–1650* ed. Stair A. Gillon (Edinburgh 1953), vol. 1, III, 137, 211, and vol. 3, 599, 813; C. K. Sharpe, *A Historical Account of the Belief in Witchcraft in Scotland* (Glasgow 1884), 159, noted that Catherine NicNiven's last name was probably bestowed upon her by her neighbours from that of the fairy queen. There is a legend that when she was led to the stake she spat out a blue stone and gave it to her family. The stone would ensure they flourished, so long as it remained in their possession.
6 Trial of Barbara (Bartie) Paterson, 18 Dec. 1607. Pitcairn vol. 2, 536. Also, C. K. Sharpe's introduction to Robert Law's *Memorialls*, (Edinburgh 1818), li; Trial of Janet Trall, *Extracts . . . Strathbogie* xi.; Trial of Jonet Morison, 18 January 1662. *Highland Papers, vol* 3, 1662–1677, ed. J. R. N. MacPhail, Scottish History Society (Edinburgh 1920), 23–4, 27; Kirk, 60; Trial of Farquhar Ferguson, 9 Dec. 1716. *Kilmory Kirk Session Minutes* NAS, CH2/214/1. Low cited an example of a woman on the island of Hoy, Orkney, who cured elf-shot wounds in the same manner. Low, *Tour through Orkney and Schetland*, 7–8. Elf-shot was also known as Troll-shot in Orkney and Shetland. For more on charms to protect or cure animals, see Thomas Davidson, 'Animal Treatment in Eighteenth Century Scotland', *Scottish Studies* 4:1 (1960): 134–49, and on musical charms see Brendan Ó Madagáin, 'Gaelic Lullaby: A Charm to Protect the Baby?' *Scottish Studies* 29 (1989): 29–38.
7 Child, vol. 1, 216. See also Dean R. Baldwin, 'Fairy Lore and the Meaning of Sir Orfeo', *Southern Folklore Quarterly* 40 (1977): 129–42.
8 Arthur Edmonston, *A View of the Ancient and Present State of the Zetland Islands* 2 vols (Edinburgh 1809), vol. 2, 76–8. *Sir Orfeo* ed. A. J. Bliss (Oxford 1954). Since the poem is preserved in the Auchinleck Manuscript it was long thought to be Scottish but that has been conclusively disproved.
9 Trial of Bessie Dunlop, Pitcairn vol. 1, 51; Trial of Janet Trall, *Extracts . . . Strathbogie*, xii.
10 The Ring of Gyges enabled the wearer to become invisible at will by turning

the stone inward or outward. The ring must be made of fixed mercury, set with a stone taken from a lapwing's nest, and engraved around the stone must be the following words 'Jesus, passing through the midst of them, went his way' (Luke iv:30). Emile Grillot De Givry, *Picture Museum of Sorcery, Magic and Alchemy* trans. J. Courtenay Locke (New York 1963), 185. English demonologist Reginald Scot refers to a conjuration which will bring forth three fairy women in possession of the Giges ring in *Discoverie* 408–10, and Thomas Ady remarked that witches could become invisible 'by the help of the Devil, especially if one of the Ladies of the Fairies will but lend her Giges invisible ring', in *A Candle in the Dark* (London 1655), 111; Kirk, 54, 69. Carlo Ginzburg, *The Night Battles: Witchcraft and Agrarian Cults in the Sixteenth and Seventeenth Centuries* trans. John and Anne Tedeschi (1966; Baltimore 1992), 76 and *passim*. Hans Peter Duerr, *Dreamtime: Concerning the Boundary between Wilderness and Civilization* trans. Felicitas Goodman (Oxford 1985), 1–11. Ability to see fairies after rubbing magical ointments on the eyes is a common motif. Kirk is reporting the abduction of women by fairies as 'ethnographic information', that is, something that really happened, but his story is also recognisable as migratory legend, ML 5070.

11 Wimberly, 275. See also E. B. Lyle 'The Teind to Hell in Tam Lin', *Folklore* 81 (1970): 177–81; Trial of Alison Peirson, Pitcairn vol. 1, 163.

12 Robert Chambers, *The Book of Days, A Miscellany of Popular Antiquities*, 2 vols. (Edinburgh 1863), vol. 1, 574.

13 Trial of Bessie Dunlop, Pitcairn vol. 1, 56. The last time Bessie saw Thomas it was the morning after Candlemas; Trial of Katherine Jonesdochter, *Court Book of Shetland*, 38–9; Trial of Katherine Caray, June 1616. In John Graham Dalyell, *The Darker Superstitions of Scotland* (Glasgow 1835), 536.

14 Kane, *Wisdom of the Mythtellers*, 103.

15 F. Marian McNeill, *The Silver Bough* (Glasgow 1959), vol. 3, 11–31; Proinsias MacCana, *Celtic Mythology* (London 1987), 127–8.

16 Kirk, 51. The Quarter Days in England are Lady Day (25 March), Midsummer Day (24 June), Michaelmas (29 September), Christmas Day (25 December). In Scotland they were different – Candlemas (2 February), Whitsun, or Old Beltane (15 May), Lammas (1 August), Martinmas, or Old Halloween (11 November). On the last evening of each quarter in parts of the Highlands urine was sprinkled on cattle, doorposts and walls of the house to keep the fairies away, Banks, *British Calendar Customs* vol. 2, 21. The Benandanti were also very active at the Quarter Days, Ginzburg, *Night Battles, passim*.

17 One of the principal laws of folk narrative, defined by Axel Olrik as encompassing 'myths, songs, heroic sagas, and local legends', is the 'law of three'. He found that repetition is almost always linked to the number three, and that three is the maximum number of characters and objects which occur in traditional narrative. 'Epic Laws of Folk Narrative', in *The Study of Folklore*,

ed. Alan Dundes (N. J. 1965), 129–41. For more on significant or magic numbers see also *A Dictionary of Superstitions* ed. Iona Opie and Moira Tatem (Oxford 1989), and Lewis Spence, *An Encyclopaedia of Occultism* (1920; Secaucus, N. J. 1960).

18 Trial of Thomas Lorn, 19 Jan. 1598–9. *Extracts . . . Aberdeen*. During his case he was warned that if he disappeared like that again he would suffer death 'as ane guilty person, dealer with spreits'; Trial of Isobel Haldane, Pitcairn vol. 2, 537.

19 That the fairies reciprocate kindness or respect shown to them is a common theme within the genre of folktale. Bruford says the gift of healing from fairies is a legend type found with most frequency in Shetland, e.g. the story of 'Farquar's Pig', Bruford, 129. Version qtd. in Black, *Folklore concerning Orkney & Shetland* 30–1; Trial of Steven Maltman, April 1628. *Stirling Presbytery Records* SCA, CH2/722/5; Trial of Isobel Sinclair, Feb. 1633. Dalyell, *Darker Superstitions*, 470.

20 For examples of fairy fiddle tunes, see Marwick, *The Folklore of Orkney and Shetland*, 34; Nicolson, *Shetland Folklore*, 76–7; Bruford and MacDonald, *Scottish Traditional Tales*, 331–3; Alexander Nicolson, *History of Skye* (1930; Portree 1994), 130.

21 Trial of Andro Man, *Miscellany*, vol. 1, part 3, 119; Trial of Elspeth Reoch, *Maitland*, 112–3; Trial of Isobell Strathaquin, alias Scudder, and her daughter (name withheld), 26 Jan. 1597. *Miscellany*, 177.

22 Bessie's patients included Lady Johnstone, Lady Blackhalls, and Lady Kilbowie. Trial of Bessie Dunlop, Pitcairn vol. 1, 54–5. On 'wise women' or 'white witches' see Keith Thomas, *Religion and the Decline of Magic*, Chapter 8, 'Cunning Men and Popular Magic'.

23 Trial of Alison Peirson, Pitcairn vol. 1, 164. Pitcairn, revealing his assumptions and his elitism, reflected, 'that such a character as his grace should have stooped to take advice of a poor witch for the cure of his bodily infirmities, appears strange indeed'. For further discussion see Chapter 5.

24 Trial of Bessie Dunlop, Pitcairn vol. 1, 53–5; Trial of Alison Peirson, Pitcairn vol. 1, 163–4.

25 Trial of Christiane Lewingston, 12 Nov. 1597. Pitcairn vol. 2, 25–6; Trial of Isobel Haldane, Pitcairn vol. 2, 537; Trial of Janet Trall, *Extracts . . . Strathbogie*, xii.

26 Helen Bull, 23 June 1647. NAS, CH2/185/5; Trial of Beatrix Lesley, 20 July 1661. NAS, JC/26/27/1; 17th c manuscript belonging to Francis Guthrie, bishop of Moray, NAS, GD/188/25/1/1 and 3; Trial of Isobell Bennet, March 1659. NAS, JC 26/26; Agnes Bennet, Oct. 1651. NAS, CH2/296/1; Horseshoes were still being used as an apotropaic device in Rousay, Orkney, in the 1890s, see Duncan J. Robertson, 'Orkney Folk-Lore' *POAS* vol. 2, 38; Kirk, 54–59. For more on 'wights' see above; Campbell, *Popular Tales of the West Highlands*, vol. 1, 49.

27 On the use of holly and rowan see Roy Vickery, *A Dictionary of Plant Lore* (Oxford 1995), 319–22, Thomas Davidson, *Rowan Tree and Red Thread* (Edinburgh 1949), 76–8, McNeill, *Silver Bough* vol. 1, 84, and Pennant, *A Tour in Scotland*, 203. Once a prevalent saying in Scotland was 'Rowan-tree and red thread, Put the witches to their speed'. Chambers, *Popular Rhymes*, 328; Campbell, *Popular Tales of the West Highlands*, vol. 1, 434.

28 Evans-Wentz, *The Fairy Faith*, 112–3.

29 Kirk, 55, 57; Briggs, *Dictionary*, 145–7.

30 A Gaelic incantation used when a Highlander attended court in some ways parallels the sequence in the ballad. 'I go forth in the name of God/in the likeness of iron; in the likeness of the horse/ in the likeness of the serpent; in the likeness of the deer/ stronger am I than each one . . . I will wash my face/ that it may shine like the nine rays of the sun/ as the Virgin Mary washes her Son with boiled milk'. W. MacKenzie, 'Gaelic Incantations, Charms, and Blessings of the Hebrides', *TGSI* (1891–2) 112.

31 A remarkable, though an obscene and sexist, poem 'Of a wenche with chyld' discusses substances that could be used for purposes of abortion, *Bannatyne MS* vol. 2, 336–9.

32 Child [28] 'Bird Ellen and Young Tamlane'; *The Book of Scottish Poems Ancient and Modern* ed. J. Ross (Edinburgh 1884), 663–4.

33 Halyrudhous Kirk Session Records. 12 March, 1633, qtd. in Dalyell, *Darker Superstitions*, 358. Dalyell also cites 'Ane elf-arrow set with silver', in Camden's *Britannia* by Gough v.iv., 232; Low, *A Tour Through the Islands of Orkney and Schetland*, 17.

34 Trial of Euphemia Makcalzane, 9 June 1591. Pitcairn vol. 1, 252; Alexander MacKenzie, *The Prophecies of the Brahan Seer*, (Stirling 1899; rep. Golspie 1970), 13–4; William Matheson, 'The Historical Coinneach Odhar and Some Prophecies Attributed to Him', *TGSI*, 46 (1971).

35 J. Geoffrey Dent, 'The Holed Stone Amulet and its Uses', *Folk Life* 3 (1965): 68–78; Pennant was told by a farmer in the Borders that a cure for a horse that was 'hag-ridden' was to hang a naturally perforated stone over it, *A Tour in Scotland*, 76. An in-depth study on a variety of charms and talismans was made by George F. Black, 'Scottish Charms and Amulets', *PSAS* 27 (1892–3): 433–526.

36 Trial of James Knarston, 1633. Dalyell, *Darker Superstitions*, 508–9; Trial of Katherine Cragie, 1640. *Abbotsford Club Miscellany* vol. 1, 135–42; For 'Trowieglive' Ernest W. Marwick, *The Folklore of Orkney and Shetland*, (London 1975), 33; W. B. Cook, ed., *Stirling Antiquary*, 4 vols. (Stirling 1893–1908). Vol. 4, 187, 190; Simpkins, *Folk-Lore Concerning Fife*, 80–81.

37 *Scottish population history from the 17th century to the 1930s* ed. Michael Flinn (Cambridge 1977), 132 and 116–200; Ian D. Whyte *Scotland Before the Industrial Revolution An Economic and Social History c.1050–c.1750* (London 1995), 111–131.

38 MacDonald, *Fairy Tradition*, 11–2. According to Briggs *Dictionary* the earliest account of a changeling is 'Malekin', recorded by 13th c. chronicler Ralph of Coggeshall. See also Bruford and MacDonald, *Scottish Traditional Tales*, 345–51; On midwives see *Malleus Maleficarum*, 41, 140–1; Simpkins, *Folk-Lore Concerning Fife*, 160; On changelings see *Malleus Maleficarum*, 105.
39 Wimberly, *Folklore in the English and Scottish Ballads*, 285, 325.
40 *A Book of Scotish Pasquils 1568–1715* ed. William Maidment (Edinburgh 1868), 65; Alasdair Maclean, *Night Falls on Ardnamurchan The Twilight of a Crofting Family* (London 1984), 35; On Montgomerie see Chapter 5.
41 Trial of Janet Trall, *Extracts . . . Strathbogie*, xii; Trial of Isobel Haldane, Pitcairn vol. 2, 538. Pitcairn suggests 'sochsterrie leaweis' are the leaves of a herb, perhaps star-grass, bog-star-grass. The *SND* gives sharg as 'a tiny mischievous creature; a puny, stunted or weakly creature, an ill-thriving child'.
42 Trial of Margaret Dickson, NAS, CH2/185/5 *Haddington Presbytery Records*. The significance of fire is also encountered in the trial of Andrew Aiken who burned the clothes of the sick person because 'this being an evill mind by the fairie folk must be helpit be fyre'. SCA, CH2/722/5 *Stirling Presbytery Records*. We are indebted to Joyce Miller for drawing these cases to our attention.
43 Martin, *A Description of the Western Isles of Scotland*, 117–8; Grant, *Parish of Suddie*, 1732, qtd. in Dalyell, *Darker Superstitions*, 539.
44 Miller, *Scenes and Legends of the North of Scotland*, 101. Robert Kirk mentions the order of St. Bennet with regard to a spell to 'expel the unbeast'. See Kirk, 110–1; W. J. Watson, *Place Names of Ross & Cromarty* (Inverness 1904), 60, James M. Mackinlay, *Folklore of Scottish Lochs and Springs* (Glasgow 1893), 84, 104, 192, Mary Beith, *Healing Threads. Traditional Medicines of the Highlands and Islands* (Edinburgh 1995), 141–2.
45 Trial of Barbara Thomasdochter or Scord, 2 Oct. 1616. *Court Book of Shetland*, 40. See below on 'Bowman'; Robert Chambers, *Popular Rhymes of Scotland* (Edinburgh 1870), 70; Simpkins, *Folk-Lore Concerning Fife*, 398. See also Angela Bourke, *The Burning of Bridget Cleary: A True Story* (London 1999) on the burning of a Tipperary woman Bridget Cleary, a suspected changeling, in 1895.
46 William Collins, *Edinburgh Magazine* April 1788, qtd. in *Minstrelsy* vol. 1, 198–9; Simpkins, *Folk-Lore Concerning Fife*, 32, 112, 113, 158, 398; Aldous Huxley, *The Devils of Loudun* (1952; Harmondsworth 1971), 273.
47 Duncan J. Robertson 'Orkney Folk-Lore', *POAS* vol. 2, (1923–4) 38–9. This was a fairly common tale type see e.g. 'A Dead Wife among the Fairies' in Bruford and MacDonald, *Scottish Traditional Tales*, 357.

CHAPTER FOUR

The Rise of the Demonic

> The Reformation swept away many of the corruptions of the Church of Rome; but the purifying torrent remained itself somewhat tinctured by the superstitious impurities of the soil over which it passed. The trials of sorcerers and witches, which disgrace our criminal records, become even more frequent after the Reformation of the Church; as if human credulity, no longer amused by the miracles of Rome, had sought for food in the traditionary records of popular superstition.
>
> Sir Walter Scott[1]

By the eve of Reformation the fairies were well and truly established in Scotland, acknowledged, accepted and best avoided by people at all levels of society who apparently took them quite seriously, save for a small group of intellectuals who hovered in court circles. However, in the period between c.1560 and c.1700, beliefs as to what fairies actually were and how detrimental, even dangerous to society they could be, came under the scrutiny of the political and religious elite, and an ever-widening gulf began to grow between learned and folk opinion. In essence, the fairies came to be presented as agents of the Devil and all those who had traffic with them as co-conspirators in his grand plan to wreak havoc on good and godly citizens. As the fear of witches increased, spreading like an epidemic across most of Europe, the fairies swiftly became so enmeshed with witchcraft that it is often difficult to distinguish them from Satan's unholy regiments. Of course, fairy belief was by no means paramount on the list of evils thought to be infesting the country and leading to the downfall of society. Many areas of popular belief, pastimes, activities and lifestyle fell under the hammer of the judges and the proselytising of religious reformers. As late as 1591 the presbytery of Haddington, close to Edinburgh, was concerned about the 'greit abus and superstitioun' within its bounds. Matters of concern were the keeping of 'superstitious days', the playing of timbrels and 'wechts', a type of tambourine, on the Sabbath, and the mounting of plays at Easter and Christmas.[2] In short, there was a movement, instigated mainly by the elite and aided by the pious (who were often one and the same), to suppress the practices of the folk majority and to give predominance to the cultural ideas of the elite minority. King James VI of Scotland was very much involved in this cultural process, the significance of his role reflected in his slight, but influential, tract *Daemonologie*, published in 1597.

The Reformation Centuries

Some have blamed the repressiveness of the age on the Reformation, which for Scotland, virtually the last country in Europe to undergo the process, came in August 1560 when the country finally broke its ties with Rome and set up a protestant establishment. Such an approach is, however, too simplistic. The medieval church throughout Europe had experienced a crisis of authority ever since the late fourteenth century when the so-called 'Great Schism' produced, at one time, no fewer than three competing popes. Meanwhile early reformers such as John Wycliffe in England and John Huss in Bohemia were knocking at the gates. Some of Wycliffe's followers, known as Lollards from a Dutch word meaning mumblers, acquired a toehold in Scotland, specifically in Kyle, Ayrshire, if John Knox is to be believed. The damaging years of 'schism' were followed by a disruptive debate which gripped and consumed ecclesiastics, about where ultimate church authority reposed. Some argued for the supremacy of the papacy, others for the college of cardinals, while yet others opted for conciliar theory which advocated the superiority of church councils. One manifestation of the angst experienced by the late-medieval church was the papal bull of Innocent VIII in 1484 which commissioned the Dominicans, Kramer and Sprenger, as inquisitors in north Germany, the two individuals who went on to produce the handbook for witch-finders known as the *Malleus Maleficarum*. This loathsome tome played a significant role in launching the witch-hunt as a means of reinforcing ecclesiastical authority at the expense, in the main, of female victims and folk belief, for much of the latter was demonised in their treatise. Copies of the book reached Scotland.

In Scotland during the same period the laity, the monarchy included, was concerned to place in its own hands as much church wealth as possible, through the feuing of church lands, the acquisition of monastic commendatorships and downright corruption. Idle-bellies at the top of the kirk-tree, such as bishops and abbots, grew fat on holy revenues. The Crown's allegiance to holy mother church was bought for the privilege of making ecclesiastical appointments, which allowed it to further milk the richest institution in the land. By the eve of reformation some 85% of the revenues of the parish churches had been appropriated elsewhere, which is to say that the funds which should have maintained individual parish priests, as well as the fabric and furnishings of their church buildings, had been diverted to monasteries, cathedrals and universities. Priests were so starved of financial support that they often had to take on secondary occupations, buildings were in a ruinous condition, and church vessels minimal or altogether absent. Many of the laity possibly did not have great expectations of their church, for things appeared to have always been thus, but there are signs of increasing popular piety in the century before Reformation, of a desire to resist the exportation of wealth to Rome and of a wish to divert charitable donations to the adornment of local buildings such as burgh and city churches. In part, at least, the Reformation came about because folk felt the need for more spirituality and for more structure in their lives. People are often anxious to discover the regulatory parameters, or the limits, which govern their existence; they crave order. On all counts the reformed church was more than happy to oblige.

The Scottish medieval church took a dim view of popular festivals, in the towns collaborating with the burgesses to restrain the wilder excesses of celebration through riotous banqueting, drinking, play-acting and processing. The Abbot of Unreason, or Lord of Bonacord in Aberdeen (elsewhere he frequently had other names), had become known as Robin Hood, with his assistant Little John, by 1508. His responsibilities included organising the May games, overseeing dancing and sports for the city, including the upkeep of playing fields, and the supervision of pageants. In some places a Queen of May was appointed. Such festivals were in a reasonably flourishing state throughout the fifteenth century, but by the 1530s men were being fined for refusing to serve as the unruly abbot. This one-time honour may have been avoided for at least three reasons – on grounds of cost since the abbot had to fork out for the festivities with no guarantee of compensation from tight-fisted local dignitaries; for reasons of piety because the celebrations appeared increasingly irreligious; and to reflect status since the payment of a fine for non-participation was an advertisement of wealth. By 1552 the Abbott's office was suppressed in Haddington, while an act of parliament three years later abolished it altogether nation-wide.[3] Clearly popular culture was under attack long before the Reformation, while the assault can be seen to have intensified as the church considered its position progressively beleaguered.

The historiography of the Scottish Reformation has been plagued by a sectarian approach, usually exemplified by worthy ministers attempting to justify to themselves and others the present status of their particular denomination. As a result many studies are stultifyingly obsessed with institutional aspects of the subject. Although matters have improved during the last forty years or so, there are still too many studies which fail to take account of the situation at grassroots level.

Martin Luther nailed his 95 theses, statements to be defended in theological debate, on the church door at Wittenberg in 1517 after a lengthy and painful process of reflection, study and self-analysis. His dilemma was that ever since the incident in the Garden of Eden humanity had been programmed to sin, and all poor sinners must inevitably be confronted by a wrathful, righteous God who had no option but to punish them. Officially sanctioned methods of appeasing the godhead, such as pilgrimages, the purchase of pardons, or the multiplicity of masses, good works as they were called, seemed to lack scriptural authority. Luther returned to the New Testament in which he was able to distinguish a god of love to replace the hopelessly judgemental deity of Old Testament notoriety, a god who was prepared to extend grace to the sinner right up until the last possible moment to any who would believe, thus offering the opportunity for justification, or salvation, by faith alone. What he discovered was hope for those who hitherto had faced only despair, at the same time eradicating all of the man-made accretion and detritus that passed for religious observance. So impressed by such ideas (and many others) was the young Patrick Hamilton of St Andrews that he went to the stake for them in 1528.

Lutheran ideas had penetrated Scotland, if not the consciousness of the Scots at large, by 1525. Political, diplomatic and economic considerations conspired to delay reformation for another generation. Ideas, especially of the theological variety, are notoriously difficult for most people to grasp, but popular and educated preachers gradually spread the word, which appealed in particular to the bourgeois and landed classes with something of a disposable income, small though it may have been, people with a taste for vernacular literature and who aspired to send their sons to university. John Knox was originally Luther-inspired but a spell in Geneva exposed him to the awesome influence of John Calvin. Luther actually liked people; Calvin did not. But Calvin produced a systematised programme for reformation in his *Institutes of the Christian Religion* which Luther failed to do. Calvin believed that all human beings were the creatures of Eden who were ever on the brink of a return to nature. He argued that the elect were predestined for salvation. Faith involved the certainty of such knowledge; to doubt was to deny God. Convinced calvinists thus became engaged in a kind of sanctimonious struggle for survival against the forces of the unregenerate. The reformation of society and of morals was as paramount as the reformation of religion. Calvin considered that the people at large constituted the monster with many heads, whereas monarchy tended towards tyranny and absolutism. His compromise was oligarchy, rule by the few, an idea which seems to have struck a chord among certain of the Scottish aristocracy who had for so long been at loggerheads with their kings.[4] Calvin undoubtedly had theocratic tendencies but his more radical followers wished to advance much further in the direction of republicanism at the expense of monarchy.

It has been argued that the Reformation was an aristocratic-led movement and there is some truth in this, but the kin-based system of Scottish society allowed the nobility to say one thing and do very little. When John Knox realised that there was no point in appealing to the monarchy, as represented by the young Mary, Queen of Scots, who was being raised a catholic in France, to bring about perfect reformation, he then addressed the nobility who likewise failed to respond. His final overture appeared in a 'Letter to the Commonalty of Scotland', the folk at large, many of whom would now be termed middle class, by asking 'Was Adam noble or not?' and pointing out that they had an obligation to act when their superiors manifestly failed to do so. Thus Reformation was achieved in 1560 through popular revolt. The poor were invoked when the 'Beggars' Summons' ordered all churchmen out of burgh almshouses, usurped from the poor for their own selfish use. There was a significant incidence of rioting leading to iconoclasm in which a portion of the nation's medieval heritage was tragically destroyed. Much was very likely accomplished with the connivance, if not the participation, of sympathetic nobility who, as in the Wars of Independence, lurked on the sidelines, while their social subordinates took the risks.

The years that followed were steeped in religious turmoil and conflict; and not only between protestants and catholics. Knox and his cohorts produced a programme for reform, never fully implemented, in their *Book of Discipline*. For a decade they squabbled about whether there was a place for bishops in the kirk, concluding in their favour. In 1574, Andrew Melville left Geneva, returning to Scottish soil with a new polity of presbyterianism, which in a second *Book of Discipline* (1578) advocated the setting up of a full system of church courts, extending from the kirk session at parish level, to presbyteries, synods and the general assembly of the Church of Scotland. Melville preached the doctrine of parity, namely that there was no distinction in the scriptures between the offices of bishop and priest, *episcopus* and *presbyter*, hence presbyterian. Not surprisingly the Crown took offence, the young James VI shrewdly suspecting that if hierarchies were abolished in the kirk, it would only be a matter of time before the state was expected to follow suit, hence 'No bishop, no King!' After a number of hair-raising scuffles and altercations, James gained the better of the Melvillians, though political expediency forced their return to very temporary favour in 1592, after which he designed a system of 'bishops in presbytery'.

Further tension developed as a result of the Union of the Crowns in 1603 when the Scots feared that their laws, institutions and culture would be assimilated with those of England. When James's schemes for an incorporating union between the two kingdoms were foiled he set about the anglicisation of the Scottish Church. On his one and only return visit to Scotland in 1617 he attempted to impose the infamous 'Five Articles of Perth' upon the kirk, including such malodorously popish observances as kneeling at communion, the readoption of the christian year, private communion and baptism, and confirmation.

It is always said that James knew when to back off but the same did not hold true for his son, Charles I, who rapidly alienated his Scottish subjects in numerous ways, both secular and religious, but mainly through his underlying presumption of divine-right kingship. Charles's extreme views, adequately reflected in his outrageous political behaviour, directly inspired the subscription of the National Covenant in 1638 which signalled the commencement for many Lowland Scots of a period of religious mania. The subsequent civil wars in the name of religion took a terrible toll. In one year, 1644–5, the Marquis of Montrose defeated six successive covenanting armies in a series of devastating battles. A covenant was a contract for eternity into which one entered with God, suggesting notions of a chosen people and a second Israel, while Edinburgh briefly became the new Jerusalem, but bewilderingly, the Amalekites triumphed again and again over Gideon's army.

After the execution of Charles I the covenanting movement was seriously split, its army demolished at the Battle of Dunbar in 1650 by Oliver Cromwell who brutally remarked 'there may be a covenant made with God or Hell'. After the misery of the Cromwellian occupation moderate covenanters managed a compromise with Charles II while their more radical brothers and sisters set up a resistance movement in the south-western counties. State terrorism led to the Killing Times when humble folk, and sometimes their children, suffered persecution, transportation and death for adhering to their faith. Their leaders were often university-educated and fanatical, hiding out in the hills where they penned radical tracts favouring the creation of a republic of Jesus Christ in opposition to the twin evils, as they saw things, of Stewart despotism and the forces of the catholic counter-reformation. Their apologists would later claim, with some truth, that in part (excluding, of course, their republican sentiments) they anticipated the principles, if such there were, behind the Glorious Revolution of 1688–9, when the catholic James VII was forced off the throne, his torch thereafter to be borne aloft by the Jacobites, while his replacement, William II, secured the presbyterian establishment in 1690.[5]

Those who later looked back on this highly troubled period, such as Robert Wodrow, something of a folklorist himself, who ransacked oral testimony in compiling his massive *History of the Sufferings of the Church of Scotland*, distinguished the previous two hundred years as the Reformation Centuries; they saw the period as having a unity because to them the struggle throughout was about the same issues. It was also a time, perhaps the most intensively religious of any period in Scottish history, when 'superstition' was most rife, a phenomenon discerned, not by the folk themselves, but by the devout, who were relentless in combating folk belief and popular culture due to an overwhelming conviction that all superstitious practices or attitudes nurtured the most sinister and fearful of all superstitions, those which had supported for a millennium and half 'the brood of the bowels of the Whore of Babylon', none other than Antichrist, as represented by the Church of Rome.

While it is true to say the Scottish Reformation took its toll of the people's culture, contrary to modern perception it did not eradicate it completely. The reformers might decree of feast days and festivals, 'such as be all those that the Papists have invented . . . we judge them utterly to be abolished from this realm', but such days continued to be observed for the practical reason that many rents and leases came due at term days and also because it went against human nature to surrender holidays. Music, song, plays and dancing were all potential targets for zealous reformers, as was folk belief. Bishop Carswell's preface to the Gaelic Prayer Book (1567) criticised the Gaels for finding more pleasure in tales of the fairies, or the *Tuatha de Danann* as he calls them in a unique Scottish reference, than in the holy word of God:

Great is the blindness and darkness of sin and ignorance and understanding among composers and writers and supporters of the Gaelic, in that they prefer and practice the framing of vain, hurtful, lying earthly stories, about the Tuath de Danand, ... with a view to obtaining for themselves passing worldly gain, rather than to write and compose and to support the faithful words and the perfect way of truth.

During the twentieth century it became fashionable for certain *literati* to deplore the blight which descended upon Scottish culture as a consequence of the Reformation. One such was Edwin Muir who, musing on a past that never was, echoed the ballad of Thomas Rhymer:

> A simple sky roofed in that rustic day,
> The busy corn-fields and the haunted holms,
> The green road winding up the ferny brae.
> But Knox and Melville clapped their preaching palms
> And bundled all the harvesters away.
> Out of that desolation we were born.[6]

Great poet though he was, his ignorance on this matter was as profound as the obduracy of the reformers, for in point of fact there have been disappointingly few studies of the cultural impact of reformation, a failure to be laid at the door of historians much too fixated on politics and polity.

Between about 1500 and 1750 the elite, including the clergy, orchestrated a redefinition of their own traditions and beliefs. Many of them withdrew from any involvement they did have with folk culture and, for the first time, began to draw clear distinctions between the sacred and the secular worlds. The Reformation unquestionably played a huge part in this process, attempting as it did to make a clean break between the sacred and the profane, eliminating any middle ground that existed. The more radical protestants attacked not only folk magic but ecclesiastical magic as well. However, shattering an entire worldview is no easy task, so not surprisingly their success was limited. Recent work on Germany suggests that the lessening of the sacramental or 'superstitious' beliefs may not have been due to reformation at all, but rather the people found other ways to create order in their daily lives. It is argued that there was no sudden shift from one set of beliefs to another, nor was there a loss of belief in the sacred and 'superstitious', only a restructuring and curtailment of their field of activity. Similar conclusions have been reached regarding England, questioning whether the official campaign against magic by the church had much of an effect on its popular appeal, in the absence of any more attractive alternative.[7] Scotland does not quite fit either pattern since views were so polarised that the intensity of opposition on the part of Church and State may have served actually to reinforce the very beliefs they were intent upon destroying.

One of the functions of the medieval church, besides of course offering the chance of salvation, was to mark out key events in the human life cycle and the seasons, thus providing 'cosmic order for human existence'.[8] It also attempted to counter folk magic by providing a rival system of ecclesiastical magic. Protestantism taught that all sacred action was a one-way system, from God to human. The idea of salvation based upon good works was replaced by predestination, notably in Scotland. This was a system based upon self-help and prayer to an omnipotent God, but it was rather difficult to fathom. When John Davidson, the fiery minister of Prestonpans, asked what happened if he doubted his own predestination, he was informed that he was no longer a believer. Calvinism, therefore, could be regarded as somewhat exclusive, indeed hopeless, so far as most frail human beings were concerned. To make matters worse Calvin's followers, like all reformers, believed they were living in the Last Days, that the world as they knew it was coming to an end, as prophesied in the *Book of Revelation*. It was necessary to prepare for the most momentous event in history, the second coming of Jesus Christ, which would also end all history. Such apocalyptic provision involved the eradication of all ungodly elements from society, be they witches, catholics or vulgar superstitions; it was all somewhat analogous to tidying the house in anticipation of a very important visitor. As the great moment approached, it was believed that the struggle unloosed between God and Satan would intensify, and clues as to its imminence could be detected on a daily basis. In this system there was no room for manoeuvre; anything deemed magical or superstitious had to be eradicated. Yet the calvinists did not initiate this programme, rather they refined an agenda which had been in place for over a century.

According to *The Complaynt of Scotland* (1550), pre-Reformation Scotland enjoyed 'sueit melodius sangis of natural music of antiquite'. Thirty-eight songs and ballads, including 'Thomas Rhymer', are recorded in this account. The degradation of the position and value of the music-makers, particularly in the Lowlands, began as early as 1449 when

Parliament legislated against bards and other wanderers. A few years later an inquisition was ordered into the activities of 'bards and masterful beggars', a significant pairing.[9] In 1549 the provincial council of the Church denounced 'all the books of rhymes and popular songs' which, when found, would be 'confiscated and burned'. In 1551 Parliament followed up by censoring many ballads, songs, blasphemies, and rhymes.

The legislation continued as urban communities joined in the assault. Dumfries council in 1548 outlawed minstrels, unless they were appointed by the burgh. In 1574 Glasgow attempted to banish 'all pyparis, fidleris, menstrales, or any other vagabondis'. In the same year an act of parliament was enacted against all those who were idle, 'menstrallis, sangstaris, and taill tellaris'. Obviously such acts were directed solely at the unattached bards and minstrels of the folk, rather than towards those who were officially sanctioned by authority, since burgh records show that many towns employed entertainers throughout pre- and post-Reformation times. The legislation targeted those who were regarded as the custodians of the folk tradition; to eradicate the bearers was to eradicate their lore.

Complete annihilation, however, was seldom the aim of the early reformers. They made strenuous efforts to change the meaning or the context of many folk customs and beliefs, refurbishing them with a veneer of morality and edification, a time-honoured ploy which the medieval church had successfully manipulated ever since the conversion by, for example, distinguishing the already existing midwinter festival as Christmas and moving All Saints' Day from February to 1 November in order to capitalise on the popularity of Halloween. They did not object to plays as such, or music for its own sake, but rather sought to exchange the meaning or content for their own. The propaganda value of such media could not be dismissed. The adaptation of profane ballads as sacred songs was a widespread convention. Rather than seek to obliterate the songs and ballads, they were used as convenient vehicles for propaganda. John Wedderburne's *The Good and Godlie Ballads* (1542) 'turned manie bawdie songs and rymes in godlie rymes',[10] at least thirty of which derived from traditional ballads and songs. The popular folk message was supplanted by a religious one. Nevertheless, many words from the original ballads survived, proving that such methods actually 'reinforced, rather than threatened, that tradition', the point being that people never actually forgot the original words.

It is symptomatic of new regimes that, in order to legitimise themselves, they impose tighter social controls, but the calvinist ascendancy was not a catalyst in the suppression of folk culture, it was part of an ongoing process. What it represented was a period of heightened social control which, in turn, led the Church and State to demand a higher level of conformity in folk belief and culture.

Redefining the Supernatural

High on the agenda of reformed proselytisers was the desire to root out and destroy all vestiges of 'pagan' superstitions and supernatural creations, though paganism frequently existed only in the eye of the beholder, as so often in the history of the Church. This process is sometimes referred to, thanks to Max Weber's inspired coinage, as the 'disenchantment of the world': no easy undertaking for, as the zealots discovered, it was not practical, or even possible, to eradicate 'superstitions' by simply telling the people that their beliefs were misguided or erroneous.

The objectives of the reformers were undoubtedly well-intended and sincerely inspired, but by reinventing a world where there could only be the forces of good, upheld by God, and the forces of evil, controlled by the Devil, they destroyed the grey area once inhabited by fairies, ghosts, and witches, and relegated them all to the dominion of Satan, whose power appeared to be growing ever stronger. The new 'moralized universe' placed more and more responsibility on the shoulders of the individual. War, famine, plague, pestilence or death would result if God's laws failed to be observed, an idea with which medieval churchmen were quite familiar. The protestant doctrine of providence could not have afforded much comfort under such conditions, nor could it have allayed the growing sense of fear and anxiety:

> The traffic between the supernatural and the natural worlds had perhaps become one-way, but the boundaries between sacred and secular remained highly porous and the seepage of the one into the other was highly unpredictable, incalculable, and even dangerous. It was for this reason that Protestants were tempted to turn to Catholic means of protection and also forms of popular magic.[11]

Of course religious revolution cannot be held accountable for all of the changes taking place. Another revolution, that of science and philosophy, must also be considered. The new science of the seventeenth century, from Galileo to Newton, revolted against the medieval worldview and

1. Hawthorn at Merlin's Grave, Drumelzier

2. The Fairy Hills, Balnaknock, Skye

3. Eildon Hills from Scott's View, Bemersyde

4. The Rhymer's Stone, Melrose

5. Tamlane's Well, Carterhaugh, Selkirk

6. Lynn Glen, haunt of Bessie Dunlop

7. Robert Kirk's Bell, Balquhidder

8. Doon Hill, Hill of the Fairies, Aberfoyle

9. The Clootie Tree, Doon Hill, Aberfoyle

10. Grave of Robert Kirk, Kirkton, Aberfoyle

11. Grave of Will o' Phaup, grandfather of James Hogg, Ettrick

called for the 'despiritualization of nature'. George Sinclair, professor of natural philosophy at Glasgow University, in some respects a pragmatist who designed pumps for coal mines, was profoundly unnerved by what he perceived to be the atheistic ramblings of Hobbes, Spinoza and Descartes.[12] In Scottish terms Sinclair, although with hindsight fighting a rearguard action which he was bound in the longer term to lose, was nonetheless initiating a debate which would blow the church apart in the nineteenth-century – the relationship between science and religion. These developments forced some supernatural beliefs to change with the times while others effectively became more entrenched.

The problems that arose from redefining supernatural agencies have been discussed in the context of ghost traditions in England.[13] Ghosts (as, indeed, all other supernatural effects and entities) were a key issue in theological debates in the years following the Reformation. They were used initially to prove the existence of Purgatory (later, of God), and subsequently as proof of witchcraft and the supernatural. The protestants argued that there could be no such things as ghosts since the soul was dispatched straight to Heaven or Hell. The difficulties they faced become apparent when it is realised that not only were ghosts deeply rooted in the oral tradition of the folk, but the bible had its fair share of them too. A much more practical approach was to redefine what ghosts actually were, or were popularly believed to be. As Gillian Bennett has shown, Ludwig Lavater's *Of Ghostes and Spirites Walking by Nyghte* translated into English in 1572, was part of the investigative process as he sought to prove that ghosts were not 'the souls of dead men, as some men have thought, but either good or evill angels, or else some secrete and hid operations of God'.[14]

The issue of what supernatural entities such as ghosts, spirits, or fairies actually constituted was widely debated by clerics, demonologists, scholars, and by at least one monarch. James VI took a very hard line approach, insisting that 'since the comming of Christ in the flesh . . . all miracles, visions, prophecies, and appearances of angels or good spirites are ceased. Which served only for the first sowing of faith, and planting of the Church'.[15] Any such supernatural visitation could only be, in his view, from the Devil. For James at least, the age of christian miracles was over.

Fairies and ghosts were not the only entities subjected to the redefining process. Elsewhere in Europe werewolves, for instance, underwent a similar metamorphosis. Portrayed in medieval texts and cherished in the folk tradition as beneficent figures who actually fought the legions of Hell on behalf of their communities, it was not until the mid-fifteenth century that the benign nature of the werewolf was obliterated to be usurped by the vicious and terrible evil-doer intent upon devouring livestock and children; at approximately the same time the hostile image of the witch crystallised.[16]

The extent to which belief traditions, in witches, ghosts, werewolves, or fairies, were redefined or reinvented is immense but also immeasurable. What can be said with confidence is that, if nothing else, popular or folk culture in pre-industrial Scotland was far from moribund.

The Scottish Witch-Hunt

Attempts to explain the roots and the reasons behind the European witch-hunt, which consisted of an estimated 100,000 trials between 1450 and 1750,[17] have recently attracted considerable scholarly interest and have generated a vast quantity of books and publications. Although it is not the intention of this book to delve into the hows and whys of the witch-hunt, some discussion of this sordid event cannot be avoided. It is an unhappy fact, and a cruel twist of fate, that so much of our best evidence on the nature of fairy belief in this period has come down to us through judicial records of testimonies taken from savagely tortured women and men accused of witchcraft. Also, the circumstance that belief in fairies became hopelessly entangled with the crime of witchcraft is sufficient reason to warrant consideration.

As already stated, although much has been written on the witch-hunts, precious little has so far been done on the content of the Scottish trials, though several projects are currently underway. Scotland is a particularly interesting place to study the witch-hunting phenomenon, representing as it does a 'middle ground' between the extremes of continental persecutions and the relatively tame hunts of England. The fullest study, and to date the most accomplished work on the subject, is Christina Larner's *Enemies of God*, though her lack of interest in the fairy material is to be regretted. When she did encounter information about fairy belief in the records she invariably dismissed it as relating only 'to dreams, nightmares, and collective fantasies',[18] an inadequate assessment to say the least. The argument adopted in the present study is that all texts have meaning and that they can be deconstructed to shed light on Scottish folk belief in the period under review. Within the trial evidence it is possible to recognise 'a more complex stratification', in which the words of the accused are covered by a 'thin diabolical crust'.[19]

The Scottish witch-hunt was initially inspired by the elite but they rapidly entered into an alliance with their subordinates, the folk at large, who sincerely wished to purge their communities from the destructive threats of deviance and evil. Both Church and State became deeply anxious and fearful about the levels of non-conformity within Scotland and a purposeful suppression was begun of any unofficial source of empowerment that might be acknowledged by the people. Panic-mongering about the threat posed by witchcraft, as exemplified in James VI's treatise, was rampant: 'I pray God to purge this cuntrie of these divellishe practises: for they were never so rife in these partes, as they are now'. But witch-hunting both nurtured and fed upon the fears and hostilities which perennially plagued the peasant community. Accusations frequently reflect the conflicts, both personal and cosmological, experienced within rural life. The disappointments, frustrations, jealousies and rivalries of daily existence are often manifested in the evidence. Many poor souls must have attempted to seek solace in alternatives when God so clearly failed them.[20]

There was not one continuous witch-hunt in Scotland. As on the Continent, persecutions underwent considerable fluctuations. Five peaks of intensive witch-hunting have been distinguished: 1590–1, 1597, 1629–30, 1649, and 1661–2. Before the passing of the Witchcraft Act in June 1563, there is little trace of the crime in the Scottish records. Within a fortnight of the passing of Queen Mary's new law, two witches were burned, though executions *en masse* did not ensue. What had significantly changed was that consulters, or clients, of witches were now deemed to be as guilty as the practitioners of witchcraft.[21] The gap between white and black magic was hastily blurred, and folk-healers were caught up in the same judicial snare as malevolent miscreants. Of equal significance was that the crime remained defined as malefice, with any suggestion of the Devil or the demonic pact only gradually emerging.

The first mass trial to strike Scotland, in 1590–1, following the alleged activities of the infamous North Berwick coven, reflects, for the first time, the importation of full-blown, educated, continental witch beliefs. In the same year as the publication of King James's treatise, *Daemonologie*, in 1597, another major witch-hunt took place. It came to the attention of the king and council that innocent people were being caught up in the panic, forcing the revocation of all standing commissions and the inauguration of a new policy of granting individual commissions upon application to the privy council.[22]

The worst episode of witch persecutions followed shortly on the heels of the Restoration (1660). Between April 1661 and the autumn of 1662, over 600 cases and approximately 300 executions took place. One of the most insidious revelations to come out of this period of hysteria was that several 'witch-prickers' were found to be frauds. Faith in the system had been unhinged – unfortunately not enough to put an end to witch-hunting altogether – but the number of cases did radically decline. It was long ago noted that after 1678, witch trials brought before the high court were rare, possibly due to the publication of John Webster's treatise, *The Displaying of Supposed Witchcraft* (1677). It has also been observed that although executions for witchcraft still occurred, cases coming into the high court of justiciary from 1678 to 1680 were more likely to end in an acquittal rather than a burning. Such verdicts probably had the effect of reducing the number of cases brought to court.[23] The last person executed for witchcraft in Scotland was Janet Horne from Dornoch in 1727, or such, at least, is the received view, for there is precious little evidence about the event. One point of interest is that Robert Kirk's son, also Robert, was minister at Dornoch from 1713 to 1758. The Witchcraft Act of 1563 was finally repealed in 1736.

Between 40,000 and 50,000 people were burned at the stake for alleged witchcraft throughout Europe. Sadly, it is impossible to know with any precision how many people were tried and executed for the crime in Scotland. A systematic study of the Scottish criminal records still awaits proper investigation. Larner's approximation is probably the most reliable at present. She estimated no more than 2,000 people were executed for witchcraft, allowing for all areas of doubt, but that a figure around 1,500 or under was more likely.[24]

Popular conceptions of witches, the Devil, and fairies before the Reformation were a lot less terrifying than they subsequently became. Traditionally Scottish witches had been regarded as members of the community, as had the fairies their respected neighbours. Though believed to be capable of harm, the witch and the fairy provided a bridge between this world and the supernatural world. The witch was often a consultant on all matters supernatural as well as a healer, dispensing medicines and charms, while even the most reputedly malignant of witches could be extremely powerful figures in the community.[25] As the worldviews of the learned and the peasantry became increasingly polarised, large areas of what had once been accepted belief were stigmatised under the catch-all phrase of 'superstition', so contaminating and blurring the distinctive roles of witches and fairies.

While trials did take place in Gaelic-speaking regions, witch panics were fewer though the precise reasons for this are unknown. It is possible that Gaelic society enjoyed a higher level of toleration of the occult and so managed to retain a certain level of acceptance or, perhaps large parishes and the fewer number of kirk sessions in the Highlands decreased the chances of major outbreaks of panic. The activities of the kirk session do indeed seem inextricably linked to witch-hunting and the changing attitudes to folk culture generally.

The kirk session, which consisted of the minister and his elders, met to decide upon disciplinary procedures and methods of public worship. By the mid-seventeenth century it had spread over most of Lowland Scotland and had ventured into Argyll and Inverness-shire. The elders monitored the lives of their parish and were endowed with powers to punish any wrongdoing as they saw fit; they would handle anything from Sabbath-breaking, fighting and drunkenness, to adultery. The punishment given to the guilty person could range from being made to perform various degradation rituals, such as the wearing of sackcloth in the presence of the congregation, to a fine.[26]

The emergence of this new system of social control, combined with the changes taking place within central administration, led to a full-scale attack on folk beliefs and customs. The use of judicial torture, which was not abolished in Scotland until 1709,[27] must also, crucially, be considered. However, the most significant causal factor of all lies in the rise and fall of official interest in abolishing ballads and songs, legislating against feast days and plays, prosecuting practitioners of witchcraft, and persecuting believers in fairies. In the years between 1590 and 1662 – the time when witch persecutions peaked – witchcraft was seen as the ultimate in social deviance, representing disorder, chaos and evil. The witch was not only a danger to the individual, but a threat to society, the state, and the church, a veritable enemy of God.

Satan's Greatest Enemy: King James VI

Many historians have had a tendency to view James's interest in witchcraft as anomalous and therefore to play down or ignore his involvement with it. James, contrary to much twentieth-century scholarship, thought that *Daemonologie* was one of his most important works. It has been convincingly argued that this tract was integral, not only to James's political career, but to his mental world as well.[28]

Fig. 2. King James interrogates Agnes Sampson, from *Newes from Scotland*, 1591.

There is considerable evidence to indicate an upsurge of interest in continental witch beliefs following James's return to Scotland after a six-month stay at the Danish court in the winter of 1589, at which time he celebrated his marriage to Anne of Denmark. There he met Niels Hemmingsen, the Danish theologian, and an authority cited in *Daemonologie*. Despite the well-known Witchcraft Act of 1563 there was not a great deal of persecution, although there were notably more cases from the 1570s, most of which were either political in nature or concerned maleficium. The North Berwick trial would significantly alter both context and perception by reinforcing the concept of the demonic pact as the first phase of intensive persecution was begun and was given official approval.

On arrival in Scotland James became convinced that his stormy voyage from Denmark had been due to witchcraft, but, doubtful that only Danish witches were to blame, he did not take long to uncover

Scottish suspects. A great coven, over three hundred in number, had allegedly met at North Berwick kirk to plot the demise of the king. The trials were held in Edinburgh in 1590–1, and among those accused of principal involvement were Agnes Sampson, John Fian, Euphemia Makcalzane, and the king's own cousin, Francis Stewart Earl of Bothwell. In co-operation, the Danes held parallel witch trials, a development that is unique in the history of European witch-hunting.[29]

The events of 1590–1 reflect the changing attitudes taking place among the educated classes towards witches. Whether or not the North Berwick 'coven' had been involved in a genuine conspiracy against King James VI or was symptomatic of a government plot to incriminate the Earl of Bothwell remains unclear. James took charge of the hunt himself, determined to stamp out this threat of treasonable sorcery. The level of his involvement in the trials allowed him to play the part of a Solomon or David, caring for the welfare of his people and defending the protestant faith against the minions of Hell.[30] If his actions were to be seen as a political ploy, then it was quite successful. It definitely gained him some welcome publicity. An English chapbook, entitled *Newes From Scotland*, printed in 1591, had the effect of furthering James's growing reputation as witchfinder extraordinaire by heralding him as Satan's most formidable opponent: '. . . the witches demaunded of the Divel why he did beare such hatred to the King, who answered, by reason the King is the greatest enemy he hath in the worlde'. Furthermore, the tract upheld James's claim to be a godly king on the grounds that his christian righteousness guarded him from the machinations of the Devil, whose prime target he allegedly, and preposterously, was. The account purported to be written 'according to the Scottish Coppie', though no such original has as yet been found. In all likelihood it was composed with the English reading public in mind. Not only was it highly flattering to James, but it included a good dose of titillation and gruesome detail to make it newsworthy.[31]

Set out as a conversation between Epistemon, the demonologist, and Philomathes, the doubting sceptic, *Daemonologie* was first published in Edinburgh in 1597. It went through two London editions in 1603, and was later translated into Latin, French and Dutch. Originality is by no means the striking feature of this treatise, which like many of its type is set out in the form of a Socratic dialogue. Though it is much shorter than most demonological works of the period, containing fewer examples and citations than is customary, it is fairly typical of the genre. Its most interesting facets are its defence of continental witchcraft beliefs, its use as a political tool, and the basic fact that it was written by a monarch.[32] James claimed that his motives for writing the book were primarily to refute the ideas of Reginald Scot and Johann Weyer, in his view the two major sceptics of the witch-hunt. His concerns derived from his awareness of 'the fearefull aboundinge at this time in this countrie, of these detestable slaves of the Deuill, the witches or enchaunters'. It was his intention to prove 'that such divelish artes have bene and are' and to outline 'what exact trial and punishment they merite'. James must also have wished *Daemonologie* to be seen as proof of his intellectual and religious capabilities, but, as has been sensibly suggested, the treatise, 'in genesis and in content', can be read as a testimonial about ideal monarchy.[33]

After the Union of the Crowns in 1603 the book was reprinted in London with anglicised spelling. *Daemonologie* continued to have some influence in Scotland throughout the seventeenth century, and was frequently referred to at trials for witchcraft. However, though James's reputation as a demonologist lived on, his interest in the subject waned once in England.[34] He became sceptical of witchcraft after some English cases, such as the Lancashire trials of 1612, were proven to be fraudulent. The witch-hunting atmosphere had, in any case, never been so fervent as it was in Scotland. The use of torture was much rarer, the courts more lenient, and charges were generally concerned with maleficium rather than the demonic pact. There was also a sizeable group of demonologists, such as Reginald Scot, George Gifford and William Perkins, proclaiming their scepticism about the existence of witches and deploring the barbarity of the witch trials. The different climate James encountered in England may well have played a part in his change of attitude towards the supernatural as it did to a whole range of subjects and ideas. It has been suggested, not altogether convincingly, that James became involved in the witch-hunt, and built up his reputation as a demonologist, as a vehicle to promote his ideals of kingship.[35] If so, then once securely ensconced on the English throne, there was less reason to try as hard. But James had been reacting against Buchanan's theories of resistance ever since the death of his old tutor and he constantly refined his ideas on divine-right kingship in order to prove that he would make a worthy successor to Elizabeth. His notions of kingship undoubtedly informed his ideas about witchcraft but his interest in the subject must have derived from his own unnerving experiences as the target of the biggest witch conspiracy ever to hit Scotland in the shape of the North Berwick coven.

The Assault on Fairy Belief

The aftermath of the North Berwick trials left James VI of the opinion that he was living in the midst of a diabolical crisis, for which he laid full blame squarely on the heads of his subjects:

> the greate wickednesse of the people . . . procures this horrible defection, whereby God justlie punisheth sinne, by a greater iniquitie . . . the consummation of the worlde, and our deliverance drawing neare, makes Sathan to rage the more in his instruments, knowing his kingdome to be so neare an ende.[36]

As James's text demonstrates, reformers were not the only ones to be concerned about the Apocalypse: he was prepared to place himself in the forefront of the last great cosmic battle.

Daemonologie, with its strongly protestant bias, argued that brownies and fairies had first come to light in a period of 'papistry and blindness'. Fairies appeared 'to the innocent sort', either to frighten them, or to pretend to be superior to others types of spirit. He thought that people in these circumstances, 'for being perforce troubled with them ought to be pittied'. But James had no mercy for those who made such claims, presuming that accused witches cited their experiences with the fairies, hoping for leniency, 'to be a cullour of safetie for them, that ignorant Magistrates may not punish them for it'.

Following the Socratic model, Philomathes, the sceptic, asks Epistemon, the demonologist, the essential question which everyone who has ever investigated this subject feels compelled to probe – how it can be that witches have gone to their deaths confessing to such events as,

> they have ben transported with the Phairie to such a hill, which opening, they went in, and there saw a faire Queene, who being now lighter, gave them a stone that had sundrie vertues, which at sundrie times hath bene produced in judgment.

Epistemon's response is to view the entire alleged experience as nothing more than a trick of the Devil:

> their senses being dulled, and as it were a sleepe, such hilles & houses within them, such glistering courts and traines, and whatsoever such like wherewith he [the Devil] pleaseth to delude them. And in the meane time their bodies being senselesse, to convey in their hande

any stone or such like thing, which he makes them to imagine to have received in such a place.

James's tract, which is mostly about witches, is interesting for several reasons, not least of which is that he attempted to explain why people believed in fairies, adopting an almost rational approach to the phenomenon – not that understanding made him any more forgiving. To Philomathes' request for more strange tales of fairy, Epistemon, who is of course James himself, replies that their debate had been predicated on the question of whether there were such things as witches and fairies and whether they had any power. To that effect 'I therefore have framed my whole discours, only to prove that such things are and may be, by such number of examples as I show to be possible by reason'. He is worried, however, by the implications of delving any further, 'in playing the part of a dictionarie, to tell what ever I have read or harde in that purpose, which would both exceede fayth, and rather would seem to teach such unlawfull artes, nor to disallow and condemne them, as it is the duetie of all Christians to do'. He was perfectly aware that heightened interest in such matters might actually have the effect of diffusing and popularising information about the subject, the very opposite of his intent.[37]

James had an unenviable upbringing. He never knew his parents, though his tutor George Buchanan, who was known on occasion to 'skelp the airse of the Lord's anointed', poisoned his mind with accounts of how his mother, Mary, had been responsible for the murder of his father, Henry Darnley. Buchanan was on hand to reinforce any unease that the young king may have felt about the legitimacy of his own regnal situation as a result of Mary's deposition at the hands of her own subjects in 1567. The tutor's tract, *The Art of Government Among the Scots*, was designed to show how unsatisfactory kings might share Mary's fate, drawing upon examples from the Scottish past. The king suffered another blow when Andrew Melville returned from Geneva full of ideas about parity in the kirk, a dangerous concept that might be transposed to the secular sphere, resulting in the destruction of monarchy. It was largely as a defence against the twin threats posed by his old tutor and by presbyterianism that he revived the medieval notion of divine-right kingship, the idea that kings were appointed by God so that to resist them was not only treason but heresy. Hence the great appeal of the extravagant fiction that James was Satan's most formidable enemy. The king's despotic tendencies were augmented once he inherited the vast resources of the English crown, and these he promptly exploited to launch a massive attack on the traditional societies of the Borders, the Gàidhealtachd and the Northern Isles. Though he was not uninterested in the culture of the folk, he was happy to eradicate it in the interests of the greater glory of the British *imperium* and his own reputation.

It was long ago pointed out that because christianity would accept only two categories of spirits, angels and devils, and as fairies belonged to neither, 'the fulminations of the church were, therefore, early directed against those who consulted or consorted with the Fairies'. However, during the fourteenth century, at around the same time as some notion of the witches' Sabbat began to take shape, toleration of a belief in creatures which seemed to fit into neither category lessened, and they were increasingly viewed by officialdom with fear and suspicion. For example, among the charges laid upon Joan of Arc, burned for heresy and sorcery in 1431, was familiarity with the fairy folk.[38]

The reformers, faced with the task of eradicating all vestiges of competing pagan beliefs, were confronted with a daunting task. The persecution of witchcraft was the most odious, as it was the most conspicuous, mechanism for rooting out such a rival belief system. Once fairy belief became identified as demonically inspired, it too was a target for reformers. What must have caused intolerable headaches for the prosecutors were the many inherent contradictions this belief had already accumulated. Traditions about fairies had effectively blended christian elements, leaving the fairies in a morally ambiguous position. The rise of the demonic, and the subsequent demonisation of the fairies, can be traced in Scotland through the witch trials, but it can also be shown to predate the king's visit to Denmark. The association between fairies and the Devil was stirring among some of the authorities at least twenty years earlier and was probably a precondition which allowed for the full crystallisation of this demonic connection so soon after James's return.

Admittedly it is not certain that Satan himself actually figured in the case of Jonet Boyman of Canongate, Edinburgh, accused in 1572 of witchcraft and diabolic incantation, the first Scottish trial for which a detailed indictment has so far been found. Indeed it is one of the richest accounts hitherto uncovered for both fairy belief and charming, suggesting an intriguing tradition which associated, in some way, the fairies with the legendary King Arthur. At an 'elrich well' on the south side of Arthur's Seat, Jonet uttered incantations and invocations of the 'evill spreits quhome she callit upon for to come to show and declair' what would happen to a sick man named Allan Anderson, her patient. She allegedly first conjured 'ane grit blast' like a whirlwind, and thereafter appeared the shape of a man who stood on the other side of the well, an interesting hint of liminality. She charged this conjured presence, in the name of the father, the son, King Arthur and Queen Elspeth, to cure Anderson. She then received elaborate instructions about washing the ill man's shirt, which were communicated to Allan's wife. That night the patient's house shook in the midst of a huge, and incomprehensible, ruckus involving winds, horses and hammering, apparently because the man's wife did not follow the instructions to the letter. On the following night the house was plagued by a mighty din again, caused, this time, by a great company of women.

When Allan fell sick again three years later, he once again sent for Jonet who protested that she could do nothing for him since it was past Halloween, on which day she had more acquaintance with the good neighbours than on any other. Allan's wife had a child which would not suck and subsequently died. When Janet was asked how she knew the bairn would die ('tak the paine to foster that barne for it hes not ane hart and can not life'), she 'ansurit that it had gottin ane blast of evill wind for the moder had not sanit [blessed] it well aneuch' before leaving the house, and so the 'sillyie wychs', or seelie wichts, had found it unsained and had given it the blast and so it was taken away. There is much more in this incredibly rewarding source, which requires much fuller analysis. One of the good neighbours was 'wele anewch cled . . . wele faceit with ane baird [beard]', but wasted like a stick when viewed from behind, possibly meaning hollow and boss-backed like Isobel Gowdie's elf-boys. Jonet had witnessed the evil blast twenty times. On the last occasion before her interrogation, a Newbattle woman who hanged herself was buried 'in ane litill chapel' since she was forbidden burial in the churchyard. Jonet was condemned as 'ane wyss woman that culd mend diverss seikness and bairnis that are tane away with the faryie men and wemin'.[39] This fascinating case raises a number of intriguing points. A charmer or healer is examined to determine the source of her occult knowledge. At an eldritch well she conjures spirits, the evil blast and an entity in the shape of a man who is charged in the name of Arthur – on the very edge of Arthur's Seat – to cure her patient. There are numerous parallels for sark-washing. Supernatural blasts affect Anderson's house. Fairies are explicitly mentioned when the patient has a relapse. Had he called her before Halloween, the good neighbours might have helped. She has foreknowledge of the death of a child who is seized by the fairies with overtones of the changeling phenomenon. The fairy man's physical description has other parallels. To crown all there is mention of a suicide, while Jonet herself is condemned and burned as a wise woman who knows about children stolen by the fairies. This was clearly a case that involved the fairfolk rather than the Devil. While the demonic is present, it is not nearly as intrusive as it would become in a famous case that took place only four years later.

Much clearer evidence that fairy belief had become entangled with the demonic, before the full-blown assimilation of continental witchcraft beliefs, is recorded in the fascinating trial of an Ayrshire healer by the name of Bessie Dunlop, strangled and burned in 1576. The sentence given to Bessie was harsh, considering that she protested to her judges that she refused any offer to go to Fairyland. No doubt to the dismay of the ministers, she was readily sought after by personages of high standing for her medications and second sight. Her alleged crime lay in the 'using of sorcerie, witchcraft, and incantatioune, with invocatioun of spretis of the devill; continewand in familiaritie with thame, at all sic tymes as sche thought expedient'. But the trial record indicates that she was not guilty of actually practising maleficium; she did not harm anyone. In other words, the mere fact that Bessie claimed to have anything to do with fairies, not to mention the ghost world, was considered criminal, regardless of her refusal to join with them in any unholy pact.

There are several instances in Bessie's confession where statements made about fairies and witches overlap. Her contact with the Otherworld was made through her acquaintance with Thomas Reid, a dead man who now resided with the fairies. She claimed that all of her skills in second sight and healing were purely attributable to advice and medicinal knowledge communicated by Reid with whom she associated over a period of four years. On one occasion he took her, on the twelfth hour of the day, to meet twelve of his friends from Fairyland. She was told that the eight women and four men to whom she was introduced were 'gude wychtis that wynnit in the Court of Elfame'. These fairies, since 'wychtis' in this context are supernatural beings rather than specifically witches, wanted Bessie to accompany them, presumably to join their society in Elfame.

An interesting passage in Bessie's confession seems to reflect a measure of discontent with the new reformed faith and its aversion to folk belief. When her interrogators asked for her opinion on the 'new law', Bessie confessed she had consulted her fairy contact on the matter. Reid, who clearly adhered to catholicism and would greet her with 'Sancta Marie' when they met, advised that the new law was not good and the old faith should come home again but not as it was before. The reported exchange most likely suggests that Bessie was looking back affectionately to the days before the Reformation when the articulation of such beliefs was not so risky.[40]

It is still possible to retrace Bessie's steps in Ayrshire beginning at the magical Lynn Glen with its waterfalls and dense vegetation on the Caaf Water at the very edge of modern Dalry in whose graveyard she saw Tom Reid. A little to the south is Monk Castle, just over a mile from the Blair Estate, a couple of miles to the south east of which is situated Auchenskeith. Kilwinning is about four miles from Dalry and both communities are some six miles from the sea. On one occasion she met with Reid on the High Street of Edinburgh. On another when she and her husband had ridden to Leith to trade oatmeal she saw a group of riders disappearing into Restalrig Loch, later identified by Reid as the 'gude wychtis'. Just why Bessie and her husband should have made the long journey to Edinburgh for trading purposes is something of a mystery but their action suggests that they were persons of some status who were also, conceivably, quite prosperous.

In 1588, another woman was burned for 'hanting and repairing with the gude nychtbouris and Quene of Elfame', and other charges of familiarity with the increasingly indistinguishable witches, ghosts, and fairies. Alison Peirson, whose fame as a healer was widespread, was immortalised as a witch, thanks to Robert Sempill's satirical poem, 'The Legend of the Bishop of St. Andrews', which commemorated her most famous patient. Like Bessie Dunlop, Alison's supernatural contact had been a mortal man before living with the fairies: William Simpson, her uncle, was the source of her medicinal knowledge and he it was who supposedly told her that bishop Patrick Adamson 'had many seiknessis' and prescribed the appropriate salves and medicines to cure him.[41]

Another instance of skills attributed to fairy instruction occurs in the confession of John Stewart, tried in Irvine in 1618. His interrogators described him as a vagabond, professing skills in jugglery and palmistry, and arrested on suspicion of having used sorcery with his accomplice Margaret Barclay in sinking her brother's ship. When asked by what means he acquired a knowledge of things to come, he divulged that twenty-six years earlier, while travelling through Galway, in Ireland, on the night of Halloween, he met the king of fairies and his court. The king touched his forehead with a white rod, which had the effect of taking away the sight of one eye and his ability to speak. Three years later at Halloween, John once again met the fairy king in Dublin. On this occasion the king restored John's speech and vision. From that time onward, John averred he met with the fairies every Saturday at seven o'clock. He also saw them every Halloween, sometimes on Lanark Hill and other times on Kilmaurs Hill. John asserted that it was during his time with the fairy court that he learned his skills. He also claimed that he saw 'many persons' in the company of the fairies, and declared that all people who had been 'taken away by sudden death' went to Elfland.

A demonic interpretation was imposed upon John Stewart's explanation of his abilities. After showing the place where he had been touched by the fairy king's wand, the spot was pricked, no differently than if the Devil's mark had been sought. When the area was indeed found to be insensible, suspicions were confirmed, but John committed suicide before any of his interrogators were given the opportunity to make a pronouncement on his case. Likewise, in the case of Steven Maltman, a charmer from Gargunnock, it was the all-important detail that he had acquired his skills of healing from the fairies that led to the more serious accusation of witchcraft, rather than the lesser crime of charming. Steven appeared before the Gargunnock kirk session in 1626, to answer a specific complaint that he had instructed a woman on how to restore milk to her cows that had been stolen by earthly and unearthly 'wights'. Two years later the indictment against this popular and much-sought-after healer was advanced to include witchcraft once it had been learned that his curative powers were derived from a demonic source, namely the fairies.[42]

There are many good examples of the similarity in language in accusations of Devil worship and of consulting with fairies. The trial of Alexander Drummond of Auchterarder, held in 1629, does not refer to any fairy involvement but is noteworthy nonetheless. Alexander was accused of being 'ane manifest sorcerar and abusar' over a period of fifty years. His crime was curing 'all sort of diseases be sorcerie and witchcraft, and ane consulter with the devill and seiker of responses frome him'. Like Bessie Dunlop and Alison Peirson, he admitted to 'having also ane familiar spreit attending him to give him instructions in the practeis of all his diabolical and unlauchfull cures'.[43]

Though inquisitors would repeatedly alter or distort the words of their victims, or torture them till they uttered the desired confessions, many people tenaciously held on to the conviction that what they had experienced represented encounters with the fairies rather than with the Devil and his monstrous retinue. A story of uncertain provenance relates how 'a rustic, . . . taxed with magical practices, about 1620, obstinately denied that the good King of the Fairies had any connection with the devil'.[44] The witch trials are full of such stubborn denial or general confusion between fairies and demons. Agnes Sampson of Nether Keythe, tried in 1590–1 for her alleged membership of the North Berwick coven, confessed that she had been called upon, on more than one occasion, to give her prognosis on various illnesses. On one occasion she was able to diagnose elf-shot, simply by examining the victim's shirt. When Agnes was asked to give her prognosis about a certain woman:

> sche tauld to the gentilwemene, that sche sould tell thame that nycht quhidder the Lady wald haill or nocht; . . . Sche passit to the gairdene, to devyise upoun hir prayer, one quhat tyme sche chargeit the Dewill, calling him 'Elva,' to cum and speik to hir, qua come in ower the dyke, in liknes of ane dog.

While most of this passage seems to reflect the type of questions and forced response demanded by Agnes's prosecutors, her naming of the Devil as Elva would strongly suggest that she was in fact describing a fairy encounter, or was at least drawing upon a knowledge of fairy traditions that were familiar to her, unlike the demonic traditions recently adopted by her jurors. Euphemia Makcalzane, another accused member of the North Berwick coven, was indicted for attending a gathering at the Fairy Hills, Newhaven, on Lammas (1 August). The festival was one of several celebrating the harvest but it was also an occasion on which to choose a partner for handfasting or trial marriage of one year's duration, at the end of which, if there was no conception, the couple were free to part. A shocked but fascinated canon breathlessly speculated of the famous Tailltenn Fair, held in Ireland at Lammas, that 'promiscuous love-making resulted from the frenzied festival of gladness or with the object of magically assisting the fruitfulness of the soil'. Lammas celebrations seem to have been particularly prevalent in Lothian. There survives a lengthy detailed account from 1785 of an annual sporting contest between the herd boys of Cramond and Corstorphine near Edinburgh. Another custom was the washing of horses in the sea, a practice frowned upon by the synod of Lothian and Tweeddale in 1646, subsequently reiterated by the kirk session of St Cuthbert's, also Edinburgh. Newhaven, on the Forth shore, just to the north of the city, was well placed for such activity.[45] Horses and love-making made a powerful combination, attractive alike to both fairies and witches.

It is unclear, in the 1597–8 confession of Andro Man, to what extent the extraordinary mingling of fairy and witch beliefs was a product of Andro's ideas or those of his judges. He claimed to have been in a lengthy relationship with the fairy queen for some thirty years, summoning her by uttering the word 'Benedicite'. He was also in communication with an angel by the name of Christsonday of whom he affirmed, 'the Quene of Elphen hes a grip of all the craft, bot Christsonday is the gudeman, and hes all power under God'. The inquisitors, however, had a different opinion, telling Andro that Christsonday was 'the Devill, thy maister' a statement which has been interpreted, none too plausibly, as an example of how the queen had been relegated to a position subordinate to that of the Devil. Christsonday could shape-shift, appearing on one occasion in the likeness of a stag. Andro's experience with the fairies was not entirely negative. They danced and sang and banqueted together and he even fathered children with their queen. But the description of the fairy revels that he attended on Halloween are strikingly similar to a witches' Sabbat: 'thay com to the Binhill, and Binlocht, quhair thay use commonlie to convene, and . . . all thay quha convenis with thame kissis Christsonday and the Quene of Elphenis airss', an account that surely implies the equality of the two recipients rather than the subordination of one to another![46]

Beigis Tod of Longniddry suggestively claimed in 1608 to have met the Devil at 'Seaton-thorne', a possible fairy site. Further afield in Shetland, Katherine Jonesdochter was accused in 1616 of 'converversing [sic], lying, keiping companie and societie with the devill quhom she callit the bowman of Hildiswick and Eschenes'. In Norn, the elements 'bo' and 'boki' both convey the sense of bogey, bogle or ghost. Katherine claimed that her first encounter with the bowman had taken place in her mother's house some forty years earlier (c. 1576) and that she had continued to see him every year since. Also in 1616 Elspeth Reoch, tried in Orkney, confessed that 'on yule day . . . the devell, quhilk she callis the farie man, lay with hir'.[47]

By the early seventeenth century the image of the Devil was as stereotyped as it was ever to become, but while in some confessions of the period he was quite recognisable, his depiction in others was much more ambiguous. In the cases of three women, tried in 1661, Janet Paxton spoke of a man 'with grein cloaths' who gave her money which disappeared after his departure; Helen Casse described the Devil as a tall man in green clothes; and Jonet Watson attested that he appeared to her 'in the liknes of ane prettie boy, in grein clothes . . . and ane blak hatt upone his head'.[48] Cumulatively such references recall the anthropology of the good neighbours rather than Auld Nick.

Isobel Gowdie interspersed fairy and diabolical beliefs in her confessions of 1662 to a degree that is unrivalled in any other known witch trial. Though Isobel came from Auldearn in the North of Scotland, an area slow to experience the full force of the presbyterian system, her confession can surely be seen as indicative of the extent to which such phenomena had become assimilated into folk culture. It can certainly be taken as evidence of the tenacity of fairy traditions within Scotland, still clinging on despite almost a century of intensive persecution. Isobel affirmed she was a member of a coven consisting of thirteen people, each of whom had a named spirit to wait upon them. She spoke of riding 'wild-strawes' and 'corn-strawes' through the air with this coterie of witches, shooting elf-arrowheads at those the Devil had instructed them to harm. The production of these missiles seems to have been a combined effort between the Devil, who shaped them in his hand, and the elf-boys, who trimmed them with a sharp object, like a packing needle. Isobel's descriptions of coven meetings allude to a feeling of festivity. She told her inquisitors that a woman, Jean Martin, named 'Maiden' by the Devil, was so called because the 'Divill always takis the Maiden in his hand nixhim, quhan we daunce Gillatrypes'. This piece, 'Gillatrypes', was the same as that played by Gellie Duncan when she led the diabolical procession into North Berwick kirk in 1589. King James, 'in a wonderfull admiration . . . in respect of the strangeness of these matters', was so fascinated that he had her play it for him. Four years later three women from Elgin 'confessit thame to bein ane dance callit gillatrype singing a foull hieland sang'.[49] There is nothing quite like the disapproval of the righteous when it comes to popularising a tune. When Isobel met the queen and king of fairy inside the Downie Hills, they treated her to a feast of meat. While in this case the fairies and the Devil co-operated, Jonet Morison of Bute, tried in the same year, gave evidence indicating the Devil could, on occasion, work in opposition to the fairy folk by disclosing their secret activities to the witch: 'the devill told her that it was the fayries that took John Glas child's lyfe'.[50]

The notorious and repugnant case of Major Weir and his sister Jean

(1670) involved accusations of incest, sorcery and witchcraft. The unfortunate Jean testified that a strange visitor, a 'tall woman', who carried one child on her back with two at her feet, asked her if she would speak on her behalf to the 'queen of ferrie, meaning the devell', a completely explicit identification. This encounter, which took place at a school in Dalkeith where Jean was a teacher, was promptly followed by another the following day when a 'little woman' came to her house who gave her 'the root of some herb or tree' that would enable her to do whatever she desired. The stranger placed a cloth on the floor near the door and instructed Jean to put her foot on the cloth and her hand upon the crown of her head and repeat three times 'All my cross and trubles goe to the door with thee'. Before the mysterious visitant left, Jean gave her all the silver she had and some meal. When Jean sat down to spin she discovered that she had acquired an extraordinary ability for the craft and had soon spun much more yarn than was humanly possible. She claimed, however, that she was not especially pleased with her new-found talent; rather she was quite perplexed, for she took it as a sign that she had renounced her baptism.[51]

Descriptions of Scottish sabbats and encounters with the fairies frequently portray an image of revelry and general 'disorder'. Whereas continental descriptions of sabbat gatherings are often filled with horrific details of infant sacrifice, cannibalism, wild sexual orgies, and formal worship of the Devil, the Scottish meetings are more like a social gathering for eating, drinking and dancing. Ironically, they reflect the pleasures in life of which the Scottish peasantry were steadily being deprived through government legislation.[52]

The intermingling of fairies and witches is also found in belief traditions about the goddess, clearly derived from the world of learning. William Hay, who lectured on marriage in 1564, counselled:

> there are certain women who do say that they have dealings with Diana the queen of the fairies. There are others who say that the fairies are demons, and deny having any dealings with them, and say that they hold meetings with a countless multitude of simple women whom they call in our tongue 'celly vichtys' [seely wichts].

James VI was of the opinion that the court of the goddess Diana was composed of fairies:

> That fourth kinde of spirites, which by the Gentiles was called Diana, and her wandring court, and amongst us was called the Phairie . . . or

our good neighboures, was one of the sortes of illusiones that was rifest in the time of Papistrie.[53]

Three centuries later, Walter Scott similarly made the connection between the goddess of the witches and the queen of fairies:

> Like Diana, who in one capacity was denominated Hecate, the Fairy Queen is identified in popular tradition with the Gyre-Carline, Gay Carline, or mother witch, of the Scottish peasantry ... She is sometimes termed Nicneven.

Here Scott has added another dimension, the gyre carline. 'Gyrekarling' has been claimed as an Orkney term for a female giant, derived from Old Norse *gygr* (ogress) and *kerling* (old woman). The derivation is acceptable but, whatever its origin, the appellation was well-known throughout the Lowlands and the giantess was the subject of a medieval poem of the same name.[54]

Carlo Ginzburg has asserted that the Scottish fairy queen corresponds to the European nocturnal goddess. Many of the key motifs are unequivocally compatible, such as women (and at least in Scotland, men) who testified to night-time excursions, following the goddess, or, in Scotland, the fairy queen, and travelling great distances through the air, sometimes on the backs of animals, sometimes by other means. They obeyed the orders of the goddess and generally met her on particular nights. She appears under various names according to region. Diana, Herodias, Oriente, Richella, the 'good mistress', Habonde, Matres, are but a few examples. Titles given to her supernatural or mortal followers are equally numerous, 'women of the good game', 'the game of the good society', the *bonae res* (good things), *bonnes dames* (good women), *bona gens* (good people), 'women from outside', and so on. Ginzburg demonstrates how the folkloric figure of the goddess became connected with witchcraft and was demonised alongside those who adhered to her, but he is not alone. A strong case has also been established for the attempted demonisation of the Sicilian fairy cult, the *donas de fuera*, in the inquisitorial records. In such attributions learned intervention is clearly to be detected since it is extremely unlikely that Scotland harboured any folk memories of the likes of Diana or her cohorts. More convincing parallels to the Scottish situation are perhaps to be discerned in the rich researches of Éva Pócs on fairies and witches in Central and Southeast Europe.[55]

Motifs in Common

In 1659 Andrew Hay of Craignethan, Lanarkshire recorded in his diary a conversation over dinner with a minister in Skirling, Peeblesshire:

> we were also informed that Jon Cleghorn, Kirklawhill, did one dark nyt see a good many men and women dancing, and with a great lyt wt them, which imeditlie disappeared, and which he sayes were witches.[56]

This description, notwithstanding Cleghorn's interpretation of what he had seen, is remarkably close to accounts of interludes with the fairies. What such narratives have in common are shared motifs.

There are several motifs familiar to both the fairy and the witch. The power to shape-shift or render oneself invisible; travelling through the air in a whirlwind or on straws or stalks; stealing food or taking the substance from foodstuffs; turning milk or butter bad and destroying crops; abducting children, sometimes replacing them with one of their own, or leaving a stock; injuring horses and cattle by shooting them with elf-shot and witch-shot. The time of day or year, such as noon or midnight, May-eve, Midsummer-eve, Halloween, is when they are at their most active. Particular locations are associated with them; hills, wells, and hawthorn trees are all common haunts. The circular impressions found in grass, often called fairy rings, are also associated with marks left by dancing witches. Both enjoy making music, dancing and feasting. Both have a fondness for indulging in houghmagandie, fairies preferring to take a mortal lover while witches endure sex with the Devil. Special skills, such as those associated with medicine, music, and second sight, are attributed to fairies and witches, though often it is the fairy who is thought to bestow these gifts on the witch. Paralysis, problems in childbirth, or sudden death, are frequently blamed on their intervention.

A great number of fairy and witch narratives stress the significance of gender. It is noteworthy that humans who become involved with the fairies often rely upon a go-between of the opposite sex for their contact with Fairyland. Fairies and the dead share an equally close relationship, the difference being that, unlike the dead, the fairies had never been human. Indeed fairies are often seen to act as intermediaries between the living and the dead, as in the cases of Bessie Dunlop and Alison Peirson who encountered the ghosts of people they had once known. In this context the fairy association with hawthorn is intriguing because the tree or bush was often thought to smell of death. It was through such fairy contact with the world of the dead that both women, neither of whom were previously aware of any unique poweres or gifts, obtained their occult knowledge. A strong distinction between witches and fairies was that the former were believed to be mortals whose power derived from a connection with a supernatural agency, but they themselves never became supernatural creatures. The witch was generally a known member of a community, while the fairy was a stranger from 'another country'.

It has been observed that 'folklore was picked over, elaborated, polished up and used for specific purposes in theological politics'. The result was the polarisation and secularisation of supernatural traditions.[57] The Scottish experience reveals that folklore was politically and culturally manipulated not only by the Church but also by the State. James VI contributed to the international debate on the subject of witchcraft with the publication of *Daemonologie*. He also left an indelible mark on the way in which the witch-hunts would unfold in Scotland. There was no doubt in the mind of the king that the phenomenon of fairies was little more than an illusion created by Satan: 'the devil illuded the senses of sundry simple creatures, in making them beleeve that they saw and harde such thinges as were nothing so indeed.'[58] The redefinition of fairies as demonically inspired hallucinations, as actual agents of the Devil's work, ensured that all who believed in them were potentially in danger of their lives.

The impact of the assault on folk culture was, however, less striking than it might at first appear. The gap between elite and folk concepts of the nature of reality undoubtedly widened in this period, and the consequent repercussions on everyday life and activity were felt at all levels of society. But folk culture is the product of collective *mentalité*. Though attitudes might change, mindsets remained. The reformers may have tried to depreciate fairy belief and suppress folk culture, but they could not destroy it. Beneath the 'thin diabolical crust' that covers the tortured voices of accused witches, is confirmation of the tenacity and endurance of fairy belief.

Notes

1 *Minstrelsy*, vol. 2, 337.
2 *The Records of the Synod of Lothian and Tweeddale 1589–1596, 1640–1649* ed. James Kirk *Stair Society* (Edinburgh 1977), 27.

3 T. Edward Milliner, *The Decline of Popular Festivals in Pre-Reformation Scotland* M. A., (University of Guelph 1991), 49–67.
4 Edward J. Cowan, 'The political ideas of a covenanting leader: Archibald Campbell, marquis of Argyll 1607–1661', in *Scots and Britons. Scottish Political Thought and the Union of 1603* ed. Roger A. Mason (Cambridge 1994), 258–9.
5 Standard works that may be safely recommended are Gordon Donaldson, *The Scottish Reformation* (Cambridge 1960), Michael Lynch, *Edinburgh and the Reformation* (Edinburgh 1981) and Ian B. Cowan, *The Scottish Reformation Church and Society in Sixteenth-century Scotland* (London 1982). See also Gordon Donaldson, *Scotland James V to James VII* (Edinburgh 1965) and Edward J. Cowan, *Montrose For Covenant and King* (London 1977).
6 Stern, *Die Ossianischen Heldenlieder*, trans. J. L. Robertson, *TGSI* vol. 22, 1897–8, 293; Edwin Muir, *Selected Poems* ed. T. S. Eliot (London 1965), 34.
7 Keith Thomas, *Religion and the Decline of Magic* (1971; Harmondsworth 1991), 304, 331; Robert Scribner, *Popular Culture and Popular Movements in Reformation Germany* (London 1987), 15.
8 Robert Scribner, 'The Reformation, Popular Magic, and the 'Disenchantment of the World', *Journal of Interdisciplinary History* 23 (Winter 1993) 477.
9 J. H. Murray, ed., *The Complaynt of Scotland* (1549; Early English Text Society 1872), 64; For this and what follows see Edward J. Cowan, 'Calvinism and the Survival of Folk or 'Deil stick da minister'', in *The People's Past* (Edinburgh 1980), 30–53.
10 David Calderwood, *History of the Kirk of Scotland*, ed., T. Thomson 6 vols. (Edinburgh 1842–9), vol. 1, 142.
11 Scribner, 'The Reformation, Popular Magic, and the 'Disenchantment of the World'', 485–7.
12 Harry Girvetz, George Geiger, Harold Hantz and Bertram Morris, *Science, Folklore, and Philosophy* (New York 1966), 163; George Sinclair, *Satan's Invisible World Discovered* (1685; rep. Edinburgh 1871), Preface.
13 Bennett, *Traditions of Belief*, 157–62.
14 Bennett, *Traditions of Belief*, 159; Ludwig Lavater, *Of Ghosts and Spirites Walking by Nyghte* (London 1572), Author's Epistle.
15 *Daemonologie*, 66.
16 Ginzburg, *Ecstasies*, 154; Ginzburg, *The Night Battles*, 28–32.
17 Robin Briggs, *Witches and Neighbours* (London 1996), 8.
18 Larner, *Enemies of God*, 152.
19 Ginzburg, *Ecstasies*, 97.
20 Larner, *Enemies of God*, 1; *Daemonologie*, 81; Briggs, *Witches and Neighbours*, 7.
21 George F. Black, *A Calendar of Cases of Witchcraft in Scotland 1510–1727* (1938; New York 1971), 9–12; Larner, *Enemies of God*, 9.
22 Brian P. Levack, *The Witch-Hunt in Early Modern Europe* (London 1987), 167.
23 Chambers, *Domestic Annals* vol. 2, 395; Larner, *Enemies of God*, 76–7.

24 Briggs, *Witches and Neighbours*, 8; Larner, *Witchcraft and Religion*, 27–8.
25 This does not imply that we accept all the theories on this topic advanced by certain recent feminist writers. See for example Anne Llewellyn Barstow, *Witchcraze: A New History of the European Witch Hunts* (San Francisco 1994).
26 Larner, *Enemies of God*, 55–56. For more on the Kirk Session see Anne Gordon, *Candie for the Foundling* (Edinburgh 1992).
27 Levack, *The Witch-Hunt in Early Modern Europe*, 216.
28 Stuart Clark, 'King James's *Daemonologie*: Witchcraft and kingship', in *The Damned Art: Essays in the Literature of Witchcraft* (London 1977), 157.
29 Edward J. Cowan, 'The Darker Version of the Scottish Renaissance: the Devil and Francis Stewart', in *The Renaissance and Reformation in Scotland* eds., Ian B. Cowan and Duncan Shaw (Edinburgh 1983), 125–40; E. William Monter, 'Scandinavian Witchcraft in Anglo-American Perspective', in *Early Modern European Witchcraft: Centres and Peripheries* eds., Bengt Ankarloo and Gustav Henningsen (Oxford 1993), 431. P. G. Maxwell-Stuart, 'The fear of the King is death: James VI and the witches of East Lothian', in *Fear in early modern society* eds. William G. Naphy and Penny Roberts (Manchester 1997), 209–25 has questioned some widely held assumptions about the case or cases. His book, *Satan's Conspiracy* (East Linton 2001), has just been published. See too Jenny Wormald, "Tis true I am a Cradle King': the View from the Throne' in *The Reign of James VI* eds. Julian Goodare and Michael Lynch (East Linton 2000), 241–56.
30 Larner, *Witchcraft and Religion*, 9.
31 *Newes From Scotland*, 1591 (London 1924), 15, and frontispiece; Larner, *Witchcraft and Religion*, 15.
32 Clark, 'Witchcraft and kingship', 156–7.
33 *Daemonologie*, xi-xii; Clark, 'Witchcraft and kingship', 156.
34 Larner, *Enemies of God*, 31.
35 Clark, 'Witchcraft and kingship', 161–164.
36 *Daemonologie*, 81.
37 *Daemonologie*, 65, 74–7.
38 *Minstrelsy*, vol. 2, 337; MacCulloch, 'The Mingling of Fairy and Witch Beliefs', 230–1; On the witches' Sabbat see Ginzburg, *Ecstasies*, 63–80, 97.
39 Trial of Jonet Boyman, 1572, NAS, JC/26/1/67.
40 Trial of Bessie Dunlop, Pitcairn vol. 1, 51–3, 56; Athol Gow, 'Prophetic Belief in Early Modern Scotland, 1560–1700', M. A. (University of Guelph, 1989), 186.
41 See Chapter 6.
42 Trial of Alison Peirson, Pitcairn vol. 1, 162–163. On Adamson and Sempill's poem see pp 165–8 below; Trial of John Stewart, *Trial . . . Irvine*, 9, and *Letters*, 134–5; Trial of Steven Maltman, May 1626. SCA, CH2/1121/1, April 1628 CH2/722/5. The latter indicates that fairies feared drawn swords. For more on this case, and the important distinction between witchcraft and

The Rise of the Demonic

charming, see the forthcoming article by Joyce Miller in *The Scottish Witch-Hunt in Context* ed. Julian Goodare (Manchester 2001).

43 Trial of Alexander Drummond, 1629. From *Books of Adjournal* and extracted in A. G. Reid *The Annals of Auchterarder and Memorials of Strathearn* (Perth 1989), 70.

44 *Minstrelsy*, vol. 2, 349.

45 Trial of Agnes Sampson, 27 Jan. 1590–1. Pitcairn vol. 1, 230–41; Trial of Euphemia Makcalzane, Pitcairn vol. 1, 254; McNeill, *Silver Bough*, vol. 2, 94–101; *Records of the Synod of Lothian and Tweeddale*, 189.

46 Ginzburg, *Ecstasies*, 97; Trial of Andro Man, *Miscellany*, vol. 1, part 3, 120–121.

47 Trial of Beigis Tod, 27 May 1608. Pitcairn vol. 2, 542–4; Jakob Jakobsen, *An Etymological Dictionary of the Norn Language in Shetland* 2 vols (1928; Lerwick 1985), *loc. cit.*; Trial of Katherine Jonesdochter, *Court Book of Shetland*, 38–9; Trial of Elspeth Reoch, *Maitland*, 114.

48 Trial of Janet Paxton or Paiston, July 1661, NAS, JC/26/27/9; Trial of Helen Casse, 20 Aug. 1661, NAS, JC/26/27/1; Trial of Jonet Watson, 16 June 1661. Pitcairn vol. 3, 601, and NAS, JC/26/27/1. See also Larner, *Enemies of God*, 147.

49 Trial of Isobel Gowdie, Pitcairn vol. 3, 606–607; Cowan, 'Calvinism and the Survival of Folk', 42.

50 Trial of Elspeth Reoch, *Maitland*, 114. In Orkney and Shetland it was believed the trows were most dangerous at Yule. See Saxby; Marwick; Trial of Jonet Morison of Bute, 18 January 1662. *Highland Papers*, 23.

51 Trial of Jean Weir, NAS, JC/2/13. Excerpts from this case can also be found in Robert Law's *Memorialls; or, the memorable things that fell out within this island of Brittain from 1638 to 1684*, ed. Charles Kirkpatrick Sharpe (Edinburgh 1818), 27, and *Minstrelsy*, vol. 2, 338–9.

52 Larner, *Enemies of God*, 200.

53 *William Hay's Lectures on Marriage*, 1564, ed., and trans. John C. Barry (Edinburgh 1967), 127; *Daemonologie*, 73–4.

54 *Minstrelsy*, vol. 2, 326; Marwick, *The Folklore of Orkney and Shetland*, 32; See pp 153 below.

55 Ginzburg, *Ecstasies*, 89–121; MacCulloch, 'The Mingling of Fairy and Witch Beliefs', 230; Gustav Henningsen, "The Ladies from Outside': An Archaic Pattern of the Witches' Sabbath', in *Early Modern European Witchcraft: Centres and Peripheries*, 191–215; Éva Pócs, 'Fairies and Witches at the Boundary of South-Eastern and Central Europe', *FF Communications* No. 243 (Helsinki 1989) and *Between the Living and the Dead* (Budapest 1999).

56 A. G. Reid, ed., *The Diary of Andrew Hay of Craignethan, 1659–1660* (Edinburgh n. d.), 158.

57 Bennett, *Traditions of Belief*, 167.

58 *Daemonologie*, 74.

CHAPTER FIVE

Writing the Fairies

> Though the Scottish Muse has loved reality, sometimes to maudlin affection for the commonplace, she has loved not less the airier pleasure to be found in the confusion of the senses, in the fun of things thrown topsyturvy, in the horns of elfland and the voices of the mountains.
>
> Gregory Smith[1]

Scottish fairies are first found in medieval poetry. They were fictionalised from the beginning, fairies and poetry enjoying a symbiotic relationship personified (in Scottish terms) by Fairyland's most famous visitor, Thomas Rhymer, who was regarded down to the time of Walter Scott as the father of Scottish poesy. Poetry provided a sort of lens through which people viewed the elfin kingdom and its inhabitants, a beguilingly wondrous, if dangerous, place which exercised its fascination upon poets and people alike. The makars, steeped in the classics as they were, provided a learned context for much of the folk tradition, self-consciously linking native supernatural phenomena to those of Greece and Rome. Societal concerns were, of course, reflected in literature. One development that can be convincingly demonstrated is the demonisation of fairy belief during the course of the sixteenth century.

True Thomas

The Romance and Prophecies of Thomas of Erceldoune[2] survives in at least five English manuscripts, the earliest dated to c. 1440. It begins, conventionally enough, on a beautiful May morning alive with birdsong. It appears to be Thomas himself who tells the story in the first person singular, though he regularly moves into the third person. While reclining beneath a tree on Huntly Banks, he beheld a fair lady riding over the lea, a spectacle of such stunning beauty that, were he spared until Doomsday, he could never adequately describe it, a disclaimer which, nonetheless, does not prevent him from valiantly making the attempt.

She sang and blew on her hunting horn from time to time, mounted upon her bejewelled and ornately decorated steed, an image which should have sounded alarm bells in the beholder, for in medieval symbology a bridled horse signified female domination. Seven hounds accompanied her. Well and truly smitten, or more accurately glamoured, Thomas made haste to intercept her at the Eildon Tree and knelt to greet this dazzling figure whom he could only assume to be Mary Queen of Heaven. Swiftly disabused of this notion – rather she was 'of ane other countree' – his immediate follow-up was to request sex. Such an act, she protested, would ruin her beauty but he promised that in return he would live with her forever be it in Heaven or Hell. Lust knows few limits and he lay with her seven times under the Eildon Tree, his willing partner coquettishly remarking that he obviously enjoyed their love-making since it had lasted all day long: 'I pray thee, Thomas, let me be!'

But her prediction had come true for she proved a 'dullfull syghte', hair dishevelled, gray eyes tearful, clothing awry, one leg black the other gray, and 'her body blue as beaten lead'. She advised her vigorous lover to bid farewell to the sun and the leaves on the trees for he must accompany her for twelve months 'and Middle Earth sall thou none see'. For his part he believed he deserved whatever was coming to him:

> She ledde hym in at Eildon Hill,
> Undir-nethe a derne [secret] lee,
> Whare it was dirke als mydnyght myrke,
> And ever the water till his knee.

For three days he heard the 'swoghynge' or the booming of the waves. Ever practical, Thomas complained that he was dying for lack of food. To make matters worse, and temptation the greater, they had just entered a lush garden of pears, apples, damsons, figs and grapes where nightingales, parrots and thrushes abounded. As the salivating Thomas reached for the fruit, he was informed it was forbidden; to consume it was to consign himself to Hell for eternity.

The queen bade him instead lay his head on her knee and she revealed to him the paths of fate that awaited all humankind. One road led to Heaven, another to Paradise, yet another to a place where sinful souls suffered (Purgatory was probably intended) and the last to Hell. This is all a little confusing since Heaven and Paradise are different places. The latter probably represented her own country although she did not make that specific identification. Finally she showed him a splendid castle wherein resided her husband 'the king of this country' who, she confided, not unreasonably, would be violently upset to learn of her recent liaison. She therefore cautioned Thomas to answer only to her and to act normally in the banqueting hall where the king was served by thirty-three knights. He could only stare and marvel as the lady regained her looks and her composure; he was mystified. Why had she blamed him for her previous disorderly appearance? She avoided answering but divulged that had she remained as she was she would have invited an immediate despatch to Hell, an ever-threatening presence in this poem:

> My lorde is so fers and fell,
> That is king of this contre,
> And fulle sone he wolde have the smell,
> Of the defaute I did with thee.

They entered the stately hall to be greeted by curtsying ladies, the music of harps, fiddles and lutes 'and all manere of mynstralsye', a massive feast of venison; knights danced; there was 'revelle, gamene and playe'. Thomas the hedonist happily participated in the merrymaking until the queen suddenly told him it was time to return to the Eildon Tree. A residence of what seemed like three days turned out to have been seven years. Furthermore 'the foul fiend of hell' would imminently descend upon the revellers to claim his fee, selecting someone from the court, and since Thomas was such a fine specimen he would almost certainly be taken.

Back in Middle Earth Thomas asked for a token by which he might remember his lover. She offered the choice of harp or carp, music or speech and, memorably, he chose: 'harping keep I none, for tongue is chief of minstrelsy'. He was assured that whether indulging in prophecy or in the telling of tales he would never lie. The word was paramount, and for the rest of his life the word was with Thomas.

The queen was anxious to be on her way – 'Fare weel Thomas, withowttyne gyle/I may no lengare dwell with thee' – but he besought her to tell him of one more 'ferly' or wonder. She responded by predicting the downfall of the Balliol family, the arch-enemies of Robert Bruce. John Balliol was selected as King of Scots by Edward I of England in 1292, reigning in person until 1295 when he was deposed by his own subjects before being forced to surrender his kingship to Edward. In the eyes of many King John remained the legitimate monarch of Scotland until his death twenty years later, while his son, also Edward, was to lead armies into Scotland in the mid-fourteenth century, seeking restitution:

> Thomas, harken what I say:
> When a tree root is dead,
> The leaves fade then and wither away;
> And fruit it bears none, white or red.
> Of the Balliols' blood so shall it fall:
> It shall be like a rotten tree.

Prescience can be painful. Throughout the remainder of the poem Thomas was given a vision of the calamities that were to befall Scotland roughly from the Battle of Falkirk (1298), where Wallace suffered defeat, through Bannockburn and the death of Bruce, the invasions of Edward Balliol, the return of David II from France and his disastrous capture at Neville's Cross in 1346, the succession of the Stewarts in 1371, to the Battle of Otterburn in 1388, the latest datable event to be mentioned and one which thus provides a useful *terminus a quo* for the composition of the poem. Each time the queen expressed a wish to depart, Thomas demanded another chunk of prophecy and it did not make for pleasant listening. His acquisition of this painful knowledge was a kind of curse, the bane of visionaries from the dawn of time – 'This world, Thomas, truly to tell/ Is nought but wondering and woe'. There was no comfort in the future:

> Then Thomas a sorry man was he,
> The tears ran out of his een gray:
> Lufly lady, yet thou tell me,
> If we shall part forever and ay?

For once there was reassurance. One day, she said, when Thomas was dwelling at Ercildune, he should make his way to Huntly Banks and there, if all went well, she would await him. With that she gave a final blow on her horn, wheeled round on her magnificent horse and, leaving Thomas at the Eildon Tree, rode off to Helmsdale in Sutherland which, from the perspective of someone in Earlston, in Lauderdale, was just about as far away from anywhere as it was possible to go.

There is much that is noteworthy in this remarkable poem. One version is prefaced by a prologue, presumably a later addition, which twice assures the listener or reader that Jesus Christ is committed to the salvation of the English who obviously have nothing to fear from the prophecies. All versions begin with a variant of 'As I went . . .', implying that the piece was composed by Thomas himself. As early as the mid-fourteenth century it was believed that he was the author of the *Romance of Sir Tristrem*, the story of Tristan and Iseult, a view shared by Scott and one that is still not entirely discounted. Poetry and truth-telling are, after all, soulmates. The remarkable powers which Thomas acquired in 'another country' serve to authenticate his narrative. The association between sexual experience and the obtaining of knowledge, together with the mention of forbidden fruit, all recall the Garden of Eden. Indeed the fair lady whom the narrator mistakes for Mary is a veritable Eve. But perhaps what is most remarkable is that the queen and the king of the poem are not actually stated to be the rulers of Elfland although that is clearly where they reside, in a subterranean paradise which can be reached only with the greatest difficulty, a place of pleasure and enchantment which Thomas is extremely reluctant to leave. Threatened by the foul fiend, in a version of what would later be known as the 'teind to hell' though not explicitly described as such, he is forced to flee. There is an element of menace in the king's potentially violent response to his queen's adultery should he learn of it, though it seems that less blame attaches to Thomas than to the lady, a highly sensual creature reminiscent of the heroine of 'Sir Gawain and the Green Knight' who shockingly inverts the conventions of courtly love by aggressively pursuing her pursuer, or of the determined Janet in 'Tam Lin'. The fairy queen was undoubtedly the subject of medieval male sexual fantasy and men, whatever the century in which they live, seldom pause to count the cost in pursuit of immediate gratification. Sex alone, however, did not result in Thomas's new-found skills; a residence in Fairyland was also necessary. The fascination of the story for successive generations was wondrously enhanced by the widespread acknowledgement that the visitant was a man who actually lived.

'Thomas Rhymour of Ercildune' witnessed a charter in the earlier thirteenth century by which one Petrus de Haga agreed to pay half a stone of wax per annum to the abbot of Melrose. That Rhymour was dead by 1294 is suggested by a charter of that year in which his son and heir conveyed his lands in Earlston to the hospital at Soutra, in the Lammermuir hills. One or other of these Thomases, though we know not which, has always been regarded as the convenient peg on which to hang the prophecies, and so far there are no better candidates. Either way his *floruit* can be placed, at least partially, in the late thirteenth century, in which period tradition also situates him. Neatly enough the prophecies in *The Romance* seem also to be located in the early 1290s during the kingship of King John. The remains of Rhymer's Tower can be seen at Earlston, a village which still clusters on the banks of the Leader Water, while a modern stone at the local kirk pronounces that

'Auld Rymers race/Lies in this place'. Hector Boece in his *Historia* (1527) reported, most likely erroneously, that Thomas's surname was Learmont, and from him that family has long claimed descent, notably one of its luminaries, the Russian poet Mikhail Yuriyevich Lermontov (1814–41), born in Moscow to Scottish parents.

There is no reason to doubt that True Thomas enjoyed a reputation for prophecy in his own lifetime. If the dating and ruling theories about the provenance of Harleian Manuscript 2253 are correct, an English prophecy composed on the eve of the Battle of Bannockburn was already attempting to exploit Thomas's reputation for prognostication against the Scots themselves, much as the prophecies of Nostradamus were used for propaganda purposes by both sides in World War II. All vaticination is obscure and open to rival interpretation. Harleian relates that the Countess of Dunbar asked Thomas when the Scottish war would end, and his reply suggested that it would last forever since the conditions for termination seemed so unlikely and so unattainable:

> When people have made a king of a capped man:
> When another man's thing is dearer to one than his own;
> When London is Forest and Forest is field;
> When hares litter on the hearth-stone:
> When Wit and Will war together:
> When people make stables of churches, and set castles with styes;
> When Roxburgh is no burgh, and market is at Forwylee;
> When the old is gone and the new is come that is worth nought;
> When Bannockburn is dunged with dead men;
> When people lead men in ropes to buy and to sell;
> When a quarter of indifferent wheat is exchanged for a colt of
>   10 merks;
> When pride rides on horseback, and peace is put in prison;
> When a Scot cannot hide like a hare in a form that the English shall
>   not find him;
> When right and wrong assent together;
> When lads marry ladies;
> When Scots flee so fast, that for want of ships, they drown
>   themselves.
> When shall this be? Neither in thy time nor in mine;
> But shall come and go within twenty winters and one.[3]

Thomas Gray, who completed his *Scalacronica* in 1355 while a captive in Edinburgh Castle, referred to 'Thomas Erceldoune whose words were spoke in figure, as were the prophecies of Merlin'. John Barbour, writing his great poem in the 1370s, asserted that Thomas had foretold that Robert Bruce would be king. He inserted a lengthy discourse on prophecy, a phenomenon which could be accessed, he disclosed, through the medium of either astrology or necromancy, the latter involving, among other things, the conjuring of spirits. 'Man is always in fear of things that he has heard tell of', he wrote, 'and especially of things to come, until he knows the certainty of the outcome'.[4] Andrew Wyntoun (c.1420) had Thomas predict the Battle of Culblean (1335) in which the patriots defeated the supporters of Balliol – 'bot, how he wyst it, was ferly [wondrous]'.[5] Walter Bower's *Scotichronicon*, written in the 1440s, related the well-known story, as had John of Fordun in the 1360s, of how Thomas, *vates ruralis*, country prophet, had predicted the death of Alexander III on that fateful March night of 1286. When the Earl of March, 'half-jesting as usual', asked what the morrow would bring, Thomas responded:

> Alas for tomorrow, a day of calamity and misery! because before the stroke of twelve a strong wind will be heard in Scotland the like of which has not been known since times long ago. Indeed its blast will dumbfound the nations and render senseless those who hear it; it will humble what is lofty and raze what is unbending to the ground.

Sure enough, at noon the next day news came of the tragedy, and so the earl and his household 'discovered by experience that the prophecies of Thomas were to become all too credible'.[6]

Blind Harry in his poem *Wallace* preserved a somewhat convoluted anecdote about how Thomas at Fail, a Trinitarian monastery near Ayr, had a sense that Wallace, who had been taken for dead, was, in fact, alive. He then prophesied:

> Forsuth, or [before] he deceas,
> Mony thousand in feild sall mak thar end.
> Off this regioune he sall the Sothroun send;
> And Scotland thrise he sall bryng to the [peace],
> So gud off hand agayne sall nevir be kend.[7]

This was sufficient to convince some writers that Tammie and Willie were the best of friends. John Mair had the same story of Thomas *Rhythmificator* presaging the death of Alexander III, adding that he (Mair) himself laughed at such tales: 'For that such persons foretold things purely contingent before they came to pass I cannot admit; and if only they use a sufficient obscurity of language, the uninstructed vulgar will twist a meaning out of it somehow in the direction that best pleases them'.[8]

John Bellenden, who translated Boece's *History* into Scots, betrayed a slight scepticism when he acknowledged that Thomas was greatly admired by the people at large and 'schew sindry thingis as they fell; howbeit thai wer ay hyd under obscure wourdis'. It was, of course, that very obscurity which explains the extraordinary shelf life which these prophecies enjoyed. The prophetic material which the queen communicated to Thomas resurfaced again and again, from generation to generation, each of which did not scruple to add to the canon, as and when they saw fit, so that a substantial bedrock of Rhymer material, as revealed in the romance, can be detected in *The Whole Prophecies of Scotland, England, France, Ireland and Denmark* which was published by royal command in 1603 to prove that James's accession to the English throne had long been anticipated.

During the sixteenth century, prophecy, particularly of the political variety, greatly troubled the authorities who did their utmost to discourage it. The Prophecies of Merlin which predicted that one day a second Arthur would rule over the British Isles and Ireland proved particularly popular. Robert Bruce had tried to manipulate the Arthurian material in support of his cause. Both Henry VII of England and James IV of Scotland named their eldest sons Arthur in the hope of thereby hastening vaticinatory fulfilment. Long after 1603 the *Whole Prophecies* remained highly popular, reappearing in whole or in part as chapbooks and proving highly inspirational to such groups as the Jacobites. So prevalent was this material that a stern Lord Hailes in 1773 thought it worth his while to offer a reasoned rebuttal:

> . . . let it be considered that the name of Thomas the Rhymer is not forgotten in Scotland, nor his authority altogether slighted, even at this day. Within the memory of man, his prophecies, and the prophecies of other Scotch soothsayers, have not only been reprinted, but have been consulted with a weak, if not criminal curiosity. I mention no particulars: for I hold it ungenerous to reproach men with weaknesses of which they themselves are ashamed. The same superstitious credulity might again spring up. I flatter myself that my attempts to eradicate it will not prove altogether vain.[9]

Of course he *did* flatter himself because the more Thomas's notoriety was known, so the number of prophecies attached to his name increased, a process that probably began in his lifetime. The folk at large believed that any unusual event which impacted nationally or locally, or impinged upon their own domestic existence, must have been foretold. Past prophecy served to legitimise present calamities, the unusual, the exotic, or the incomprehensible: even, on occasion, what might appear to outsiders as the unutterably mundane.

The individual who, incomparably, did most to circulate Rhymerian lore was, predictably enough, Sir Walter Scott through the publication of *Minstrelsy* and his personal obsession with recreating an antique landscape. He it was who purchased Dick's Cleugh as an addition to his Abbotsford estate, promptly renaming it Rhymer's Glen and shifting Huntly Banks from the Eildon Tree to the same locality. As late as 1875 various old worthies were trotted out to verify relevant locations to the satisfaction of James Murray, editor of the *Romance and Prophecies*. It is noteworthy that such informants were always 'old'; age authenticated while young people who could well have been in receipt of oral tradition were never consulted, nor were women who were frequently depended upon for ballad transmission but who were apparently considered less reliable on matters of topography and local history. Andrew Currie of Darnick recalled, in 1839, his excitement at having witnessed the accomplishment of Thomasian prophecy: 'two young hares in a nettle bush in the fire place of Rhymer's Tower'.

But it was Scott and Scott alone who, in *Minstrelsy*, first recorded the tradition concerning Thomas's return to Fairyland. One night as the prophet and his friends were partying in Rhymer's Tower, word came that a hart and hind were slowly wandering along the village street. Thomas recognised the sign and followed the deer into the forest, whence he never returned. 'According to the popular belief, he still "drees his weird" in Fairy Land, and is one day expected to revisit earth'. One venerable worthy, Rob Messer, was 85 when he told Andrew Currie his version of events: 'aw had it frae ma graanfaither, an nae doot he had it frae his fore-bears'. According to him, Thomas set off to visit Thirlestane Castle near Lauder bearing money for the local laird when he was set upon, robbed and murdered, his body being tossed into the floodwaters of the Leader which swept it to Berwick. So said his grandfather – 'an nae doot he had it handed doon . . . An that's likker-like than the Fairy story! Sae ye hae'd, as aw had it, frae thaim 'at was afore us'.[10] So far as Murray was concerned, the use of vernacular lent credibility and authenticity to the story almost in the way that earlier generations had revered Latin.

If to some he was Tammy-tell-the-truth, to others he was Thomas the Lyar. According to the chronicle tradition which dates to the fourteenth-century, the Earl of March used to treat the seer in a 'jocular' fashion. He is something of a comic figure in the *Romance and Prophecies* too. At some stage the embellishment was added that Thomas was a horse dealer to trade and that he protested to the fairy queen that the powers which she conferred on him would ruin his business! In 1598 Andro Man's dittay stated that the accused had been assured by the queen of fairy as a boy that he would know all things, would be able to cure all kinds of sickness and would be well looked after but 'wald seik thy meit or thow deit, as Thomas Rymour did', that is, he would be forced to beg his bread before he died. What, after all, shall it profit a man if he shall gain the whole world and lose his own soul? In acquiring the gift of truth, Thomas lost a part of his own small world since truth is precisely what the world at large does not want to hear.

Rather similar in tone though grander in its descriptions and more morally uplifting in the outcome is the lay of 'Sir Orfeo', which has been dated a little earlier than the 'Romance of Thomas'. The former is a tale of 'fairy' concerning Orfeo, whose skill at harping transported listeners to Paradise and engendered thoughts of eternity. He and his lovely wife Heurodis, both lived happily at Winchester, presiding over their kingdom until one day Heurodis fell asleep, in an orchard, under an ympe tree, one that had been grown from a cutting rather than from seed. She was visited by the king of Fairyland who then transported her to his realm, revealed a few of its mysteries, and returned her to Middle Earth, announcing that he would collect her the following day to live with him eternally. If she refused to comply, she would be torn apart, limb from limb, in which condition they would take her in any case. Despite Orfeo's best efforts she was duly taken away, whereafter he abandoned his kingdom, dressed as a beggar and, armed only with his harp, set off through the wilderness to search for his beloved. When the mood was on him, and the weather kind, he would harp for an audience of beasts and birds.

Sometimes he saw the fairy king hunting, at others fairy knights and ladies dancing. One day he encountered sixty ladies, 'not a man in all their band', out hawking. Among them was Heurodis and he decided to follow the troop through a rock and back to Fairyland. There on a bright sunlit plain he beheld a splendid castle of amazing height, whose walls of a hundred towers glittered like crystal. 'By every sign one might surmise/It was the court of Paradise'. Once inside he confronted 'a host of people, thither brought/As being dead though they were not':

> Some, though headless, stood erect,
> From some of them the arms were hacked,
> And some were pierced from front to back,
> And some lay bound and raging mad.
> And some on horse in armour sat,
> And some were choked while at their food,
> And some were drowning in a flood,
> And some were withered up by fire;
> Wives lay there in labour-bed,
> Some raving mad, and others dead.[11]

He also spied his wife who mercifully was still alive but once again asleep. When Orfeo played for the fairy court he enchanted the enchanters and he was asked to name his reward, which predictably was his lovely wife and, his earthly kingdom restored to him, they all lived happily ever after.

Eldritch Explorations

The words 'fairy' and 'elf' have been used interchangeably in Scotland. The earliest recorded usage of 'fairy' appears in an anonymous poem entitled 'King Berdok' written c. 1450; 'elf' is first noted in the poetry of Robert Henryson. Berdok belongs to the category of eldritch poems – comic, weird, fantastical and sometimes nonsensical – which often gain their effect through the juxtaposition of the real and the ridiculous. The word also connotes uncanny, elfish or otherworldly. William Dunbar wrote of Pluto, 'that elrick incubus, in cloke of grene', while Gavin Douglas evoked an owl's 'elrische skreik'. Eldritch poetry hardly constitutes the best evidence for those in pursuit of the fairies, but it is in such verse, appropriately enough, that the first references to fairies and elves occur.

It might be suspected that Berdock himself was a fairy since in summer he dwelt in a cabbage stalk, while he spent winter in a cockleshell. When he falls in love, it turns out that the object of his affections is the daughter of the fairy king who strongly disapproves of the courtship: 'The king of Fary hir fader then blew out, And socht Berdok all the land about'. To escape his wrath Berdok takes refuge in the fireplace of a kiln where he is besieged by the king of the Picts among others. He is eventually saved when Mercury turns him into a bracken bush which, when it sways in the wind, appears to his enemies to be a ghost. The poem ends with the reflection that 'though love be sweet, often it is full sour', a line, we may think, that must have been penned by a Scot, as indeed it was since the credit for scribing this depressing, if truistic and stereotypical sentiment is attributed, in this case, to the historian Hector Boece.

Other poems in the usually anonymous eldritch group are equally unhelpful in tracing fairy belief. 'Lichton's Dreme' opens by asking who can doubt that dreams are fantasy. All sorts of adventures befall the dreamer after he imagines that he has been captured by the king of fairy who binds him in a rope of sand in a delusory prison. 'Ane Little Interlude', otherwise known as 'The Maner of the Crying of the Play', contains a reference to a whirlwind, usually associated with fairies or witches, but otherwise it is about giants. Another giantess is celebrated in 'The Gyre-Carling' who survived on the flesh of christian men, evidently sound nourishment, for when she farted she deposited North Berwick Law on its present site. 'The king of Fary [then] come with elffis mony ane' to set a siege which succeeded in driving her abroad where she married Mohammed.[12] These unusual, not to say bizarre, poems are generally dated to the late fifteenth and early sixteenth centuries.

Robert Henryson tackled the perennial favourite, 'Orpheus and Eurydice', though in his version Orpheus did not succeed in bringing Eurydice back. In Scotland there was no point in a happy ending if a sad one was available. Henryson, who wrote in the late fifteenth century, adhered much more closely to the classical version of the tale. Eurydice went forth one May morning to 'a medow grene' to take the air and see the flowers bloom.

> A wicked herd-boy,
> quhen he saw this lady solitar,
> bairfut, with schankis [legs] quhyter than the snaw,
> preckit with lust, he thocht withoutin mair
> hir till oppress, and to his cave hir draw.

His quarry fled, but in so doing she stepped on a venomous serpent with dire results. When Orpheus questioned Eurydice's maidservant she replied, distraught, 'Erudices, your quene, Is with the phary tane befoir myne ene', subsequently reinforcing the point, 'the quene of fary clawcht [snatched] hir (up), and furth with hir cowth cary'. When Orpheus eventually penetrated to the very depths of the underworld, he found his beloved in a state of languor, Pluto reassuring him that 'thocht scho be lyk ane elf, Scho hes no causs to plenye [complain]', since she was just like everybody else confined down below, though he predicted that she would recover if she returned to her own home. His brilliant harping convinced her captors to let Eurydice go, on condition that Orpheus never looked back, but alas he did, and in Hell she remained.[13]

The first Scottish appearance of the term 'fairfolks' occurs in Gavin Douglas's translation of Virgil's *Aeneid* in 1513. The woods were for long occupied by 'nymphis and fawnys apon euery syde, Quhilk fairfolkis, or than elvys, clepyng we (which we call fairfolks and elves)'. He noted also that some stern critics disapproved of the content of Book VI of the *Aeneid*: 'Al is bot gaistis and elrich fantasyis/Of browneis and of bogillis ful this buke'; the latter line was famously to inspire Burns in composing 'Tam o Shanter'. Douglas went on to note that while such critics contrasted 'vayn superstitionys' with true belief, they clearly misunderstood Virgil who spoke of the universal beliefs and condition of humanity. An early reference to the brownie is found in the writings of historian and theologian John Mair. Commenting in his treatise *Expositio in Matthaeum* (1518) on his native region of East Lothian, he attested to the firm belief in brownies, stating, 'those fauns called *brobne* [brownies] can perform a multiplicity of tasks in the course of a single night'.[14]

Though the point cannot be made too dogmatically, William Dunbar tended to keep the worlds of fairy and diablerie separate. The abbot of Tongland, John Damian, experimenter in alchemy and flight, was of Satan's seed. Dunbar hated him because he received preferment over himself, a point explicitly made in 'Lucina schyning in silence of the nycht', but the poet had little to fear in the longer term:

> He sall ascend as ane horrible griphoun.
> Him meit sall in the air ane scho dragoun.
> Thir terribill monsturis sall togidder thirst,
> And in the cluddis get (beget) the Antechrist,
> Quhill all the air infect of thair poysoun.

Damian also had impending appointments with such luminaries of the nether world as Simon Magus, Mohammed, Merlin and a witch 'on a besum hame rydand/Off witches with ane windir [marvellous] garesoun', a line notable for containing the first Scottish reference to a witch on a broomstick. Mohammed also figures in 'Fasternis Evin in Hell' alongside the 'feindis fell', Belial and the Devil.

Dunbar uses the word 'fairy' in different senses. In the poem 'Full oft I muse and hes in thocht' it signifies illusion or enchantment:

> How ever this warld dois chynge and varie,
> Let us no moir in hart be sarie,
> Bot ay reddie and addrest
> To pas out of this fraudfull farie.
> For to be blyth me think it best.

It is more recognisable, to modern eyes, in the account of the parents of Tammie Norny[15] the court fool, whose father was a giant and whose mother was 'ane farie queyne/Gottin be sossery [sorcery]'. The poem 'This hinder nycht, halff sleeping as I lay' describes a dream sequence which could easily fit the fairy archetype, especially since the sleeper at first seems to welcome the vision, but then, having viewed it, his innate pessimism sobers him up and he wonders if it might be malevolent:

> Me thocht the lift all bricht with lampis lycht,
> And thairin enterrit many lustie wicht,
> Sum young, sum old, in sindry wyse arayit,
> Sum sang, sum danceit, on instrumentis sum playit,
> Sum maid disportis with hartis glaid and lycht.
>
> Thane thocht I thus: this is ane felloun [great] phary,
> Or ellis my witt rycht woundrouslie dois varie.
> This seimes to me ane guidlie companie,
> And gif it be ane feindlie fantasie,
> Defend me Ihesu and his moder Marie!

The sense of fairy as enchantment persists until, at the end of the poem, the somewhat subdued revellers, 'as ane fary', make a rush to the door.[16] On balance, given the volume of poetry which he produced, it must be concluded that Dunbar the Makar, while welcoming the artistic opportunities which the 'eldritch' afforded his poetic imagination, was not altogether charmed by the fairies.

It remains a matter of controversy whether the three female characters in his 'Tretis of the Tua Mariit Wemen and the Wedo' are indeed fairy women, as has been argued.[17] The poem was composed, before 1507, possibly for the court of James IV:

> Apon the Midsummer Ewin, mirriest of nichtis
> I muvit furth allane in meid [meadow] as midnicht wes past,

> Besyd ane gudlie grein garth [garden], full of gay flouris,
> Hegeit [hedged] of ane huge hicht with hawthorne treis,
> Quhairon ane bird, on ane bransche so birst out hir notis . . .

Attracted by the scene and the birdsong (probably that of a nightingale), the poet approaches, hiding himself under a hawthorn tree. In a green arbour are three gay ladies, sitting down to a fine feast, while engaged in animated conversation. The women are

> All grathit [adorned] in to garlandis of fresche gudlie flouris.
> So glitterit as the gold wer thair glorius gilt tressis,
> Quhill all the gressis did gleme of the glaid hewis.
> Kemmit [combed] war thair clier hair and curiouslie sched,
> Attour [over] thair schulderis doun schyre schyning full bricht,
> With curches [head-dresses] cassin thair abone of kirsp cleir and thin
> [delicate transparent fabric].
> Thair mantillis [mantles] grein war as the gres that grew in May
> sessoun . . .

There are many indications that what the narrator describes is more than just three upper-class Edinburgh ladies having a girls' night out. The audience would be aware that the time, midnight on Midsummer's Eve, was one when fairies could be expected to be abroad. The place, a holly and hawthorn grove, is a location commonly associated with fairy trysting sites. The attire of the women, who are all wearing green dresses and have their hair combed out and hanging down their backs, is unusual. Wearing the hair combed down was ordinarily the custom for unmarried women in fifteenth- and sixteenth-century Scotland, while married women generally wore their hair up or completely covered. Fashionable ladies would be unlikely to dress in this way. It is almost as if they are kitted out in fairy-like gear for one special night of the year. The bright, shining light which emanates from the ladies could possibly be interpreted as fairy light.[18] The narrator's retreat under the 'plet thorn', or tangled hawthorn, may have the counter-magical significance of protecting him from enchantment.

The date and the setting seem also to confer a measure of libidinous licence upon the ladies whose promiscuous talk over copious quantities of wine suggests yet another link with the fairies: 'syn [in time] thai spak more spedelie and spairit no matiris [no holds barred]'. Both of the younger women are unhappily married. One is saddled with an ancient husband who thoroughly disgusts her, 'ane wallidrag, ane worme, ane auld wobat carle', impotent, done and used up. The other is wedded to a rake, 'a hur [whore] maister . . . He has beyne lychour [lecher] so lang quhill lost is his natur, His lwme [tool] is vaxit larbar [enfeebled] and lyis in to swoune'. He swaggers around as the consummate ladies' man but in private he is always 'drup fundin'. Like her friend she advocates something like annual marriage to keep her satisfied. The widow is the ultimate dissembler, pretending love for one husband while taking a lover and acting the shrew with the second though keeping him sweet until she acquired his property. He too was a drone who was useless in bed; when he made love to her she would imagine another. Now mercifully a widow, she dresses in mourning as the grieving spouse though beneath her weeds she pampers and adorns her body, in preparation for the lovers that she takes as she pleases. Such is the legend of her life though, as she defiantly adds, it is not written in Latin; the vernacular is perfectly acceptable so far as the merry widow is concerned.

There is an element of inversion in all of this, of the carnivalesque, the women taking the opportunity to unburden their frustrations through the most efficacious mechanism known to humanity, namely conversation. They confirm contemporary male assumptions and suspicions about female sexual inexhaustibility, and the audience may harbour a notion that at dawn they all return to the tedium of everyday existence, having bluffed one another as they have fooled the eavesdropper. The poem fits well with the *querelle des femmes* tradition, which was essentially a debate as old as time itself – about the nature of women and wedlock. Although he was not discussing 'The Tua Mariit Wemen and the Wedo', the words of Mikhail Bakhtin are particularly apposite as a gloss on the poem:

> Womanhood is shown in contrast to the limitations of her partner; she is a foil to his avarice, jealousy, stupidity, hypocrisy, bigotry, sterile senility, false heroism and abstract idealism . . . She represents in person the undoing of all pretentiousness, of all that is finished, completed, and exhausted. She is the inexhaustible vessel of conception, which dooms all that is old and terminated.[19]

If such was Dunbar's message, then his voice was unique in sixteenth-century Scotland. Part of his achievement could be described as truly 'eldritch', and for that the fairies are to be thanked, for it was their trope or metaphor which permitted him to draw in his audience, so forcing women and men alike to reconsider certain basic assumptions about their own natures.

Fig. 3. 'The Fairy Rade', by K. Halsewelle.

Fairies in Flyting

A demonisation of sixteenth-century fairy belief, parallel to that which was emerging in the witch-hunts, is also to be detected in the literature of the period, as exemplified in Alexander Montgomerie's 'Flyting of Montgomerie and Polwart'.[20] Flyting was a medium in which two competing poets verbally slandered one another with the aim of reducing one's opponent to subhuman levels through the manipulation of hyperbolic and scatological language. However obscene and extreme the abuse heaped by the one upon the other, these agonal contests were ludic in nature, subject, like other games, to their own rules and formal space, often ending, we may think, in the two protagonists adjourning for a drink like rival football players after a match or politicians fresh from vitriolic debate. There is a suggestion that flytings were actual performances. They have been compared to linguistic tournaments, jousts of reciprocal contempt, the best of which were written down, possibly posted for wider consumption, and subsequently printed. Few Scots would have had any difficulty in recognising, or enjoying, the genre which represented elaborate sophistications of daily exchanges in the tavern or the market place.

Writing the Fairies

Montgomerie's opponent was Sir Patrick Hume of Polwarth, a well-established poet in his own right and master of the household of James VI, a monarch who would become no stranger to flyting himself. Born about 1550 at Hessilhead Castle, Ayrshire, Montgomerie was related to James. By the time he arrived at court in 1580 he could poetically boast:

> I haiv bene in mony cuntrey strange
> Through all Europe, Afrik, and Asia,
> And throu the new fund out America.

There is some evidence that he saw military service in both Argyll and on the Continent, attaining the rank of captain. While abroad, probably in the Low Countries, he became attracted to catholicism, thus eschewing, at least in part, his calvinist upbringing. His almost certain involvement in a catholic plot of 1580 did not interfere with the royal favour which he immediately enjoyed upon his return home. James was a highly impressionable, if deeply learned thirteen-year old at this time, spellbound by his cousin Esmé Stewart, Sire d'Aubigny, the first human being to whom the young king gave his love. But d'Aubigny was a catholic with literary interests, and though his presence doubtless provided a congenial environment for Montgomerie, the Frenchman's ascendancy at court generated paranoia among the protestants. Such was the fear of Counter-Reformation that in 1581 the royal household was forced to subscribe the Negative Confession, a total abjuration of popery, considered so comprehensive that it was to become the first part of the National Covenant in 1638. When d'Aubigny was created Duke of Lennox, the Ruthven Raiders were spurred into expelling him, having seized the person of the king. In the interval, however, James assumed the role of apprentice to Montgomerie, the master poet, his 'Beloved Sanders', a period during which the king penned his first poems and the master flyted Hume of Polwarth. After the king escaped the clutches of the Raiders, Montgomerie became chief poet of the Castalians, a talented group of writers, presided over by James himself, which sought to foster literature, song and music. The remainder of Montgomerie's career involved almost as many plots as it did poems. His overt catholicism can be convincingly dated to the withdrawal of his pension and subsequent disfavour. At his death in 1598, however, he received a privilege unusual for a known catholic in the aftermath of the Spanish Armada. Following a decade of conspiracy, real and imagined, when Jesuit shocktroops moved freely through Scotland, he was buried in the Canongate Kirk, Edinburgh, lamented by his one-time royal prentice.

When, in 1584, James wrote his treatise on poetry, *The Reulis and*

Cautelis, he quoted as an example of 'Tumbling verse' the description in the Flyting of the fantastic birth of 'elfgett Polwart' (to use an appellation in one of James's poems). The allusions in this passage to 'the king of pharie with the court of the elph quene', he would later condemn in his *Daemonologie* as illusions 'rifest in time of papistrie'. Polwarth was, according to Montgomerie's acerbic and scurrilous pen, conceived and born in exaggeratedly eldritch circumstances:

> Into the hinderend of harvest, on ane alhallow evin,
> When our goode nichtbouris ryddis, if I reid richt,
> Sum buklit [mounted] on ane bunwyd [flax stalk] and sum on ane bene,
> Ay trippand in trowpis fra the twie-licht;
> Sum saidlit ane scho aip [she-ape] all grathit [clad] into grene,
> Sum hobling on hempstaikis, hovand on hicht [rising on high].
> The king of pharie, with the court of the elph quene
> With mony alrege [eldritch] incubus, ryddand that nicht.
> Thair ane elph, and ane aip ane unsell [wretch] begate,
> In ane peitpot [pot-hole in a peat bog] by Powmathorne;
> That brachart [brat] in ane buss wes borne;
> They fand ane monstour on the morne,
> War [worse] facit nor ane cat.[21]

The mentions of harvest and Halloween, the good neighbours engaged in the twilight Fairy Rade, well-mounted on their plant stalks, some grounded, some flying, some riding on an ape clad in green and the elfin court accompanied by sundry eldritch *incubi* are all conventional enough. What is significant is that in subsequent passages (not quoted by James) the 'Weird Sisters' and the entire diabolic panoply also get in on the act.

Birth in the sixteenth century, even for such supposedly unnatural creatures as Polwarth, was a highly dangerous time. The sisters 'mused at the mandrake unmade lik a man . . . how that gaist had been gotten, to gesse they began'. Since the mandrake root, throughout Europe, was thought to resemble human form, it was often used by witches to represent their victims. It supposedly shrieked when it was pulled from the earth because it was rooted in a human heart; whoever uprooted the plant would fall down dead, while those hearing its scream would be driven mad. In a horrific inversion of the stereotypical benign godmother the sisters conferred birth gifts of monumental repugnance upon the newborn – every possible type of disease or affliction that they could command. The creature, furthermore, was to be outlawed; any who cared for it were to be cursed: 'ay the langer that thou lives thy lucke be the lesse'. He was condemned to be driven mad at each full moon and, suffering utter destitution, to wander with werewolves and wildcats. The malignant sorority visited further predictive curses upon the infant Polwarth who was to be nursed by none other than Nicneven the demon queen who had much experience of riding post to Elphin. They then withdrew to make way for Nicneven herself:

> Thair a cleir cumpany cum eftir close,
> Nickniven with hir nymphis in nomber anew,
> With chairmes from Cathnes and Chanrie of Ross,
> Whais cunning consistis in casting a clew [thread];
> Sein that sarrie [sorry] thing they said to thameself:
> 'This maikles [matchless] monstour is meit for us
> And for our craft commodious;
> And uglie aip and incubus,
> And gottin of Elf.'

These nymphs of darkness were well-armed with spells and charms from the north country, areas famed as the abodes of witches. They were expert in predicting the future (casting a clew).

'Thir venerable virgines whom the world call witches' rode backwards on pigs, dogs, stags and monkeys, or hobbled along, some as if crippled, glowering at the moon or the ground. Harnessing the four winds, they rode 'widdershins' – that is against the direction of the sun – round the thorn at whose roots ravens rived at the rat-like runt. They proceeded to baptise the bairn in their own hellishly inimitable fashion, calling upon three-headed Hecate, who was assured that Polwarth had forsaken his faith in favour of allegiance to herself, an action sanctified – obscurely it must be said – by some thirty knots tied in blue thread or yarn and by men's members taken from over a hundred presumably involuntary donors and well-sewed to a shoe. The former is a type of *les novements d'arquillettes*, knot magic, the idea being that the victim was condemned until the knots were untied. The second is less obvious since Victorian editors scrupled to explain such matters, but an explanation may be sought in an age when Jacobean men, possibly seeking to compensate for nature's underendowment, were fond of displaying their supposed attributes by means of elaborate codpieces. A concomitant anxiety may have been shared with the presumably celibate authors of *Malleus Maleficarum, The Hammer of Witches* (1486):

What is to be thought of those witches who sometimes collect male organs in great numbers, as many as twenty or thirty members together, and put them in a bird's nest, or shut them up in a box, where they move themselves like living members, and eat oats and corn, as has been seen by many and is a matter of report? It is to be said that it is all done by devil's work and illusion, for the senses of those who see them are deluded in the way we have said. For a certain man tells that, when he had lost his member, he approached a known witch to ask her to restore it to him. She told the afflicted man to climb a certain tree, and that he might take which he liked out of a nest in which there were several members. And when he tried to take a big one the witch said: You must not take that one; adding, because it belonged to a parish priest.[22]

The shoe, for its part, symbolised female reproductive anatomy. There was an element of, at best, the erotic, at worst the pornographic, associated with witches but it was not entirely absent from fairy lore either as when Montgomerie mentions the *incubi* who accompanied the Fairy Rade. The entire 'baptismal ceremony' was sealed by words, hyperbolic and hellish:

> Be the hight of the heavens, and be the howness [hollowness] of hell,
> Be the winds, and the weirds, and the Charlewaine [the Plough],
> Be the hornes, the handstaff, and the king's ell,
> Be thunder, be fyreflaughtes [lightnings], be drouth, and be raine,
> Be the poles, and the planets, and the signes all twell,
> Be the mirknes of the moone – let mirknes remaine -
> Be the elements all, that our crafts can compell,
> Be the fiends infernall, and the Furies in paine -
> Gar all the gaists of the deid, that dwels there downe,
> In Lethe and Styx that stinkand strands,
> And Pluto, that your court commands,
> Receive this howlat [owl] aff our hands,
> In name of Mahowne [Mohammed];
>
> That this worme, in our worke, some wonders may wirk;
> And, through the poyson of this pod, our pratiques prevaile
> To cut off our cumber [burden] from comming to the kirk,
> For the half of our helpeand hes it heir haill.
> Let never this undought [puny creature] of ill doing irk,
> Bot ay blyth to begin all barret and baill [strife and mischief].

Of all blis let it be als bair as the birk,
That tittest [soonest] the taidrell [weakling] may tell ane ill taill:
Let no vice in this warld in this wanthrift [unthriven creature] be
                                                                              wanted.

Mahowne or Mohammed, oft cited by Dunbar, was regarded by christians as the Devil himself, particularly after the Fall of Constantinople in 1453 until well into the seventeenth century when Islam seemed to threaten the very existence of christendom. The disaster at Flodden deprived James IV of his sworn intent to lead a crusade, while Andrew Fletcher of Saltoun fought against the Turks in Hungary in the 1680s. The witches were determined that Polwarth would commit every imaginable type of crime and would be in possession of all known vices. NicNeven would nurse him, teaching him how to master such impossible accomplishments as sailing in a sieve. Nourishment would be provided in the shape of milk stolen by witches from nursing mothers or filched by the fairies. In short, the creature would be raised as the most vicious unnatural monster, 'and ay the langer that it live, the warld sould be the war [worse]'.

Polwarth, needless to say, was having none of Montgomerie's nonsense. This is not the place to investigate the later flyting's possible debt to William Dunbar's 'Flyting of Dunbar and Kennedie', which more than matches it in outrageous scatology and taunting obscenity. Suffice it to say that the elf and the ape which notionally conceived Polwarth are mentioned early in Dunbar's poem whose 'wanfukkit funling' (misbegotten foundling) may have inspired Montgomerie's tirade.[23] Kennedy describes Dunbar as mandrake and 'mymmerkin' (dwarf), which parallels Montgomerie's demeaning of Polwarth as 'little cultron cuist', which renders something like 'little wee nyaff'. To be small was to be despicable; clearly size did matter in Stewart Scotland. Dunbar responds with 'cuntbitten crawdoun', or coward, and 'mismaid monstour'. Arse-kissing, later associated with the diabolic kiss, appears in both poems, as do Mohammed, werewolves and the dreaded cockatrice mentioned four times in the bible, a fabulous creature hatched by a serpent from a cock's egg and able to inflict death with its breath or a glance. It is true that vituperative rhetoric perhaps required no model, but it is tempting to believe that in his flyting Montgomerie paid some homage to Dunbar. What is to be noted is that although Dunbar was perfectly familiar with the world of Fairy, he does not link it with weird sisters, witches and the Devil in the way that Montgomerie does.

Just how the later flyting poem was received is problematical. James was clearly smitten by it, yet ten years after its composition he would preside over a sensational series of trials in which people were accused of doing the very things described by Montgomerie, sailing in sieves, moving widdershins and uttering spells or charms, to name only a few. As we discuss elsewhere in this study, Bessie Dunlop had been executed, most likely for fairy belief, a mere five years before Montgomerie wrote the 'Flyting'. There were witch cases in 1577 and 1580, while in 1581 Bessie Robertson in St Andrews was 'delatit' for witchcraft. It is not entirely clear therefore whether Montgomerie's effusion is to be seen as entirely 'jocound and mirrie', as Bannatyne described Dunbar's composition.

The question of what exactly constituted humour in a past age is extremely fraught, though it is a pretty safe assumption that the Rabelaisian extravagance of Montgomerie's piece was meant to be entertaining. If he really did have recusant sympathies, he might be expected to be even more wary of the material which he was satirising. It is more likely, however, that he fell into the category of *politiques*: those people who believed that religion had already cost too much blood in the century of reformation and who preferred to seek more of a middle way. Francis Stewart Earl of Bothwell seems to have been so minded, as was William Alexander Earl of Stirling and Viscount Canada, while James, left to himself and free from the constraints of the Kirk, appears to have shared such sympathies, later manifested in his desire to promote himself as a kind of European *Rex Pacificus* after 1603.

It may be that Montgomerie in 1580–2 should be viewed, rather like Bothwell a decade later, as one of a group of young intellectuals who defied convention and who saw themselves as somehow unconfined by the constraints which governed lesser mortals. He and his peers may have shared a couple of the premises put forward by the authors of the pernicious *Malleus Maleficarum* which, amongst much other nonsense, argued that 'certain abominations are committed by the lowest orders, from which the higher orders are precluded on account of the nobility of their natures', an invitation, if ever there was one, by the Church to the dominant classes to enter into an alliance in the witch-hunt conspiracy. Furthermore it was asserted that 'witchcraft is not taught in books, nor is it practised by the learned but by the altogether uneducated', a comforting thought for a group of young poets trying to resurrect the glorious traditions of Scottish literature. As is notoriously known, the sickeningly misogynistic *Malleus* demonstrated to its own satisfaction that women were much more susceptible to the snares of the

Devil than men. It also noted that 'it has never yet been known that an innocent person has been punished on suspicion of witchcraft and there is no doubt that God will never permit such a thing to happen', so proving a crucial premise while consigning thousands of poor souls to perdition.[24]

The importance of Montgomerie's account is that it provides a snapshot of fairy belief around 1581, belief which was inevitably becoming contaminated, as perhaps it always had been, and always would be, by innovatory material from the world of learning but which nonetheless accurately reflected the folk tradition, since poets like himself fed upon their environment. If he really was ridiculing elite beliefs about witches, then he was a remarkable breath of fresh air, and it may be that for a time he carried the king with him. Certain it is that he was the first poet, so far as is known, to explicitly link fairies and witches, at least in Scotland, for there were similar trends in England and elsewhere.

The trial of Alison Peirson in 1588 caused a sensation when it was revealed that among her clients was one of the greatest and most controversial figures in the land, Patrick Adamson, bishop of St Andrews. He was said to have first consulted a nameless witch, his Phetanissa or pythoness, derived from the prophetic priestess of the Pythian or Delphic Apollo, so affording one of his bitterest critics, the poet Robert Sempill, the opportunity to accuse him of indulging in almost the entire range of occult practices:

> sorcerie and incantationes,
> Reasing [raising] the devill with invocationes,
> With herbis, stanes, buikis and bellis,
> Menis members, and south rinning wellis;
> Palm croces, and knottis of strease [straws],
> The paring of a preistis auld tees.[25]

To the last-mentioned priestly toenail clippings he added St John's nut – two nuts growing together supposedly had protective qualities – a four-leafed clover, heather cut at the crescent moon, holy water, and amber beads which were popularly believed to derive from the tears of seabirds, all of which, when they were applied to Adamson's horse, killed the beast. He then consulted a witch in Anstruther whose powers exceeded those of Circe, Medusa, Hecate, Mercury and Zoroaster, who 'first inventit magica'. She made him a potion of wine dregs, dried frogs and black hens' eggs. Sempill's poem, condemnatory and salacious though it was, implied that Adamson refused to act against the witches, allowing them to escape from prison while putting it about that they had been rescued by Pluto, their master. The bishop may, in reality, have been totally sceptical about witch accusation. He was not to be put off, for Alison was the third witch that he consulted, introduced by Sempill in glorious fashion as a member of the Fairy Rade, riding around Breadalbane at Halloween:

> Ane carling of the Quene of Phareis,
> That ewill win geir to elphyne careis.
> Through all Braid Abane scho hes bene
> On horsback, on Hallow ewin;
> And ay in seiking, certayne nyghtis,
> As scho sayis, with our sillie wychtis;
> And names out nytboris sex or sewin,
> That we belevit had bene in heawin.[26]

She had seen the dead among the fairies and she relied on a book of spells given to her by her uncle, William Simpson, also mentioned in her dittay. After she became a prisoner in the bishop's own castle, he allegedly did not scruple to seek her out for other nefarious purposes:

> Closing the door behind his back
> And quietly to her he spak,
> And said his tool was of no worth:
> Loosing his breeks he laid it forth.
> She sained it with her holy hand,
> The pure pith of the prior's wand:
> When she had sained it twice or thrice,
> His rubigo began to rise:
> Then said the bishop to [his] 'John Bell',
> Go take the first sight of her yoursel.
> The witch to him her vessel gave,
> The bishop's blessing to receive.

Sex is a wonderful source of satire and invective, perhaps even more so when occult creatures are involved.

Patrick Adamson was one of the most outrageous individuals in the galaxy of eccentrics and non-conformists which populated James's court. Graduating from St Andrews in 1558, he became minister of Ceres in Fife but soon quit and went off to France as tutor to the son of a laird. There he wrote an incriminating poem lauding Mary Stewart as rightful ruler of

England and France as well as Scotland, an effusion which earned him six months' imprisonment. After studying law at Bourges, he returned to Scotland in 1570, his services much sought after due to the shortage of talented manpower in the Kirk. When his first bid to secure the bishopric of St Andrews failed, he resoundingly traduced episcopacy and secured a charge at Paisley. Although appointed private chaplain to the Regent Morton, he worked hard to secure the acceptance of the *Second Book of Discipline* to which his patron was opposed. As the poem states, Adamson was highly capable, in sermon or debate, of pleasuring folk on both sides. When Morton eventually rewarded him with the bishopric, he refused to submit to the General Assembly, but since the Book of Discipline would disenfranchise the episcopate, he now opposed it so that this Machiavelli now found himself, through a series of contorted machinations, in the position of illegally exercising his episcopal functions. An attempt to excommunicate him was frustrated when he preached before the king in favour of the lately exiled Duke of Lennox who, he claimed, was a good protestant. Sent by the king on a mission to England, he disgraced himself through his beggarly behaviour and his disgusting personal habits. On his way to a personal audience with Elizabeth he responded to the call of nature:

> His pintle against the palice wall
> Puld out to piss, and wold not spair,
> Which is a thing inhibit thair.

Both Sempill and the historian David Calderwood gleefully accepted that such an event really took place, the poet reporting that he repeated the offence as he left Whitehall. As a result the English attendants 'maid a mydwife of him', which was to say that as a midwife is brought with all haste and honour, on horseback, to a woman in childbirth, she is made to trudge home alone on foot when her work is done. Back in Scotland he was deposed in 1586 as an 'ethnic', that is a heathen, but he responded by excommunicating his opponents, notably the great Andrew Melville and his nephew James, and succeeded in having the sentence of deposition quashed. Further chicaneries and subterfuges absorbed the remainder of his life, which ended in 1592. He is an excellent example of the bewildering uncertainties and shifts which marked the early years of Reformation.

In 1588 he suffered from a great 'feditie', a foul sickness described in Alison Peirson's dittay as 'ripples, trembling, fever and flux' which she treated with a posset and a salve used to annoint his body. His numerous enemies put his illness down to 'drunkenesse and gluttonie'; as one report stated, the physicians could scarce understand the nature of it. Robert Sempill's poem, which Calderwood entitled from its third line 'The Legend of a Lymmeris Lyfe', reads like one half of a flyting. Adamson was a respected Latin poet whose paraphrase of the *Book of Job* was sanctioned by the Assembly, so he probably perfectly understood the convention. The poem manages to combine poetic invective with the scurrilous rhetoric which the clergy were accustomed to hurl at one another. Thus Adamson and his kind are described as 'pestiferous prelatis . . . veneriall pastoris . . . scabbit sheip . . . servants to satan . . . untruthful teachers . . . fraudulent fellows . . . voracious wolves . . . libidinous drunkards . . . bastard brethren'. A dreadful pun on bishop makes Adamson a 'bytescheip' but he is also 'an elphe, ane elvasche incubus'. He is, furthermore an Eulenspiegel, *scottice* Holyglass or Owlglass, the German prankster. Sempill's poem is, without question, uproariously funny, reminiscent as it is of some of the best of Burns, but the humour was, in certain respects, deadly, as was the outcome of these events for some of the participants. Adamson the prankster went on to further vacillation and duplicity while Alison Peirson, the familiar of the fairies, was sent to the stake.

The laughter in the poems of both Montgomerie and Sempill is highly ambiguous; it is no longer as folksy or homely as it was, for example, in 'Kynd Kittock' when the latter's actions caused God to laugh his heart sore. Perhaps the learned were more adept at verbal cruelty, at wounding and destructive character assassination which simultaneously, through the use of scabrous rhetoric, mocked the ridiculous superstitions of the folk tradition. It has been observed that 'all the acts of the drama of world history were performed before a chorus of the laughing people. Without hearing this chorus we cannot understand the drama as a whole'.[27] Laughter can also function to combat ordinary human fears, to disguise doubts and hide unease about certain subjects. Many of those who heard the effusions of this merry pair of poets may have chuckled self-consciously, but at the very moment of conceptualisation and composition the laughter was already sounding fatally hollow.

Notes

1 G. Gregory Smith, *Scottish Literature Character & Influence* (London 1919), 20.
2 *The Romance and Prophecies of Thomas of Erceldoune printed from five manuscripts with Illustrations from the Prophetic Literature of the 15th and*

16th Centuries ed. James A. H. Murray, *Early English Text Society* (London 1875), 1–47. All references are from this edition, but see also *Minstrelsy*, vol. 4 , 91–7, Robert Jamieson, *Popular Ballads and Songs from Tradition, Manuscripts and Scarce Editions; with Translations of Similar Pieces from the Ancient Danish Language, and a Few Originals by the Author 2* vols. (Edinburgh 1806), vol. 2, 3–43. James Murray, later editor of *OED*, had an excellent knowledge of the Borders and their lore. He was born at Denholm and spent the first 27 years of his life in Teviotdale. See K. M. Elisabeth Murray, *Caught in the Web of Words; James Murray and the Oxford English Dictionary* (Oxford 1979).
3 *Romance and Prophesies*, xviii-xix, lxxxvi.
4 John Barbour, *The Bruce* ed. A. A. M. Duncan (Edinburgh 1997), 83, 182–7.
5 Andrew of Wyntoun, *The Orygynal Cronykil of Scotland* ed. David Laing 3 vols. (Edinburgh 1872), vol. 2, 427.
6 Walter Bower, *Scotichronicon* ed. D. E. R. Watt, 9 vols. (Aberdeen and Edinburgh 1987–98), vol. 5, 429.
7 *Harry's Wallace* ed. M. P. McDiarmid 2 vols. *Scottish Text Society* (Edinburgh 1968–9), vol. 1, 28–9.
8 *A History of Greater Britain as well England as Scotland By John Major by name indeed a Scot, but by profession a Theologian* 1521 trans. Archibald Constable, Scottish History Society (Edinburgh 1892), 190.
9 David Dalrymple, Lord Hailes, *Remarks on the History of Scotland* (Edinburgh 1773), 3.
10 *Romance and Prophecies*, xliv-lii and notes; *Minstrelsy*, vol. 4, 83.
11 *Medieval English Verse* trans. Brian Stone (Harmondsworth 1964), 224. For text see *Sir Orfeo*, ed. A. J. Bliss (Oxford 1954).
12 *The Bannatyne Manuscript Writtin in Tyme of Pest 1568 by George Bannatyne* ed. W. Tod Ritchie 4 vols. *Scottish Text Society* (Edinburgh 1928–34), vol. 2, 269, 315–6.
13 *The Poems and Fables of Robert Henryson Schoolmaster of Dunfermline* ed. H. Harvey Wood (Edinburgh 1933), 129–48.
14 Gavin Douglas, trans. *Virgil's 'Aeneid'*, 1513. ed. David F. C. Coldwell *Scottish Text Society* 4 vols. (Edinburgh 1957–64), vol. 3, 7. Also in the text: 'I wirschip nowder ydoll, stok nor elf', vol. 3, 154; *History of Greater Britain*, xxx.
15 'Tam-o'-Norrie' is the Scots word for puffin, the 'clown' of sea-birds (Tammie Norrie in Shetland).
16 Priscilla Bawcutt, *The Poems of William Dunbar* 2 vols *Association for Scottish Literary Studies* (Glasgow 1998), vol. 1, 40–44, 56, 80, 133, 115, 149–56. Priscilla Bawcutt, *Dunbar the Makar* (Oxford 1992), 260–92.
17 A. D. Hope, *A Midsummer Eve's Dream: Variations on a theme by William Dunbar* (Edinburgh 1971), 7–28 and *passim*.
18 William Dunbar, 'The Tretis of the Tua Mariit Wemen and the Wedo', *The Poems of William Dunbar*, vol. 1, 41–55; Hope, *A Midsummer Eve's Dream*, 10–11, 16.

19 Mikhail Bakhtin, *Rabelais and His World*, trans. Helene Iswolsky (Bloomington 1984), 240.
20 The following discussion is based upon *Poems of Alexander Montgomerie* ed. James Cranstoun *Scottish Text Society* (Edinburgh 1887), *Poems of Alexander Montgomerie Supplementary Volume* ed. George Stevenson, *Scottish Text Society* (Edinburgh 1910), Helena Mennie Shire, *Song, Dance and Poetry of the Court of Scotland Under King James VI* (Cambridge 1969), 80–99, R. D. S. Jack, *Alexander Montgomerie* (Edinburgh 1985) *passim*. See also *Scottish Literary Journal Alexander Montgomerie (1598–1998)* Special Number eds. Theo van Heijnsbergen and Murray G. Pittock, vol. 26 (Winter 1999).
21 Montgomerie, *Poems* ed. Cranstoun, 69. All quotations are from this edition, *Alexander Montgomerie A Selection of from his Songs and Poems*, ed. H. M. Shire, (Edinburgh 1960) states that there was at Polwarth an old thorn associated with fertility rites, 82 note.
22 *Malleus Maleficarum*, 121.
23 Bawcutt, *Dunbar the Makar*, 220–56; *Poems of William Dunbar*, vol 1, 200–218 and notes.
24 *Malleus Maleficarum*, 29, 45–8, 95, 136.
25 'The Legend of the Bischop of St Androis Lyfe, callit Mr Patrik Adamsone', *Satirical Poems of the Time of the Reformation*, ed. James Cranstoun, 2 vols *Scottish Text Society* (Edinburgh 1891), vol. 1, 362 and notes.
26 Robert Sempill, 'Heir Followis the Legend of the Bischop of St Androis Lyfe, Callit Mr Patrik Adamsone, alias Cousteane', *Satirical Poems of the Time of the Reformation*, ed., James Cranstoun, vol. 1, 365.
27 Bakhtin, *Rabelais and His World*, 474.

CHAPTER SIX

The Reinstatement of Fairy Belief: Robert Kirk and *The Secret Common-Wealth*

> It may be supposed not repugnant to reason or religion to affect ane invisible polity, or a people to us invisible, having a commonwealth laws and oeconomy, made known to us but by some obscure hints of a few admitted to their converse . . . And if this be thought only a fancy and forgery becaus obscure and unknown to the most of mankind for so long a time, I answer the antipodes and inhabitants of America, the bone of our bone, yet their first discovery was lookt on as a fayrie tale, and the reporters hooted at as inventers of ridiculous Utopias.
>
> Robert Kirk[1]

Throughout the Reformation centuries, the whole of Scottish society shared a providential cosmology – a view of the universe in which God had absolute control over his creation. Since God's power was thought to supersede the natural laws of the universe, in theory, nothing was truly impossible. As the seventeenth-century progressed, the concept of an omnipotent God was relegated by the great philosophical minds of the age to the role of initial creator behind the construction of the universe, but one who no longer intervened in the world's affairs. The supreme power of God appeared, to some, in danger of being supplanted. A clash between these systems of belief was inevitable and is seen in a number of Scottish writings of the period. One book of particular interest, which has been cited throughout the present investigation, Kirk's *The Secret Common-Wealth of Elves, Fauns and Fairies*, was written in defence of the providential view of the universe. His text is a useful counter to the assault on fairy belief since he argues that to disbelieve in fairies is to doubt the very existence of God.

Kirk had an almost neo platonic concept of the universe, assuming 'orders and degrees of angels' between humans and God, with fairies occupying one of the lowest strata in such a formulation. He set out, with near-scientific precision, to collect and record 'evidence' of fairy belief (and other related phenomena such as second sight) in part to uphold and strengthen belief in the existence of angels, the Devil, and the Holy Spirit. By calling for the reinstatement of fairy beliefs, Kirk intended nothing less than to 'supress the impudent and growing atheisme of this age'.[2]

'The Fairy Minister': Robert Kirk

Our knowledge of fairy belief in the seventeenth century would be much slighter had not Robert Kirk, a minister successively in the parishes of Balquhidder and Aberfoyle, pursued his interests in the *sluagh sith*, the people of peace. This man not only provided one of the best sources of folk belief in pre-modern Scotland, but he also became personally entwined with the very traditions that he dedicated the latter part of his life to studying, a paradoxical situation in which the historical figure was absorbed as part of the folk tradition. Kirk would perhaps not be surprised to know of his adoption into these traditions. It was thought unwise to speak of one's knowledge of the fairy folk, for revelation of their secrets would incur their displeasure and subsequent infliction of punishment. Donald McIlmichall, convicted in 1677 for consulting with evil spirits, was made to swear an oath of secrecy by his fairy contacts. He broke his oath by confiding in a friend and was duly punished: 'He was engadgeit to conceall them [the fairies] and no to tell other. Bot that he told it to . . . Robert Buchanan once for which he was reproved and stricken be them in the cheik and other pairts'. Furthermore, it was commonly held that those who had been in some way close to fairies would end up in the fairy realm at the termination of their earthly existence: 'those who had an intimate communication with these spirits, while they were yet inhabitants of middle earth, were most apt to be seized upon and carried off to Elfland before their death'. Such was the popular view of Thomas Rhymer's fate which, as Sir Walter Scott affirmed, was still believed by 'the vulgar' down to his own time.[3]

On the evening he died, Kirk had taken a stroll on Doon Hill behind his manse. He collapsed and was subsequently buried in the Kirkton graveyard, Aberfoyle. Sometime later, the deceased was seen by a relative to whom he gave a message, to be passed on to his cousin, Graham of Duchray. Kirk explained that he was not dead, but was held hostage in Fairyland. He said he would appear again, at the baptism of his posthumous child, only this time Graham was to throw a dagger above the apparition of himself, thus releasing him from the fairies. When the day arrived, Kirk did indeed appear, but his cousin was so startled that he forgot to throw the dagger. The spectre vanished and 'it is firmly believed . . . that he is, at this day, in Fairyland'. This account was given (possibly invented)[4] by Patrick Graham more than a century after Kirk died. Scott included the details of the story in his *Letters on Demonology and Witchcraft*. Over two centuries after Kirk's death W. Y. Evans-Wentz was in Aberfoyle asking locals for information about the minister. Most of them were familiar with Patrick Graham's account. Wentz asked questions specifically about Kirk's grave and was told by some that his coffin was filled only with stones. Others shared Mrs. Margaret MacGregor's opinion that the 'good people took Kirk's spirit only', leaving his body. Another woman, who kept the keys to the Kirkton churchyard, was able to point to Doon Hill where she said the fairies lived and to which Kirk had been taken. Wentz also spoke with Rev. William M. Taylor who reported that at the time of Kirk's death people believed that he had been taken by the fairies because he had been prying too deeply into their secrets.[5] Taylor related that he had searched the presbytery records but found nothing to indicate how Kirk had actually died, though his theory was that he had suffered some sudden illness, such as apoplexy. In 1943, Katharine Briggs heard another version from a pregnant woman who had rented the Old Manse at Aberfoyle. The expectant mother knew of a local tradition to the effect that

> if her baby was born in the Manse and christened there, Kirk could be freed from fairyland if a dirk was thrust into the seat of his chair. The chair was still there – or the chair supposed locally to have been his – so that it would have been still possible to disenchant him.

Briggs was of the opinion that 'this was only a whimsical belief on her part, but she had learnt it from the local people, for she was a stranger in the place'. When, in 1990, Margaret Bennett carried out fieldwork on fairy belief in Balquhidder, Kirk's first parish, she ascertained that while a fair number of the children believed in fairies and were familiar with Kirk, the adult population shared neither the belief nor much knowledge of the minister.[6]

Although the details of Kirk's life are unfortunately scanty, it is possible to piece together some sort of biography. He was the youngest, and the seventh, son of Rev. James Kirk, minister of Aberfoyle; he was thus assumed to have the power of second sight. The exact date of his birth is unknown but he was probably born in Aberfoyle in 1644. He was a student of theology, graduating with an M.A. from Edinburgh University in 1661; afterwards he studied at St. Andrews. In 1664 he became minister of Balquhidder. The visitor to Balquhidder today, who is usually there to view Rob Roy's grave, can see the ruins of the church in which he served for twenty years, and the old church bell that bears his name. He married Isobel Campbell, daughter of Sir Colin Campbell of Mochaster, in 1678 and a son soon followed. After her untimely death on Christmas Day 1680, he married a cousin of his first wife, Margaret, daughter of Campbell of Fordie.[7] She too had a son, called Robert. In 1685 Kirk was appointed to his father's old charge at Aberfoyle where he remained until his death, or his abduction, on 14 May 1692. There is a grave marker at the east end of Kirkton church bearing an inscription to 'Robertus Kirk', though it is unlikely that this is his authentic gravestone,[8] the style of lettering indicating that the stone was carved at the end of the eighteenth century, if not later.

Kirk was an accomplished Gaelic scholar. He worked toward the evangelisation of the Highlands through Gaelic translations of holy works. Among his achievements, he was responsible for the first complete translation into Gaelic of the Scottish Metrical Psalms, *Psalma Dhaibhidh An Meadrachd*, published in Edinburgh in 1684, and, on the instruction of Sir Robert Sibbald, collected specimens of Perthshire Gaelic for inclusion in John Ray's *Dictionariolum Trilingue*. In 1689 he went to London to oversee the printing of the Irish Bible, in Roman type, prepared under Bishop Bedell. The costs of this publication were initially met by Robert Boyle, originator of Boyle's Law stating that the pressure and volume of gas are inversely proportional. Curiously Boyle was also a seventh son – of the first Earl of Cork – and, among other things, a self-confessed alchemist who was a devoted member of the Royal Society. Others would eventually follow Boyle's lead and contribute to the printing expenses of the bible, three thousand copies of which Kirk finished printing in the spring of 1690.[9] His growing reputation as a Gaelic scholar, and the time spent working on the bible's distribution, gave him the opportunity to make new associates. Fortunately, Kirk was in the habit of keeping a notebook, so we have some idea of his acquaintances, his conversations and his interests. Soon after his arrival in London he was introduced to Edward Stillingfleet, the Bishop of Worcester, an individual with whom he subsequently had regular discussions, often on the subject of the supernatural. The bishop declared himself a non-believer in such things as apparitions and second sight, though he was interested to hear about Kirk's research on the subject from an antiquarian point of view. While he may well have been unswayed by Kirk's defence of the supernatural, he was not unimpressed by the man himself, donating the sum of ten guineas toward the printing of the Gaelic Bible. A copy of the finished manuscript of *The Secret Common-Wealth* was, for reasons unknown, later sent to Stillingfleet's wife.[10]

It is unclear when Kirk actually started to write *The Secret Common-Wealth*, though he must have completed it during 1691. These were difficult years for someone of Kirk's religious persuasion since when presbyterianism was re-established in 1690 over half of the ministers were deprived. Kirk, who had spent his entire career under the episcopalian system, was clearly not one of them, suggesting that he was something of a moderate in matters of religion. Much of his material was lifted, with little alteration, straight out of the notebooks he so studiously kept. Though handwritten copies of this text were made and circulated, it remained in manuscript form until 1815 when Sir Walter Scott published an edition of one hundred copies, based upon an incomplete manuscript in the Advocates' Library. It is likely that Scott had someone else transcribe the document for him, possibly the ballad editor, Robert Jamieson, a native of Morayshire, who, after a spell in England, secured a post as depute-clerk-register in General Register House, Edinburgh. Unfortunately, the manuscript used by Scott is missing, if indeed it was ever returned after copying.[11]

In 1893, Kirk's text was reprinted, with a lengthy commentary by Andrew Lang, and *A Study in Folk-Lore and Psychical Research* appended to the title. This edition was based on the 1815 printing although, considering that the original manuscript was lost, the minor changes that he made must have been guesswork. Lang, who regarded Kirk as an early 'student in folk-lore and in psychical research', was particularly interested in the second sight material. He was, among other things, president of the Society for Psychical Research, and he embraced Kirk's findings to further his own scientific approach to such investigations. Eneas MacKay of Stirling published a third reprinting in 1933, with an introduction by R. B. Cunninghame Graham. Regrettably, the latter took no part in the preparation of the text, and Lang's errors were retained while further mistakes were added.[12]

While the quality and accuracy of Kirk's treatise deteriorated during successive printings, another manuscript languished in Edinburgh University Library. Written in the hand of Robert Campbell at Inshalladine in 1691,[13] it consisted of a complete text, an appended letter from Lord Tarbat, later Earl of Cromarty, to Robert Boyle with Kirk's response, and *A Short Treatise of the Scotish-Irish Charms and*

Spels. It was upon this manuscript that the first, and best, complete edition was based, published by the Folklore Society in 1976, edited with a commentary by Stewart Sanderson.

The importance of *The Secret Common-Wealth*, to folklorists and historians alike, cannot be overestimated. This treatise provides a first-hand account of the belief in fairies and second sight in the area of Perthshire where Kirk lived and worked. He was, of course, not alone in his desire to preserve, for posterity or any other reason, the beliefs and traditions of his countrymen and women. Such contemporaries as George Sinclair, *Satan's Invisible World Discovered* (1685), Martin Martin, *Description of the Western Isles of Scotland* (1703), Robert Wodrow, *History and Sufferings of the Church of Scotland from the Restoration to the Revolution* (1721-2) and many others shared his interests. All of these men detected a value in folklore. Sinclair was an eclectic who drew material from Scotland and beyond. Martin based his accounts on personal interviews and empirical observation, one of the few informants who was himself the object of second sight. Wodrow used oral tradition in compiling his history of atrocities during the covenanting persecutions, and he was an avid recorder of prodigies and portents of all kinds. Many of those investigators were either members of, or were loosely associated with, the Royal Society, founded in 1660, whose first president, Sir Robert Murray, was a Scot.

The Secret Common-Wealth is of particular note in that it not only describes fairy beliefs but argues, from a metaphysical standpoint, for the existence of fairies. Kirk did not perceive a dichotomous relationship between christian doctrine and folk belief, a polarisation that had been so rigorously asserted by the reformed church during the past century and a half. He maintained that fairy belief was not inconsistent with christianity.[14] His arguments in support of the interchange and co-existence of the two worlds or spheres are carefully reasoned, using first-hand eye-witness accounts, supported by biblical and classical evidence.

The War Against Atheism and the Sadducees

As Sanderson remarked, 'one hardly expects to find a minister of the Kirk advocating, as a counterblast to godlessness, such Pagan superstitions as belief in fairies'. Initially, Kirk's beliefs may indeed appear incongruous but, when seen in the context of a man determined 'to suppress the impudent and growing atheisme'[15] of his era, he was not so unusual. Such pursuits were not wholly uncommon at this time. There was a small, but not insignificant, number of learned men in Scotland and England who, like Kirk, attempted to conquer the rise of atheism and materialism by upholding and defending the actual existence of witchcraft, ghosts, and the entire world of spirits. Incredulity of the supranatural world, for these men, equated with disbelief in God. They sought to authenticate and offer proof of the existence of supernatural phenomena, and thus combat the tide of scepticism among educated men and women. Case histories of alleged metaphysical experiences were compiled and offered as empirical evidence. In order to establish the intellectual atmosphere in which Robert Kirk lived and wrote, it is helpful to explore the wider circle of some of these men of letters.

Richard Baxter, Richard Bovet, Robert Boyle, Meric Casaubon,[16] Joseph Glanvill, and Henry More were but a few of those, furth of Scotland, who engaged in the battle against Sadducism and unbelief. The term Sadducism is derived from the ancient Jewish sect, the Sadduccees, who denied the resurrection of the dead, immortality, and the existence of angels and spirits. Joseph Glanvill was distressed that 'there is no one, that is not very much a stranger to the world but knows how atheism and infidelity have advanced in our days, and how openly they now dare to show themselves in asserting and disputing their vile cause'.[17] The great danger to christian belief, which so disquieted Glanvill and like-minded others, came in part from the new 'mechanical philosophy' of Descartes, Hobbes, and Spinoza. Sometimes called the 'father of modern philosophy', René Descartes' notion of a separation of matter from spirit – thus excluding the possibility of mysterious entities, powers, or demons – was at the heart of the controversy. Cartesian philosophy appeared to reduce living creatures and the natural world to mechanistically driven automatons. Steering dangerously close to atheism, Descartes, and some of his followers, did not openly dispute the reality of God but rather cast him in the role of the great clockmaker and initial creator of the universe.

Earlier debunkers and sceptics of the witch-hunt were also criticised as promoters of atheism and Sadducism, men such as Reginald Scot, *Discoverie of Witchcraft* (1584), who denied, at great length and with considerable persuasion, the reality of spirits and witches. George Gifford, author of *A Discourse of the Subtill Practises of Devilles by Witches and Sorcerers* (1587) and *A Dialogue Concerning Witches and Witchcraftes* (1593), believed in the existence of witches but had reservations about the validity of the witch-hunt. John Webster, in his *The Displaying of*

Supposed Witchcraft (1677), argued: 'there is nothing but couzenage [deceit] and melancholy [mental illness] in the whole business of the feats of witches'.[18] The driving force behind much of this enquiry, for both supporters and sceptics of paranormal phenomena, was the Royal Society, which could boast among its members such luminaries as John Aubrey, Isaac Newton, and Samuel Pepys.[19]

In Scotland, fulminations against Sadducism can be found as early as the sixteenth-century. King James VI had used the scriptures to prove the existence of spirits in his *Daemonologie*, framing his discourse not 'only to prove that such things are and may be', but also as a rebuttal of the arch-sceptic of witchcraft in Britain, Reginald Scot. James was clearly incensed by the *Discoverie*, which was written before the Scottish witch-hunt was truly underway: 'Scot an Englishman, is not ashamed in publike print to deny, that ther can be such a thing as witch-craft: and so mainteines the old error of the Sadducees, in denying of spirits'.[20]

By the mid to late seventeenth century the debate was in full swing. A letter written in 1659 to Richard Baxter, by John Maitland second Earl, later first Duke of Lauderdale, began with a statement of the problem:

> It is sad that the Sadducean, or rather atheistical denying of spirits, or their apparitions, should so far prevail; and sadder, that the clear testimonies of so many ancient and modern authors should not convince them. But why should I wonder, if those who believe not Moses and the prophets, will not believe though one should rise from the dead?

Lauderdale's religious bias became evident as he continued:

> One great cause of the hardening of these infidels is, the frequent impostures which the Romanists obtrude on the world in their exorcisms and pretended miracles. Another is the too great credulity of some who make everything witchcraft which they do not understand; and a third may be the ignorance of some judges and juries, who condemn silly melancholy people upon their own confession, and perhaps slender proofs. None of these three can be denied, but it is impertinent arguing to conclude, that because there have been cheats in the world, because there are some too credulous, and some have been put to death for witches, and were not, therefore all men are deceived.[21]

In 1676 Joseph Glanvill, the English philosopher and an active member of the Royal Society, a man clearly concerned about the decline of belief in witchery, opined, 'those that deny the being of witches, do it not out of ignorance of those Heads of Argument of which they have probably heard a thousand times; But from an apprehension that such a belief is absurd, and the thing impossible'. The arguments to which Glanvill referred were furnished by such men as his friend Henry More. A letter which he wrote to Glanvill, included in the highly influential book *Saducismus Triumphatus* (1681), reveals that More regarded as providential the inexhaustible supply of examples of apparitions and witchcraft, 'as may rub up and awaken their [the sceptics'] benummed and lethargick minds into a suspicion at least, if not assurance that there are other intelligent beings besides those that are clad in heavy earth or clay'. It is 'the common consent and agreement of mankind that these things exist or happen; to deny them is contrary to experience'. Emphatically he argued, 'that there are bad spirits, which will necessarily open a door to the belief that there are good ones, and lastly that there is a God'.[22]

Henry More, the philosopher known as the 'Cambridge Platonist', collected many of the stories which appeared in *Saducismus Triumphatus*. Glanvill originally published *Saducismus* in 1666 under a different title, *Philosophical Considerations Touching Witchcraft*. After his death it was reissued twice (1681, 1688), co-authored by More, who supplied additional material. In essence the book purported to prove, firstly, that active, immaterial spirits existed and were known to humankind; secondly, that witchcraft and other forms of demonic activity were genuine occurrences providing indisputable evidence of the existence of spirits and, naturally, of God. The *Saducismus* was very popular in Scotland where it almost certainly inspired the investigations of such enquirers as Sinclair, Martin and Kirk.[23]

More had been protesting against what he saw as the growing incredulity of his age long before his involvement with Glanvill's compelling tome. Initially a supporter of Descartes' mechanical philosophy, he soon came to the conclusion that though this theorisation was persuasive within certain limits, too much of it was, in his view, invalid. In *An Antidote against Atheism* (1653) he asserted the primacy of spirit over matter. A chapter heading in this, his first major book, reads:

> That the evasions of atheists against apparitions are so weak and silly, that it is an evident argument that they are convinced in their own judgment of the truth of these kinds of phenomena, which forces them to answer as well as they can, though they be so ill provided.

The bible was frequently used as supporting evidence of the spirit world in the compilation of these demonological and philosophical tracts, More's being no exception. In 1681, he wrote of his great indignation at 'the men of these times, that are so sunk into the dull sense of their bodies, that they have lost all belief or conceit that there are any such things as spirits in the world'. Yet, as More saw it, 'if there were any modesty left in mankind, the histories of the Bible might abundantly assure men of the existence of angels and spirits'.[24]

Richard Bovet, a great admirer of Glanvill and More, produced *Pandaemonium, or the Devil's Cloyster* (1684), which, unfortunately for the author, did not sell well. Using a combination of biblical authority and his own acquaintance with popular attitudes towards witchcraft, he upheld his firm belief that the 'Prince of Darkness hath a very large dominion among the sons of men', having his familiars in the dark region to assist him in the execution of his hellish purposes.[25]

George Sinclair, professor of natural philosophy at Glasgow and author of *Satan's Invisible World Discovered* (1685), compiled a 'Choice Collection of Modern Relations, proving evidently against the atheists of this present age, that there are devils, spirits, witches, and apparitions, from authentic records and attestations of witnesses of undoubted veracity'. In his view there was:

> a monstrous rabble of men who, following the Hobbesian and Spinozian principles, slight religion and undervalue the Scripture, because there is such an express mention of Spirits and Angels in it, which their thick and plumbeous capacities cannot conceive. Whereupon they think, that all contained in the Universe comes under the nature of things material, and bodies only, and consequently no God, no Devil, no Spirit, no witch.

This tract proved popular, at least in Scotland, and extracts of Sinclair's work were readily transferred to the flourishing Scottish market for chapbooks dealing with superstition.[26] It is just possible that Sinclair's work partially inspired Kirk's treatise, for in the invisible world of Satan, as conceived by the Glasgow professor, the fairies are conspicuously absent. In the same year that Kirk was writing his tract, Richard Baxter produced a digest of supernatural encounters, *The Certainty of the World of Spirits Fully Evinced* (1691). Baxter explained nearly every one of the experiences he collected for his compilation as either the providence of God or the work of the Devil.[27]

Three years after Kirk's death Alexander Telfair, minister of the parish of Rerrick, Kirkcudbright, felt a similar compulsion to engage this threat to christianity. He wrote a small pamphlet about a family in his parish which was haunted by a poltergeist. Telfair modestly admitted that he had little desire to appear in print but certain motives had compelled him to publish. One of these motives he clearly stated as

> the conviction and confutation of that prevailing spirit of atheism and infidelity in our time, denying, both in opinion and practice, the existence of spirits, either of God or Devils; and consequently a Heaven and Hell; and imputing the voices, apparitions, and actings of good or evil spirits to the melancholick disturbance or distemper of the brains and fancies of those who pretend to hear, see, or feel them.[28]

Though the bulk of material written against Sadducism appeared in the seventeenth-century, the debate continued into the eighteenth. Two relatively late Scottish tracts defending witchcraft were the anonymous *Witch-Craft Proven* (1697), the author given only as a 'lover of truth', and John Bell of Gladsmuir's *The Tryal of Witchcraft* (1705).[29] Forbes' *Institutes of the Law of Scotland* in 1730 spoke of witchcraft as 'that black art whereby strange and wonderful things are wrought by power derived from the devil', adding: 'nothing seems plainer to me than that there may be and have been witches, and that perhaps such are now actually existing'. Seceders from the Church of Scotland published a pamphlet in 1743 complaining about the repeal of the Witchcraft Act (1736) as 'contrary to the express letter of the law of God'. It was reprinted at Glasgow as late as 1766.[30]

What is of particular interest in these examples is the way in which folk beliefs have been utilised and defended as essential to christian orthodoxy.[31] Though many of these books were written with the intention of providing propaganda in the fight against atheism, they are also invaluable repositories of folk belief and custom. Robert Kirk was writing at a time when the Scottish elite had lost, or were rapidly losing, their convictions about the reality of witchcraft, the number of persecutions having steeply declined since the 1660s. He was battling against the tide of 'rationalism', but he was clearly not fighting alone.

Seers, Second Sight, and the Subterranean People

It has been seen that, in the later seventeenth century, there was a great surge of elite interest in the supernatural belief traditions of the subordinate classes, so much so that these beliefs were being used as propaganda in the polemics of the day. Aspects of popular (and elite) belief that received particular attention were second sight and prophecy. The demonisation of fairies, and the prosecution of witches, had a concomitant impact upon popular seers and prophets, for these gifts of prescience had been associated with the fairies. In 1574 and again in 1579, parliamentary legislation decreed that persons claiming 'knowlege of prophecie, charming or utheris abusit sciences quhairby they persuaid the people that they can tell thair weirdis, deathes and fortunes and sic uther fantasticall Imaginationes' would, on a first offence, lose an ear, but if repeated would be hanged.[32]

It was James VI's opinion in *Daemonologie* that second sight was not a genuine human capability but, like encounters with fairies and spirits, was a trick of the Devil. When the curious Philomathes asks, 'what say ye to their fore-telling the death of sundrie persones, whome they alleage to have seene in these places?', Epistemon responds, 'I thinke it likewise as possible that the Devill may prophesie to them when he deceives their imaginationes in that sorte'. Those who claimed an ability to foresee the future through the agency of fairies were by no means spared James's cruel pronouncement to be 'punished as any other witches'. On the king's interpretation, even Thomas Rhymer was no more than an unwitting pawn of the Devil. Ironically, after James succeeded to the English throne, the elite were quick to identify the Union of the Crowns as a fulfilment of Arthurian prophecy, while James wholeheartedly embraced this identification which he enthusiastically promoted.[33]

The double standard of the age was revealed: while associations between reigning monarchs and fashionable courtly prophecy were encouraged, and indeed received with eager interest by the elite, ordinary women and men were being persecuted on grounds of possessing demonically inspired, and in some cases fairy-related, second sight. Accused witches, such as Bessie Dunlop (1576), Alison Peirson (1588), Christiane Lewingston (1597), Andro Man (1598–9), Elspeth Reoch (1616), John Stewart (1618), Isobel Haldane (1623), and Isobel Sinclair (1633), all claimed that their foreknowledge of future events was derived from their fairy contacts.

Towards the end of the seventeenth-century and the beginning of the eighteenth, as rationalism and scepticism were beginning to make their impact, scholarly inquisitiveness about Gaelic culture, and especially second sight, was very much on the increase. Among the many who collected incidences and examples of the latter phenomenon were George Sinclair, Lord Reay of Durness, Lord Tarbat, Martin Martin, John Frazer author of *Deuteroscopia* (1707), and Theophilus Insulanus, whose *A Treatise on the Second Sight* was published in 1763. Kirk was similarly interested in this subject and devoted a great deal of attention to it in *The Secret Common-Wealth*. So that he would 'not be thought singular in this disposition', Kirk appended a letter written by George Mackenzie, Lord Tarbat, to Robert Boyle, in which he related stories he heard while 'confined to abid in the North of Scotland' during the Cromwellian occupation (1651–60). Initially a sceptic – 'I heard verie much but beleived verie litle of the second sight' – Tarbat was to change his mind, relating occurrences of second sight told to him by Sir James MacDonald, Sir Norman MacLeod, and Daniel Morison, and also incidents which he himself witnessed.[34]

What was particularly intriguing about Kirk's inquiry into second sight was his insistence that only those persons who had the gift were able to see and communicate with the fairy folk; never before had anyone suggested such a co-dependent relationship. Furthermore, Kirk insisted that, in virtually all cases, men alone were gifted with this faculty, 'females being but seldom so qualified'.[35] These observations were not consistent with those of other commentators on the subject. There were plenty of documented examples of alleged interludes with fairies by people who did not claim to have 'the sight', just as there were several women who professed an ability to prophesy and foretell future events. It may be, of course, that Kirk was reporting ideas about the second sight which were then current in such places as Balquhidder and Aberfoyle and which were not representative of other parts of the country.

That fairies were usually only seen by seers or men of the second sight, did not, according to Kirk, necessarily preclude others from sharing the experience. Those not invested with this particular power could, if they so wished, witness the subterranean dwellers if they touched the second-sighted person, thus, as it were, channelling some of the seeing power. The 'curious person' must 'put his foot on the Seers foot, and the Seers hand is put on the inquirers head, who is to look over the wizards right shoulder'. The commingling or sharing of this special, ocular ability through physical contact is a relatively common theme also found in folktale and legend. For instance, there is a Shetland legend about a woman from Papa Stour who watched the trowies dance every Yule from the brig-stanes, or stepping stones, in front of her house. Her husband would join her on occasion but could not see the dancing spectacle until he held his wife's hand or placed his foot on her's. Similarly, other kinds of visions could be shared in this way, as in a legend from Arran about a man who saw his own wraith though it was invisible to his brother until he placed a foot upon his. To see one's own wraith was an omen of impending death, and in this case, true to tradition, sure enough the man died at the very location where he had his vision.[36]

Scott thought the bestowal of the 'gift of prescience', or the obtaining of any kind of supernatural power, from fairies became

> the common apology of those who attempted to cure diseases, to tell fortunes, to revenge injuries, or to engage in traffic with the invisible world, for the purpose of satisfying their own wishes, curiosity, or revenge, or those of others. Those who practised the petty arts of deception in such mystic cases, being naturally desirous to screen their own impostures, were willing to be supposed to derive from the fairies, or from mortals transported to fairyland, the power necessary to effect the displays of art which they pretended to exhibit.

Scott was unimpressed, it would seem, by both seers and their alleged fraternity with the fairy folk: 'some of the Highland seers, even in our day, have boasted of their intimacy with the elves, as an innocent and advantageous connection'. He cited one Macoan, from Mull, 'the last person eminently gifted with the second sight', who according to Ramsay of Ochtertyre, owed his prophetic visions to fairy intervention.[37] Scott, of course, was obsessed with the 'last' of anything, be they minstrels or seers. That the ability to see into the future was called a 'gift' can at times be misleading. Kirk comments that seers 'have verie terrifying encounters with them [fairies]'. Martin Martin, probably the single most informative individual on this topic, observed that 'seers are generally illiterate and well meaning people, and altogether void of design, nor could I ever learn that any of them make the least gain by it, neither is it reputable among 'em to have that faculty'.[38]

Robert Kirk and Fairy Belief

The Secret Common-Wealth has been described as 'a remarkable mixture of neoplatonic science, Highland mythology and fantasy which focused on fairyland and bore only a slight relationship to the material coming up in the criminal courts'. It would be true to say that the treatise illustrates the author's own distinct ideas about fairy belief and second sight, but a counter-argument can be made that, on the whole, Kirk's material shares a strong relationship with the witch-trial evidence and, for that matter, other material from the period. Without a doubt, the sheer volume and detail of information which the tract imparts concerning seventeenth-century beliefs about fairies is unparalleled in any other source, as Kirk busily scrutinised 'their nature, constitutions, actions, apparel, language, armour, and religion'.[39]

The area in which Kirk lived and worked and had his being was, in Scott's view, 'the most romantic district of Perthshire'. Sir Walter's proclivity to poetic flourishes and romanticised notions of landscape is well known, and is garnered to full effect in the description he gave of the Trossachs:

> These beautiful and wild regions, comprehending so many lakes, rocks, sequestered valleys, and dim copsewoods, are not even yet quite abandoned by the fairies, who have resolutely maintained secure footing in a region so well suited for their residence.

The feeling that particular areas and places are host to more supernatural creatures than others is not uncommon, but Kirk would probably have thought Scott's remark, or any others like it, absurd. He certainly would not have denied that the fairies lived within his parish, but he would not have thought them somehow unique to his area either. He believed that fairies were everywhere, above ground, under the ground, moving unseen amongst the human population, 'as thick as atomes in the air'.[40] Why they should have revealed themselves to any 'superterranean' at all, was, he assumed, due to

> the courteous endeavours of our fellow creaturs in the invisible world to convince us (in opposition to Sadducees, Socinians and Atheists) of a Dietie, of spirits; of a possible and harmless method of correspondence betwixt men and them, even in this lyfe.

It was his contention that the fairies were a race of beings, living unseen by most mortal eyes only because they dwelled in another region or sphere of the world. This division between worlds was, for him, no different to the separation between humans and the undersea world. In his own lifetime sea-diving trials were underway. For example, underwater contraptions had been designed to allow the exploration of the Tobermory galleon, off Mull, a relic of the Spanish Armada which, the Campbells were convinced, was stuffed full of treasure. The fairies lived in another state, 'as some of us men do to fishes which are in another element'. In the course of time, Kirk envisaged an open correspondence between humans and these 'nimble and agil clans', the fairies, once they were uncovered like any other of the world's many mysteries:

> Every age hath som secret left for it's discoverie, and who knows, but this entercourse betwixt the two kinds of rational inhabitants of the same Earth may be not only beleived shortly, but as freely intertain'd, and as well known, as now the art of navigation, printing, gunning, riding on sadles with stirrups, and the discoveries of the microscopes, which were sometimes as great a wonder, and as hard to be beleiv'd.

In such a passage Kirk's debt to Glanvill can be traced. The Englishman thought that much would be proved by 'microscopical observations', that it was no more possible to argue against the world of spirits than against the most ordinary effects of nature: 'We cannot conceive how the foetus is formed in the womb, nor as much as how a plant springs from the earth we tread on'; nor did anyone understand how souls move the body, nor what united these different and extreme natures.[41] The details and observations that Kirk provided about what fairies are, and what they do, have been scattered throughout this book and integrated with various other materials. Much of what he wrote tells us something about the general conceptions which his contemporaries had of the fairies. His comments also reveal something deeper and more personal. Kirk expressed, not just his belief in the actual reality of fairies and second sight, but how such phenomena fitted into his own worldview, displaying glimpses of an even wider cosmology and the adoption of an almost philosophical stance. His approach to the life and death of fairies incorporated reincarnation, and projected a notion of the great circle of life:

> they live much longer than wee, yet die at last, or least vanish from that state: For 'tis one of their tenets, that nothing perisheth, but (as the Sun and Year) everie thing goes in a circle, lesser or greater, and is renewed and refreshed in its revolutiones, as 'tis another, that every body in the creatione, moves, (which is a sort of life:) and that nothing moves but what has another animall moving on it, and so on, to the utmost minutest corpuscle that's capable to be a receptacle of lyfe.

Kirk's neo platonism is in evidence here. In descending order, he described seven major spheres: Heaven existed in the circumference of the earth; living in the highest region of the air was the 'Manucodiata' or Bird of Paradise; followed by common birds; then flies and insects at the lowest region. On the earth's surface there were humans and beasts; under the surface of the earth and water were worms, otters, badgers, and fishes. At the centre of the earth was Hell. He believed that there was 'no such thing as a pure wilderness in the whol Universe'. Not even the middle cavities of the earth remained empty in his view, pointing to the caves of Wemyss in Fife as his proof. The parish of Wemyss derives its name from Gaelic *uaimh* (cave), from the spectacular rock caves along the shore, according to tradition fashioned by the Picts, 'short wee men wi red hair and long arms and feet sae broad that when it rained they turned them up ower their head, and then they served for umbrellas'.[42] Many of the caverns contain inscriptions from the early christian era but they were obvious places to encounter fairies or to hear tunes played by spectre pipers. People who ventured too far into the Forbidden Cave near Arbroath in Angus, 'were met by horrible spectres, and heard dismal yellings'. The folklore of caves is voluminous but it is salutary to remember that many of them were permanently occupied as domiciles down to the nineteenth century and possibly, in some instances, well beyond.

The fairies were, in Kirk's view, part of God's creation yet had an ambiguous relationship with christianity. They had 'nothing of the Bible' but used 'collected parcels', or portions of the good book, for charms and counter-charms. These charms could not be used to protect themselves, probably because they were not christian, but were used 'to operat on other animals'. But whatever their precise relationship to christianity, the fairies were still subject to God's command. 'Our verie subterraneans are expresly said to bow to the nam of Jesus',[43] an interpretation he derived from a line in Philippians 2:10, 'that at the name of Jesus every knee should bow, in heaven and on earth and under the earth'. Since he also mentioned that fairies would vanish on hearing God's name, 'bow' seems to convey a sense of deference rather than obeisance.

Overall, Kirk portrays the fairies in a kinder and more sympathetic role than is typical of other descriptions from the period. He states that although 'one of them is stronger than manie men, yet [they] do not inclyne to hurt mankind, except by commission for a gross misdemeanor'. However, he was very aware of the potential danger fairies posed to humans. He personally examined a woman by the name of 'NcIntyr', in the presence of another clergyman.[44] Rather like people such as Alison Peirson or Elspeth Reoch, this woman of forty had never recovered from years of abductions and abuses. Based on her own accounts and those of her family, Kirk outlined her condition:

> she took verie litle, or no food for several years past, that she tarry'd in the fields over night, saw, and convers'd with a people she knew not, having wandred in seeking of her sheep, and slept upon a hillock, and finding hirselfe transported to another place befor day, The woman had a child sinc that time, and is still prettie melanchollious and silent, hardly ever seen to laugh.

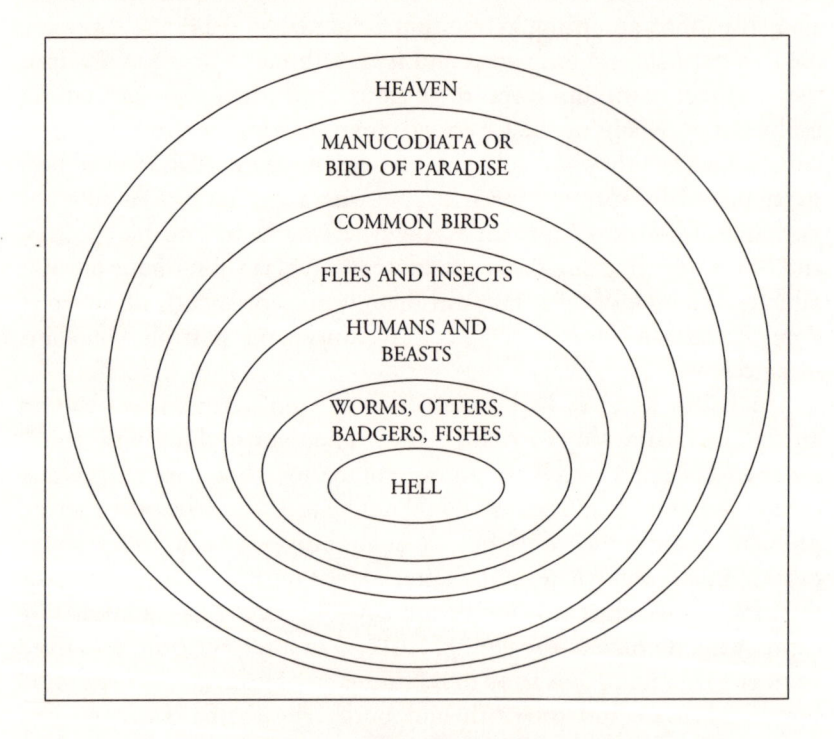

Table 2. Robert Kirk's Universe

(concentric ovals from outer to inner: HEAVEN; MANUCODIATA OR BIRD OF PARADISE; COMMON BIRDS; FLIES AND INSECTS; HUMANS AND BEASTS; WORMS, OTTERS, BADGERS, FISHES; HELL)

There are several themes, motifs, and concepts which emerge from Kirk's *Secret Common-Wealth*. Fundamentally, he argued that the fairies were a distinct species, possessing intelligence, endowed with supernatural powers, and having 'light changable bodies . . . best seen in twilight'. They were liminal creatures *par excellence*.[45] Using biblical authority to back him up, he defended the existence of fairies in order to prove the reality of spirits, angels, demons, and the Devil. To disbelieve in fairies was, in Kirk's reasoning, the first step to atheism and a threat to God. His treatise was, in part, intended to save christianity from what he saw as the impending mood of scepticism and Sadducism.

Fairyland itself existed in the 'other' space. Kirk believed that this enchanted zone was located underground, and usually inside particular fairy hills. The fairies frequently moved around and amongst the folk, unseen by most human eyes, except for the second-sighted. It was possible for humans to physically pass over the boundary demarcating this world from the Otherworld, though generally this occurred accidentally or involuntarily. The spirits of the dead were also connected to this underworld, yet they were distinct from the fairy race. Impressionistically, the fairies were not christian but, as part of Creation, they were still answerable to God.

The Secret Common-Wealth is an incomparable legacy of the fairy belief traditions of Reformation Scotland. As Stewart Sanderson said of Kirk, 'he was, in the truest sense, a scholar, a gentleman, and a Christian, who strove in all humility to discharge his duties and exercise his talents in the cause of his faith'. Perhaps the finest tribute comes from Andrew Lang:

> He heard, he saw, he knew too well
> The secrets of your fairy clan;
> You stole him from the haunted dell,
> Who never more was seen of man,
> Now far from heaven, and safe from hell,
> Unknown of earth, he wanders free.
> Would that he might return and tell
> of his mysterious company!
>
> And half I envy him who now,
> Clothed in her Court's enchanted green,
> By moonlit loch or mountain's brow
> Is Chaplain to the Fairy Queen.[46]

Notes

1 From a notebook of Robert Kirk, Edinburgh University Library MS. La.III.545., qtd. in Kirk (Sanderson), 15.
2 Kirk (Sanderson), 38–9; Kirk, 1, 83.
3 Trial of Donald McIlmichall, *Highland Papers*, 38; *Letters*, 108–9; *Minstrelsy*, vol. 4, 83.
4 See Below p. 198.
5 Graham, *Sketches of Perthshire*, 253–5; Kirk (Sanderson), 18. An idiosyncratic, not

to say a totally unacceptable, explanation for the disappearance of Kirk is given by Archie McKerracher. He claims that the fairy hill at Aberfoyle is situated on one of many lines which follow the faults in the rock structure of the earth. Pressure on these faults has created an electro-magnetic field. He speculates that Kirk was caught in one of these fields. An iron knife, passed over his head, would short circuit this field. Archie McKerracher, 'The Minister of Fairyland', *Fate* 43 (1990): 59–64; *Letters*, 138; Evans-Wentz, *The Fairy Faith*, 89–90.

6 Communicated to Stewart Sanderson from Katharine Briggs in a letter dated 10 March 1964, qtd. in Kirk (Sanderson), 19; Margaret Bennett, 'Balquhidder Revisited: Fairylore in the Scottish Highlands, 1690–1990', in *Good People*, 94–115. The children had very precise ideas as to what fairies were, blending Kirk's descriptions with contemporary notions.

7 On Kirk's ecclesiastical career see D. MacLean, 'The Life and Literary Labours of the Rev. Robert Kirk of Aberfoyle', *TGSI* vol 31, 1922–4 (1927), 328–66; Mario Rossi suggests 6 August, 1644 as Kirk's probable birth date, 'Text-Criticism of Robert Kirk's Secret Commonwealth', *Edinburgh Bibliographical Society Transactions* vol 3. part 4. Sessions 1953–4, 1954–5, (1957), 253–68; He was about 47 years and 5 months old when he died, Kirk (Sanderson), 3–6; His wife Isobel's grave stone can also be seen in Balquhidder churchyard. Tradition has it that Kirk carved the inscription on her grave marker; Lewis Spence, *The Mysteries of Britain* (London 1994), 132.

8 The inscription reads:
>   HIC SEPULTUS
>   ILLE EVANGELII
>   PROMULGATOR
>   ACCURATUS
>   ET
>   LINGUAE HIBERNIAE
>   LUMEN
>   M. ROBERTUS KIRK
>   ABERFOILE PASTOR
>   OBIIT 14 MAII 1692
>   AETAT 48.

9 Kirk's Gaelic glossary was published posthumously, under the title 'A Vocabulary of the Irish Dialect, spoken by the Highlanders of Scotland; collected by Mr Kirk, publisher of their Bible', in W. Nicolson, *The Scottish Historical Library* (London 1702); Kirk (Sanderson), 7–8, 10–12, 17. John Lorne Campbell has suggested that Kirk may have been mostly responsible for the material in *A Collection of Highland Rites and Customes*, ed. J. L. Campbell, The Folklore Society (Cambridge 1975).

10 Rossi, 'Text-Criticism of Robert Kirk's Secret Commonwealth', 257. Rossi speculates that Kirk wrote *The Secret Common-Wealth* 'to send to Lady Stillingfleet', a conjecture which Sanderson rejects. Kirk (Sanderson), 16, 28.

11 Kirk (Sanderson), 16, 21–2.
12 Kirk (Sanderson), 23; Robert Kirk, *The Secret Commonwealth of Elves, Fauns, and Fairies. A Study in Folk-Lore and Psychical Research* 1691, ed. and commentary Andrew Lang (London 1893), xv; For more on Andrew Lang see Richard M. Dorson, *The British Folklorists: A History* (London 1968), 206–20, and Roger Lancelyn Green, *Andrew Lang: A Critical Biography* (Leicester 1946); A recent contribution, *Robert Kirk. Walker Between Worlds* by R. J. Stewart in 1990, translates the text into modern English and is furnished with a detailed commentary. A forthcoming edition, *The Occult Laboratory* by Michael Hunter, is eagerly awaited.
13 Inshalladine was the name of Kirk's manse in Aberfoyle. Kirk (Sanderson), 25.
14 Kirk (Sanderson), 39.
15 Kirk (Sanderson), 1.
16 Meric Casaubon (1599–1671) *Of Credulity and Incredulity Against the Sadducism of the Times in Denying Spirits, Witches, etc.* (1668).
17 Joseph Glanvill, *Saducismus Triumphatus* (London 1682), 3.
18 Sidney Anglo, 'Reginald Scot's *Discoverie of Witchcraft*: Scepticism and Sadduceeism', in *The Damned Art: Essays in the Literature of Witchcraft* ed. Sidney Anglo (London 1977), 129; Alan MacFarlane, 'A Tudor Anthropologist: George Gifford's *Discourse* and *Dialogue*', in *The Damned Art*, 140–55; John Webster, *The Displaying of Supposed Witchcraft* 1677, qtd. in Hall, *Henry More*, 140.
19 On 10 May 1663, the Royal Society was formally incorporated by a charter granted by Charles II. Hall, *Henry More*, 169; Edward J. Cowan, 'The Supernatural in Scottish History', in *'Fantasticall Ymaginatiounis': The Supernatural in Scottish Culture*, ed. Lizanne Henderson (East Linton: Tuckwell Press, forthcoming 2002).
20 *Daemonologie*, xi, 58, 76.
21 Lauderdale, (letter) March 12, 1659, qtd. in Sharpe, *Historical Account of the Belief in Witchcraft in Scotland*, 219–20.
22 Joseph Glanvill, *Essays on Several Important Subjects in Philosophy and Religion* (London 1676), 3; Henry More in a letter to Joseph Glanvill, *Saducismus Triumphatus* (London 1682), 14.
23 'Saducismus Triumphatus' is literally 'Agnosticism Overcome'. A. Rupert Hall, *Henry More: Magic, Religion and Experiment* (Oxford 1990), 137–8; Cowan, 'The Supernatural in Scottish History'.
24 Hall, *Henry More*, 129; Henry More, *Antidote Against Atheism* (1653; London 1655), 269. More reissued an expanded edition in 1662; Henry More, preface to *Saducismus Triumphatus* (1681).
25 Richard Bovet, *Pandaemonium, or the Devil's Cloyster* (London 1684), 162.
26 George Sinclair, *Satan's Invisible World Discovered* (1685; rep. Edinburgh 1871), preface. Sinclair was appointed to the chair at Glasgow in 1654, but was removed from office in 1662 for non-compliance with episcopacy; William

Harvey, *Scottish Chapbook Literature* (Paisley 1903), 107.
27 Bennett, *Traditions of Belief*, 166.
28 Alexander Telfair, *A True Relation of an Apparition, Expressions, and Actings, of a Spirit, which infested the House of Andrew Mackie, in Ring-Croft of Stocking, in the Paroch of Rerrick, in the Stewardy of Kirkcudbright, in Scotland* (London 1696).
29 Christina Larner, 'Two Late Scottish Witchcraft Tracts: *Witch-Craft Proven* and *The Tryal of Witchcraft*, in *The Damned Art*, 227–45; The founder of Methodism, John Wesley, bemoaned the sceptical climate in England 'and indeed most of the men of learning in Europe, have given up all accounts of witches and apparitions, as mere old wives' fables. I am sorry for it; . . . the giving up of witchcraft is, in effect, giving up the Bible', *The Wesley Journal* 25 May 1768.
30 W. H. Davenport Adams, *Witch, Warlock, and Magician: Historical Sketches of Magic and Witchcraft in England and Scotland* (London 1889), 376.
31 Chambers, *Domestic Annals*, vol. 2, 475.
32 The scholarly study of Scottish second sight and prophetic belief is a relatively overlooked phenomenon. The best modern study is an unpublished dissertation by Athol Gow, 'Prophetic Belief'. See also Elizabeth Sutherland, *Ravens and Black Rain: The Story of Highland Second Sight* (London 1987); *APS* vol. 3, 140.
33 *Daemonologie*, VI, 75; Gow, 'Prophetic Belief', 78, 119–27.
34 Kirk, 73–80.
35 Kirk, 51. He cites one woman from Colonsay as an exception to the rule, 68.
36 Kirk, 64; John Nicholson, *Folk-Tales and Legends of Shetland* (N.p. 1920), 10; W. M. MacKenzie, *The Book of Arran* 2 vols. (1914; Glasgow 1982), vol. 2, 288.
37 *Letters*, 120; *Minstrelsy*, vol. 2, 349. John Ramsay of Ochtertyre, *Scotland and Scotsmen in the Eighteenth Century* ed. Alexander Allardyce 2 vols (Edinburgh 1888), vol. 2, 470–2.
38 Kirk, 51; Martin, *A Description of the Western Isles of Scotland*, 309.
39 Larner, *Enemies of God*, 33; Kirk, 102. Cowan, 'The Supernatural in Scottish History', suggests that Kirk's scientific approach derives from his association with members of the Royal Society.
40 *Letters*, 136; Kirk, 64.
41 Kirk, 82, 90, 95; Glanvill, *Saducismus Triumphatus*, 7–8.
42 Kirk, 51, 55–6, 87–88. He also refers to the caves in Malta. See also Simpkins, *Folklore Concerning Fife*, 9–11; Robert Edward, *The County of Angus 1678* (Edinburgh 1883), 53.
43 Kirk, 57, 92.
44 Kirk, 70, 95. 'Nic' is the female patronymic prefix, 'daughter of', equivalent of male 'Mac', 'son of'.
45 Kirk, 49–51, 70.
46 Kirk (Sanderson), 20; 'The Fairy Minister' by Andrew Lang in *The Secret Commonwealth of Elves, Fauns and Fairies* (Stirling 1933).

CHAPTER SEVEN

Farewell Lychnobious People

'What are ye, little mannie? and where are ye going?' inquired the boy, his curiosity getting the better of his fears and his prudence. 'Not of the race of Adam', said the creature, turning for a moment in his saddle: 'the People of Peace shall never more be seen in Scotland'.

Hugh Miller[1]

One Sunday morning, in the small hamlet of Burn of Eathie, in the Black Isle, while all the inhabitants were in church, two children, a boy and girl, stayed behind. Just as the shadow on the sundial fell on the noon hour, the siblings observed a number of figures riding by on horseback:

> The horses were shaggy, diminutive things, speckled dun and grey; the riders, stunted, misgrown, ugly creatures, attired in antique jerkins of plaid, long grey cloaks, and little red caps, from under which their wild uncombed locks shot out over their cheeks and foreheads.[2]

As the last in the procession of 'uncouth and dwarfish' riders went by, the boy plucked up the courage to ask who the riders were, to be told that what the children had witnessed was the departure of the last fairies from Scotland. This story was recorded, at the beginning of the nineteenth century, by Hugh Miller. The final farewell of the fairies is a theme that has always been a part of the tradition, just as new encounters are reported in every generation.[3]

Fantastical Fictions

The fairies, of course, did not disappear. They hovered around to further haunt the literature of Scotland whence they cast a spell on the world which is not yet broken. One scion of a prominent Scottish noble house who is celebrated for his contribution to the French tradition of fairy tales is Anthony Hamilton who died in 1720 at the Jacobite Court in exile. Best remembered for his *Mémoires* of the Comte de Grammont his tales were both parodic and erotic.[4] While, back home in Scotland, the Renaissance poetry was not forgotten, surfacing from time to time in various publications which self-consciously attempted to advertise the literary achievements of a former era, a further fictionalisation of the fairies was initiated by the publication of James Macpherson's *Fragments of Ancient Poetry* in 1760. These fragments were passed off as translations of Gaelic originals composed by a bard named Ossian in the early centuries A.D. Their translator conspired with Hugh Blair, Professor of Rhetoric and Belles-Lettres at Edinburgh University, who vouched for the authenticity of his work by providing a critical and cultural context which depicted Ossian as a second Homer. The *Fragments* and further works satisfied a huge public appetite, throughout the English-speaking world and subsequently through the medium of translation, for a nativist literature which was believed to be the match in accomplishment of those of Greece and Rome. Between them Macpherson and Blair orchestrated the Celtic mania which continues to burgeon at the present time.[5]

As it happens, fairies as such were not mentioned in Macpherson's texts but there were frequent references to departed spirits,

> represented not as purely immaterial, but as thin airy forms, which can be visible or invisible at pleasure; their voice is feeble; their arm is weak; but they are endowed with knowledge more than human. In a separate state, they retain the same positions which animated them in this life. They ride on the wind; they bend their airy bows; and pursue deer formed of clouds. The ghosts of departed bards continue to sing. The ghosts of departed heroes frequent the fields of their former fame ... Ossian's mythology is founded on what has been the popular belief, in all ages and countries, and under all forms of religion, concerning the appearances of departed spirits.

Equally significant was the setting for such activities:

> The extended heath by the sea shore; the mountain shaded with mist; the torrent rushing through a solitary valley; the scattered oaks, and the tombs of warriors overgrown with moss; all produce a solemn attention in the mind, and prepare it for great and extraordinary events.[6]

Herein was a reinforcement of the entrenched idea that fairies favoured remote fastnesses and confirmation of the suspicion that they had certain scenic preferences. What was novel was their association with all of the ingredients which Blair tipped into his Celtic cauldron – druids, bards and lamentations for past times, as well as weather and landscape.

A book could easily, and should, be written about fairies in Scottish literature. If Scotland was the land of Calvin, oatcakes and sulphur, it was also, during the century and a half following Macpherson, the country of couthy sentimental poetry which was frequently fixated on fairies, though fortunately there was a fairly hefty infusion of accomplished verse to accompany the dross.

John Leyden produced his 'Ode to Phantasy' in 1796, a fanciful piece written in a sort of sub-Ossianic style that drew upon traditional and classical material. The poet imagines himself flying with the fairies:

> then I seem in wild vagary,
> Roving with the restless fairy;
> Round and round the turning sphere,
> To chase the moon-beams glancing clear.
> Where ocean's oozy arms extend,
> There our gliding course we bend;
> Our right feet brush the billows hoar,
> Our left imprint the sandy shore.

He wrote a number of poems on this and parallel themes including the 'The Elfin King', 'The Cout of Keeldar', 'The Celtic Paradise' and 'Scenes of Infancy'. He was born at Denholm in Teviotdale in 1775 and was brought up at Henlawshiel at the foot of Rubers Law. He attended Edinburgh University where he studied theology and medicine, attending meetings of the Literary Society by way of recreation. He once said of himself, 'I often verge so nearly on absurdity, that I know it is perfectly easy to misconceive me, as well as misrepresent me'; he does seem to have had a rather lonely existence. He eventually went off to India where he studied Asiatic languages and literatures. He died of fever in Java in 1811.

Leyden was not only an accomplished poet; he was also a brilliant scholar. He studied Hebrew and Arabic at Edinburgh and produced an edition of *The Complaynt of Scotland* which led to an acquaintance with Scott. Sir Walter invited his assistance with *Minstrelsy of the Scottish Border* for which he was at that time collecting materials. The poet was only too happy to oblige since he had been absorbing local lore since boyhood, and he eventually supplied a few poems and the bulk of the material on fairy lore that was attached to the ballad of Tamlane in Scott's ground-breaking publication. Scott, however, did not publicly acknowledge Leyden's contribution until 1830.[7]

The *Minstrelsy* was the single most influential publication on the subject of fairies, frequently reprinted and perennially plundered by would-be authorities. Robert Jamieson had already planned to publish a collection of ballads but Scott beat him to it, publishing the first two volumes in 1802. William Laidlaw, James Hogg and several others also contributed. Leyden no doubt shared Scott's desire to 'preserve some of the most valuable traditions of the south of Scotland, both historical and romantic', an endeavour in which Walter brilliantly succeeded, drawing upon the rich ballad traditions which had haunted him ever since his boyhood days at Sandyknowe in the shadow of Smailholm Tower.

It has recently been pointed out that in 1802 Scott was preparing his edition of *Sir Tristrem* and he had also started work on *The Lay of the Last Minstrel* which was to gain him worldwide renown as a poet.[8] The former was, of course, conceived as a scholarly enterprise while the latter was poetic fiction very loosely based on historical events. *Minstrelsy* was something of a blend of the two. The first part of the work was devoted to historical ballads, the second to those of the romantic type and the third part to imitations. In each separate section Scott very cleverly blended landscape, poetry and literature, often with reference to himself and his own forebears, in a fashion which readers then, and since, were to find irresistible. What he achieved was the conferring of authority upon the texts and, through a process of reciprocation, upon his commentary also, so that the one complemented the other. He did not deliberately set out to mislead but he did use slight of hand, here and there, to cut corners or to make assertions that others would have considered questionable at best, but for this he could claim privilege because the various literary activities upon which he was engaged in 1802 conspired to convince him that he really was the Last Minstrel. Someone once unkindly suggested that *Minstrelsy* was Scott's greatest work of fiction, a remark which, however jocular in intention, was well wide of the mark. Walter once confessed that there was a period in his life 'when a memory that ought to have been charged with more valuable matter' was so crammed with ballads 'as would have occupied several days in the recitation'. That extraordinary memory was also crammed with historical, genealogical, onomastic and traditional information which, with the verification of people like Leyden and Hogg, conspired to create an invincible authority.

Although the Leyden-Scott collaborative essay was entitled 'On the Fairies of Popular Superstition', almost half of it is devoted to learned theories about fairy origins, rather than beliefs, formulated in exactly the same way as they might have written about the antecedents of the Celts, the Teutons or any of the other peoples of early Europe. Thus, in something of a *tour de force*, they cite Gothic roots from the Icelandic sagas, distinguish Finnish parallels, suggest that *fairy* derives from *peri*, a Persian word transmitted through Arabic, investigate examples from medieval romance, consider evidence from England and the Isle of Man – though curiously they ignore Ireland – trace the classical heritage identifying the fairy queen with Habundia, Diana and Hecate, not forgetting Pluto and Mercury, and they end with a brief notice of biblical references. All of this deeply learned apparatus was, needless to say, quite irrelevant in the context of Scottish fairy belief past or present, but, as with the ballads, the scholarly dissertation conferred a certain degree of respectability upon the study of the subject. Dozens of popular and pseudo-academic works, from that day to this, have ruthlessly and uncritically plagiarised the corpus of information assembled by Leyden and Scott. One other publication worthy of note was John Jamieson's *Etymological Dictionary of the Scottish Language* (1808–9), which represented over twenty years of toil. Jamieson, a Secession minister born in Glasgow and a prolific writer of theological works, was greatly influenced by the Icelandic scholar, Grimur Thorkelin, to the extent that the dictionary exaggerates the Scandinavian influence upon the Scots language, but the work is also valuable as the equivalent of an encyclopaedia of Scottish folklore which can still be consulted with profit. Scott and a host of others were to be significantly indebted to Scotland's scholarly Icelandic connection in pursuit of the supernatural.[9]

The fairies are never far away in Scott's poetry because we know that they lurk in the rugged landscapes of which he was so fond. In *The Lady of the Lake* the ballad of 'Alice Brand' tells the story of how the heroine transforms Urgan, the hideous dwarf, into her brother Ethert, believed to be dead. The episode takes the form of a Fairy Rade:

> Tis merry, tis merry, in Fairy-land,
> When fairy birds are singing,
> When the court doth ride by their monarch's side,
> With bit and bridle ringing.
>
> And fading like that varied gleam,
> Is our inconstant shape,
> Who now like knight and lady seem,
> And now like dwarf and ape.'

Banal and mechanical though the verse now seems, it was wildly popular when published in 1810. Scott claimed that he modelled his ballad on 'The Elfin Gray', translated from the Danish by Robert Jamieson. In the voluminous notes he took the opportunity to recycle material from the *Minstrelsy*.

The extent to which Scott fed, and indeed was responsible for the creation of, tradition may be indicated by the publications of one of his informants. When Patrick Graham, minister of Aberfoyle, produced his *Sketches Descriptive of Picturesque Scenery* in 1806, he included much information about the supernatural but nothing whatsoever about Robert Kirk. But the version reissued and expanded as *Sketches of Perthshire* (1812) not only contains a stanza from *The Lady of the Lake* to describe Kirk's fate but also the story of Graham of Duchray failing to free Kirk from Fairyland. What had happened in six years to inspire Patrick Graham, who was not only minister at Kirk's old church but who shared Duchray's surname, to suddenly unearth this supplementary information? Since Graham was so flattered to have been invited to communicate his lore of the Trossachs to Scott, and since he actually included material in his second edition because it furnished 'an opportunity of pursuing an ingenious idea suggested by Scott, in one of his learned notes to *The Lady of the Lake*', we may be forgiven the suspicion that the learned minister was inventing, rather than preserving, tradition.

By 1830, when he wrote *Letters on Witchcraft and Demonology* and supplied the final notes for the collected poems, Scott had spurned the traditions which had made him so famous. He betrayed the snobbery of his class when he reviewed John Galt's Gothic novel, *The Omen*, in 1826. While Gothic sensibility was quite acceptable in writers such as Galt or Byron, men of breeding could no longer sustain 'any belief in the superstition of the olden time, which believed in spectres, fairies, and other supernatural apparitions. These airy squadrons have long been routed, and are banished to the cottage and the nursery'.[10] He had travelled far from the *Minstrelsy* in pursuit of his ideas of progress and improvement but the price was the betrayal of the folk, and their lore, both of which had sustained his art.

Two almost exact contemporaries of one another, both aristocratic, leisured dilettantes with interests in Scottish history, literature and culture, and both of whom could have been characters in Scott's peerless *The Antiquary*, were Charles Kirkpatrick Sharpe and John Graham Dalyell. Sharpe in 1819 published an edition of Robert Law's

Memorialls; or the Memorable Things that fell out Within this Island of Brittain from 1638 to 1684, a most odd enterprise for a Jacobite since, as the dates indicate, the book was primarily concerned with the covenanters. The introduction by Sharpe was later published separately as *A Historical Account of the Belief in Witchcraft in Scotland*. He contributed to *Minstrelsy*, wrote undistinguished poems, dabbled in ballads and executed engravings of historical themes but, whether on his estate at Hoddam, Dumfriesshire, or at home in Drummond Place, Edinburgh, his artistic and aristocratic sensibilities removed him pretty far from the folk tradition. Dalyell, a scholar of wider range, published his *Essay on the Darker Superstitions of Scotland* in 1834 after most of a lifetime spent in the Advocates' Library. His best-known publication was the superb *Rare and Remarkable Animals of Scotland* (1847). It could be said of both men that their folklore researches reeked more of the lamp than of the peat fire.

The incomparable James Hogg was the self-proclaimed 'King o' the Mountain and Fairy School', of whom it was said that he was more at home among the fairies than with the folk of Middle Earth. The supernatural traditions of his native Border country, particularly the sweeping haunted valleys of Ettrick and Yarrow, informed a great deal of his work, notably his later stories and poems when he may have been attempting to feed what he perceived as a public appetite for such material. Born about 1770, he received a minimal education and was largely self-taught, his lifelong occupation giving rise to his designation, the Ettrick Shepherd. A highly gifted and multi-faceted writer, he self-consciously cultivated a personal role as custodian of, and spokesperson for, the traditions of his people, many of which he learned from his mother, Margaret Laidlaw, who was famously one of Scott's ballad informants. He was also much indebted to his grandfather, William Laidlaw, or Will o' the Phaup, 'the last man of this wild region who heard, saw and conversed with the fairies'. Hogg told a story of how one Halloween Will came across a gathering of the fairfolk feasting and making merry at the foot of a deep cleuch. When they repeated his name twice, Will's 'hair stood all up like the birses on a sow's back, and every bit o his body, outside and in, prinkled as it had ben burnt wi nettles'. He beat a hasty retreat before he could be named on a fateful third occasion.

Hogg was frequently ridiculed by the *Noctes* group, a circle of writers associated with *Blackwood's Magazine*, for his peasant cunning and boorish manners. One fictive episode portrayed the shepherd recounting how he fell into a dwam, 'a kind of inspired dream', during which he was visited by the green lady of the forest, the fairy queen herself, direct from the land o' peace. She planted a kiss on his temple: 'just where the organ of imagination and identity lies, fra which I became ane o' the immortals'. His most popular poem, the much-loved 'Kilmeny', he admitted owed much to 'Thomas Rhymer' and 'Tam Lin', the latter of which he reworked in 'The Haunted Glen'. In another poem it was the fairies who taught the witches of Fife to fly through the air.

A visit to remote Loch Avon in the heart of the Cairngorms, the 'summer haunt of innumerable tribes of fairies', inspired the ninth bard's song in *The Queen's Wake*. He collected stories of the dreadful fahm, a troll-like mountain creature whose head was twice the size of its body. To cross its tracks before the sun shone on it was fatal, the victim's head swelling until it burst, an affliction the learned shepherd observed, which actually affected sheep, a condition he knew about as the author of a practical tract on sheep diseases. 'Old David' preserved stories that would 'make even Superstition blush'. Ettrick, sweetest glen, was apostrophised – 'Thy fairy tales, and songs of yore/Shall never fire my bosom more' – an idea reflected in another poem: 'fears of elf, and fairy raid/Have like a morning dream decayed'. 'The Spectre's Cradle Song' derived from lore he heard in Glen Dochart, Perthshire, concerning the abode of the fairies, and an elfin mother and her babe. One of his finest poems was 'May of the Moril Glen', a supernatural being of uncertain origin as stunningly beautiful as she was conspicuously wealthy:

> Some said she was found in a fairy ring,
> And born of the fairy queen;
> For there was a rainbow behind the moon
> That night she first was seen.

The king in the story was initially less impressed:

> If I find her elfin queen,
> Or thing of fairy kind,
> I will birn her into ashes small,
> And sift them on the wind.

There is adequate compensation for the utterly tedious 'Origin of the Fairies' and the equally wearisome 'Song of the Fairies' in the excellent 'Superstition', a hymn to the passing of tradition, which could be seen as a statement of Hogg's personal *credo* on such matters. Superstition is personified as a deity who once ruled over mountains and glens but who is now banished by corruption and sadducism. He seems to be condemning modern values, and probably his own snobbish tormentors, who allow no room for wonder in their arid lives. Superstition has preyed upon the imaginations of countless generations who thus come to terms with their environment, its topographical features, such as with the graves and howes of long ago, and with such natural disasters as a storm at sea, or a blinding blizzard keeping a shepherd from his sheep. Superstition fuelled the witch-hunts, something of which Hogg approved, for he was convinced that while the fairies were fading, witchcraft was on the increase. 'All these are gone – the days of vision o'er/The bard of fancy strikes a tuneless string':

> She is gone that thrilled the simple minds
> Of those I loved and honoured to the last;
> She who gave voices to the wandering winds,
> And mounted spirits on the midnight blast.
> At her behest the trooping fairies passed,
> And wayward elves in many a glimmering band;
> The mountains teemed with life, and sore aghast
> Stood maid and matron neath her mystic wand,
> When all the spirits rose and walked at her command.

The supernatural informs his fiction as well, not only his masterpiece, *Confessions of a Justified Sinner*, but such stories as *Ewan M'Gabhar*, *The Hunt of Eildon* and *The Brownie of Bodsbeck*, all of which tales served to feed traditions back into folklore. A Rhymer-like seer appears in the first chapter of the exhilarating *Three Perils of Man*, incidentally illustrating very neatly how easy it was for a man of Hogg's talents to add to Thomas's prophetic corpus. Michael Scot the wizard figures prominently in the tale, he who was responsible for dividing the single Eildon Hill into three, a story which possibly originates with Hogg who may have derived it from traditional material, communicating it to Scott who noticed it in *Minstrelsy* but which, at any rate, has now become part of the legend of the Borders.

Though Hogg was perfectly happy to use fairy lore for literary effect, he was so steeped in it that we may suspect it meant a great deal to him, that alongside the other supernatural traditions which were part of his heritage, it symbolised, in his more vulnerable moments, a culture and a past which Scott and people such as the insufferable John Wilson of the *Maga* circle were intent upon junking. Deep down James Hogg was resisting the idea that the lore and beliefs which had sustained his ancestors were now considered only fit for the nursery: in his view, they deserved to be treated with respect as enshrining the modes by which the folk of Scotland had sought to come to terms with their world. There is some exaggeration, but also considerable merit in the considered opinion of Hogg's editor:

> Shut up within a limited range, and almost wholly secluded from the world of reality, he turned with double ardour to a world of his own; so that, while his temporary hut was in Ettrick Forest, his home was in Fairyland, where he could roam at will, and create according to his good pleasure. Such was the man and such the poet; one to whom the supernatural was worth a whole universe of common-place realities, and who welcomed fays, phantoms and wizards, as the most congenial of all associates. In this consisted his poetical life, as well as poetical superiority.[11]

However that may be, Hogg's world was undoubtedly being overtaken. John Galt, the novelist, wrote to him about his recent experiences in Canada with the observation, 'one remarkable thing in the American woods is their entire freedom from fairies and all sorts of hobgoblins'.[12]

William Nicholson, the packman bard of Galloway, was, however, on hand to preserve traditional lore in his enduring and delightful poem 'The Brownie of Blednoch' which beautifully tells the story of Aiken Drum. The brownie, who 'lived in a lan where we saw nae sky (and) dwalt in a spot where a burn rins na by', laboured willingly, true to his kind, for no more reward than a dish of brose until one day a demure wife, offended by his nakedness, left out an old pair of her husband's breeks which meant that Aiken Drum must part:

> Let the learned decide, when they convene,
> What spell was him and the breeks between;
> For frae that day forth he was nae mair seen.
>
> Awa, ye wrangling sceptic tribe,
> Wi your pros and your cons wad ye decide
> 'Gainst the 'sponsible voice o the hale country-side
> On the facts 'bout Aiken Drum.[13]

Poor Nicholson, in another time, might have been deemed to be affected by the fairies, for in later life he tragically lost his wits. A contemporary who made his name as a novelist was the somewhat overlooked George MacDonald from Huntly, who was, perhaps, more than slightly touched by the fairies, about whom he wrote a very great deal from *Phantastes: a Faery Romance for Men and Women* (1858) to *Lilith* (1895) as well as children's books such as *At the Back of the North Wind* and *The Princess and the Goblin*. He is generally written about as an individual who had great influence on others such as C. S. Lewis and J. R. R. Tolkien but he is an interesting study in his own right as one of a number of prominent Victorians who sought a mystical, or fantastical, retreat from the crass materialism of their world. An older and less romantic contemporary of MacDonald's was Hugh Miller of Cromarty, devout christian, respected geologist and compassionate folklorist who preserved much fairylore the passing of which he, like Hogg, regretted. G. K. Chesterton remarked of MacDonald that he 'really did believe that people were princesses and goblins and good fairies and he dressed them up as ordinary men and women'.[14]

Women are not absent from the annals of Scottish fairyology. One of Catherine Sinclair's earliest publications was *Holiday House* (1839) which contains 'Uncle David's Nonsensical Story About Giants and Fairies'. Dinah Maria Craik was English but she married a Scot and sometimes wrote on Scottish themes. Although better known as the author of *The Ogilvies* (1849) and *John Halifax, Gentleman* (1857) she also produced *Alice Learmont* (1852) which derived from and was inspired by 'Thomas Rhymer'; she went on to write books about fairies and brownies. Eleanor vere Boyle, born at Auchlunies, Kincardineshire, illustrated a number of fairy tale collections during the second half of the nineteenth century.

An illustration in Scott's *Letters on Demonology* had been supplied by George Cruikshank who was born in London to Scottish parents. He was to become the best-known engraver of fairy material during the nineteenth century. His style influenced many of the illustrations, by Edward Burne-Jones, in a most peculiar production, Archibald Maclaren's *The Fairy Family* (1857). Maclaren was born in 1819 at Alloa, Clackmannanshire and became, in time, a fencing master at Oxford, a keen gymnast and fitness fanatic who published *A System of Physical Education* (1869). He became great friends with Burne-Jones and William Morris. His fairy book was a truly bizarre production. Among those who influenced him were Scott, Leyden, and Robert Chambers, a close contemporary, but he was also indebted to Thomas Keightley, author of *The Fairy Mythology* (1828), the brothers Grimm, and Paul Henri Mallet whose *Northern Antiquities* had been translated by Bishop

Percy, he of ballad fame. Maclaren's philosophy is indicated in his preface:

> The author has been led to the composition of this work chiefly by the fact, that while Fairy Lore possesses a charm and attraction above all others for young people, and while its value and importance as a means of moral instruction are fully recognised, much of our Fairy Literature, so eagerly longed for and so greedily devoured, is but moral poison, – weakened by unmeaning extravagances, polluted by indelicate allusions, and disfigured by purposeless cruelties and crimes.

Since he clearly wanted sound minds to accompany healthy bodies, he attempted to adapt the fairy mythology 'for virtuous teaching . . . in tales of a pure moral character'. The moral was to be worked out in the development of the story while preserving 'the true mythologic character of the various personages'. His method involved a brief introduction to separate sections of the book on different types of fairy followed by the direst verse of his own composition. Mercifully the book was a failure, for Maclaren sought nothing less than the total sanitisation of fairy belief.[15]

The illustrated *Book of British Ballads* (1842) contained Scottish contributions by the painters W. Bell Scott and Noel Paton. The latter, a lifelong resident of Dunfermline, was Scotland's most famous painter in the second half of the nineteenth century and especially renowned for his fairy pictures. As a boy he devoured Ossian and Scott. In manhood he became a great friend of John Everett Millais though he stood outside the Pre-Raphaelite circle. His brother-in-law was David Octavius Hill, perfecter of the calotype and pioneer photographer. Paton enjoyed the patronage of Queen Victoria and between 1858 and 1863 painted his famous 'The Fairy Raid, Carrying off the Changeling, Midsummer Eve', based on Scott's 'Alice Brand' and the whole heritage of fairyology, a magnificent picture which, unlike his earlier studies such as 'The Reconciliation of Oberon and Titania' and 'The Quarrel of Oberon and Titania', superb though they are, is unmistakably Scottish, complete with standing stones, twilight, scenery and moss-covered tree roots. Much to their amusement he put his children into the piece 'scuddy-duddy' or naked. On a flying visit to Edinburgh Oscar Wilde expressed the hope, 'perhaps I may find you out of Fairyland'. Acquaintances included Lewis Carroll and Scots, Alexander Anderson, the poet who published as 'Surfaceman', Andrew Carnegie, and

William Sharp who, writing under his female persona as Fiona Macleod, was to eventually completely lose himself in a Celtic phantasmagoria, in which fairies were by no means inconspicuous.

A contemporary of Paton was Richard Doyle, the talented illustrator of *The Fairy Ring* (1846) and *In Fairyland* (1870). His nephew was Conan Doyle, born in Edinburgh where he later studied medicine under the professor upon whom he modelled Sherlock Holmes. In 1922 he introduced his book on the Cottingley Fairies with the observation:

> It is hard for the mind to grasp what the ultimate results may be if we have actually proved the existence upon the surface of this planet of a population which may be as numerous as the human race, which pursues its own strange life in its own strange way, and which is only separated from ourselves by some distance of vibrations.[16]

Doyle was a member of the Society for Psychical Research, founded in 1882. During the 1890s it attracted a fair number of celebrities and scholars as it probed various supernatural phenomena. At the same time it began a series of investigations in Gaelic-speaking Scotland.

The approach of the millennium witnessed a host of publications on mythology and the occult. Sir James George Frazer published his twelve volumes of *The Golden Bough* between 1890 and 1915, a monumental work which is still not without influence. From the 1880s Andrew Lang, one of a seeming legion of Borderers who contributed to the fairy genre, published a steady flow of books on mythology, history, anthropology, ballads and many other subjects. He is now best remembered for his anthologies, his Blue, Red, Green, Yellow, Pink, Grey, Violet, Crimson, Brown, Orange, Olive and Lilac Fairy Books which have been credited in some quarters with reviving interest in the fairy tale, in others with practically inventing it in the form in which it is now known.[17] J. M. Barrie from Kirriemuir, who was educated at Glasgow, Forfar, Dumfries and Edinburgh, launched his play *Peter Pan, or The Boy who Wouldn't Grow Up* upon the world in 1904; it appeared in story form in 1911. The book is much darker than the annual Christmas reruns on stage, a work of imaginative brilliance and sympathy tinged with bitterness. Peter was thought to live with the fairies but when children died 'he went part of the way with them so that they should not be frightened'. Each child had different notions of Neverland. Tinker Bell had an unusual attribute for one of her kind and size since she tended to *embonpoint* or plumpness. Peter's address was 'Second to the right and then straight on till morning'. Fairies originated when the first baby laughed for the first time and its laugh broke into a thousand pieces. Peter, for whom 'make-believe and true were exactly the same thing' believed that to die would be an awfully big adventure. Some of the mother-child role play involving Wendy, a name which did not exist before Barrie invented it, appears somewhat bizarre in modern eyes but what is most chilling is perhaps the last sentence which relates that the Peter Pan story will be played out in every generation 'so long as children are gay and innocent and heartless'. Critics have probably read too much of Barrie's autobiography into these words which link innocence and selfishness, the unconscious, unthinking and non-malicious latter generating the agony and eternal anxiety of parenthood. What is clear is that Peter Pan is unmistakably Scottish, inheritor as he is of the traditional associations that are hundreds of years old.

Of Lang Barrie wrote, 'there was a touch of the elf about him'. When Lang died in 1912, the torch was passed to Lewis Spence of Broughty Ferry, a journalist whose output was not as prodigious as Lang's but was, nevertheless, impressive. There are numerous others who could be mentioned, such as Kenneth Graham, born in Edinburgh, who wrote about the fairfolk before penning his masterpiece *The Wind in the Willows* (1918) into which he may have imported some dim childhood memories of Argyll. The twentieth century would add its store to the lore. Suffice it to suggest that the fairies retained a significant hold on the Scottish literary and creative imagination, first captured once upon a distant time, and that they continued to exercise their glamour long after True Thomas had his fateful engagement with the fairy queen under the Eildon Tree.

Folklore and Fairyology

In folklore, fairy and other supernatural beliefs, once shunned as absurdities or impossibilities, have survived the twin onslaught of authoritarian disapproval and Victorian artifice, to continue unabated, if constantly updated and remodified, 'like elastic, stretching and thinning out rather than letting itself be severed completely'. One reason fairy belief has endured for so long is that 'belief in the existence of spirits is founded not upon loose speculation, but upon concrete, personal experiences, the reality of which is reinforced by sensory perception'.[18]

A possible explanation for its apparent decline in the last century is not, perhaps, that people are no longer experiencing the fairy phenomenon, but that the language and referents used to express similar experience have changed. A theory that has gained ground in recent years is that fairy belief has never really disappeared, it has simply adapted to the modern, technological age and been transposed into UFO sightings and abduction narratives. The first person to consider fairy belief and UFO lore together argues that UFOs are 'nothing but a resurgence of a deep stream in human culture known in older times under various names . . . the modern, global belief in flying saucers and their occupants is identical to an earlier belief in the fairy faith'. A convincing number of analogies between the two traditions has been distinguished, though important phenomenological differences should not be ignored.[19] It is imperative that folklore keeps pace with such up-to-the-minute developments.

The word 'folklore' is one of the most misunderstood and misapplied terms in the English language. Like 'superstition', it is often used to denote someone else's beliefs and traditions. It is something which happens somewhere else. This sentiment is by no means new. James VI's opinion has been widely shared. Why should it be, he wondered, that superstition should be more prevalent in such wild parts of the world as Lapland, Finland, Orkney or Shetland? 'Because where the Devill findes greatest ignorance and barbaritie, there assayles he grosseliest, as I gave you the reason wherefore there was moe witches of women kinde nor men'.[20]

An eighteenth-century chapbook entitled *History of the Haverel Wives* reflects the prejudice, not only of 'superstition' considered as a foreign problem but also as a statement of anti-catholicism: 'most of the priests . . . are dead and rotten, and the rest o' them gade awa to Italy, where the auld Pape their faither, the deil, the witches, brownies, and fairies dwal'. The folk were confident in their assumption that witches, brownies, and other 'unco bodies' were inhabitants of foreign countries. *The History of John Cheap the Chapman* relates that when Cheap informed a woman at Tweedside that he had been in London, she responded, 'Yea, yea, lad, an ye cum'd frae London ye're no muckle worth, for the folks there awa' is a' witches and warlocks, deils, brownies, and fairies'.[21]

Scott, to be sure, established the part of Scotland most dear to his heart as the centre of supernatural activity, 'but though the church, in the border counties, attracted little veneration, no part of Scotland teemed with superstitious fears and observances more than they did'. Furthermore, nowhere had 'the belief in Fairies maintained its ground with more pertinacity than in Selkirkshire'. Scott was perhaps unusual in identifying his own back yard as a great repository of superstition, but in his case the distance was temporal. By recording the folklore of the Borders, he both controlled and, in a sense, ended it, fossilising the material on the page with no expectation or encouragement of furthering the organic process. It was a common view among educated Scots that Scotland had always been a peculiar haunt of supernatural entities; many subscribed to Scott's view that 'fairy superstition in England . . . was of a more playful and gentle, less wild and necromantic character, than that received among the sister people'.[22]

The sentiment that there is 'a natural connection . . . between wild scenes and wild legends' is by no means only the judgement of past commentators.[23] At the present time fairy belief, and indeed 'folklore' generally, is still sometimes pushed out to geographically remote areas. Time and again assertions are made that 'old Celtic strongholds' remain the favoured haunts of the fairies: the Scottish Highlands, the Welsh mountains, the West of Ireland, and the West Country in England. Another cliché is that 'actual belief in fairies and the related Second Sight survived latest among the Gaelic-speaking Highlanders of Scotland because they lived in the most inaccessible part of Britain, further out of the reach of authority and more remote from the 'civilizing' influences – including the English language – than the rest of the population'.[24] The tone of cultural imperialism in this last pretentious nugget beggars belief, but is sadly familiar, the implication being that countries which retain a store of supernatural belief traditions are culturally, and in every other sense, backward.

It is not particularly difficult to understand why the fairies are consistently consigned to a supposedly dim and distant place or past. Frequently, though not necessarily intentionally, a patronising image of a quaint, rural, untarnished and 'simple' time or place is constructed. In other instances, it is a hearkening back to something that appears to have been lost in one's own lifetime or immediate surroundings. One recent investigator finds, for example, that by pushing fairies back in time, the Newfoundlanders' narratives about fairies became 'emblematic' of a 'vanished happy past'.[25]

The fairies have been, in the main, connected with the concept of 'wildness' or 'wilderness'. However, like foxes and squirrels, some fairies are moving into the cities and towns. In March of 1966 Ogilvie Crombie, while sitting on a bench in Edinburgh's Royal Botanic Gardens, met a faun called Kurmos. He was a boy, about three feet tall, who wore no clothing but had shaggy legs and cloven hooves, pointed chin and ears, and little horns on his head. Ogilvie conversed with the creature, who confided that he lived in the Gardens and helped the trees to grow. Nature spirits, said the faun, had lost interest in humans 'since they have been made to feel that they are neither believed in nor wanted'. Kurmos then accepted an invitation back to Ogilvie's flat. On a later occasion, near the National Gallery, Ogilvie met another creature of the same description as Kurmos, but this one was taller than himself. They walked together through the streets of Edinburgh, the being questioning Ogilvie as to whether he was afraid of him. It played the pipes for him, and then left. Ogilvie continued to meet a variety of Otherworldly creatures including the Elf King at Rosemarkie, and, on the island of Iona, Pan, whom he maintained was the god of all nature spirits.[26]

While we have been researching this book, we have met many people who have confided a belief in fairies. One person told us that he encountered one of the fairfolk near the top of Schiehallion, another that fairies still occupy the 'Picts' Houses' on Skye. We have been assured that fairies intervene in human affairs and they have been cited in explanation of unusual phenomena, including illness. The need to explain, from a 'scientific' or 'rational' perspective, what fairies are and why people believe in them is something that this book has avoided. What is important is that they are real to those who believe in their existence or have experienced the phenomenon first-hand. Nonetheless, some comment on the various 'roles' or 'functions' that have been ascribed to fairy belief in Scottish history is in order.

Figuring the Fairies

Alleged fairy intervention can offer explanations for the inexplicable: 'there is a human need to come to terms in some way with eternal mysteries . . . the unpredictable intervention of the unknown in our daily life'. In folk belief, the fairies 'constitute a threat to humankind: they represent hidden and inimical powers, ever ready to disturb the tenor of daily life'. Fairies also make 'excellent scapegoats for human failings and problems, and have taken the blame for illness, violence, disability and death'. Fairy legends, tales, poems, ballads, lullabies, charms, and so on, can be seen as conveyors of useful cultural knowledge, a suggestion also made about ballads which take the Otherworld as their theme. Since 'folklore operates within a society to insure conformity to the accepted cultural norms', the fairies could serve 'as a pedagogic device'.[27]

There are many possible reasons for putting a fairy interpretation on an event: 'to have a good story, to make things exciting, to make one's self interesting', as an excuse for getting lost, 'showing up where one should not be, or not showing up where one should'. Scott related the story of a man, employed to pull heather from Peatlaw Hill, near Carterhaugh, who fell asleep on a fairy ring and awakened to find himself in Glasgow. 'That he had been carried off by the Fairies, was implicitly believed by all, who did not reflect, that a man may have private reasons for leaving his own country, and for disguising his having intentionally done so'. The fairies could also act as a cover for 'violence, abductions, or other deviant behaviour'.[28]

Evidence of fairies being used as a cloak for human crimes is almost impossible to confirm. J. G. Dalyell noted the 1624 Orkney trial of James Houston, who may have murdered his own grandson, but told the boy's mother 'the fairie had tane him away'. Sudden illness or death was often thought to be the handiwork of supernatural agents. Thomas Cors, tried in Orkney in 1643, testified that to be struck dumb or suffer paralysis was called 'the phairie'. Changelings have been the subject of much theorising, ranging from the plausible to the utterly improbable, or totally unprovable, such as the suggestion that children were kidnapped by pre-Celtic peoples or Druids, as recruits for their diminished force, or that specially chosen, healthy children were used in sacrificial rituals, while sick children were rejected. Another notion was that the soul of the human had been abstracted by disembodied spirits or magicians. A further theory was concerned with demonic possession.[29]

Explanations as to what changelings 'really' were often involve medical interpretations such as deformity or disease. That changelings were a 'folk explanation' for disabled children with 'identifiable congenital disorders' is another contention, as is the idea of an infant's 'failure to thrive'. By no means all investigators are convinced of the value of such approaches:

> while there can be little doubt that such 'fairy' afflictions have their origin in physical and mental disturbances, to say that their main role is etiology, that is, to 'explain' the disturbances to tradition-bearers, is a limited view which ignores the important contextual fact that the stories are told long after the original event, by people with no particular need to explain anything.

That changeling narratives only 'explain' mental and physical conditions is inadequate, in this view: the 'narrative value' must, therefore, derive from another, or additional, source. One suggested possibility is the 'tension between nature [fairies] and culture' which, it is argued, is one of the 'underlying dynamics' of, once again, Newfoundland fairy tradition. Furthermore,

> as applied to 'normal' children – cranky, crying, wakeful, tiresome – changeling tales could express normal, but personally and socially unacceptable, parental feelings of anger and rejection. As a sublimating device, they are a model of structural economy: the 'real' child (beautiful, happy, lovable) is safely removed, and abuse heaped upon the ugly, cantankerous substitute.[30]

But perhaps there is a fifth possibility – the cultural legitimisation of infanticide. It may be that unwanted or sickly children were given fairy origins and subsequently left out, or exposed, to be taken by those alleged to be their own kind. The death of the child thus provided a socially acceptable method of ridding the community, and the parents, of potential burdens upon themselves.

The fairy world is an inversion of the human world, the unpredictability of daily existence reflected in fairy belief. Nearly everything in Elfland – time, topography, even the fairies themselves – was subject to change, alteration or metamorphosis. Those who found themselves in situations of enchantment were often also in a process of transition, specifically alienation from their communities – a familiar theme in fairy narratives. To be separated or distinguished in some way, or to break with conformity, was to be endangered. Yet even here the inversion principle can be distinguished. Removal from the community, or to be marked out in some way from its members, could sometimes attract increased power or status. To be alone in fairy places, and to have communication with fairy folk, often left the individual with special gifts, such as second sight, prophecy, an ability to heal, or unusual musical talent.

Fairies were firmly connected to the landscape and deeply rooted in the soil. The importance of respecting the land which they frequented was widely recognised. It was bad luck to interfere with, or try to remove, trees, bushes, stones, ancient buildings, or anything else believed to have fairy associations. Misfortune, illness, or even death might result from tampering with fairy property. In Ireland a number of Iron Age ring forts, which came to be known as 'fairy forts', were preserved from demolition because of their Otherworld associations. Roads in Iceland have had to be rerouted to avoid known habitations of the trolls.[31] That some Scots shared similar sentiments is indicated by the tale of Sir Godfrey MacCulloch of Galloway. One evening, near his home, he was accosted by a 'little old man, in green and mounted upon a white palfrey'. He told MacCulloch that he lived underneath his house and that he had 'great reason to complain of the direction of the drain, or common sewer', which emptied itself directly into his best room. A concerned MacCulloch assured the old man that he would redirect the offending drain, which he promptly did. Several years later, MacCulloch was brought to trial for the murder of a neighbour and condemned to be beheaded on the Castle-hill, Edinburgh. As he approached the scaffold, his 'good neighbour' suddenly appeared on a white horse. Sir Godfrey jumped up behind him, and they sped off 'and neither he nor the criminal were ever again seen'. In actual fact, Sir Godfrey MacCulloch was found guilty of murdering William Gordon in October, 1690. He escaped abroad, thus averting justice for some years but later returned to Scotland where he was apprehended and brought to trial in Edinburgh. On 25 March, 1697 he was executed.[32]

Other sites were associated with more mundane matters:

> He wha gaes by the fairy ring,
> Nae dule nor pine shall see;
> And he wha cleans the fairy ring,
> An easy death shall dee.

The same dire warning is conveyed in a Berwickshire rhyme recorded by George Henderson:

> He who tills the fairies' green,
> Nae luck again shall hae;
> And he who spoils the fairies' ring,
> Betide him want and woe;
> For weirdless days and weary nights
> Are his till his dying day.

Likewise, 'Where the scythe cuts, and the sock rives/Hae done wi' fairies and bee-bykes!' In other words, mowing or ploughing leads to the eradication of beehives and fairies alike, for, in various places, fairies were said to have been seen, gathered together, to 'take a formal farewell of the district, when it had become, from agricultural changes, unfitted for their residence'.[33]

Some commentators have been puzzled by the christian elements that emerge in the witch confessions, such as those of Bessie Dunlop and Andro Man, but it should be kept in mind that christianity represented a mere veneer upon beliefs which in some cases had been in existence for thousands of years. Belief in christianity and belief in the fairies were not necessarily incompatible. People were, as they still are, quite capable of adhering to more than one belief system, no matter how incongruous they may seem. Martin Martin's account of his summer visit to St. Kilda in 1697 revealed that though the people were staunch christians, they believed that the rocks and hills were places where 'spirits are embodied', and that these spirits could appear instantaneously whenever and wherever they chose. The suggestion that there is an element of individual choice involved in 'which aspects of a body of tradition are accepted for 'belief'' can be applied here. 'People do not unthinkingly accept a whole 'set' of traditions, but evaluate them according to experience, authenticity, and other criteria; they are selective in what they take from the reservoir of available ideas and how they use it'.[34] Selectivity is obvious in two cases probably involving adultery from the Isle of Bute. In 1650 Finwell Hyndman in Kingarth was questioned about why she disappeared for a twenty-four hour period about once every quarter year, particularly since when she returned she had upon her 'such a wyld smell that none could come neire her, and that she was all craised [crazed] and weary as if it were one after a farr journey'. Since no satisfactory explanations were forthcoming, she was 'bruted for a witch or (as the commone people calls it) being with the fayryes'. Twenty years later a man objected that he was accused of having a mistress 'among the furies commonly called Fairfolks' to the detriment of his good name.[35]

This book has attempted to investigate fairy belief, mainly, but not exclusively, in sixteenth- and seventeenth-century Scotland. The connection of the fairies with the landscape has been explored, as has the journey to Fairyland, fairy society, and the association between fairies and the dead, with witches, and with second sight. The process of enchantment, and its corollary disenchantment, has also been discussed, as have the 'marvellous gifts' thought to have been conferred upon humans by the fairies. The assault on fairy belief, mainly in the post-Reformation era, took place at the same time as the attack upon folk culture in general, but, despite the best efforts of Church and State, fairy belief survived. Perhaps even more remarkable were the efforts of Robert Kirk, and others, to assert the reality of fairies in mounting a rearguard action against the forces of Enlightenment. The fairies who, in Scottish terms, first appear in medieval literature, continued to haunt the medium throughout the centuries, 'The horns of Elfland' proving a potent source of inspiration to some of our finest writers. The nature of fairy belief from the eighteenth century to the present remains to be investigated; some of its potential richness for future research has been indicated.

It has been remarked that 'as we have grown in civilization we have lost many instincts once granted to mortals', implying that the fairies are still present but folk no longer have the ability to recognise them. Such an observation was apparently not shared by an old lady from Quarff, Shetland who when told that people in the twentieth-century no longer saw fairies answered, 'Yea, dat dø dey, bit dir faird ta tell onybody', (that they do but they're afraid to tell anyone).[36] It may be that they tell themselves. At the top of Doon Hill in Aberfoyle, where Kirk breathed his last, a tall pine is now said to entrap his soul. The place may have functioned as a clootie den for many years, but we first noted the practice in 1996 following the Dunblane massacre: hundreds of scraps of ribbon or cloth offering touching prayers for the dead and the injured. On a recent visit (July 2000), the observance continues: branches and bushes adorned with messages, including one for Fairy Rose of whom we had, hitherto, never heard. The fairies, it would seem, have not departed quite yet.

Notes

1 Hugh Miller, *The Old Red Sandstone* (1841; London 1922), 215.
2 Miller, *The Old Red Sandstone*, 215.
3 There is a similar tradition in England where the fairies were said to have taken their leave at the Rollright Stones, Oxfordshire. This was witnessed by an old man called Will Hughes who saw the fairies dancing around the King Stone. See A. J. Evans, *Folk-Lore Journal* 6 (1895), 6.
4 Robert Chambers, *A Biographical Dictionary of Eminent Scotsmen*, 3 vols (London 1870) *loc. cit.*; *The Oxford Companion to Fairy Tales* ed. Jack Zipes (Oxford 2000), 223, a work which incidentally minimises the Scottish contribution to the genre.
5 Edward J. Cowan, 'The Invention of Celtic Scotland', in *Alba: Celtic Scotland in the Medieval Era*, eds. Edward J. Cowan and R. Andrew McDonald (East Linton 2000), 18–19.
6 James Macpherson, *The Poems of Ossian and Related Works*, ed. Howard Gaskill (Edinburgh 1996), 356, 366. The supposed grave of the Cout, or Colt

Farewell Lychnobious People

– a reference to his strength and agility – is still to be seen on the banks of Hermitage Water in which the warrior drowned.

7 James Morton, *The Poetical remains of the late Dr. John Leyden with Memoirs of his Life* (London 1819), 10, 29, 147, 295–415, i-lxxxv; *Letters*, 102n; *Minstrelsy*, vol. 2, 300–407.

8 Jane Millgate, *Walter Scott: The Making of a Novelist* (Edinburgh 1984), 3–18.

9 Edward J. Cowan, 'Icelandic Studies in Eighteenth and Nineteenth Century Scotland', *Studia Islandica* 31 (1972), 109–51.

10 James Hogg, *The Three Perils of Man: War, Women and Witchcraft*, ed. Douglas Gifford (Edinburgh 1996), xvii. We are indebted to Douglas for drawing Scott's review to our attention.

11 Hogg, *Works*, vol. 2, 13, 18, 24, 26, 32–6, 58, 61, 97, 100–3, 323, 374, 392–4; Mrs Garden, *Memorials of James Hogg The Ettrick Shepherd* (Paisley 1904), x, xx, 61; Edith C. Batho, *The Ettrick Shepherd* (New York 1927), *passim*; Douglas Gifford, *James Hogg* (Edinburgh 1976), *passim*.

12 *Memorials of James Hogg*, 173.

13 Harper, *Bards of Galloway*, 72–6.

14 Elizabeth Saintsbury, *George MacDonald: A Short Life* (Edinburgh 1987), *passim*.

15 Archibald Maclaren, *The Fairy Family. A Series of Ballads and Metrical Tales Illustrating The Fairy Faith of Europe*, illustrated by Edward Burne-Jones (1857: London 1985), ix-xvii, 3–11.

16 *Victorian Fairy Painting*, ed. Jane Martineau (London 1997), 11–21, 101–13; M. H. Noel-Paton and J. P. Campbell, *Noel Paton 1821–1901* (Edinburgh 1990), *passim*; Richard A, Schindler 'Joseph Noel Paton's Fairy Paintings: Fantasy Art as Victorian Narrative', *Scotia. Interdisciplinary Journal of Scottish Studies* xiv (1990) 13–29; Sir Arthur Conan Doyle, *The Coming of the Fairies* (1922: London 1996), 7.

17 *The Oxford Companion to Fairy Tales*, 290; Green, *Andrew Lang*, 82.

18 Bennett, *Traditions of Belief*, 118–9; Honko, 'Memorates and the Study of Folk Beliefs', 10.

19 Jacques Vallee, *Passport to Magonia, From Folklore to Flying Saucers* (Chicago 1969), qtd. in Peter M. Rojcewicz, 'Fairies, UFOs, and Problems of Knowledge', in *Good People*, 480–1, 508, note 12.

20 *Daemonologie*, 69.

21 William Harvey, *Scottish Chapbook Literature* (Paisley 1903), 53.

22 *Minstrelsy*, vol. 1, 139–40, vol. 2, 377–8, 351; MacCulloch, 'The Mingling of Fairy and Witch Belief', 231–2; *Letters*, 150.

23 Miller, *The Old Red Sandstone*, 214.

24 Patrick Harpur, 'Away with the Fairies', *Country Living* May 1996; Jennifer Westwood, foreword, *Robert Kirk. Walker Between Worlds*, ed. R. J. Stewart (Longmead, Dorset 1990), ix.

25 Rieti, *Strange Terrain*, 99. See also Linda-May Ballard, who notes that on

Rathlin Island, situated off the coast of Northern Ireland, fairies are probably 'less part of the actual belief system of the islanders than they were a generation ago'. However, she wonders if an increasing reluctance to admit to belief in fairies is a part of the complex of the 'idea that fairy belief is fading and belongs to the past'. 'Fairies and the Supernatural on Reachrai', in *Good People*, 48, 91.

26 Paul Hawken, *The Magic of Findhorn* (1975; Glasgow 1983), 134–69.
27 Kirk (Sanderson), 45; Rieti, *Strange Terrain*, 212. See also Narváez, 'Newfoundland Berry Pickers', 354–8; Buchan, 'Taleroles and the Otherworld Ballads', 254; Bascom, 'Four Functions of Folklore', 293, 297.
28 *Minstrelsy*, vol. 2, 378; Rieti, *Strange Terrain*, 120. See also Narváez, 'Newfoundland Berry Pickers', 354–8.
29 Trial of James Houston, 22 Jan. 1624, and of Thomas Cors, 6 April 1643. *Records of Orkney*, 57, 261, qtd. in Dalyell, 539; Evans-Wentz, *The Fairy Faith*, 245–51.
30 Edwin Sidney Hartland, *The Science of Fairy Tales* 1891 (Detroit 1986), 110; Susan Schoon Eberly, 'Fairies and the Folklore of Disability: Changelings, Hybrids, and the Solitary Fairy', in *Good People*, 227; Joyce Underwood Munro, 'The Invisible Made Visible: The Fairy Changeling as a Folk Articulation of Failure to Thrive in Infants and Children', in *Good People*, 251–83; Barbara Rieti, ' "The Blast" in Newfoundland Fairy Tradition', in *Good People*, 287; Rieti, *Strange Terrain*, 43–4.
31 Ó Giolláin, 'The Fairy Belief and Official Religion in Ireland', 199.
32 *Minstrelsy*, vol. 2, 359–61; Chambers, *Domestic Annals of Scotland*, 174–6.
33 George Henderson, *The Popular Rhymes, Sayings, and Proverbs of the County of Berwick* (Newcastle-on-Tyne 1856), 111–2; Chambers, *Popular Rhymes of Scotland*, 324.
34 Martin Martin, *A Voyage to St. Kilda*, 1697, 1753 (Edinburgh 1986), 43; Rieti, *Strange Terrain*, 98.
35 *Kingarth Parish Records: The Session Book of Kingarth, 1641–1703*, ed. Henry Paton (n.p. 1932), 19–21, 57–8; J. King Hewison, *The Isle of Bute in Olden Time*, 2 vols. (Edinburgh 1895), vol. 2, 261–9.
36 Simpson, *Folklore in Lowland Scotland*, 89; Reid Tait, *Shetland Folk Book*, vol. 2 (1951), 24–5.

Table 3. Witch Trials

All witch trials so far found that contain references to fairy belief.

Name	Place	Date
Jonet Boyman	Canongate, Edinburgh	29 Dec. 1572
Bessie Dunlop	Lyne, Ayrshire	8 Nov. 1576
Alison Peirson	Byrehill	28 May, 1588
Katherine Ross Lady Fowlis	Ross-shire	22 July, 1590
Agnes Sampson	Nether Keythe	1590–1
Euphemia Makcalzane	Cliftonhall	9 June, 1591
Isobell Strathaquin (and her daughter)	Dyce, Aberdeen	Jan.-Feb., 1597
Christiane Lewingston	Leith	12 Nov., 1597
Andro Man	Aberdeen	1597–8
Thomas Lorn	Overton of Dyce	19 Jan., 1598–9
Walter Ronaldson	Kirktown of Dyce	20 Nov., 1601
Barbara (Bartie) Paterson	Newbattle	18 Dec., 1607
Jonet Drever	Orkney	1615
Katherine Caray	Orkney	June, 1616
Katherine Jonesdochter	Shetland	2 Oct., 1616
Barbara Thomasdochter	Delting, Shetland	2 Oct., 1616
Elspeth Reoch	Caithness/Orkney	1616
John Stewart	Irvine	1618
Isobel Haldane	Perth	15 May, 1623
Janet Trall	Blackruthven/Perth	22 May, 1623
James Houston	Orkney	22 Jan., 1624
Steven Maltman	Gargunnock	April, 1628
James Knarston	Orkney	1633
Isobel Sinclair	Orkney	Feb., 1633
Katherine Cragie	Orkney	1640
Thomas Cors	Orkney	6 April, 1643
Margaret Alexander	Livingstone	12 March, 10 April, 1647
Barbra Parish	Livingstone	10–17 April, 1647
Finwell Hyndman	Kingarth	17–19 March, 1650
Isobell Bennet	Stirling	March, 1659
Beatrix Lesley	Dalkeith	20 July, 1661
Bessie Flinkar	Libberton	7 Aug., 1661
Jonet Morison	Bute	18 Jan., 1662
Isobel Gowdie	Auldearn	13 April, 3 and 15 May, 1662
James M'Phie (scandal)	Kingarth	3 Jan., 1670
Jean Weir	Dalkeith	6 April, 1670
Donald McIlmichall	Appin/Inveraray	27 Oct., 1677
Farqhar Ferguson (charming)	Kilmory/Arran	9 Dec., 1716

Table 4. Folk Motifs

Migratory Legend
Reidar Th. Christiansen, *The Migratory Legends*, Folklore Fellows Communications 175 (Helsinki 1958).

ML 4075 Visits to fairy dwellings.
ML 4077 Caught in Fairyland.
ML 5006 The ride with the fairies.
ML 5050 The fairies' prospect of salvation.
ML 5055 The fairies' attitude to the Christian faith.
ML 5070 Midwife to the fairies.
ML 5075 Removing a building over a Fairy's house.
ML 5080 Food from the Fairies.
ML 5081 Fairies steal food.
ML 5082 Fairies borrow food.
ML 5085 The Changeling.
ML 5086 Release from Fairyland.
ML 5095 Fairy woman pursues man.
ML 6045 Drinking-cup stolen from the fairies.
ML 6050 The Fairy Hat.
ML 6055 The fairy cows.
ML 7012 The Fairy revenge for negligence.
ML 8010 Hidden Treasures.

Motif
Stith Thompson, *Motif-Index of Folk Literature*, 6 vols. (Indiana 1955–8).

A1135 Origin of winter weather.
A1535.5 Beltane.
B120.0.1 Animals have second sight.
B733 Animals can see spirits and scent danger.
C46 Taboo: offending fairy.
C51.4.3 Taboo: spying on fairies.
C211.1 Taboo: eating in Fairyland.
C311.1.2 Taboo: looking at fairies.
C420 Taboo: uttering secrets.
C420.2 Taboo: not to speak about a certain happening.
C433 Taboo: uttering name of malevolent creature.
C515 Taboo: plucking flowers.
C523.2 Taboo: disturbing fairy ring.
C532 Taboo: digging in fairy haunts.
D562 Transformation through bathing.

Table 4. Folk Motifs

D610 Repeated transformations from one form into another.
D631 Fairy changes size at will.
D661 Transformation as punishment.
D700 Disenchantment.
D757 Disenchantment by holding enchanted person during successive transformations.
D766 Disenchantment by liquid.
D926 Magic well.
D931 Magic stone.
D950 Magic tree.
D950.6 Magic ash tree.
D950.10 Magic apple tree.
D950.13 Magic hawthorn.
D965 Magic plant.
D978 Magic herbs.
D1030 Magic banquet.
D1162 Magic light.
D1184 Magic thread.
D1222 Magic horn (musical).
D1242 Magic fluid.
D1244 Magic salve (ointment).
D1273.1.1 Three as a magic number.
D1273.1.3 Seven as a magic number.
D1273.1.5 Twelve as a magic number.
D1381 Magic object protects from attack.
D1385 Magic object protects against evil spirits.
D1385.2 Plant as antidote to spells and enchantments.
D1385.2.5 Ash (quicken rowan) protects against spells and enchantments.
D1500.1.1.2 Well with curative powers.
D1500.1.3 Magic trees heal.
D1500.1.4 Magic healing plant.
D1500.1.4.2. Magic healing leaves.
D1500.1.11 Magic healing drink.
D1516 Charms against elf-shot.
D1786 Magic power at crossroads.
D1825.1 Second sight.
D1896 Magic ageing after years in Fairyland; person crumbles to dust.
D1960.2 King asleep in mountain.
D2011 Years thought days.
D2031 Magic illusion.
D2031.0.2 Fairies cause illusions.
D2066 Elf-shot.
D2083.3 Milk transferred from another's cow by magic.
D2087.6 Food stolen by magic.
D2098 Ships magically sunk.
D2120 Magic transportation.
D2125 Magic journey over water.
D2161 Magic healing power.
F81 Descent to lower world of dead (Hell, Hades).
F81.1 Orpheus.
F92 Entrance to lower world through spring, hole, or cave.
F103.1 (Baughman) 'Green children' visit world of mortals; continue to live with them.
F141 Water barrier to the Otherworld.

F162.1 Garden in Otherworld.
F162.2 Rivers in Otherworld.
F211 Fairyland under hollow knoll.
F211.0.1 Fairies live in prehistoric mounds.
F211.3 Fairies live under the earth.
F212 Fairyland under water.
F213 Fairyland on island.
F221 House of fairy.
F221.1 Fairy house disappears at dawn.
F222 Fairy castle.
F230 Appearance of fairies.
F233.1 Green fairy.
F233.6 Fairies fair (fine, white).
F234.0.2 Fairy as shape-shifter.
F234.1 Fairy in form of an animal.
F235.1 Fairies invisible.
F235.4.1 Fairies made visible through use of ointment.
F236.1 Colour of fairies' clothes.
F236.1.3 Fairies in white clothes.
F236.1.6 Fairies in green clothes.
F236.3.2 Fairies with red caps.
F236.6 Fairies wear gay clothes.
F239.4.1 Fairies are the same size as mortals.
F239.4.2 Fairies are the size of small children.
F239.4.3 Fairy is tiny.
F241 Fairies' animals.
F241.1 Fairies' horses.
F241.1.0.1 Fairy cavalcade.
F241.1.1.1 Fairies ride white horses.
F241.1.7 Fairies turn sticks and straws into horses.
F241.2 Fairies' cows.
F243 Fairies' food.
F244 Fairies' treasure.
F251.2 Fairies as souls of the departed.
F251.3 Unbaptised children as fairies.
F251.4 Fairies are children Eve hid from God.
F251.6 Fairies are fallen angels.
F251.10 Fairies are not children of Adam.
F251.11 Fairies are people not good enough for Heaven and not bad enough for Hell.
F252.1 Fairy King.
F252.2 Fairy Queen.
F253.1.1 Fairy with extraordinary physical strength.
F254.1 Fairies have Physical disabilities.
F257 Tribute taken from fairies by fiend at stated periods.
F261 Fairies dance.
F261.1.1 Fairies dance in fairy rings.
F262 Fairies make music.
F262.1 Fairies sing.
F262.2 Fairies teach bagpipe-playing.
F262.8 Fairy horns heard by mortals.
F263 Fairies feast.
F271.0.1 Fairies as craftsmen.

Table 4. Folk Motifs

F271.4 Fairies work on cloth.
F271.4.3 Fairies spin.
F271.10 Fairies bake bread.
F282 Fairies travel through air.
F282.2 Formulas for fairies' travel through air.
F282.4(a) Mortal travels with fairies: feasts with them in various spots.
F301 Fairy lover.
F301.1.1.2 Girl summons fairy lover by plucking flowers.
F301.2 Fairy lover entices mortal girl.
F302.3.1 Fairy entices man into Fairyland.
F305 Offspring of fairy and mortal.
F320 Fairies carry people away to Fairyland.
F321 Fairies steal child from cradle.
F321.1 Changeling. Fairy steals child from cradle and leaves fairy substitute.
F321.1.2.2 Changeling is always hungry.
F321.1.2.3 Changeling is sickly.
F321.1.3 Exorcizing a changeling.
F321.1.4 Disposing of a changeling.
F321.1.4.3 Changeling thrown on fire, and thus banished.
F321.2 Charms against theft of children by fairies.
F322 Fairies steal man's wife.
F322.2 Man rescues his wife from Fairyland.
F328 Fairies entice people to their domains.
F329.1 Fairies carry off youth; he has gift of prophecy when he returns.
F330 Grateful fairies.
F332 Fairies grateful for hospitality.
F332.0.1 Fairy grateful to mortal for daily food.
F333 Fairy grateful to human midwife.
F335 Fairy grateful for loan.
F338 Fairies grateful to man who repairs their utensil or implements.
F340 Gifts from fairies.
F342.1 Fairy gold.
F343.21 Fairies give mortal skill in music.
F344 Fairies heal mortals.
F346 Mortals helped by fairies.
F347 Fairy as guardian spirit.
F348.7 Taboo: telling of fairy gifts: gifts cease.
F352 Theft of cup from fairies.
F352.1 Theft of cup from fairies when they offer mortal drink.
F360 Malevolent or destructive fairies.
F361 Fairy's revenge.
F361.3 Fairies take revenge on person who spies on them.
F361.3.3 Fairies blind person who watches them.
F361.4 Fairies take revenge on person who trespasses on their land.
F361.4 (c) Fairy complains of drain; man changes it; fairy later saves his life.
F362 Fairies cause diseases.
F363 Fairies cause death.
F365 Fairies steal.
F369.7 Fairies lead travellers astray.
F370 Visit to Fairyland.
F372 Fairies take human nurse to wait on fairy child.
F372.1 Fairies take human midwife to attend fairy woman.

F375 Mortals as captives in Fairyland.
F377 Supernatural lapse of time in Fairyland.
F377 (c) Person is in Fairyland for duration of one dance; months or years have passed.
F377 (d) Person returns from Fairyland; crumbles to dust.
F378.1 Taboo: touching ground on return from Fairyland.
F378.7 Taboo: eating fairy food while with fairies.
F379.1 Return from Fairyland.
F379.1.1 No return from Fairyland.
F379.3 Man lives with fairies seven years.
F380 Defeating or ridding oneself of fairies.
F382.1 Fairies fear the cross.
F382.2 Holy water breaks fairy spell.
F382.3 Use of God's name breaks fairy spell.
F382.4 Bible breaks fairy spell.
F383.2 Fairy unable to cross running stream.
F383.4 Fairy power ceases at cockcrow.
F384.2 (a) Knife powerful against fairies.
F384.3 Iron powerful against fairies.
F388 Fairies depart.
F391 Fairies borrow from mortals.
F399.4 Playful or troublesome fairies.
F451 Dwarfs.
F451.2 Appearance of dwarfs.
F460 Mountain spirits.
F480 House spirits.
F621 Strong man: tree puller.
F721.1 Underground passages.
G225 Witch's familiar spirit.
G241.4 Witch rides on object.
G243 Witches' Sabbath.
G263.4 Witch causes sickness.
G265.4 Witch causes disease or death of animals.
G265.9 Witch ruins crops.
G266 Witches steal.
G272.2.1 Rowan wood protects against spells.
G275.8.2 Witch overcome by help of fairy.
G283.1.2.3 Witches raise wind to sink ships.
G303.3.1 Devil in human form.
G303.3.3 Devil in animal form.
N411.12 Curse by witch.
N512 Treasure in underground chamber.
N538 Treasure pointed out by supernatural creature.
N570 Guardian of treasure.
N815 Fairy as helper.
R112.3 Rescue of prisoners from fairy stronghold.
V70.1.1 Beltane (May Day).
V70.3 Midsummer.
V70.6 Candlemas (Imbolg).
V70.50 Samhain (Halloween).
V134 Sacred wells.
V134.2 Offerings to holy wells.
Z72.1 A year and a day.

Tale Type
Antti Aarne and Stith Thompson, *The Types of the Folktale* (Helsinki 1961).

AT 400 (variant) The man in quest for his lost wife.
AT 425 (variant) Search for lost husband.
AT 503 Gifts of the Little People.
AT 930 The Prophecy.

Bruford index
Alan J. Bruford, 'Trolls, Hillfolk, Finns, and Picts', in *Good People*, 116–41.

F21 Absence for many years in the fairy hill, which seems only hours or minutes to the victim.
F22 Dancing in the Fairy Hill.
F34 Fairy host or sluagh.
F62 Fairy changeling.
F103 Learning tunes from the fairies.
F105 The gift of healing from the fairies.

Bibliography

Unpublished Manuscripts

NAS, CH2/1/2 *Presbytery Records of Aberdeen*
NAS, CH2/185/5 *Haddington Presbytery Records.*
NAS, CH2/214/1 *Kilmory Kirk Session Minutes*
NAS, CH2/296/1 *Pencaitland Kirk Session Records*
NAS, JC/2/13 *Edinburgh Justiciary Court Records*
NAS, JC/26/1/67 *Edinburgh Justiciary Court Records*
NAS, JC /26/26 *Stirling Justiciary Court Records*
NAS, JC/26/27/1, 9, 10 and 13 *Edinburgh Justiciary Court Records*
NAS, GD/124/15/1263 MS. 'An Account of Highlanders by Lord Grange for Viscount Townshend', 1724, 1725.
NAS, GD/188/25/1/1 and 3 MS. of Francis Guthrie, bishop of Moray
SCA, CH2/722/5 *Stirling Presbytery Records*
SCA, CH2/1121/1 *Gargunnock Kirk Session Records*

Primary Material

Aberdeen Presbytery Records. Aberdeen 1846.
Asloan, John. 'The Maner of the Crying of ane Playe'. *The Asloan Manuscript. A Miscellany in Prose and Verse. Written by John Asloan in the Reign of James the Fifth.* 1515. ed. W. A. Craigie. 2 vols. *Scottish Text Society.* Edinburgh 1925.
Barry, John C., ed. *William Hay's Lectures on Marriage.* 1564. Stair Society. Edinburgh 1967.
Bawcutt, Priscilla, ed. *The Poems of William Dunbar.* 2 vols. Glasgow 1998.
Bliss, A. J., ed. *Sir Orfeo.* Oxford 1961.
Boswell, James. *Journal of a Tour to the Hebrides with Samuel Johnson.* 1785. ed. R. W. Chapman. Oxford 1979.
Bovet, Richard. *Pandemonium, or the Devil's Cloyster.* London 1684.
Brand, John A. *A Brief Description of Orkney, Zetland, Pightland Firth and Caithness.* 1701. Edinburgh 1883.
Calderwood, David. *History of the Kirk of Scotland.* ed. T. Thompson. 6 vols. Edinburgh 1842–9.
Campbell, John Francis. *Popular Tales of the West Highlands.* 1860–1. 2 vols. Edinburgh 1994.
——. *More West Highland Tales.* 1940. 1960. 2 vols. Edinburgh 1994.

Carmichael, Alexander. *Carmina Gadelica*. 6 vols. Edinburgh 1928–54.
Catton, James. *The History and Description of the Shetland Islands*. London 1838.
Coldwell, David F. C., ed. Gavin Douglas *Virgil's Aeneid*. 1513. 4 vols. Edinburgh 1957–64.
The Court Books of Orkney and Shetland, 1614–1615. ed. and transcriber, Robert S. Barclay. Scottish History Society. ser. 4. vol. 4. Edinburgh 1967.
Court Book of Shetland, 1615–1629. ed. Gordon Donaldson. Lerwick 1991.
Cranstoun, James, ed. *Poems of Alexander Montgomerie*. Scottish Text Society Edinburgh 1887.
——. *Satirical Poems of the Time of the Reformation*. Scottish Text Society. Edinburgh 1891.
Edmonston, Arthur. *A View of the Ancient and Present State of the Zetland Islands*. Edinburgh 1809.
The English and Scottish Popular Ballads. ed. Francis James Child. 5 vols. Boston and New York 1882–1898.
Extracts From the Council Register of the Burgh of Aberdeen, 1570–1625. Spalding Club 1848.
Fox, Denton, ed. *The Poems of Robert Henryson*. Oxford 1981.
Gerald of Wales. *The Journey Through Wales*. 1188. Trans. Lewis Thorpe. Harmondsworth 1978.
Gillon, Stair A. ed. *Selected Justiciary Cases, 1624–1650*. Edinburgh 1953.
Glanvill, Joseph. *Saducismus Triumphatus: or, Full and Plain Evidence concerning Witches and Apparitions*. London 1682.
——. *Essays on Several Important Subjects in Philosophy and Religion*. London 1676.
James VI, King. *Daemonologie in forme of a Dialogue 1597*. London 1924.
Johnson, Samuel. *A Journey to the Western Isles of Scotland*. 1774. ed. R. W. Chapman. Oxford 1979.
Kirk, James, ed. *The Records of the Synod of Lothian and Tweeddale 1589–1596, 1640–1649*. Stair Society. Edinburgh 1977.
Kirk, Robert. *The Secret Common-Wealth*. 1691. ed. and Commentary by S. Sanderson. Cambridge 1976.
Lavater, Ludwig. *Of Ghostes and Spirites Walking by Nyght*. London 1572.
Law, Robert. *Memorialls; or, the memorable things that fell out within this island of Brittain from 1638 to 1684*. ed. Charles Kirkpatrick Sharpe. Edinburgh 1818.
Low, George. *A Tour Through the Islands of Orkney and Schetland, containing hints relative to the ancient, modern and natural history collected in 1774*. Kirkwall 1879.
MacPhail, J. R. N. ed. *Highland Papers, vol 3, 1662–1677*. Scottish History Society. Edinburgh 1920.
Maitland Club Miscellany. Edinburgh 1833.
Major, John. *A History of Greater Britain*. 1521. ed. and trans. Archibald Constable. Edinburgh 1892.
Martin, Martin. *A Description of the Western Islands of Scotland*. (London: 1703. Second edit. 1716.) Edinburgh 1976.

———. *A Voyage to St. Kilda, 1697.* 1753. Edinburgh, 1986.
Miscellany of the Spalding Club. Aberdeen 1841.
Monro's Western Isles of Scotland. 1549. ed. R. W. Munro. Edinburgh 1961.
More, Henry. *An Antidote Against Atheism.* London 1655.
Murray, James A. H. ed. *The Romance and Prophecies of Thomas of Erceldoune.* Early English Text Society. London 1875.
Pennant, Thomas. *A Tour in Scotland and Voyage to the Hebrides, 1772.* ed. Andrew Simmons. 1774. Edinburgh 1998.
Perth Kirk Session Records. Spottiswoode Club Miscellany. Aberdeen 1845.
Pitcairn, Robert. *Ancient Criminal Trials in Scotland.* 4 vols. Edinburgh 1833.
Robinson, F. N. ed. *The Complete Works of Geoffrey Chaucer.* Oxford 1957.
Scot, Reginald. *The Discoverie of Witchcraft.* 1584.
Scott, Sir Walter. *Minstrelsy of the Scottish Border.* 3 vols. 1802–3. 4 vols. Edinburgh 1932.
Sinclair, George. *Satan's Invisible World Discovered.* 1685. Gainesville 1969.
Sinclair, John, ed. *The Statistical Account of Scotland.* 21 vols. Edinburgh 1771–1799.
Stevenson, George. *Poems of Alexander Montgomerie Supplementary Volume.* Scottish Text Society. Edinburgh 1910.
Stoddart, Sir John. *Remarks on Local Scenery & Manners in Scotland during the years 1799 and 1800.* 2 vols. London 1801.
Stuart, John. ed. *Extracts from the Presbytery Book of Strathbogie.* Aberdeen 1843.
Telfair, Alexander. *A True Relation of an Apparition, Expressions, and Actings, of a Spirit, which infested the House of Andrew Mackie, in Ring-Croft of Stocking, in the Paroch of Rerrick, in the Stewardy of Kirkcudbright, in Scotland.* London 1696.
Thompson, T. and C. Innes, eds. *Acts of Parliament of Scotland.* 12 vols. London 1814–75.

Secondary Material

Anglo, Sydney. *The Damned Art: Essays in the Literature of Witchcraft.* London 1977.
———. 'Reginald Scot's *Discoverie of Witchcraft*: Scepticism and Sadduceeism', in *The Damned Art: Essays in the Literature of Witchcraft.* ed. Anglo, 106–39.
Ankarloo, Bengt and Gustav Henningsen, eds. *Early Modern European Witchcraft: Centres and Peripheries.* Oxford 1993.
Bakhtin, Mikhail. *Rabelais and His World.* trans. Helene Iswolsky. Bloomington 1984.
Ballard, Linda-May. 'Fairies and the Supernatural on Reachrai', in *The Good People.* ed. Narváez, 47–93.
Banks, Mary MacLeod. *British Calendar Customs.* 3 vols. Glasgow, 1939–46.
Bascom, William R. 'Four Functions of Folklore', in *The Study of Folklore.* ed. Alan Dundes. N. J. 1965. 279–98.
Bawcutt, Priscilla. 'Elrich Fantasyis in Dunbar and Other Poets', in *Bryght*

Lanternis: Essays on the Language and Literature of Medieval and Renaissance Scotland. eds. J. Derrick McClure and Michael R. G. Spiller. Aberdeen 1989.

Beith, Mary. *Healing Threads. Traditional Medicines of the Highlands and Islands.* Edinburgh 1995.

Bennett, Gillian. *Traditions of Belief: Women, Folklore and the Supernatural Today.* London 1987.

Bennett, Margaret. *Scottish Customs: From the Cradle to the Grave.* Edinburgh 1992.

——. 'Balquhidder Revisited: Fairylore in the Scottish Highlands, 1690–1990', in *The Good People.* ed. Narváez, 94–115.

Black, George F. collector. *A Calendar of Cases of Witchcraft in Scotland, 1510–1727.* 1938. New York 1971.

——. *Examples of Printed Folklore Concerning the Orkney & Shetland Islands.* 1903. ed. Northcote W. Thomas. London 1994.

——. 'Scottish Charms and Amulets'. *Proceedings of the Society of Antiquaries of Scotland* 27 (1892–3): 433–526.

Bourke, Angela. *The Burning of Bridget Cleary: A True Story.* London 1999.

Briggs, Katharine M. *The Vanishing People: A Study of Traditional Fairy Beliefs.* London 1978.

——. *A Dictionary of Fairies.* London 1977.

——. *The Personnel of Fairyland.* Detroit 1971.

——. 'The Fairies and the Realm of the Dead'. *Folklore* 81 (1970): 81–96.

——. *The Fairies in Tradition and Literature.* London 1967.

——. *The Anatomy of Puck.* London 1959.

Briggs, Robin. *Witches and Neighbours.* London 1996.

Bruford, Alan James and Donald Archie MacDonald, eds., *Scottish Traditional Tales.* Edinburgh 1994.

Bruford, Alan James. 'Trolls, Hillfolk, Finns, and Picts: The Identity of the Good Neighbours in Orkney and Shetland', in *The Good People.* ed. Narváez, 116–41.

Buchan, David. 'Ballads of Otherworld Beings', in *The Good People.* ed. Narváez, 142–54.

——. 'Taleroles and the Witch Ballads', in *Ballads and Other Genres.* ed. Zorica Raj Kovic. Zagreb 1988.

——. 'Taleroles and the Otherworld Ballads', in *Tod und Jenseits im Europäischen Volkslied.* ed. Walter Puchner. Ioannina 1986. 247–61.

——. *The Ballad and the Folk.* London 1972.

Burke, Peter. *Popular Culture in Early Modern Europe.* New York 1978.

Campbell, John Gregorson. *Superstitions of the Highlands and Islands of Scotland.* Glasgow 1900.

Campbell, J. L., ed. *A Collection of Highland Rites and Customes.* The Folklore Society. Cambridge 1975.

Chambers, Robert. *Domestic Annals of Scotland: From the Reformation to the Revolution.* 3 vols. Edinburgh 1874.

——. *Popular Rhymes of Scotland.* 4th ed. Edinburgh 1870.

Clark, Stuart. 'King James's *Daemonologie*: Witchcraft and kingship', in *The Damned Art*. ed. Anglo, 156–81.
Cohn, Norman. *Europe's Inner Demons*. St. Albans 1976.
Cook, W. B., ed. *Stirling Antiquary*. 4 vols. Stirling 1893–1908.
Cowan, Edward J. 'The Supernatural in Scottish History', in *'Fantasticall Ymaginatiounis': The Supernatural in Scottish Culture*. ed. Lizanne Henderson. East Linton: Tuckwell Press, forthcoming 2002.
——, ed. *The Ballad in Scottish History*. East Linton 2000.
——. 'The Invention of Celtic Scotland', in *Alba. Celtic Scotland in the Medieval Era*. eds. E. J. Cowan and R. A. McDonald. East Linton 2000. 1–23.
——. 'Burns and Superstition', in *Love and Liberty. Robert Burns: A Bicentenary Celebration*. ed. Kenneth Simpson. East Linton 1997. 229–238.
——. 'Myth and Identity in Early Medieval Scotland'. *Scottish Historical Review* vol. LXIII. (1984): 111–35.
——. 'The Darker Version of the Scottish Renaissance: the Devil and Francis Stewart', *The Renaissance and Reformation in Scotland*. eds. Ian B. Cowan and Duncan Shaw. Edinburgh 1983. 125–40.
——. 'Calvinism and the Survival of Folk or 'Deil stick da minister'', in *The People's Past*. ed. Edward J. Cowan. Edinburgh 1980. 32–57.
Cromek, R. H. *Remains of Nithsdale and Galloway Song: with Historical and Traditional Notices Relative to the Manners and Customs of the Peasantry*. London 1810.
Dalyell, John Graham. *The Darker Superstitions of Scotland*. Glasgow 1835.
Davidson, Thomas. 'Animal Treatment in Eighteenth-Century Scotland'. *Scottish Studies* 4:1 (1960): 134–49.
——. *Rowan Tree and Red Thread*. Edinburgh 1949.
Dennison, Walter Traill. *Orkney Folklore and Traditions*. Kirkwall 1961.
——. *Orkney Folklore & Sea Legends*. Compiled by Tom Muir. Kirkwall 1995.
Duffy, Maureen. *The Erotic World of Faery*. London 1989.
Dundes, Alan, ed. *The Study of Folklore*. N. J. 1965.
Eberly, Susan Schoon. 'Fairies and the Folklore of Disability: Changelings, Hybrids, and the Solitary Fairy', in *The Good People*. ed. Narváez, 227–50.
Edwards, Gillian. *Hobgoblin and Sweet Puck: Fairy Names and Natures*. London 1974.
Evans-Wentz, W. Y. *The Fairy Faith in Celtic Countries*. 1911. New York 1990.
Febvre, Lucien. *The Problem of Unbelief in the Sixteenth Century: The Religion of Rabelais*. 1942, 1968. Trans. Beatrice Gottlieb. Cambridge 1982.
Fergusson, R. Menzies. *Rambling Sketches in the Far North and Orcadian Musings*. Kirkwall 1883.
Firth, John. *Reminiscences of an Orkney Parish together with Old Orkney Words, Riddles and Proverbs*. Stromness 1920.
Flinn, Michael, ed. *Scottish population history from the 17th century to the 1930s*. Cambridge 1977.

Freedman, J. R. 'With Child: Illegitimate Pregnancy in Scottish Traditional Ballads'. *Folklore Forum* 24:1 (1991): 3–18.

Ginzburg, Carlo. *Ecstasies: Deciphering the Witches' Sabbath*. Trans. R. Rosenthal. New York 1991.

——. *Clues, Myths, and the Historical Method*. 1986. Trans. John and Anne Tedeschi. Baltimore 1992.

——. *The Cheese and the Worms: The Cosmos of a Sixteenth-Century Miller*. Trans. John and Anne Tedeschi. 1976. Harmondsworth 1982.

——. *The Night Battles: Witchcraft and Agrarian Cults in the Sixteenth and Seventeenth Centuries*. 1966. Trans. John and Anne Tedeschi. Baltimore 1992.

Gordon, Anne. *Candie for the Foundling*. Edinburgh 1992.

Gow, Athol. 'Prophetic Belief in Early Modern Scotland, 1560–1700'. M. A. University of Guelph 1989.

Graham, Patrick. *Sketches of Perthshire*. London 1812.

——. *Sketches Descriptive of Picturesque Scenery on the Southern Confines of Perthshire*. Edinburgh 1806.

Green, Roger Lancelyn. *Andrew Lang: A Critical Biography*. Leicester 1946.

Gunnyon, William. *Illustrations of Scottish History, Life and Superstition from Song and Ballad*. Glasgow 1879.

Haden, Walter D. 'The Scottish 'Tam Lin' in the Light of Other Folk Literature'. *Tennessee Folklore Society Bulletin* 38 (1972): 42–9.

Hall, A. Rupert. *Henry More: Magic, Religion and Experiment*. Oxford 1990.

Hartland, Edwin Sydney. *The Science of Fairy Tales*. 1890. London 1925.

Harvey, William. *Scottish Chapbook Literature*. Paisley 1903.

Hawken, Paul. *The Magic of Findhorn*. 1975. Glasgow 1983.

Henderson, George. *The Popular Rhymes, Sayings, and Proverbs of the County of Berwick*. Newcastle-on-Tyne 1856.

Henderson, Lizanne. 'The Road to Elfland: Fairy Belief and the Child Ballads', in *The Ballad in Scottish History*. ed. Cowan, 54–72.

Henderson, William. *Notes on the Folk Lore of the Northern Counties of England and the Borders*. London 1866.

Henningsen, Gustav. "'The Ladies from Outside': An Archaic Pattern of the Witches' Sabbath', in *Early Modern European Witchcraft: Centres and Peripheries*. eds. Ankarloo and Henningsen, 191–215.

Hogg, James. *The Three Perils of Man: War, Women and Witchcraft*. ed. Douglas Gifford. Edinburgh 1996.

——. *The Works of the Ettrick Shepherd*. ed. Thomas Thomson. Glasgow n. d.

Honko, Lauri. 'Memorates and the Study of Folk Beliefs'. *Journal of the Folklore Institute* 1 (1964): 5–19.

Hope, A. D. *A Midsummer Eve's Dream: Variations on a Theme by William Dunbar*. Edinburgh 1971.

Hufford, David J. 'Rational Scepticism and the Possibility of Unbiased Folk Belief Scholarship'. *Talking Folklore* 9 (1990): 19–33.

——. *The Terror that comes in the Night: An Experience-Centered Study of Supernatural Assault Traditions*. Philadelphia 1989.

——. 'Reason, Rhetoric, and Religion: Academic Ideology Versus Folk Belief'. *New York Folklore* 11:1–4 (1985): 177–94.

——. 'The Supernatural and the Sociology of Knowledge: Explaining Academic Belief'. *New York Folklore* 9: 1–2 (1983): 21–30.

——. 'Traditions of Disbelief'. *New York Folklore* 8: 3–4 (1982): 47–56.

Jansen, Wm. Hugh. 'The Esoteric-Exoteric Factor in Folklore', in *The Study of Folklore*. ed. Alan Dundes. N. J. 1965. 43–51.

Johnston, Alfred and Amy Johnston, eds. *Old-Lore Miscellany of Orkney, Shetland, Caithness and Sutherland*. London 1912.

Jolly, Karen Louise. *Popular Religion in Late Saxon England: Elf Charms in Context*. Chapel Hill 1996.

Kane, Sean. *Wisdom of the Mythtellers*. Peterborough 1994.

Keightly, Thomas. *The Fairy Mythology*. 1828. London 1981.

Kvideland, Reimund and Henning Sehmsdorf, eds. *Scandinavian Folk Belief and Legend*. Minneapolis 1991.

Larner, Christina. *Witchcraft and Religion: The Politics of Popular Religion*. ed. Alan MacFarlane. Oxford 1984.

——. *Enemies of God: The Witch-Hunt in Scotland*. London 1981.

——, Christopher Hyde Lee and Hugh V. McLachlan. *A Source-Book of Scottish Witchcraft*. Glasgow 1977.

——. 'Two Late Scottish Witchcraft Tracts: *Witch-Craft Proven* and *The Tryal of Witchcraft*', in *The Damned Art*. ed. Anglo, 227–45.

Levack, Brian P. *The Witch-Hunt in Early Modern Europe*. London 1987.

Lyle, Emily B. "'King Orpheus' and the Harmony of the Seasons', in *The Ballad Image: Essays Presented to Bertrand Harris Bronson*. ed. James Porter. Los Angeles 1983. 20–9.

——. 'The Burns Text of Tam Lin'. *Scottish Studies* 15 (1971): 53–65.

——. 'The Teind to Hell in Tam Lin'. *Folklore* 81 (1970): 177–81.

——. 'A Reconsideration of the Place-Names in 'Thomas the Rhymer''. *Scottish Studies* 13 (1969): 65–71.

Lysaght, Patricia. *The Banshee*. Dublin 1986.

MacCulloch, J. A. 'The Mingling of Fairy and Witch Beliefs in Sixteenth and Seventeenth Century Scotland'. *Folk-Lore* 32 (1921): 227–44.

MacFarlane, Alan. 'A Tudor Anthropologist: George Gifford's *Discourse* and *Dialogue*', in *The Damned Art*. ed. Anglo, 140–55.

MacDonald, Isabel. *The Fairy Tradition in the Highlands and Some Psychological Problems*. Keighley 1938.

MacKenzie, Donald A. *Scottish Folk Lore and Folk Life: Studies in Race, Culture and Tradition*. London and Glasgow 1935.

MacKenzie, W. 'Gaelic Incantations, Charms, and Blessings of the Hebrides'. *Transactions of the Gaelic Society of Inverness*. 18 (1891–2): 97–182.

MacKenzie, W. M. *The Book of Arran*. 2 vols. 1914. Brodick 1982.
Mackinlay, James M. *Folklore of Scottish Lochs and Springs*. Glasgow 1893.
MacLean, Calum I. 'Fairy Stories from Lochaber'. *Scottish Studies* 4 (1960): 85–95.
MacLean, D. 'The Life and Literary Labours of the Rev. Robert Kirk of Aberfoyle'. *Transactions of the Gaelic Society of Inverness* vol. 31. 1922–4 (1927): 328–66.
MacLeod, Finlay, ed. *Togail Tìr, Marking Time: The Map of the Western Isles*. Stornoway 1989.
MacManus, Diarmuid. *Irish Earth Folk*. New York 1959.
McNeill, F. Marian. *The Silver Bough*. 4 vols. Glasgow 1959.
MacRitchie, David. *Fians, Fairies, and Picts*. London 1893.
——. *The Testimony of Tradition*. London 1890.
Marshall, George. *In a Distant Isle: The Orkney Background of Edwin Muir*. Edinburgh 1987.
Marwick, Earnest W. *The Folklore of Orkney and Shetland*. London, 1975.
——. 'Creatures of Orkney Legend and their Norse Ancestry'. *Norveg Folkelivsgransking* 15 (1972): 177–204.
Mill, Anna. *Medieval Plays in Scotland*. London 1969.
Miller, Hugh. *The Old Red Sandstone*. 1841. London 1922.
——. *Scenes and Legends of the North of Scotland*. 1835. Edinburgh 1994.
Monter, E. William. 'Scandinavian Witchcraft in Anglo-American Perspective', in *Early Modern European Witchcraft: Centres and Peripheries*. Eds. Ankarloo and Henningsen, 425–34.
Muchembled, R. *Popular Culture and Elite Culture in France, 1400–1750*. Baton Rouge 1985.
Munro, Joyce Underwood. 'The Invisible Made Visible: The Fairy Changeling as a Folk Articulation of Failure to Thrive in Infants and Children', in *The Good People*. ed. Narváez, 251–83.
Napier, James. *Folk Lore in the West of Scotland*. 1879. Wakefield 1976.
Narváez, Peter. 'The Fairy Faith'. *Ideas*. CBC Transcript (Montreal 29 June 1989).
——, ed. *The Good People: New Fairylore Essays*. New York and London 1991.
——. 'Newfoundland Berry Pickers 'In the Fairies': Maintaining Spatial, Temporal, and Moral Boundaries Through Legendry', in *The Good People*, 336–68.
Nelson, C. E. 'The Origin and the Tradition of the Ballad of "Thomas Rhymer"', in *New Voices in American Studies*. eds. Ray B. Browne, Donald M. Winkelman and Allen Hayman. Purdue 1966. 138–50.
Nicholson, John. *Folk-Tales and Legends of Shetland*. N.p. 1920.
Nicolson, James R. *Shetland Folklore*. London 1981.
Niles, J. D. 'Tam Lin: Form and Meaning in a Traditional Ballad'. *Modern Language Quarterly* 38 (1977): 336–47.
Noel-Paton, M. H. and J. P. Campbell. *Noel Paton, 1821–1901*. ed. Francina Irwin. Edinburgh 1990.
Ó Giolláin, Diarmuid. 'The Fairy Belief and Official Religion in Ireland', in *The Good People*. ed. Narváez, 199–214.

Olrik, Axel. 'Epic Laws of Folk Narrative', in *The Study of Folklore*. ed. Alan Dundes. Englewood Cliffs, N. J. 1965. 129–41.

Ó Madagáin, Brendan. 'Gaelic Lullaby: A Charm to Protect the Baby?' *Scottish Studies* 29 (1989): 29–38.

Peel, J. D. Y. 'Understanding Alien Belief-Systems'. *British Journal of Sociology* 20: 1 (1969): 69–84.

Pócs, Éva. *Between the Living and the Dead*. Budapest 1999.

——. 'Fairies and Witches at the Boundary of South-Eastern and Central Europe'. Folklore Fellows Communications No. 243 Helsinki 1989.

Polson, Alexander. *Our Highland Folklore Heritage*. Dingwall 1926.

Ralls-MacLeod, Karen. *Music and the Celtic Otherworld: From Ireland to Iona*. Edinburgh 2000.

Rees, Alwyn and Brinley Rees. *Celtic Heritage: Ancient Tradition in Ireland and Wales*. New York 1989.

Reid, A. G. *The Annals of Auchterarder and Memorials of Strathearn*. Perth 1989.

Reid Tait, E. S., Ed. *Shetland Folk Book*. 9 vols. Lerwick 1947–95.

Rieti, Barbara. *Strange Terrain: The Fairy World in Newfoundland*. St. John's 1991.

——. "The Blast' in Newfoundland Fairy Tradition', in *The Good People*. ed. Peter Narváez, 284–97.

Ritchie, Anna. *Perceptions of the Picts: From Eumenius to John Buchan*. Rosemarkie 1994.

Robertson, Duncan J. 'Orkney Folk-Lore'. *Proceedings of the Orkney Antiquarian Society*. Vol. 2. (1923–4).

Rojcewicz, Peter M. 'Fairies, UFOs, and Problems of Knowledge', in *The Good People* ed. Narváez, 479–514.

Rossi, Mario M. 'Text-Criticism of Robert Kirk's Secret Commonwealth'. *Edinburgh Bibliographical Society Transactions*. Vol. 3, part 4. Sessions 1953–4, 1954–5 (1957). 253–68.

Sahlins, Peter. 'Deep Play in the Forest: The 'War of the Demoiselles' in the Ariège, 1829–31', in *Culture and Identity in Early Modern Europe (1500–1800): Essays in Honor of Natalie Zemon Davies*. Eds. B. B. Diefendorf and Carla Hesse. Ann Arbor 1993.

Saxby, Jessie M. E. *Shetland Traditional Lore*. Edinburgh 1932.

Schofield, William Henry. *Mythical Bards and the Life of William Wallace*. Cambridge 1920.

Scott, Sir Walter. *Letters on Demonologie and Witchcraft*. 1830. London 1884.

Scribner, R. 'The Reformation, Popular Magic, and the 'Disenchantment of the World''. *Journal of Interdisciplinary History* 23 (Winter, 1993): 475–94.

——. *Popular Culture and Popular Movements in Reformation Germany*. London 1987.

Sharpe, Charles Kirkpatrick. *A Historical Account of the Belief in Witchcraft in Scotland*. Glasgow 1884.

Shire, Helena Mennie. *Song, Dance and Poetry of the Court of Scotland Under King James VI*. Cambridge 1969.

Sikes, Wirt. *British Goblins*. 1880. N. p. 1991.
Simpkins, John Ewart. *Strange Tales of Bygone Fife*. 1912. Midlothian 1976.
——. *Examples of Printed Folk-Lore Concerning Fife with some notes on Clackmannan and Kinross-shires County Folk-Lore. Vol vii*. Publications of the Folklore Society lxxi. London 1914.
Simpson, Eve Blantyre. *Folklore in Lowland Scotland*. 1908. Wakefield 1976.
Spence, Lewis. *The Fairy Tradition in Britain*. London 1948.
——. *British Fairy Origins*. 1946. Northamptonshire 1981.
——. 'The Fairy Problem in Scotland'. *Hibbert Journal* 36 (1938): 246–55.
Stewart, William Grant. *The Popular Superstitions and Festive Amusements of the Highlanders of Scotland*. 1822. London 1851.
Sutherland, Elizabeth. *Ravens and Black Rain: The Story of Highland Second Sight*. London 1987.
Thomas, Keith. *Religion and the Decline of Magic*. 1971. Harmondsworth 1991.
Thompson, David. *The People of the Sea: A Journey in Search of the Seal Legend*. London 1980.
Thompson, Francis. *The Supernatural Highlands*. London 1976.
Toelken, Barre. 'Figurative Language and Cultural Contexts in the Traditional Ballads'. *Western Folklore* 45: 2 (1986): 128–42.
Tolkien, J. R. R. *Tree and Leaf*. London 1964.
Ward, Donald. 'The Little Man Who Wasn't There: Encounters With the Supranormal'. *Fabula* 18: 3–4 (1977): 212–25.
White, Carolyn. *A History of Irish Fairies*. 1976. Dublin 1992.
Whyte, Ian D. *Scotland Before the Industrial Revolution An Economic and Social History c.1050–c.1750*. London 1995.
Williams, Noel. 'The Semantics of the Word *Fairy*: Making Meaning Out of Thin Air', in *The Good People*. ed. Narváez., 457–78.
Wilson, William. *Folklore and Genealogies of Uppermost Nithsdale*. Dumfries 1904.
Wimberly, Lowry C. *Folklore in the English and Scottish Ballads*. Chicago 1928.
Winberry, John J. 'The Elusive Elf: Some Thoughts on the Nature and Origin of the Irish Leprechaun'. *Folklore* 87 (1976): 63–75.
Wood, J. Maxwell. *Witchcraft in South-West Scotland*. Wakefield 1975.

Index

Abbotsford 150
abduction 22, 60, 76, 80, 81, 83, 86–8, 96–100, 102, 128–9, 137, 172, 174, 188, 210
Aberdeen 54, 61, 83, 84, 108
Aberfoyle 8, 172–4, 183, 190, 191, 198, 214
Adamson, Patrick (Bishop of St. Andrews) 85, 130, 165–8
Aiken Drum 16, 202
Alexander III 148
Alexander, Margaret 58, 61, 66
Alexander, William Earl of Stirling 164
All Saints' Day 115
America 54, 159, 171, 202
angels 18, 19, 21, 23, 44, 117, 127, 133, 171, 177, 180, 188
Angus 9, 187
animals 1, 15, 16, 23, 29, 33, 36–8, 40–2, 44, 46–8, 57–8, 63, 69, 71, 76–9, 81, 83–4, 88, 90–3, 96, 98–9, 101–2, 104, 128, 131–3, 136, 137, 143, 147, 150–3, 156, 160–3, 165, 166, 168, 169, 186–8, 193, 197, 199, 200
antiquarian 2, 3, 9, 22, 28, 53, 174
Appin 42
Arbroath 187
archaeology 9–10, 15, 19, 21–2, 24, 29, 33, 52, 63, 201, 211
Ardnamurchan 96
Argyllshire 9, 89, 121, 206
Arran 79, 184
Arthur, King 24, 42, 127–8, 149, 182
Aubrey, John 37, 178
Auldearn 37, 41, 134
Ayrshire 31, 41, 56, 84, 107, 129, 130, 148, 159

Baillie, Joanna 93
Bakhtin, Mikhail 10, 157
ballads 4–5, 8, 9, 16, 35–7, 39, 40, 42, 45, 49–50, 55, 57, 61–2, 75–6, 79–83, 87, 90–2, 96, 101, 114–15, 121, 150, 175, 195–9, 204, 205, 209
Balliol, Edward 144–5, 148
Balliol, John 144, 146, 148
Balquhidder 172–4, 183, 190
Bannockburn, Battle of 145, 147
banshee 15–16, 32, 33
Barra 23, 89
Barrie, J. M. 9, 47, 205–6
Baxter, Richard 177, 178, 180
Bellenden, John 149
Beltane 49, 81–2, 90, 98, 102, 137
Benbecula 52, 56, 97
Bennet, Agnes 88
Bennet, Isobell 88
Bennett, Gillian 117
Bennett, Margaret 173
Berwick 150
Bible 10, 23, 87, 100, 117, 163, 174–6, 180, 187, 188, 192, 197
Billie Blin 49–50, 70
birth (see also childbirth) 15, 26, 41, 80, 86–7, 95, 100, 160, 172
Black Isle 193
Blair, Hugh 22, 194
blast 75, 78–80, 85–6, 128
Blind Harry 17, 45, 49, 70, 148
Boece, Hector 147, 149, 153
Borders 9, 16, 44, 104, 127, 169, 199, 201, 208
Bovet, Richard 64, 177, 180
Bower, Walter 148
'Boy of Borgue' 64–5
'Boy of Leith' 64
Boyle, Eleanor vere 203

Boyle, Robert 174, 175, 177, 183
Boyman, Jonet 127–9
Brahan Seer 93
Brand, John 23, 59
bread 87, 97, 100
Breadalbane 166
Briggs, Katharine 4, 173
brownies 15, 16, 21, 25, 26, 32, 35, 49–50, 54–6, 72, 125, 154, 201, 202, 203, 207
Bruce, Robert 144–5, 149
Buchan, David 5, 67
Buchanan, George 50, 81, 92–3, 124, 126
Bull, Helen 87
Burgh, John 77
Burke, Peter 10
Burne-Jones, Edward 203
Burns, Robert 28, 41, 68, 154, 168
Burton, George 64
Bute 78, 134, 213

Cairngorms 200
Caithness 9, 23, 69, 161
Calderwood, David 167, 168
Calvin, John 109–110, 114, 195
Campbell, J. F. 21, 26, 46, 88–9
Campbell, J. G. 38, 56
Canada (see also Cape Breton, Newfoundland) 202
Candlemas 102
Canmore, Malcolm 100
Cape Breton 89
Caray, Katherine 82
Carmichael, Alexander 23
Carsewell, Bishop 19, 112–13
Carterhaugh 37, 44, 92, 93
Casse, Helen 134
Charles I 111–12
Charles II 111–12, 191
Chambers, Robert 4, 203
changelings 22, 90, 94–100, 105, 129, 204, 210–11
charming 27, 74–9, 83, 85, 87–8, 90, 94–100, 120, 127–31, 135, 140, 161, 164–5, 182, 187
Chaucer, Geoffrey 24–5, 33

Chesterton, G. K. 203
Child, F. J. 5, 56, 96
childbirth/labour (see also birth) 41, 50, 66, 75, 79–80, 84, 86–8, 92–100, 137, 152, 167, 188
Christmas (see Yule)
Cleland, William 25, 27, 33
Collins, William 53, 71
Colonsay 52, 56, 192
Complaynt of Scotland, The 114
Cors, Thomas 210
Cottingley Fairies 13, 205
Cragie, Katherine 83, 94
Craig, Jane 77
Craik, Dinah Maria 203
Crieff 77
Cromarty 97, 203
Cruikshank, George 203
Culblean, Battle of 148

Daemonologie (James VI) 8, 58, 107, 119, 121–6, 138, 160, 178, 182
Dalkeith 87, 135
Dalry 60, 130
Dalyell, John 3, 198–9, 210
Damian, John 154
David II 145
Davidson, John 114
dead, the 19–20, 23, 45, 46–7, 60–1, 82, 88, 129, 137–8, 152, 162, 166, 177, 189
death 26, 44, 57, 60–1, 77, 80, 86, 88–90, 95–7, 128–9, 131, 134, 137–8, 160, 172–3, 182, 184, 209–12
Denmark 122–3, 127, 149, 198
Devil 37, 41, 58, 66, 67, 77, 78, 81, 95, 96, 102, 106, 114, 116–20, 123–7, 129, 131–5, 137, 138, 154, 162, 163, 165, 171, 180–2, 188, 207
Diana (see also goddess) 62, 135, 197
Dickson, Margaret 96–7
Dickson, Tibbie 98
Dornoch 120
Douglas, Gavin 17, 152, 154

Downie Hills 9, 41, 45, 66–7, 134
Doyle, Conan 205
Doyle, Richard 205
dragon 83, 90, 154
Drever, Jonet 41
druids 19, 22, 33, 194, 210
Dumbarton 42
Dumfries 25, 95, 115, 205
Dunbar, Battle of 111
Dunbar, William 45, 66, 152, 154–7, 163–4
Dunfermline 204
Dunlop, Bessie 4, 19, 41, 46, 56, 58–60, 66, 75, 80, 82, 84–5, 129–31, 137, 164, 182, 213
Dunning 80
dwarf 49, 54, 55, 70, 163, 193, 197

Earlston 145, 146
Easter 106
Edinburgh 64, 106, 123, 127, 130, 132, 147, 156, 159, 173, 174, 175, 194, 195, 199, 204, 205, 206, 208–9, 212
Edmonston, Arthur 79
Eildon Hills (Eildon Tree) 9, 36, 42, 69, 76, 143–5, 201, 206
elf-arrows/darts 55, 75, 77, 79, 88, 93–4, 134
elf-shot 18, 32, 77–9, 83, 88, 93–4, 101, 132, 134, 137 (see also blast)
Elgin 134
Elizabeth I 124, 167
England 18, 26–7, 47, 49, 89, 93, 114, 117–8, 123–4, 147, 149, 165, 167, 177–9, 207–8
Evans-Wentz, W. Y. 20, 28, 173, 197

fairies: clothing of 57–60, 156
  death of 89–90, 97
  etymology 16–17, 32, 54, 152, 197
  hills 9, 18, 20, 22, 24, 37, 40–1, 43–6, 55, 62–4, 67–8, 73, 75, 79, 82–4, 93, 100, 125, 132, 134, 137, 172–3, 188–90, 210, 213, 214
  landscape of 9–10, 18, 37–44, 82, 185, 187–9, 201, 211–12
  names of 8–9, 14–16, 19, 31, 58, 61, 75–6, 98, 101, 133, 136, 152, 154, 172
  origins 19–24, 136, 196
  rings or circles 10, 18, 62–3, 137, 200, 210, 212
  stock/image 79–80, 137
  (see also green)
Fairy Cup 38, 67–8, 73
Fairy Darts (see elf-arrows)
Fairy King 42, 48, 57, 58, 61, 62, 65–7, 79, 81, 87, 131, 132, 134, 143–5, 151–3, 160, 209
Fairyland (Elfland) 35–7, 39–49, 56, 61, 64, 68, 129, 131, 146, 150, 151, 173, 184, 189, 197, 198, 202, 204
Fairy Queen 15, 24, 36, 37, 40, 45, 56, 57, 58, 60, 65–7, 72, 75, 80, 81, 84–5, 90, 92, 101, 125, 130, 133–6, 142–6, 151, 153, 155, 160, 166, 189, 197, 200, 206
Fairy Rade 62, 158, 160, 162, 166, 197, 200, 204
Fairy/Charm/Bored Stone 83, 93–4, 101, 104, 125–6
Fairy Tale (see Folktale)
Falkirk, Battle of 145
Fastern's Eve 86, 154
fay (fey) 16–17, 31, 83, 99, 101, 202
Ferguson, Adam 27
Ferguson, Farquhar 79
Fergusson, R. Menzies 29, 33–4
festivals 49, 81–83, 102, 108, 112, 115, 132
Fetlar 10, 63
Fife 81, 94, 99, 166, 187, 200
Fletcher, Andrew of Saltoun 163
Flinkar, Bessie 37
Flodden, Battle of 46, 163
'Flyting of Dunbar and Kennedie' 163
'Flyting of Montgomerie and Polwart' 62, 158, 160, 164
Folklore 2–3, 6, 10–11, 12, 24, 27, 39, 136, 138, 176, 187, 197, 199, 201, 203, 206–210

Folktale (fairy tale) 9, 15–16, 21, 26, 35, 38, 66, 70, 88, 103, 171, 183–4, 193, 200, 203, 205
Fordun, John of 148
Fowlis, Lady (Katherine Ross) 41, 82
France 32, 38, 64, 100, 110, 145, 149, 159, 166–7, 193
Frazer, James George 205
Frazer, John 183

Galloway 16, 18, 26, 202, 212
Galt, John 198, 202
Gargunnock 83, 131
Geace, Thomas 94
Gerald of Wales 48
Germany 56, 80, 107, 113, 168
ghosts 19–20, 25, 60, 73, 88, 116–18, 129, 130, 133, 137, 153, 154, 160, 162, 177, 194
giants 22, 31, 45, 49, 66, 136, 153, 155, 203
Gifford, George 124, 177
Ginzburg, Carlo 3–4, 10, 45, 136
Glanvill, Joseph 177, 178–180, 186
Glasgow 115, 117, 180, 181, 191, 197, 205
Glen Shee 28
goddess (see also Diana) 16, 19, 135–6
Good and Godlie Ballads, The 115
Gowdie, Isobel 4, 16, 37, 41, 45, 55, 58–9, 66–7, 77, 134
Graham, Kenneth 206
Graham, Patrick 173, 198
Graham, R. B. Cunninghame 175
Gramsci, Antonio 11
green (fairy colour) 18, 22, 25, 35, 57–8, 66, 68, 76, 90, 92, 134, 152, 156, 160, 189, 200, 212
Greenland 54
Gyar Carline (Gyre-Carling) 35, 136, 153
Gyges Ring 80, 101–2
gypsies 32, 60

Haddington 87, 106
Hailes, Lord (David Dalrymple) 149

Haldane, Isobel 41, 58, 73, 83, 86, 96, 182
Halloween 81–3, 90–1, 102, 115, 128–9, 131, 133, 137, 160, 166, 199
Hamilton, Anthony 193
Hamilton, Patrick 109
hawthorn 40, 41, 69, 89, 137, 156
Helmsdale 145
Henry VII 149
Henryson, Robert 36, 66, 152, 153
Hibbert, Samuel 62–63
Highlands and Islands 16, 21, 27, 29, 44, 50–53, 56, 59, 66, 88–9, 104, 121, 127, 174, 182–3, 208
Hogg, James 9, 14, 26, 28, 74, 196, 199–203
Holy Cross Day 82
horseshoe 88, 103
Houston, James 210
Hume, Sir Patrick of Polwarth 159–63
Huntly 203
Hyndman, Finwell 213

Iceland 23, 197, 212
Insulanus, Theophilus 183
Inveraray 42
Inverness 9, 42, 121
invisibility 14, 18, 54, 57, 64, 80, 101–2, 137, 171, 194
Ireland/Irish 15–16, 19–20, 23, 45, 53–4, 59, 62, 71, 88–9, 130–2, 149, 197, 208, 211, 215
iron 77, 87, 88, 92, 99–100, 104, 190
Irvine 41, 130
Isle of Man 18, 47, 197
Italy 80, 136, 207

James IV 46, 66, 149, 155, 163
James V 100
James VI 8, 51, 58, 62, 66, 81, 96, 107, 111, 117, 119, 121–7, 134, 135, 138, 159, 164, 166, 178, 182, 207
James VII 112
Jamieson, John 197
Jamieson, Robert 175, 196, 198

Index

Joan of Arc 127
Johnson, Samuel 71
Jonesdochter, Katherine 41, 60, 82, 133

Keightley, Thomas 203
Kelso 95
Kilmory 79
Kilwinning 85, 130
'King Berdok' 53, 66, 152
'King Orfeo' 5, 45, 77, 79, 90
Kirk, Robert 1, 8–9, 14, 17–18, 19–20, 37, 41, 44, 46, 47, 54, 56–7, 59, 61, 63, 65–6, 75, 77, 79–80, 82, 87–9, 120, 171–92, 214
Kirkwall 100
Knarston, James 83, 94
Knox, John 25, 107, 109–10, 113

Laidlaw, Margaret 199
Laidlaw, William (Will o' the Phaup) 196, 199
Lammas 82, 102, 132
landscape 9–10, 18, 27, 39–44, 82, 89, 150, 185, 194–7, 201, 208, 211
Lang, Andrew 9, 20, 175, 189, 205, 206
Larner, Christina 118, 120
Lauderdale 145
Law, Robert 198
Leith 64, 86, 130
leprechaun (luprachan, lusbartan) 14, 54
Lermontov, Mikhail Yuriyevich 147
Lesley, Beatrix 87
Lewingston, Christiane 86, 182
Lewis 50–2, 56, 71
Lewis, C. S. 203
Leyden, John 195–7, 203
liminality 39, 43–4, 82, 128, 188
Livingston 41, 58, 76
Lochaber 42
Lorn, Thomas 83
Luchruban 50–1, 53–4, 70
Luther, Martin 109
Lyndsay, Sir David 40, 81

MacCrimmon (family) 84
MacCulloch, J. A. 3, 4
MacCulloch, John 53
MacDonald, George 35, 203
McIllmichall, Donald 42–3, 46, 62, 66, 172
MacKenzie, Donald A. 66
MacKenzie, Kenneth (see Brahan Seer)
MacLaren, Archibald 203–4
MacPherson, James 9, 22, 194, 195
MacRitchie, David 21, 32
Mair, John 148, 154
Maitland, John 100, 178
Makcalzane, Euphemia 82, 93, 123, 132
Malleus Maleficarum 95, 107, 161, 164
Maltman, Steven 83, 131
Man, Andro 46, 56, 58, 62, 84, 133, 182, 213
Martin, Martin 51–4, 56, 59, 71, 97, 176, 179, 183, 184, 213
Mary Queen of Scots 81, 110, 119, 126
Melrose 146
Melville, Andrew 110–11, 113, 126, 167
Merlin 148, 149, 154
mermaid (also finnmen, finfolk) 24, 29, 33
Michaelmas 55, 102
Middle Earth 20, 37, 40, 42, 74, 143–4, 151, 172, 199
Midsummer 82, 102, 137, 155–6, 204
midwife 75, 76, 87, 95, 167
milk 19, 48, 63, 92, 104, 131, 137, 163
Miller, Hugh 24–6, 97, 193, 203
Minstrelsy of the Scottish Border 18, 150, 195–6, 198–9, 201
Mohammed 153, 154, 162–3
Monro, Donald 50, 53, 56
Montgomerie, Alexander 62, 66, 96, 158–165
Montrose, Marquis of (James Graham) 111
More, Henry 177, 179–180
Morison, John 52, 71

Morris, William 203
Morrison, Jonet 78, 134
Muir, Edwin 113
Mull 63, 184, 185
Murray, James 150

Narváez, Peter 39, 69
National Covenant 111, 159
Neville's Cross, Battle of 145
Newes from Scotland 122–3
Newfoundland 26, 39, 208, 211
Newton, Isaac 178
Nicholson, William 26, 202
NicNiven (see also fairy names) 15–16, 77–8, 136, 161, 163
NicNiven, Catherine 77–8, 101
Nisbett, Alison 77
North Berwick 119, 122–5, 132, 134, 153
Nostradamus 147

Orkney 9, 15, 21, 23, 25, 26, 28, 29, 42, 46, 54, 56, 59, 83, 94, 100, 101, 103, 127, 133, 136, 141, 207, 210
'Orpheus and Eurydice' 36, 62, 66, 79, 153–4
Oswald, Katharine 77
Otherworld 35, 36, 37, 44, 69, 75, 90, 129, 152, 189, 209, 212
Otterburn, Battle of 145

Paisley 167
Parish, Barbara 41, 76
Paterson, Bartie 77–8
Paton, J. Noel 62, 204–5
Paxton, Janet 134
Peirson, Alison 19, 37, 42, 45, 46, 60, 66, 81, 85–6, 87, 130, 131, 137, 165–8, 182, 187
Pepys, Samuel 178
Perth 41, 58, 96, 111
Picts 8, 9, 21–2, 33, 152, 187, 209
Pinkie, Battle of 60
placenames 9, 42–3
poltergeist 63–4, 181
Prestonpans 114

prophecy 83, 93, 144–51, 165, 182, 201, 211
pygmies 1, 22, 47–8, 50–4, 56, 71

Quarter Days 82, 83, 87, 97, 102
Queen of Fairy/Elfland (see Fairy Queen)

Ramsay, Allan 75
Ramsay, John, of Ochtertyre 184
Reay, Lord, of Durness 183
Reformation 25, 27, 29, 74, 106–20, 130, 167, 171, 189
Reoch, Elspeth 42, 58, 59, 60, 84, 133, 182, 187
Rhymer, Thomas (see Thomas Rhymer)
Romance and Prophecies of Thomas of Ercedoune, The 142, 150–1
Ronaldson, Walter 54
Ross 97
Rousay 100, 103
Rowan (mountain ash) 78, 89, 104
Royal Society, the 8, 174, 176, 178, 191, 192

St. Andrews 85, 109, 164, 166–7, 173
St. Kilda 213
St. Margaret 100
Sadducism 177–79, 181, 185, 189, 200
Sampson, Agnes 77, 93, 122, 123, 132
Sanderson, Stewart 176, 189, 190
Schiehallion 9, 209
Scot, Reginald 26, 102, 124, 177, 178
Scott, Sir Walter 3, 4, 9, 18, 27, 28, 53, 56, 75, 106, 136, 142, 146, 150, 172–3, 175, 184, 185, 195–9, 203, 204, 207–8, 210
seals/selkies 23, 33
second sight 17, 20, 36, 57, 75, 82–6, 88, 93, 128–31, 137, 171–6, 181–4, 208, 211
Selkirkshire 208
Sempill, Robert 130, 165–8
shape-shifting 47, 49, 55–6, 61, 80, 83, 90–2, 133, 137
Sharpe, Charles Kirkpatrick 98, 198–9

Sharpe, William 205
Shetland 9, 15, 16, 23, 26, 28, 31, 41, 56, 60, 63, 67, 79, 83–4, 98, 101, 103, 127, 133, 141, 183, 207, 214
Shrove Tuesday 86
Sibbald, Sir Robert 52, 71, 174
Simpson, William 60, 73, 85, 130, 166
Sinclair, Catherine 203
Sinclair, George 117, 176, 179, 180, 183, 191
Sinclair, Isobel 83, 182
'Sir Gawain and the Green Knight' 146
'Sir Orfeo' 151–2
Skye 28, 71, 84, 209
Smith, Gregory 142
Society for Psychical Research 175, 205
Spence, Lewis 206
Stewart, Esmé 159, 167
Stewart, Francis, Earl of Bothwell 123, 164
Stewart, John 41, 130–1, 182
Stewart, Mary 166
Stillingfleet, Edward 174–5
Stirling 88, 175
Strathaquin, Isobell 84
Superstition 10, 22, 27, 28, 29, 33, 51–2, 59, 100, 106, 112–14, 116, 120, 154, 168, 180, 198, 200–1, 207–8
Sutherland 23

taboo 75, 85
Tam Lin 5, 37, 40, 41, 44, 45, 49, 55, 56, 57, 75–6, 79, 81, 83, 90–3, 96, 146, 195, 200
Tarbat, Lord George MacKenzie 175, 183
teind 58, 75, 76, 80–1, 83, 144, 146
Telfair, Alexander 180–1
Teviotdale 169, 195
Thirlestane Castle 150
Thomas Rhymer 5, 8, 9, 36, 40, 42, 45, 46, 48, 49, 55, 69, 75–6, 83, 90, 92, 113–14, 142–51, 172, 182, 200, 201, 203, 206
Thomasdochter, Barbara 98
Tinker Bell 9, 13, 89, 205

Tod, Beigis 133
Tolkien, J. R. R. 1, 42, 47, 203
Tomnahurich Hill 9, 42
tooth fairy 13
Trall, Janet 58, 78, 80, 83, 86, 94, 96
Tranent 77
'Tretis of the Tua Mariit Wemen and the Wedo' 155–7
'Tristan and Iseult' 145, 196
Trossachs 185, 198
trows/trolls 9, 15, 16, 21, 24, 28, 29, 31, 33, 41, 55, 60, 63, 82, 83–4, 94, 141, 183
Tuatha Dé Danann 19, 112–13

UFOs 207
Uist 42
Union of the Crowns 111, 124, 182

Vikings 22, 31 (Norse 15, 62, 67)

Wales 20, 48–9, 89, 208
Wallace, William 145, 148
Watson, Jonet 134
Weber, Max 116
Webster, John 177–8
Wedderburn, John 115
Weir, Jean 135
wells 10, 37, 41, 68, 73, 75, 76, 92, 97–8, 127–8, 137
Wemyss 187
werewolves 117–18, 161, 163
whirlwind 37, 38, 49, 79, 128, 137, 153
Whole Prophecies of Scotland etc., The 149
wicht/wight 8, 15, 23, 42, 64, 65, 85, 87, 88, 97, 128–31, 135, 155
Wild Hunt 62
Wilde, Oscar 204
wilderness 23, 40, 151, 187, 207, 208
William II 112
Wilson, John 201
Wimberly, L. C. 20
witch/witch trial 3–4, 8, 15–16, 23, 26, 29, 33, 37, 41–2, 45, 47, 50, 56, 58, 61, 66, 76–90, 93, 96, 100, 104, 106–7, 116–38, 153–4, 158,

161–8, 177–82, 185, 192, 200–1, 207, 213
Wodrow, Robert 112, 176
Wyntoun, Andrew 148

Yeats, W. B. 16
Young, Isobell 77
Yule 49, 82, 102, 106, 115, 133, 141, 183, 205